NOBLE INTENTIONS

THE JACK NOBLE SERIES™ BOOK FOUR

L.T. RYAN

LIQUID MIND MEDIA

CONTENTS

EPISODE 1

EPISODE 2

EPISODE 3

EPISODE 4

EPISODE 5

THE JACK NOBLE SERIES

Purchase L.T. Ryan's Paperbacks!

The Recruit (Short Story)
The First Deception (Prequel 1)
Noble Beginnings (Jack Noble #1)
A Deadly Distance (Jack Noble #2)
Ripple Effect (Bear Logan)
Thin Line (Jack Noble #3)
Noble Intentions (Jack Noble #4)
When Dead in Greece (Jack Noble #5)
Noble Retribution (Jack Noble #6)
Noble Betrayal (Jack Noble #7)
Never Go Home (Jack Noble #8)
Beyond Betrayal (Clarissa Abbot)
Noble Judgment (Jack Noble #9)
Never Cry Mercy (Jack Noble #10)
Deadline (Jack Noble #11)
End Game (Jack Noble #12)
Noble Ultimatum (Jack Noble #13)
Noble Legend (Jack Noble #14)

EPISODE 1

CHAPTER 1

"Momma!" the little girl called out in a frightened voice.

Jack Noble looked over and saw her standing alone. She looked to be eight or nine years old. He watched people walk by the crying child, paying no attention to her. His first thought was to ignore her like the faceless others who didn't notice or care that a little girl was standing in the middle of the sidewalk alone and lost.

"Momma? Where are you?" she said through sobs.

Jack jogged over and knelt in front of the child. "What's your name, sweetheart?"

"Mandy." She wiped tears away from her big blue eyes. "Can you help me?"

Jack looked around at the crowded street and then at his watch. The old man would be there soon. The instructions were explicit; he had to be at the corner of Main Street and Roosevelt Avenue at 9:30 a.m. The old man did not like it when people were late.

Jack looked at the little girl. "Didn't anyone ever tell you not to talk to strangers?"

She stared back at him.

"C'mon, Mandy." He hoisted her onto his shoulders. "Can you see her?"

Mandy looked up and down the street. "No. I don't see her nowhere."

"How long have you been lost?"

"I dunno. A long time." Her crying had stopped.

Jack turned in a tight circle so Mandy could scout the crowd.

"I can't see her mister."

Jack pulled her down from his shoulder and held her against his chest. "Where do you live?"

"23423 52nd Street, Apartment D." She rattled the address off fast, like a robot, and he knew the address had been drilled into her by her mother or father.

"Do you know your mommy's cell phone number?"

As quickly as she offered up her address, the little girl gave him her mother's cell phone number.

Jack reached into his pocket and pulled out his cell phone, dialed the number and waited for it to ring.

"We're sorry, the number you have dialed has been disconnected. Please check the number and try again," a recorded operator told him.

He dialed again, but the same message played.

"Shit."

"Oh, you said a bad word," Mandy said.

He smiled at the girl, but his smile turned into a look of concern when he saw the white Mercedes getting closer. The old man was here, 9:30 a.m. on the dot. He looked around to see if anyone recognized the little girl. People walked by, eyes ahead staring off into the distance like zombies. It was always the same in every big city he visited. Everyone walked around with blank stares, looking straight ahead. They didn't give a care about him or his problems.

The Mercedes pulled up to the curb. The rear window rolled down. An old Asian man peered at him through thin glasses. "Hello, Mr. Jack."

Jack nodded back at the man.

"Do you have the documents with you?"

Jack held up the briefcase for the old man to see. "Right here."

"Is today bring your child to work day?"

"Condescending much?" Jack continued to look around for someone, anyone, who recognized Mandy. "I need you to give me a couple minutes here."

"There are no minutes to give, Mr. Jack. Our agreement was 9:30 a.m. It is now 9:30 a.m."

"Just give me a minute. She's lost. I need to find a safe place for her."

"I can assure you my car is the safest place for her." His sly, yellow smile was enough to put Jack on alert.

"Just give me a minute," Jack said.

He knew the old man wouldn't blink an eye at the little girl if she weren't with Jack. And if he turned her over, then the old man would drive five minutes out of the city and drop her on the curb, if he didn't kill her first.

"You have 30 seconds, Mr. Jack. Fail to return in 30 seconds and... well, I don't have to tell you what's to come. Do I?"

"No. I'm well aware of that." In six years he had done at least four dozen jobs for the old man. Jack knew the only reason the crime boss continued to give him assignments was because Jack didn't screw up. He didn't attract attention, and he most definitely didn't tell the old man to wait.

"You are wasting time, Mr. Jack."

Jack took off down the sidewalk. He recalled seeing a police officer stationed a block away. Dealing with a cop wasn't ideal. There was always a risk that Jack's face was plastered on a wanted poster somewhere. But if he wanted Mandy in a safe place, there was no other choice.

"Officer!" Jack yelled.

The police officer turned to face Jack with a look of indifference smeared across his face.

"Officer, this little girl is lost. I need you to take her. She knows her address and her mom's cell phone." Jack pushed the little girl towards the cop. She turned and reached back for Jack, apparently not wanting to leave his side.

"Whoa, whoa, wait," the policeman said. He held out his hand and shook it in Jack's face. "What the hell is going on here? You can't just dump a kid on me."

"I know how it looks, officer, but she's in danger. Just take her back to the precinct until her mother shows up."

The cop eyed Jack's six foot two inch frame up and down. His gaze lingered a second too long and Jack got the feeling the cop didn't care too much for him. He watched the policeman's eyes stop at the handcuffs attached to Jack's left wrist. They widened when the cop seemed to realize that the other end was attached to a briefcase. The cop backed up.

"What the hell is attached to your wrist?"

Jack checked to see how many people were around. It was crowded. He was in New York for Christ's sake, of course it was crowded. He preferred not to make a scene with this many people nearby, but he didn't have much choice. He looked back at the cop. The pudgy officer had his hand on his gun. Jack knew at that moment he had no other choice.

Jack slowly raised his left hand and distracted the officer by pushing Mandy toward him. The moment the cop looked down at the little girl, Jack's window opened. He reached into his pocket for a stun grenade, or flashbang as he called it. In one fluid motion he threw the flashbang at the cop's feet, pulled Mandy back, and turned so he wouldn't be blinded by the light.

The cop didn't have time to react. *BOOM!* The flashbang exploded with a burst of bright light that instantly and temporarily blinded anyone who saw it. The explosion was loud enough to upset the fluid in the inner ear, disrupting all sense of balance and direction. The officer fell back and hit his head on the sidewalk. Hours later neither the cop nor any of the bystanders would be able to describe Jack. The only thing the cop remembered was the briefcase.

Jack lifted Mandy in a fireman's carry and ran. He scoured the street for the Mercedes, but it was gone. It looked like the old man hung him out to dry.

Again.

Jack cursed out loud.

Mandy giggled.

"You think this is funny?"

She stopped laughing and pushed with her hands to get off of his shoulder. Jack tightened his grip as he looked for the Mercedes. He spotted it parked a block and a half away. He was almost out of breath when he finally reached the car.

"Mr. Jack," said the old man, "I would have thought that someone in your line of work would be in better shape."

"Dirty cigarettes," Jack said.

"You know, those will kill you." The old man reached into his shirt pocket and pulled out a cigarette, lit it with a wooden match, and threw the match out the window toward Jack.

"When?" Jack asked in a sarcastic tone. He set the girl down and ran his hand through his brown hair. "Let us in," he said, "we'll get this sorted out on the way."

"Mr. Jack, you are late. Not only that, you have attracted the attention of the police. This meeting has been compromised." He rolled up the window and the Mercedes pulled away.

"Wait!" Jack said. "Let us in. I've got what you want right here."

The Mercedes stopped and the old man stuck his head out the window, looking back at him. "Another time, Mr. Jack." The old man paused and lowered his sunglasses so Jack could look at his cataract covered eyes. "I'll be in touch soon."

The Mercedes sped away and Jack heard the sounds of sirens approaching. The cops would be here soon. He had to get moving or it would only be a matter of seconds before they found him.

"It's time for plan B, Mandy." He lifted her back onto his shoulder.

"What's plan B, Mr. Jack?"

"I'll let you know as soon as I do, sweetheart."

Jack jogged half a block and ducked into an alley. He pulled out a map of the area that was marked with the locations of places he considered safe houses. Over the last decade he had performed enough favors he could always call on someone when in a tough situation.

Clarissa's apartment was one block away. She was a friend. Truth be told, she was more than a friend. There were two people Jack trusted with his life and Clarissa was one of them. She would hide him for the night, no questions asked. He might even be able to pawn Mandy off on her. He looked at the little girl and laughed at the thought of Clarissa taking care of a kid.

"What's so funny?"

"Other than your face?"

"Hey! That's not nice!" Mandy stuck out her lower lip in an exaggerated pout.

Jack laughed. "I'm teasing sweetie. Only teasing."

They hid out in the alley until dark. Clarissa's apartment wasn't far away, but he didn't want to risk the cops spotting them. He didn't want to kill a cop in front of Mandy. He might be a killer, but he did have some morals.

CHAPTER 2

"W ho is it?" Clarissa asked from the other side of the door.

Jack held Mandy against his chest. She was asleep, had been since before they left the alley. He quietly replied, "It's Jack."

"Jack?"

"C'mon, Clarissa. I'm in trouble. Need your help."

The door opened and Jack was greeted by the gorgeous red head. There weren't many women who could look him in the eye, but at five foot ten and wearing heels, Clarissa could. She motioned with her hand for Jack to come in. As he walked past her, he noticed how great she smelled. She always smelled great. Not cheap like most of the other strippers he knew.

"Who the hell is this?"

"Her name's Mandy. She's lost." Jack paused a beat. "I was waiting for an associate and spotted her. She was standing there, crying for her mom. No one would help her."

Clarissa raised a curious eyebrow. "Ahhh, you've gone soft, baby."

"Shut up."

"So, what, you went up to her and?"

"I offered to help. Figured her mom was in a nearby store. You know something simple like that."

"I'm guessing you assumed wrong then?"

"Yeah, very wrong. Worst thing is I missed my meeting, which pissed off some very bad people." He unlocked the handcuffs and set the briefcase down.

Clarissa cast a curious eye toward the briefcase. "So why are you here? You need me to hide you?" She laughed.

"I also pissed off the cops." He looked up at the ceiling, his hands clasped behind his head.

"Let me get you a drink."

Jack nodded.

"What do you want? I got beer, whiskey, tequila."

"One of each," Jack replied. "Hey, you got somewhere she can lie down?"

"Sure, go ahead and put her in my room for now." Clarissa pointed to the back of the apartment with one hand as she filled shot glasses with the other.

Jack walked over to the couch and picked up the sleeping girl. It had been a long day for the child. She opened her eyes and stared at him, lips drawn tight and her eyebrows furrowed. He waited for her to ask him a question, but before she could open her mouth, her head fell forward on his shoulder and she went back to sleep. He stroked her hair as he took her to Clarissa's bedroom. Jack laid her down and covered her up with a blanket.

He walked back to the kitchen and went straight to the counter where his shot glasses were waiting. He threw back a shot of tequila and grimaced at the burn and aftertaste. He'd only had three jobs go bad. Two of those three had been because of tequila.

"I've never seen you that gentle with anyone," Clarissa said. She placed her hand on his shoulder and gave it a soft massage, then dragged her nails lightly across his back.

He picked up the second shot glass and held it to his lips. "I screwed up." He drank the whiskey, slammed the shot glass down and then cracked opened the bottle of beer. "Big time."

"More?"

"Yeah, one of each." He slid the shot glasses across the counter.

Clarissa poured his refills. "How bad can it be?"

Jack said nothing. He drank his shots in succession and returned to his bottle of beer. "We'll only be here tonight."

"Jack, you know you can stay as long as you need. I don't mind. Even with the kid, it's cool with me." She put her arm around his shoulders. "As much as you have done for me, it's the least I can do."

"It's the old man," he said.

Clarissa looked down at the floor, toward the briefcase. "I'm guessing that briefcase has something to do with it?"

Jack nodded and said nothing.

"What's inside?" she asked.

"Just some papers." He paused. "It's better you don't know."

"Will he try to kill you?"

Jack thought about it for a moment, shrugged. *Would he kill me?*

"If he wanted me dead he would have killed me after I botched the deal."

"So why don't you go to him tonight and complete the deal?" Clarissa asked.

"The cop on the corner. He saw enough of me to be able to identify me. Plus, the old man said he'd be in contact. Better to just wait it out."

"You want to turn on the TV? Check the news?"

"Nah, that garbage's depressing."

They both laughed but the moment was short lived, interrupted by a shrill scream. Jack raced to the back of the apartment to check on Mandy.

"Mommy!"

Jack sat on the edge of the bed and stroked her hair. "Shhh," he whispered, "we're going to get you to your momma. I promise." He sat with her until she fell back to sleep.

Clarissa greeted him with a smile when he returned to the kitchen. He smiled back. She looked good tonight. Hell, she looked good any time of day. But tonight she seemed more vibrant than usual. Even though he had ten years on her, they'd always had a connection. Things had progressed further the last few years, though, and that scared Jack. In his line of business it didn't pay to be close to anyone.

"Another drink?" she asked.

Jack nodded.

Clarissa brushed against him on her way to the fridge.

Jack followed her, waiting behind the opened door. The air escaping from the refrigerator felt cool against his flush face.

She stood, turned and stopped inches from him. Bit her bottom lip.

He lifted his hand, brushing strands of her hair behind her ear. Leaned in and kissed her neck. His hands worked down her sides. Steady fingers unbuttoned her jeans and slid them off her waist. "For a stripper you wear some pretty boring panties."

"Exotic dancer," she said in between nibbles on his ear. She wrapped a leg around his.

"The little girl," Jack said. "She's sleeping in the other room."

Clarissa waved off Jack's protest. "I'll be quiet."

"But you know I can't be," he said with a wry smile.

They found the couch and fell into one another.

CHAPTER 3

Clarissa awoke as the sun peeked through a crack in the curtains, casting long fingers of light across her body. She sat up, reached her arms out and opened her eyes to find herself alone. "Son of a bitch," she muttered as she stood. Her head throbbed from the combination of sex, alcohol and lack of sleep.

She walked to the back of the apartment to see if Jack was in the bathroom or had slipped into her bed. She had been told that she snored. It wasn't all that uncommon for her lovers to sneak off and find a quiet place to sleep.

There was a note on the bedroom door. She read it to herself:

Clarissa,

Sorry, I have to take care of something this morning. Watch over Mandy for me. Back by evening.

Jack

"Son of a bitch," she said again.

She opened the bedroom door a crack and peeked in to check on Mandy. Covers hugged the little girl as she lay sleeping. Clarissa went back to the kitchen and grabbed her cell phone. She searched for Jack's number. It was in there a few days ago, but she couldn't find it now. He must have erased his number from her phone before he left. She rolled her eyes at the thought.

"Momma?"

Clarissa slammed her phone down and bit her lip in frustration. She turned to see Mandy standing there looking timid.

"Where's my momma? Where's Mr. Jack?"

"Jack had to go out for a bit sweetie. He's looking for your mom."

"Who are you? Are you Mrs. Jack?"

Clarissa laughed. "No, baby, but we are really good friends."

"That means you're my friend, too," Mandy said.

Clarissa smiled at her. *Things are so simple for children.* "Are you hungry?"

"Mmhm." Mandy rubbed her belly.

Clarissa poured a bowl of cereal, sat it in front of the child. "Now eat up. We got to get you cleaned up. Can't have your momma show up with you looking all a mess."

Mandy looked up and smiled at her with a mouth full of cereal and milk. The milk trickled down her chin as she grinned. Clarissa couldn't help but laugh, which resulted in milk and cereal spraying across the table as the little girl joined in. Their laughter was disrupted by a loud knock on the door.

CHAPTER 4

Jack pressed the gun into the back of Lester's head. The man kneeled down on the ground, feet crossed, arms tied behind his back, his face just inches away from the cold, grey wall. Lester struggled to keep his head from touching the wall. Jack had told him if he touched it, he was dead.

The dimly lit cellar had a single yellow light bulb hanging from the ceiling. It swayed slightly, casting shadows side to side.

"I... I don't know any more than what I told you, Jack," Lester said.

"For some reason I just don't believe that, Lester." Jack looked back at Bear and nodded.

Riley "Bear" Logan was Jack's partner on most of his assignments. Bear was a big man, as one would guess based on his nickname. He stood at six foot six and weighed in at over three hundred pounds. He had a big, bushy brown beard and a heavy brow. He'd had Jack's back since they were 19 years old, fresh out of Marine recruit training.

Lester's teeth chattered and his body convulsed every ten seconds or so.

There was a time when Jack would have felt sorry for the poor bastard. Those days were long gone. In fact, it had only taken a few civilian kills to cleanse him of any feelings of remorse. Today all he wanted was a name. He really didn't care if he killed Lester or if he let him walk out of the cell. But killing him would only be fair, since Lester sure as hell didn't care that Bear nearly died a month ago due to Lester's recklessness.

"Lester, I just need a name. Any name that leads me to him. You got in contact with him to set up that job. How did that happen? Don't try and tell me telepathy or some mystical garbage."

"They'll kill me, Jack."

"I'll kill you, Lester."

Lester bowed his head. "Do what you gotta do then. At least you'll be quick about it. Those guys will torture me and probably kill my family too." His voice shook the entire time. Bravery did not befit him. He made a better computer geek than a spy.

"Why are you protecting these people?"

"Protecting them? I don't care about them. I'm protecting my wife, my kids."

Jack remained silent, pushed the barrel of his gun into the back of Lester's head.

"You're a killer, Jack, but you won't go after my family."

Jack smiled. He would go after Lester's family if it got him what he wanted. And Lester knew enough about Jack to know that. "What if I could offer you protection until this mess is cleaned up?"

"How? I thought you worked alone now?"

"Plenty of people owe me favors," Jack replied.

Just then his cell phone rang. *Christ, how did she find my number?* He took his phone out of his pocket and looked at the caller ID. It wasn't Clarissa. He didn't recognize the number at all.

He walked out of the cellar and told Bear to keep an eye on Lester. Bear was the only person other than Clarissa that Jack trusted. They had worked together as independent contractors for the better part of a decade, and Bear had saved his life at least a dozen times. In another life the two were soldiers. Trained killers. But now they killed for profit.

"Who is this?" asked Jack.

"Hello, Mr. Jack."

He recognized the voice. "You ready to finish this deal?"

"What business have you with Lester, Mr. Jack?"

Jack climbed the stairs and peeked out the tall, skinny windows next to the front door. "Not sure what you're talking about."

"Mr. Jack, you know I have eyes and ears everywhere," the old man said. "Don't try to fool me."

"My business with Lester is *my* business. I don't work for you."

"As you wish. Mr. Jack, all I want is the briefcase. I want to complete our deal."

"You left me out there to hang yesterday. Why should I trust you now?"

The old man laughed. "Trust? This is about money, Mr. Jack. Not trust."

"Where do you want to meet?" Jack asked while peeking into the cellar.

"The city is too hot right now. Your face is all over the news. Something about kidnapping a girl and attacking a cop. The horror."

"Christ. Tourists with their friggin' camera phones." Jack would have to use another favor to clean this up. "Ok, so where then?"

"I will be in touch soon, Mr. Jack," the old man replied. "Oh, and give my regards to Mr. Lester. Tell him his wife and kids didn't suffer, they went in their sleep."

Jack was silent. He worked out what had happened in his head. The old man must have had guys at Lester's house or tailing Bear. The men saw Bear go in and come back out with Lester. As soon as Bear left, they went in and killed Lester's family.

They probably have pictures of Bear going in and leaving with Lester and can use those to pin the murders on him. What a mess.

"Your silence is confirmation enough for me Mr. Jack. Goodbye."

The line went silent. Jack stood in the doorway and nodded at Bear.

The big man walked toward him. "What's the deal?"

"Seems Lester pissed off a lot of people."

"How so?" Bear asked

"That was the old man," Jack stepped back and closed the door. The cellar was soundproof as long as the door was shut. "He had Lester's family taken care of."

"You don't think he's behind—"

"No," Jack said. "It's something else. Wait here."

Jack stepped into the cellar. "You ready to give me a name?" He positioned himself behind Lester.

"I told you Jack, I got nothing."

"You know who that was?" Jack asked. He didn't wait for Lester to answer. "That was the old man. You pissed a lot of people off, Lester. Powerful people."

This was a game to Jack. Whether or not Lester gave him a name, Jack was going to kill him. He'd be doing Lester a favor. Lester's family was dead and the poor bastard would be devastated when he found out their fate. Besides, the old man would kill Lester if Jack didn't, and it sure as hell wouldn't be quick or painless. Why not save him the pain of knowing his family had been murdered?

"Do it!" Lester shouted.

Jack grabbed a piece of plexiglass to shield his body from the blood spray. He preferred to stay clean whenever possible. He fired one bullet into the back of Lester's head and stepped back.

Lester's body slumped forward against the cinder block wall, slowly falling against the wall, leaving a trail of blood.

Jack opened the door and waved Bear in the room. "Take care of that."

Jack didn't know exactly what Bear would do after he left the room, but Lester's body would never be found. That was good enough for him.

"Did you get it?" Bear asked.

"No," Jack said. "Maybe the old man knows. I'll find out when I complete this deal."

Bear nodded.

Jack climbed the stairs, noticed blood stains on his shirt. He rolled his eyes and ducked into the bathroom to wash up and change before leaving the building. They each kept a change of clothes in the linen closet. Jack grabbed a casual outfit, baseball hat and a pair of sunglasses.

He made a call to an associate who could modify the footage the news was showing and get some of the heat off of him.

"Hello?"

"Hey, Brandon. It's Jack." He put the phone on speaker so he could change and talk at the same time.

"Jesus, Jack. Your face is all over the news. What the hell you got yourself into?"

"Yeah, about that... I need a favor."

"I'm already on it. But you are gonna owe me big time for this one. I'm talking a free job type favor."

"You got it." Jack hung up the phone and cursed to himself. Then he made his way to 52nd Street to find Mandy's mom.

CHAPTER 5

"You think he took care of Lester?"

"I really don't care," the old man replied. "I pay my men to kill. If Mr. Jack didn't kill him, then they will."

Charles laughed. "I see your point, Boss." He sat back and thought for a second, rubbing his temples with his large fingers. "Hey, what are we going to do about Jack?"

"Oh, I have plans for Mr. Jack." The old man smiled and clapped his bony hands together. "Big plans."

"Care to elaborate?" Charles leaned in closer to the old man.

The old man's smile broadened. "When the time comes, Mr. Charles, you will have all the details. For now, get your smelly breath out of my face."

Charles sat back in his seat. He held his hand in front of his face and exhaled into it, checking to see how bad his breath smelled. He thought about pressing his boss for more information, but he knew that wouldn't go over well. He'd seen his boss have men killed for less. No, now was not the time, the old man had made that clear. But as soon as the old man decided to confide in him, Charles would be ready. He'd proven that over the last dozen years.

The old man turned his head away and Charles thought back to his first couple of years working for the old man...

He started off working as a mechanic for the old man. One thing that was different about this crime boss. He provided cars for his guys. And he always wanted his cars to be in top shape. He had a team of mechanics available 24 hours a day. Charles had never been involved in any criminal activity before this. He took the job for the pay. He had no idea who the old man was or what his business was, but he liked the idea of being a private mechanic. It sounded official.

He worked in the garage for two years. He was a good employee, kept his head down, and did his work. By this point he knew what was really going on and so did the other mechanics. Most of them knew before they took the job. Typically, the mechanics that worked for the old man were relatives of his more trusted employees. Only the mechanics didn't have what it took to be a killer, at least the type of killers that could get away with murder. For some it was a mental thing. Either they were careless or they were incapable of pulling the trigger or swinging a bat. For others it was physical. They'd be killed on their first assignment. But they all shared one common trait. They all thought they were bad asses.

Charles ignored the banter and slacking off that went on every day at work. Some of the other mechanics were offended by this and made remarks off to the side that Charles was too good for them. Individually, they would never think about confronting Charles. At six foot six and two hundred eighty pounds, he was massive. If he hadn't dropped out of school he would have gone to the University of Miami on a football scholarship.

One day, four of the other mechanics decided they had enough of Charles and his *my crap don't stink* attitude. They circled him with a plan to attack, all of them armed with tools. It didn't take long for Charles to realize what was going on. This wasn't the first time he'd been jumped. It wouldn't be the last.

Charles didn't wait for the other mechanics to make their move. Those four dumbasses never stood a chance. He killed two of them and put the other two in the hospital. The injuries were so bad that the old man was able to blame it on a car lift collapsing. The police asked no questions. Of course, that was nothing new when the old man was involved.

The old man reviewed the footage of the fight. He liked what he saw and summoned Charles to his office. Charles was scared as he entered. He had twelve inches and one hundred twenty pounds on the old man. But he knew that men sometimes entered that office and didn't leave under their own power. The old man was vicious and ruthless, which is exactly why he was one of the most powerful crime bosses on the east coast.

"Mr. Charles," the old man said. He sat with the back of his chair facing the doorway. "Please come in and have a seat."

Charles sank down in the chair, his heart racing. "You wanted to see me, sir?"

"What is this sir talk? Just call me Boss."

"Yes, sir. I mean, Boss."

"I heard about the garage incident. You killed four of my mechanics."

"Boss, I... I'm sorry about that. They left me no choice. They surrounded me. They were all armed with tools. I guess my, my instincts kicked in."

The old man spun around in his chair and glanced to the corner of the room, giving the man standing there a nod.

Charles tightened up and shut his eyes. He expected to feel the cold barrel of a gun press against the top of his head any second now. He raised his shoulders and hunched over slightly when he heard the door shut.

The old man laughed. "Mr. Charles, if I wanted you dead you would already be gone. Why would I invite you into my office to kill you?"

Charles slowly rose up and looked at the old man. The smile looked genuine, and he was still alive. He turned his head and saw that the room was empty. "You... You're not going to kill me?"

"Kill you? God, no! I want to promote you, Mr. Charles."

"Promote me? What?"

"Those four men you killed," said the old man, "they were not just mechanics. They were a hit team. I used them for jobs that had to look amateur. The kind of hits that would be too easy to pin on me if done by a professional. Do you understand?"

Charles shook his head at the old man.

"I know you are not stupid, Mr. Charles, so I will get right to the point. You took out four trained killers and suffered barely a scratch. I want you to be my bodyguard. You will drive my limo and accompany me all day, every day. Do you understand?"

This time Charles nodded. "Yes, sir. I mean, yes, Boss." He didn't have a choice. If he said no, the old man would kill him. Even though he liked working in the garage, this was a chance to be in the action.

THE CAR HIT A POTHOLE AND CHARLES'S HEAD BUMPED INTO the roof as the Mercedes bounced. The pain on the top of his head was enough to bring his attention back to Jack and the current situation. "He's become a pain in the ass. Jack, that is."

"But an efficient pain in the ass, Mr. Charles," the old man said. "Much like yourself." He grinned.

Charles chuckled while rubbing the top of his head. "I just don't see where he gets off being so arrogant. I wish you would let me—"

"Mr. Charles," the old man interrupted. "When the time comes, if the time should come, you will get the go ahead. For now, quit talking about Mr. Jack. It is giving me indigestion."

"Ok, Boss. What do you think about Thai for dinner?"

The old man looked at him and smiled. "Good choice, Mr. Charles."

CHAPTER 6

Jack's questioning cellar wasn't too far from the address Mandy had given him. He figured the little girl and her mother didn't have much, judging by the neighborhood and condition of the building. The neighborhood was a known rough area, with far too many drug pushers, addicts, and prostitutes. He wondered if Mandy's mother was one of those, or maybe all three.

He entered the old building and balked at the smell of stale urine. "Bums," he muttered under his breath. There was no security in a building like this. Anyone could sneak in at night and sleep in the halls. These buildings had no public restrooms, so the derelicts would just urinate in the hallway. The supers of these buildings could care less, so the whole place stunk to high hell.

The elevator had an *Out of Order* sign posted on it. Probably for the best, Jack figured. Who would want to get stuck in an elevator in a place like this? He pushed the door to the stairwell open, heard the sounds of a prostitute servicing a man underneath the concrete steps. He imagined the prostitute was a woman, but he knew he couldn't be sure of that. Around these parts, people would do anything to get their next fix.

Jack worked his way up the industrial grey painted stairs to the fourth floor, cautiously approaching every turn and doorway. Anyone could be hiding out here, just waiting for some fool to come by that they could rob, rape, and/or kill.

He reached the fourth floor, pushed open the door, entered the hallway. It was dark, most of the lights on the floor smashed out. He made his way down to apartment D and knocked on the door. No answer. He waited a minute, noticing how dented the door was and how the paint was cracked and falling off in chips. He knocked again. Still no answer.

Jack turned the doorknob, found it unlocked, pushed the door open. He had a preconceived notion of what the apartment would look like from the moment he entered the building. It didn't disappoint him. If anything, it was more disgusting than what he had imagined.

That poor girl. I can't believe she has to live in this pigsty.

It disturbed him to think that sweet little girl would probably end up like her mother, an addicted prostitute drug dealer. That was his assumption at least.

He entered the apartment and closed the door behind him. There were no signs of anyone. "Hello?" he called out.

No response.

He started to reach for the light switch but stopped himself. He had been around long enough to know that you could wire a light switch to do some pretty nasty stuff. Instead he walked over to the windows and opened the blinds.

As the light filled the room, he realized that maybe Mandy's mom wasn't the slob he thought she was. The apartment wasn't messy, it was ransacked. Jack's instincts kicked in and he went on high alert. He pulled out his gun and proceeded cautiously through the rest of the apartment.

The small dwelling only had a few rooms. He checked them all to make sure no one was hiding. He knew he wouldn't uncover any dead bodies. It didn't smell bad enough.

He entered the bedroom, which was as trashed as the rest of the apartment. On the dresser was a picture of Mandy with whom Jack guessed was her mother. He removed the picture from the frame and stashed it in his backpack. On the floor lay a tattered old teddy bear. He grabbed it as well, figuring Mandy would be happy to be reunited with her stuffed animal.

Jack searched the apartment thoroughly, didn't find anything concrete. This was a professional job, not a random break in. What had the woman done to deserve this? The thought that whoever broke in might be watching crossed his mind. On top of that, the old man knew he had Lester, which meant Bear had been followed. Whoever followed Bear had likely been positioned outside the questioning cellar, and they would have followed Jack here.

He peeked out the door and saw the hallway was empty.

Time to go.

Jack stood just inside the entrance of the apartment building. He surveyed the scene outside through the dirty window pane, looking for any sign of the old man's crew waiting for him.

A bum wearing an old fashioned hat and a trench coat pushed through the doorway.

"Hey," Jack said. "Give me your hat and coat."

"Screw you, man," the bum said.

"I'll pay you."

"Fine. One thousand dollars and it's yours, man."

Jack pulled out a wad of cash and held out a hundred dollar bill in front of the bum's face.

The bum's eyes lit up. "You got a deal, bro!" He pulled off his coat and hat and handed them to Jack.

The stench of the trench coat overwhelmed Jack, but he didn't have much choice. Without it, he'd be made the instant he walked out the door. He buttoned up the coat and put on the hat, praying that it wasn't infested with lice. He hated the shaved head look. He opened the door, turned back to the man and flipped him the baseball cap and jacket he had been wearing when he entered the building.

Jack dipped his head as he took the steps from the building to the sidewalk. He spotted two of the old man's guys out of the corner of his eye. They watched him as he walked down the stairs. He saw one of them point at him and Jack reached into his coat and grabbed the handle of his gun.

The men's eyes shifted back to the door.

Jack breathed a sigh of relief as he turned onto the sidewalk and headed back towards Clarissa's apartment.

CHAPTER 7

A couple blocks away, Jack glanced over and saw the old man's white Mercedes stop next to him. His heart sank. He *had* been spotted leaving the building.

"Heya Jack," Charles said from inside the Mercedes

"What's your ugly mug doing out here?" Jack asked.

"Picking up the old man's dry cleaning," Charles replied.

Jack faked a smile.

"I need you to get in the car, Jack." Charles rested the barrel of his gun on the window.

Jack looked for an escape route. The high walls of block-wide apartment buildings trapped him.

"There's nowhere to run, Jack. We got guys all around."

Jack felt the barrel of a gun poking his back. He slowly raised his arms. The person behind him reached around and pulled Jack's gun out of his pocket, then pushed him forward. Jack stumbled, turned, saw the bum from the building wearing his hat and jacket.

"Like, thanks for the hundred, bro," the bum said.

Charles and the bum burst into laughter.

Jack wondered how he had been so stupid. "Very clever, you got me." He heard the car door open behind him and braced himself for what was to come. Bullet to the brain? Bat to the head?

Charles placed his massive hand on Jack's shoulder. "C'mon, Jack. Why don't you get in the car?"

Jack obliged. He had no choice.

The bum closed the door behind Jack and walked away, whistling a tune.

Charles signaled to the driver and the car pulled away.

"Jack, give up the search for the girl's mother. That's a dead end," said Charles.

"What? What are you talking about?" Jack asked.

"The little girl was supposed to be a diversion. We put her there so no one would see you get into the Boss's car." Charles poked him in the chest.

Jack glared back at Charles and clenched his fists.

I was set up. They planted the little girl. And now she and her mom are in danger because of me.

Charles looked down at Jack's hands. "Don't bother Jack. You wouldn't stand a chance in the back of this car." He paused. "So anyways, when you helped the little girl, you messed up the old man's plans. The mom had done some work for him. She might be pissed that he kidnapped her and her daughter, but she wouldn't dare stand up to him."

"She was just standing there crying. She said she didn't know where her mother was," Jack said.

"Imagine you're an 8 or 9 year old kid, Jack. What'd you do if I told you 'don't tell the truth,' and that if you did I'd kill your mother? And no matter how safe you thought you were, I would be watching you and would chop your mommy's head off if you said anything. Would you talk?" Charles's eyes were wide, his hands out.

"Guess being the old man's top guy is a boring gig, huh, Chuck?" Jack said. "Getting your rocks off by scaring little girls now?"

Charles threw his head back and laughed. He didn't get dirty much anymore, but you didn't insult him like that. He stopped laughing then slammed his large elbow into Jack's face.

The impact knocked Jack's head back into the seat. The elbow smashed his nose. His eyes teared up and he felt blood pouring over his upper lip. He reached up and felt his nose. It wasn't broken. Charles didn't have enough room to strike with that kind of force. But it was a clear reminder of the disadvantage Jack was at in the backseat of a car against a man like Charles.

"You got anything else to say, Jack?" Charles chuckled.

Jack wiped his eyes and pinched his nose closed. He looked over at Charles who was still smiling. He stared at the scar that ran from an inch above Charles's right eyebrow down to his jaw.

Charles glanced over. His eyes narrowed, his lips thinned. "I ain't forgot about that night, Jack. I'll never forget that you did this." He pointed to his scar, traced it halfway down.

Jack tried to clear the blood from his throat.

"I already told the old man, the moment he decides you are worthless to us, I want the job." He flashed a smile at Jack. Charles had a smile like a hockey player. Jack counted at least four teeth missing.

Jack didn't let any man intimidate him, but from a physical standpoint, Charles had him beat. Charles knew how to fight and he could take a hell of a lot of punishment. Jack had to watch himself in this situation. It could get out of control fast. If there was one person the old man wouldn't immediately kill for disobeying his orders, it was Charles. Sure, he might get an earful for killing Jack, but that would be about it. Charles knew it. More importantly, Jack knew it too.

The two men sat in silence for a few minutes until Charles reached to the side.

Jack turned, arms up ready to defend himself.

Charles laughed. "Jesus, Jack. I'm getting a drink out for us." He pulled out a fifth of whiskey and retrieved two tumblers from the center console. He poured each of them a shot.

Jack took the glass and wiped the blood away from his lips with the sleeve of the dirty trench coat, trying not to think of what might be living on the rag. He tilted his head back, letting the whiskey burn its way down his throat, then he held out the glass for another pour.

"Thirsty?" Charles asked him.

"Just pour me another."

Charles chuckled. "Hey, the more the merrier. Just gonna make it easier to kill you if need be."

Jack forced a smile. "So what about the girl's mom?"

"She's of no use to the old man now. Garbage, that's what he called her."

"So where is she then?"

"What do you do with garbage, Jack?"

Jack reached back behind his head and grabbed a handful of his hair.

"Forget about the mother, Jack."

"Just tell me if she's dead." He locked eyes with Charles.

"Just complete the deal, Jack. Complete the deal, then you'll get the mother."

Jack held out the empty glass. "Let me out at the next corner and I'll go get the briefcase."

"You're funny," Charles said. But Charles wasn't laughing. He looked more serious now than ever. "You think I'll just let you out of this car? Have you lost your mind?"

"I'm not gonna take you there. If you want it, you let me out."

"You're in no position to demand anything, my friend," said Charles.

Jack rubbed his eyes and double checked his nose, making sure it hadn't been broken. He had a knife hidden on his leg but there was no way he could get to it without Charles noticing.

"Well? You gonna tell me where it's at?" Charles asked. "And don't tell me the whore's apartment. We already searched there. Didn't find nothing."

Jack panicked at the thought of the old man's guys in the apartment with Clarissa and Mandy. He controlled his emotions and asked, "What whore? What apartment?"

"Let's not play games." Charles shifted his drink between his hands. "We've had someone on you since yesterday. You went into the apartment last night with the little girl and the briefcase." Charles pointed to Jack's left wrist. "Then you came out this morning with nothing. My guys tore through the apartment and found nothing. No briefcase. No documents. The whore said she knew nothing about it." He stared at Jack and held out his hands.

Jack contemplated his next move. He wondered what they had done with Clarissa and Mandy. "Did you kill them?"

"Jack, we may be criminals but we don't kill innocent children." Charles said, turning his palms up. "The little girl is fine. We have her in a safe place."

"What about the woman?"

"The whore? We have her too."

Jack clenched his jaw. "Is she safe?"

"Well," Charles paused. He searched for the right words. "She's not dead, Jack. But we had to... question her."

"Bastards," Jack said.

"You have some dangerous friends, Jack. We had to make sure she wasn't a threat. And we needed to know for sure what she knew about the documents."

Jack was silent. He thought about what Clarissa had likely gone through. Tough didn't begin to define her, and Jack had seen her take down a two hundred fifty pound man. But that was a drunken customer in an alley behind a club, not a group of trained killers.

"It's nothing a little time and a few stitches aren't going to take care of. So as long as we get what we want, she'll be free to be your whore again."

Jack couldn't stop thinking about Mandy and how scared she must be.

He remembered the tattered teddy bear he found in the apartment. He reached over his shoulder to grab his bag.

"Whoa, whoa! What are you doing?" Charles shouted. He pulled his gun out and jammed it into Jack's stomach.

"Relax, Chuck," he said. "I grabbed the girl's teddy bear from her apartment. I just wanted to ask you to give it to her." He held his breath waiting for the giant to pull the trigger or remove the gun from his stomach.

"Look at you," Charles said, holstering his weapon. "Turned into a big pussy."

He knew Charles a long time ago, before the big man was a badass. The big man had a soft spot for kids. Jack felt sure that Charles hated that the old man authorized taking the little girl. But Charles was a good soldier and did what he was told.

Jack fished around the bottom of his bag until he found what he was really looking for. The brass knuckles felt cold against his sweaty palm. With his other hand he pulled out the stuffed bear. He held it up in front of Charles and beamed a big smile.

"This will make her feel better, I'm sure of it."

Charles didn't look.

"C'mon, take a look, Chuck."

"I told you not to call me Chuck, you arrogant prick. One more time…"

He didn't get to finish the sentence. As Charles turned his head, Jack met it with a brass knuckle reinforced right hook. Charles's forehead split open upon impact. Blood splattered on the ceiling, the seats, and both men. The big man's eyes rolled back in his head as he slumped back against the door.

The driver sat straight up, startled. "What the hell did you do?"

Jack reached into Charles' jacket and grabbed his pistol. He pointed it at the driver. "Don't move a muscle unless I say so."

The driver froze in place. Sweat covered his forehead. It started beading down his face.

"Unlock the door and give me your cell," Jack said.

The driver unlocked the car doors, offered up his cell phone.

Jack slowly backed out of the car, keeping his gun trained on the driver's head. He fired a shot into the navigation system and then took off.

CHAPTER 8

"Wipe the blood from your face, child."

Clarissa reached over, grabbed the towel lying next to her and wiped the blood and dirt off her face. The last eight hours had been hell. Three different interrogators had beaten her, each of them using a different tactic. They all wanted to know the location of the documents. She figured that with as much torture as she had gone through, they would believe her denials. But they all knew Jack, and anyone associated with him should be considered as trained and dangerous as him.

"Now, are you going to tell me what I want to know?" asked the mysterious man.

She pushed her head and torso off the ground and looked up at him. This man was different. Not that big when compared to the other three that had taken turns beating her. He looked to be as tall as her, but he probably didn't weigh more than a hundred fifty pounds. His face was drawn and pale, with a thin silver and grey mustache. However, he had a sinister look about him. His nose crooked like a fighter's. His left eye was completely white, highlighted by the fact that the right one looked black.

His eyes met hers and he continued. "Or am I going to have to persuade you?" He put on a pair of dark leather gloves.

Clarissa steadied herself, waiting for the room to stop spinning. She sat up and stared at the man.

"I'm waiting." He tapped his foot.

Clarissa cleared her throat to speak.

The man raised an eyebrow in anticipation.

Instead of speaking, she spat at him. She aimed for his face, but the beatings had left her weak. Her spittle sprayed onto her chest, over the floor and on his shoes.

The man looked down at the mixture of blood and saliva covering his seven hundred dollar Italian designer shoes. He shook his head and smiled at her. "If these shoes didn't cost so much, I'd break your ribs with them."

Clarissa mustered up a laugh. "Who are you?"

"Why should I tell you?" the man asked.

"The other cowards did."

"The other cowards also failed to coerce you to give up the information they were tasked to get from you."

Clarissa smiled. She'd pissed the interrogators off, no doubt about that. They couldn't get anything out of her. Not a single word.

The man smiled back. He seemed to be intrigued by her. "My name is Sinclair," he said. Sinclair stepped back and grabbed a black leather bag from the table. It resembled one of those medical bags doctors carried around a hundred years ago.

She stared intently at Sinclair as he dug around in his bag. *This is different.* None of the other men had brought anything with them, just their fists. They used brute force on her. "You're not like the others," she said.

Sinclair looked down at her, his lips pressed tight. "Thank you, dear. I'm not part of the old man's association. I work independently. People call me in when they need information extracted. They call me when no one else can crack the code." He reached into his bag again, pulled out a large hypodermic needle and a vial of liquid. "I'm a specialist," he said as he plunged the needle into the vial, filling it three quarters of the way to full. The needle slid out of the vial. He flicked the tip with his middle finger, sending a bead of fluid to the floor.

Clarissa steadied herself, removing any expression from her face. Her heart rate increased, as did her breathing. She wanted to ask what the needle was for, but she knew. Instead she asked, "Does it really do anything when you flick the end of a needle like that? I thought that was just to build a little suspense in a movie."

Sinclair laughed. "You are something else, child."

She smiled, shrugged. She felt the sincerity in his words, but she wasn't going to kid herself. In the end, this would go the same way as the other attempts to get her to talk had gone.

"Now, child, we can do this the easy way or the hard way."

Six hours ago Clarissa would have leapt at him, taken the syringe and plunged it into his neck. However, the hours of beatings had left her exhausted. She held out her arms, palms up and waited for him to inject the drug into her.

"Very nice," Sinclair said. "I'll make this quick."

Clarissa's eyelids fluttered. Her eyes reacted to the light. The world looked grey and blurry. The drug Sinclair injected into her knocked her out cold. For how long, though? She blinked and her vision started to clear. She saw his expensive shoes a few feet away from her face.

"Welcome back," Sinclair said.

She tried to lift herself up but found that her arms wouldn't move. She tried to kick her legs and nothing happened. She tried to talk but her mouth stayed shut. Her throat didn't produce a single sound. She could feel some things. Her body tingled. The sting of the cuts and bruises hadn't faded. She just couldn't move.

"Not to worry," he told her. "I've injected you with a paralytic agent. Your muscles are frozen, that is all. In a few minutes the ability to control your body will return. Try speaking now."

Clarissa tried to talk. A squeak slipped from her throat. Her mouth remained closed, though, still unable to work the muscles of her face.

"Excellent. Here's how this will work. I'm going to ask you a question and you are going to give me an answer. Failure to provide me an answer will result in pain being inflicted upon you. Understand?"

Clarissa remained still.

"Blink twice to let me know that you understand," he said.

She blinked her wide eyes twice.

His lips thinned. "Don't worry. I'm not going to hit you. I don't believe in that. I can see that they have thoroughly beaten you. Yet, where did that get them?" He shrugged. "You see, my methods are far more effective. A tough girl like you can take a fist to the face. But do you really want to lose your thumbs?" He held up a pair of garden shears, slamming the blades together to demonstrate.

A tear rolled down Clarissa's cheek. Her lips trembled. She tried to force out a word but nothing happened.

"There, there. You have nothing to be afraid of. Tell me what I want to know and I'll be on my way. Have you regained your voice?"

She looked away and closed her eyes. She enjoyed a few moments of silence, trying to convince herself this was just a dream. The hissing of a blowtorch disrupted the serenity she had built in her mind. She opened her eyes and looked up at Sinclair.

He held the end of an ice pick over a flame. "I asked if you had regained your voice."

She refused to answer, looked away.

Sinclair knelt over her and whispered in her ear, "We can do this any way you like. It makes no difference to me." He waited a few seconds for a response and then touched her cheek with the burning hot ice pick.

Clarissa gritted her teeth and did her best to hold in her scream. The pain increased with every second he held the burning ice pick to her face. She yelled out, "Bastard!"

"Now that wasn't so difficult, was it? Now that we have established you can speak, we will proceed with the questioning." He lifted her off the ground and sat her in a chair fitted with restraints. He crossed the large leather belts across her torso, wrapping them around her arms. He also placed separate belts around her waist, above her knees, and across her shins, securing them to the chair. Sinclair grabbed his chair and supply bag. He placed his chair in front of Clarissa and sat down. "I've already provided you with instructions on how this works, so let's get started."

Clarissa looked down at her bound body. The feeling returned to her arms and legs, but she was in no position to defend herself.

"First question. What is your name?"

She didn't answer.

He fired up the blowtorch and grabbed the shears. "The beauty of heating these up is that they will partly cauterize the remaining flesh after I cut off your thumb, reducing the amount of blood loss. Quite revolutionary for cleanup crews."

She watched intently as the blades turned bright red. She knew she was dead. It would just be a matter of how much suffering she could tolerate before the final blow.

Sinclair leaned in and grabbed her right hand. "I will ask one more time. After that you lose your thumb. What is your name?"

She felt the heat from the blades. She clenched her fists. "Clarissa," she whispered. "Clarissa Abbot."

"Beautiful name, Ms. Abbot. I can't believe you were almost willing to give up your thumb to withhold that information from me." He scribbled her name into a notepad.

She knew what he would do with her name. They probably figured she wasn't going to give them any information, but killing her would be a waste.

However, with her name they could track down her family and try to find someone close to her. If she wouldn't talk to save her own life, maybe she would to save someone she loved. Fortunately, she had no one, except for Jack.

"Next question. What do you do for a living?"

"I'm a dancer."

"Ah, ballet?"

She smiled at him. "Exotic."

"Intriguing. Who is the little girl?"

"Mandy?" she asked.

"Is there more than one?"

"No. Mandy is her name. I thought you would know about her. I don't know much about her. She was lost. Jack brought her to my apartment."

"Tell me about Jack. How do you know him?"

"My father. He served under my father."

"So your father introduced you to him?" he asked.

"Yes." Her eyes cast down at the floor.

"Go on," said Sinclair.

"Jack was the one who informed me that my father had been killed. And then, I don't know."

"I sense there is more, Ms. Abbot. Did Jack take you in after your father's death?"

She laughed. "I was nineteen and had been on my own for two years. I didn't need a hero to take me in. He let me know if I ever needed anything he was there and could help."

"Are you aware of Jack's job?"

Clarissa nodded. She didn't know all the details, but she knew enough.

"Jack was carrying a briefcase the night he came to your apartment. Correct?"

"Yeah, handcuffed to his wrist."

"Did he tell you what was in the briefcase?"

"No," Clarissa responded. "He never said anything about it. I didn't ask, he didn't tell."

Sinclair reached for the ice pick and blowtorch again. He repositioned himself and said, "Where is that briefcase now?"

She shook her head, eyes focused on the ice pick. The burn on her face ached and she wondered if he was going to give her a matching one on the opposite cheek.

"I don't know," she said.

"Are you sure?" he asked as he lit the blowtorch.

"Yes," she replied. "Jack was gone before I woke up. He took it with him."

"Did you see him take it with him?" Sinclair held the end of the ice pick in the flame.

"Like I said, I was sleeping. When I got up, he was gone. So was the briefcase."

"So you looked for the briefcase?"

"What? No, I mean, I just noticed it was gone."

"How long have you been working for Jack?" His tone deepened, eyes narrowed to slits, and his lips drew thin and tight.

"Work for him? I don't work for him. He's just a friend."

"Do you often let friends sleep over at your house?"

The questioning flustered her.

"I will ask you one more time, Clarissa. Where is the briefcase?" He turned off the blowtorch and put it on the table. Then he stood up and grabbed the back of her head pulling her hair back and forcing her face to look up at him. He held the ice pick inches from her eye.

Clarissa started to cry. "I don't know."

"Clarissa, don't lie to me. Where is the briefcase?"

"If I knew, I would tell you."

"Don't mess with me, Clarissa." He leaned over so his face was barely hovering over hers. "Do you see my eye? Do you see my dead eye? That is what happens when a scalding hot ice pick is inserted into an eye. Is this what you want?"

Clarissa sobbed. Her heart raced and her stomach tightened. She had never been this frightened before. "I don't know."

Sinclair backed up and reignited the blow torch. "This is your last chance." He cleared his throat and brushed strands of his silver and black hair out of his face. "Where is that briefcase?"

She said nothing and looked away. There was no hope. His gloved hand grabbed her chin and pulled her face toward him.

"So be it, Ms. Abbot." He moved the ice pick directly above her eye. "I won't do this quickly. You see, it's rather painless once the pick penetrates your eye."

The real damage was the buildup of the event, the terror of knowing that a burning piece of metal was about to be inserted into her eye, blinding her. The fear spread as the glowing red ice pick inched closer and closer.

"Enjoy these last ten seconds of sight."

The door to the cell slammed open. Sinclair let go of Clarissa's face and turned around. "What the hell are you doing?"

Clarissa saw the outline of a large man in the doorway.

Charles stepped into the light. "Give me the whore." Dried blood covered his face. A white bandage stained red covered his forehead. A trickle of blood streamed down between his eyebrows and along the right side of his nose.

"The old man called me to extract information. You can have her when I'm done," Sinclair said.

"You're done," Charles said. "I'm relieving you of your duties."

"Like hell you are. Go get the old man."

Charles grabbed Sinclair by the throat and lifted him into the air. Sinclair swung the ice pick and plunged it into the back of Charles's shoulder. Charles hurled the man against the wall. Sinclair staggered to his feet. Charles charged and slammed his shoulder into Sinclair, driving him into the wall. He lifted Sinclair by his neck, punching him twice in the face. He let Sinclair go and watched his body collapse into a pile on the floor.

Then he turned his attention to Clarissa. "You're mine." He untied her restraints, threw her over his shoulder, and carried her out of the room.

Part of her felt relieved. And the other part of her felt more terrified than ever.

CHAPTER 9

Jack stood in the shadows, half a block from Clarissa's apartment building. The briefcase and the documents it held were hidden inside an apartment. They were the key to getting Mandy and Clarissa out of the old man's compound alive.

He knew the old man would have a team watching the apartment building, waiting for him. Like any tactical team, there would be a pattern to their movements. He studied the area to locate the men and dissect their patrol pattern. Two men stood on top of the building. A gap of 15 seconds where neither man monitored the front of the building occurred every two minutes. Ground level appeared easier. Two men patrolled on the ground. They walked around the building together, leaving a large gap of time where the front was unpatrolled.

They heard about me. Must be scared to be alone.

Jack inched closer to the building, tight against a brick facade, staying out of the light. When the opportunity presented itself he sprinted to the entrance. He entered the building with the gun he stole from Charles drawn. He made his way to the apartment where he had hidden the briefcase. As he picked the lock again, he thought to himself, *Who the hell is dumb enough to not use a deadbolt in this city?* The latch clicked.

He pushed the door open and peeked inside. The large man sleeping on the couch hadn't been there when he was inside last time. It had been completely empty. Jack wished the heavy man was wearing more than a pair of boxers with cartoons of puppies.

Jack slipped to the closet in the back corner of the room. The sleeping man coughed and seemed to be waking up.

I'd kill for a suppressor for this gun.

He held his breath until the man rolled over and went back to sleep.

Jack opened the closet door and moved blankets and sheets around until he had the briefcase in his grasp. He backed out of the closet and turned to see a woman standing there, half naked. She, unlike her sleeping beau, looked good in her skivvies. At first he grinned and winked at her, but when she opened her mouth to scream he held the gun up in one hand and put his other hand to his mouth and gave her the universal signal for, *"Shut the hell up if you don't want to die!"*

She stood there, frozen. Arms held out, mouth open, eyes unblinking. Jack fully expected her to urinate on herself.

He made his way back to the door, keeping his back against the wall. He kept the gun pointed up and his finger over his mouth. She turned her body, mirroring his movements. He opened the door and slipped out. Before completely closing the door he popped his head back in and said, "You really should use your deadbolt and get a chain lock as well. Especially with a body like that. This was just too easy."

The man started to wake.

Jack smiled at the woman and closed the door. He wasn't one hundred percent sure, but he thought she might have smiled back.

Jack's smile faded as he turned his attention to getting out of the building. He climbed the stairs to the second floor and ran around back. The hallway was dimly lit. He peered out the window. The dark alley behind the apartment building provided just the kind of cover he needed. He lifted the window and climbed onto the metal fire escape. He stuck a leg over and paused. The sound of police cars approaching filled the air. Jack groaned, certain it had been the fat man that placed the call.

They actually did him a favor by calling the police. The men on the top of the building would have to hunker down so they wouldn't be spotted. The team that was patrolling outside would split, running off in two directions. At least, Jack hoped that would happen.

Jack made his way down to the ground, using the gaps between the large bricks that made up the exterior as handles and footholds. He crouched down as he heard the men on patrol approaching. Just as he expected, they each went a different direction after they reached the back of the building. He followed the heavier man, figuring he would quit running sooner. Jack Noble, above all else, considered himself a man of opportunity.

The heavy man impressed him, making it approximately a half mile before he stopped to rest and catch his breath. As Jack approached him, he deliberately stomped his feet on the sidewalk to alert the heavy man to his presence. Jack never got much pleasure out of attacking a man from behind. He'd do it if necessary. However, he liked to look his victim in the eye as he rendered them incapacitated.

The man spun. His eyes widened at the sight of Jack, and he reached for his gun in between labored breaths. Jack closed the distance with a sprint, lunged at the man and delivered a strike to his throat. The single blow collapsed the man's windpipe. He fell to his knees and onto his stomach.

Jack searched through his victim's pockets. He had never been inside the old man's compound before, but he had heard plenty of tales from his associates. You needed an access card to get through the main gate as well as to enter certain rooms. He found the card tucked in a pocket on the inside of the man's coat. He decided to keep the jacket and ditch the disgusting trench coat. Lastly, he grabbed the man's gun and wallet. He slipped into the darkness. He had one more stop to make before going to the compound.

CHAPTER 10

J ack stood behind Bear's apartment building for close to fifteen minutes, getting more agitated with every second that passed. "C'mon Bear!" he kept muttering under his breath.

"I'm right here," a deep voice said from behind.

"Jesus!" Jack said. "I would have killed you if I heard you coming up behind me like that."

"You didn't hear me, though. Did you?"

Jack wondered how a man that large could be so invisible and so quiet. He had been in several sticky situations with Bear and not once had the enemy got the drop on the big man. Jack could partner with any spy, thief, or killer-for-hire in the country, but time and time again he chose Bear.

"Did you bring everything?" asked Jack.

Bear rolled his eyes at him and sighed. "Really, Jack?" He held out a duffel bag.

Jack grabbed the bag and inspected the weapons one by one to make sure everything was there. "Ok, looks good to me."

"When will you stop doubting me?" Bear said with a laugh.

"When we can get through one of these without me having to save your ass," Jack said.

Bear laughed.

e stress of the day had finally got to Jack. These missions usually volve personal feelings. Tonight was different. It was his fault that and one little girl were in danger of losing their lives. He swore ing man stating that he would protect Clarissa. He might as well have done the same for Mandy, because there was no way he was going to let her or her mother, if she was still alive, die.

Jack shushed Bear to get him to be quiet, but the large man's full belly laugh was too much for him and he joined in. They were in hysterics, so much so that they didn't notice a man sneaking up on them.

"Freeze!"

Jack and Bear turned and saw the man standing there with a gun pointed at them. Their laughter stopped but their smiles lingered.

"What do you make of this, Jack?" asked Bear.

"Hmmm, not sure, Bear," Jack replied. "There's only one, so it's not an asshole convention."

Bear chuckled.

"You know you're not getting paid for this one, Bear. You don't have to laugh at my jokes," Jack said.

"In that case I don't know if this is worth it." Bear acted like he was going to walk away.

"You two just shut up. Shut up or I'll shoot," the man said.

Jack gave Bear a look. The two had worked together long enough that they could communicate without saying a word. Time was running out. The man's partner would be coming around soon. Jack was surprised he wasn't there already.

Bear winked at Jack. The big man clutched his chest with both hands and fell to his knees. His eyes rolled back in his head. He hit the ground while letting out a loud groan.

"Bear," Jack said.

"What the hell is wrong with him?" the man asked.

"It looks like he is having a heart attack," Jack said.

"The hell he is," the man said while pointing at Bear. "What are you two trying to pu—"

That was all the guy got out. The instant the man looked down at Bear, Jack lifted his right knee and pulled out the tactical sidekick boot knife he kept strapped to his calf. In one fluid motion he closed the gap and plunged the knife into the man's neck, severing his carotid artery. Jack regained his balance and sliced the knife across the man's neck, sealing his fate.

"Let's get the hell out of here, Bear."

They ran for a block and got in one of Bear's cars. Hopefully the old man hadn't made this one yet.

CHAPTER 11

"Y ou're a lucky lady. You know that?"

Clarissa didn't say anything. She just stared at the scar running down Charles's face.

"The old man thinks you are a valuable asset, or some garbage like that. If it were me, I'd kill you. Slowly, though. It wouldn't happen in one night." He shifted in his seat. "I'd let hope stay alive in you for a couple days. Let you keep thinking that your boyfriend was gonna show up and be the hero. Rescue you or some garbage like that. Know what I mean?"

Clarissa raised her hand to her forehead and traced an imaginary line down her face. She saw that her mocking had started to piss him off. "How'd you get that nasty, disgusting scar?" She already knew the story. Jack had told her a dozen times about the night Charles tried to kill Bear and Jack stepped in to save his friend's life. She watched with amusement as Charles's eyes widened and his nostrils flared out in anger.

He stood, took off his jacket, turned slightly and hung it over the chair he had been sitting in. He glared at her while removing the five rings that normally adorned his large fingers. Rings were a point of contention among some guys. There were those that enjoyed the extra damage a large ring could inflict on their target. But others preferred not to have to clean the blood out of their favorite rings, so when given a choice, they never wore them in a fight.

Or, as in this case, a beating.

"Afraid of getting your pretty jewelry dirty?"

Charles bared his teeth at her as he tilted his neck side to side. She cringed at the slow popping sounds that emanated as he cracked his neck. He shrugged his shoulders. *Pop, pop, pop, pop.* He looked like a fighter getting ready to go 12 rounds.

He glared at her. "You stupid twat."

"You can't touch me," she said. "I heard the old man tell you that."

"No, he said I couldn't *kill* you." Charles smiled. "There was nothing about touching you." His eyes worked over her body.

She tensed as he approached. The restraints held her tight, and there was little she could do to defend herself. She steadied herself for what was to come.

He stood in front of her, his body massive, built like a brick wall. He took a step back and leaned over her, placing his hands on either side of her head.

"You were admiring my scar earlier," he said with a smile. "You know how I got this scar?" He raised an eyebrow.

Clarissa said nothing, didn't even blink. She continued to stare him in the eye.

"Your boyfriend gave it to me, the dumb moron. He was helping us on a job..."

Clarissa interrupted him, "I don't need a history lesson, asshole. I know all about your beauty mark. So get your stank breath out of my face."

Charles smiled at her and stood up. "You're feisty." He licked his lips. "I like that."

She didn't respond. She just watched him as he unbuttoned his shirt and took it off. He reached down and grabbed her by the jaw.

"You like what you see?"

"Screw you." Her arms pulled at the restraints.

"That's the point," he said.

He leaned over and ripped her blouse open. Clarissa closed her eyes and listened to the sound of her shirt buttons bouncing around on the floor. A lump formed in her throat. Tears welled up in her eyes. *Get ahold of yourself. Don't cry in front of this guy.* She refused to allow him the pleasure of scaring her.

"Yeah, I like that," he said glaring down at her while wiping away the tears that formed in her eyes. He placed his massive hands on her shoulders and massaged her upper back and her neck.

She fought with everything she had not to cringe at his touch.

"Maybe when this is all over, you and me can take a trip to the islands. The Boss has a nice set up down there."

"Screw you," she whispered.

"That would be included in the daily activities."

Clarissa stared at the gray concrete wall. She couldn't look him in the eye anymore.

"Don't worry, I'm gonna take really good care..." His cell phone interrupted him. "For the love of God."

She watched him lumber over to his coat, pulling his pants up so he didn't trip over them. If only she could free her hand or her leg, she could surprise him when he got back. She might not be built like a boxer, but she knew where to strike a man to take him down. Her father and Jack had given her plenty of lessons in self-defense and she had no problem putting those lessons into action.

"What?" he shouted into his phone. He stood there with the cell phone pressed against his ear while holding his pants up with his other hand. "Ok, Boss. I'll be there in a minute."

"Leaving so soon?" Clarissa asked.

He said nothing. He walked back and stopped a few feet in front of her.

"Run to your boss, Sally," Clarissa said.

Charles smiled at her.

She didn't know how much antagonizing he could take.

He started to turn towards the door and then stopped. "Go to hell," he said as he delivered a kick to her chest that sent her and the chair reeling back into the wall. Her head hit the concrete wall, knocking her out. The chair tipped over onto the floor and she laid there with a small pool of blood forming around her head.

CHAPTER 12

Jack had never been inside the old man's compound. Neither had Bear. But both men had heard plenty of stories about the place: the prostitutes the old man kept on staff, the glamorous guest accommodations, the three-hole golf course, and the interrogation and prison cells underground. Jack had a pretty good idea where Clarissa and Mandy were being kept.

"So what's the plan?" asked Bear.

Jack pulled out the access card and held it up for Bear to see. "This will get us in. I swiped it off of one of the men patrolling Clarissa's building."

"And then what?"

"I've got something he wants. He won't do anything to me," Jack said.

"You got the docs with you?"

"No," Jack said. "They are hidden."

"That's comforting," Bear said. "What about me?"

Jack smiled at his large friend. "Don't worry, they won't hurt you either."

"They can't."

The compound was well guarded. In the fifteen minutes they had been scouting the entrance they counted at least four sets of patrolling guards, ensuring that the entrance remained in sight at all times. Two more guards were positioned inside the gate, and at least half a dozen cameras were perched high and scanning in all directions.

"Ten," Bear said.

"Yeah, plus the cameras."

"Even if we get in, they are gonna have us spotted, Jack. And there is no way we get in without killing at least six of those guards."

Jack started to rethink his idea. His entire plan was based on emotion. There was no logic to it. He had seen the results of plans like this. They'd be better off shooting themselves than walking into a hornet's nest unannounced. "Dammit." He pulled out his cell phone.

"What you doing?"

"I'm going to announce our presence."

"Are you friggin' kidding me? Jack, think about this for a second."

"He's not going to do anything. Those documents are worth more to him than anything else."

"What are these documents?"

Jack frowned and gave Bear a look. Not just any look, *the* look. "You know better than to ask questions like that."

Bear wiped the sweat from his large forehead. "Christ almighty. Why do I keep working with you?"

Jack laughed. "You'd be bored without me, Bear. Admit it."

The large man forced a smile while shaking his head. "Go on then. Call him up."

Jack searched through his cell's call history until he reached the old man's number. He highlighted it and hit send.

"Hello, Mr. Jack. I have been waiting for you. I'm glad to see you weren't foolish enough to use that key card to come through the front gate."

"Let them go," Jack said.

"Will you not do me the courtesy of some polite conversation first?"

"Go to hell."

"Mr. Jack, your profanity will not be tolerated. One more outburst and the little girl loses a finger."

Jack bit his tongue as anger and frustration built up. He wished they had gone through the front gate instead. He took a deep breath to settle himself. "That won't be necessary."

"Good, I am glad you see it my way, Mr. Jack."

He hated the way the old man called him Mr. Jack. For years he had put up with it and didn't even know the old man's whole name. Nobody knew his name as far as Jack was aware. He had a hunch that Charles did, but when he asked Charles, the big oaf smiled and said 'Boss.'

"Mr. Jack, you have something I want. I have some things that you want. I have a proposal for you."

"I'm listening."

"In one half hour I will send one of my employees outside. He will exit the gate and walk twenty five feet exactly. You will come down from your hiding spot at the top of the hill and hand him the documents. After Mr. Charles and I have verified the contents of the documents I will release the little girl and the whore. Are we in agreement?"

"And the girl's mother?"

The old man raised his voice. "Mr. Jack, this is not a time for questions. Are we in agreement?"

"No deal," replied Jack. "You know I can sell those docs to the highest bidder and get ten times what you're paying me."

The old man laughed. "Are you trying to play hardball with me young man?"

"What assurance do I have you will let them go?"

"Assurance? In all the years we have worked together, have we ever had an issue, Mr. Jack?"

"No. But then again, you never tried to have me killed like you did today," Jack replied.

"At least that you are aware of, Mr. Jack," the old man said.

"Hang on." Jack covered the mouthpiece of the phone and talked it over with Bear. "I don't trust him on this Bear. He wants the documents and says he'll release them after that."

Bear's advice was simple and to the point. "Tell him to shove his offer down his throat. Or better yet, down Charles's throat."

Jack returned to the phone. "I need more than that. Release one of them to me. Then I'll go get the documents. We can meet somewhere public to complete the exchange."

"Mr. Jack, you listen to me," said the old man in a tone that Jack had never heard before. "I employ over 200 of the finest hit men, thieves, and cleaners on the east coast. I can make you disappear with a snap of my fingers." He snapped his fingers close to the phone for emphasis. "Who do you think you are to demand this of me?"

"With all due respect, old man," Jack said. "If they are the best, then why did you need me for this job?"

The old man said nothing. Jack heard muffled voices in the background. The old man was discussing it with Charles. Jack had a feeling this would work in his favor. Charles would do anything to create a situation where he and Jack would meet face to face. That meant he would do his best to persuade the old man to agree to Jack's terms.

"Mr. Jack, you have a deal."

Jack breathed a sigh of relief and gave Bear a thumbs up. The big guy wiped his brow and exhaled loudly while pretending to fall over and pass out.

"Choose now," the old man said.

"Send out the little girl and her mother."

"Oh, Mr. Jack, I am sorry to tell you that while the little girl is here with me, her mother did not make it."

Jack fought back his rage. He pictured the old man sitting there with the girl next to him, stroking her hair as he talked about her mother's death. He wondered when it happened, how it happened. He felt guilty. She died because of him. Mandy was an orphan because of him.

"Do you still want the girl, Mr. Jack? Or shall I send for the whore?"

"The girl," Jack said. He knew Clarissa could take care of herself. These guys couldn't break her.

"She will be out in twenty minutes. When the gate opens she will be sent out alone. You will meet her on the other side of the street. Do not step foot in the street, Mr. Jack. If you do so, my guards will be instructed to shoot you, and the little girl."

Twenty minutes passed. Bear stayed on the hill to the north. Jack stood across the street in front of the gate. He could make out four guards flanking either side of the gate. All of them had their guns trained on him. He looked down in amusement at the red lights flickering around on his chest. *Amateurs.* He smiled and waved at the hidden gunmen.

The area behind the gate lit up when the door opened. He could make out the shape of a little girl walking through the courtyard. *Mandy.* The gate opened automatically. She slowly approached the curb, saw Jack, smiled.

He held a hand up to keep her from running into the street. He checked to make sure no cars were coming and then motioned for her to cross over to him.

Mandy ran as fast as she could and Jack knelt down, holding his arms open for her. She had the teddy bear grasped tightly in her right hand.

That softie, he gave it to her.

Jack held her tightly, kissed her forehead, and told her everything was going to be ok. "No one is ever going to take you again," he said.

The guards kept their guns trained on Jack. He saw the red lights dancing on his chest and the back of the little girl's head. "You bastards," he yelled. "She's a little girl. Put your weapons away."

They didn't budge.

Jack lifted the girl and held her close to his chest with one arm. His other hand held his gun tight. He backed up slowly, letting the night envelop them.

CHAPTER 13

Jack and Bear owned or leased more than thirty five apartments and homes. Twenty of them were located in or just outside of the city. Last night they went to the one furthest from the old man's compound. You were never fully out of his reach, though. His network was vast. He owned police precincts. He owned other criminal organizations. The Godfather had nothing on the old bastard.

Jack sat in a rocking chair on the front porch. He had been stationed there since before dawn, watching, waiting. He expected one of the old man's teams to show up any moment. He was so focused on the street and surrounding homes he didn't notice when Bear sat down next to him.

"Nice morning," said Bear.

"Jesus, Bear. Scared the tar out of me."

Bear let out a belly laugh and handed Jack a cup of coffee.

"Thanks," Jack said. He took the mug and sipped on the coffee. "She still asleep?"

"Sound."

"Poor thing. She must have been in a panic the whole time."

Bear nodded.

"I want to take him down, Bear."

Bear raised an eyebrow and looked at him out of the corner of his eye while scratching his bushy beard.

"I know it won't happen overnight, but we can do it."

"Jack, you need to relax. Get this job done and then take a few weeks to think about it. You don't just go around declaring war on the old man. He has more contacts inside the government than you and I combined."

Jack said nothing. His eyes scanned the street looking for anything out of the ordinary.

"He doesn't know about this place, Jack." Bear stood and opened the screen door. "C'mon, let's get some breakfast and get the little girl ready to move."

Jack followed Bear into the house, sat down at the kitchen table and continued to look out the window for any sign of the old man's guys.

"Mornin' Mister Jack," a soft voice said.

Jack turned and smiled. Mandy was standing there, holding her teddy bear, eyes bright and blue. "How're you, sweetheart?"

She shrugged.

"What would you like for breakfast?" He stood and walked to the cupboard to find some cereal, certain she would want something loaded with sugar.

"Can I have some eggs?"

"Sure sweetie. Bet you didn't know that Bear over there is the finest egg-chef in the northeast!"

"Your name is Bear?" she asked.

"Yeah," Bear said. "That ok with you?"

"Like Ted E. Bear." She smiled, holding up her tattered teddy bear.

The big man chuckled. "No, not teddy. More like Grizz Lee Bear." He lifted his arms, threw his head back and made a loud roaring sound.

Mandy laughed uncontrollably and before long the two men joined her.

The laughter was interrupted by the sound of Jack's cell phone ringing. "It's the old man," he said while holding up the phone.

Bear nodded. "C'mon Mandy, let's go see what's on TV."

The little girl hopped up and followed Bear into the other room.

"I'm here," Jack said into the phone.

"Mr. Jack, I will keep this brief."

"Let me talk to Clarissa."

"There is no time for that, Mr. Jack."

"You want the documents, you'll let me talk to her." Jack wasn't sure if it was the lack of sleep, but he had never talked to the old man like this before.

There was silence on the other end. Jack heard muffled voices and thought he could make out the old man telling Charles to bring the girl over.

"Jack," a soft voice said through the phone.

"Jesus, Clarissa, I'm sorry. You ok?"

"A bit banged up, slight concussion. But other than that I'm all right."

"I'm gonna clean this up," he said. "I need you to stay strong for a bit longer. He won't do anything to you until he has what he wants. Hang in there, OK?"

"OK."

"Now say goodbye. I need to wrap this up."

"Goodbye, Jack."

The old man returned to the line. "Mr. Jack. Paris. Thursday. Bring the documents. Go alone. Understood?"

"Yeah, I got it," Jack replied. "Where do you want—"

The old man cut him off. "We'll be in touch Thursday morning. Goodbye."

The line went dead.

"That old bastard," Jack said, staring at the cell phone.

Bear was leaning against the refrigerator. He stood a good six inches taller than the appliance. "What did he say?"

"I have to go to Paris... alone. I have to be there by Thursday," Jack said. He thought for a second and then started to ask, "Bear, can you—"

"You don't have to ask. I won't let her out of my sight."

Jack smiled at him. Thanks weren't necessary. "We should get out of this house. Best to consider it a compromised location from now on."

CHAPTER 14

Jack sat alone at an empty gate in the international terminal of Hartsfield-Jackson airport in Atlanta, waiting for his flight to Paris. A man had been watching him for the past twenty five minutes. The man had even followed him to the bathroom. He didn't go in with Jack, though. When Jack exited, the man followed him back to the gate, always staying fifty feet or so away. Always kept his face hidden. The man was a Fed. Maybe even a spook. The blue suit and conservative red tie with vertical blue stripes was a giveaway. Some might say he could just be a businessman. But a businessman wouldn't wear those shoes with a twelve hundred dollar suit. Jack didn't look at him long enough to be able to place him, but he knew him.

Jack feigned interest in a magazine, checking on his chaperon from time to time. He looked up and realized the man was gone. He looked around. The man was out of sight.

"Hello, Jack."

Jack turned to face the man standing behind him. "Jesus, Frank. I thought I was going to have to kill you. You look different. Not in a good way, either."

Frank laughed. "You don't stand a chance against me, Jack."

"Hey, how's that top secret non-existent agency you work for doing?"

"Don't have a clue what you are talking about, Jack. But if I did, I'd say great." Frank winked.

The small talk continued for a few more minutes. Jack was well aware who Frank was and who the man worked for. It wasn't that long ago that

Jack worked for the same agency. He hadn't dealt with his old partner in two years or so, but routinely took contracts for the agency. They called Jack in when they needed dirty work done, the kinds of jobs that they couldn't just explain away to their backers in the government.

"Cut to the chase, Frank. What do you need me to do?"

"We became aware that you're traveling to Paris this morning. We have some laundry that needs to be washed over there. Kind of thing that is right up your alley."

Jack looked over his shoulder to make sure no one was paying attention to them. "Rate?"

"One hundred."

Jack raised an eyebrow. "That is quite generous. But my reasons for traveling, you know, I'm going to be pretty tight for time. And once my business is resolved, I might be too weighed down to complete another job."

"Two hundred," Frank said.

"Deal," Jack said. He held out his hand. "Details?"

Frank pulled out a manila folder and handed it to Jack. "It's all in there. I don't need to tell you that we never had this conversation, right, Jack?"

Both men rose to their feet. Jack extended his hand. "What conversation?" He watched as Frank walked away and then peeked down at the manila folder and shook his head in amusement. All the technology available today and one of the most secret organizations in the country, hell, in the world, just gave him an assignment in a manila folder.

"Now boarding First Class passengers for Air France flight 8985, non-stop to Charles de Gaulle airport, Paris," the flight attendant said over the intercom.

Jack tucked the manila folder into his carry on and walked toward the gate. The flight attendant took his ticket and welcomed him on board. He strolled down the jetway and settled into his first class seat, ordered a drink and sat back. He felt relaxed for the first time in weeks.

Jack thought about Mandy, reassured by the fact that she was with Bear. They had flown to Atlanta together and then the trio split up. Bear and Mandy were flying to San Diego to lay low for a few days. Jack was travelling to Paris to complete the deal with the old man and get Clarissa.

He thought about Clarissa and the oath he had made to her father as the man died in his arms. He had promised that nothing bad would ever happen to her. He sipped his whiskey and winced as he came to grips with his failure to uphold his oath to Roger Abbot, his former CO during his time in the Marines.

I'm gonna rescue her, Rog. I promise you that.

He followed his first drink with two more. The alcohol did its job. He started to feel numb. He would arrive in Paris Monday afternoon. That would leave him plenty of time to take care of the job for the Feds while he scouted possible locations for the document exchange with the old man.

He figured that he better get acquainted with his new assignment and opened up the manila folder. He raised an eyebrow and his mouth hung open when he saw the photograph. "How about that, no wonder they need me." He closed the folder and glanced around to make sure no one was watching him. He caught the eye of the pretty flight attendant walking down the aisle. "Stewardess, refill please."

EPISODE 2

CHAPTER 1

Jack Noble stepped off the plane into Charles de Gaulle airport at two-thirty Monday afternoon. He had three days until his meeting with Charles and the old man. Three days until he would hand over the documents in exchange for Clarissa. In the meantime he had an assignment to carry out for a government agency so clandestine few people had ever heard of it. He still couldn't get over the fact that someone high enough in the food chain that is the United States government wanted the target taken out.

The worst of it was that he knew he'd be stopped at customs. It happened every single time. He took the documents that the old man wanted into the restroom, took photos of each and saved them deep in his phone's file folders, as well as in the cloud using a little known application reserved for certain government associates. This method worked well for his assignment information, but he had a feeling the old man would be upset at not receiving the originals.

Fine with me. He can search through airplane toilet waste for blue stained shreds if he wants.

Jack had to get through customs before he could worry about the old man. Sure, he'd head toward the sign that said, *Nothing to Declare*, but he knew he'd be stopped.

Jack made his way through the terminal, doing his best to remain inconspicuous. Not an easy feat when you are six foot two and everything about you screams government agent, a look he couldn't shake. He would have fit in perfectly with the CIA or NSA, both of which had recruited him as his term with the Marines came to an end. But he was done being a government stool pigeon. He had heard about the opportunities available to freelancers and they had sounded far more attractive. It was Riley "Bear" Logan who first turned him on to the idea.

Bear was his associate and closest friend since the age of nineteen, when they met in Marine Recruit Training. They'd been stationed together and performed missions together. Through it all, Bear always had his back.

Jack's thoughts turned to present day and he wondered if Bear and Mandy had made it to California OK. They would have landed a couple hours before he did. He figured he would make contact as soon as he settled in.

"Monsieur, s'il vous plait."

Jack looked over and saw the customs officer, flanked by two military agents. He was motioning for Jack to step over to his table.

Jack nodded and changed course. Dropped his bag on the table and pulled out his wallet.

"Passport, s'il vous plait."

"Right here," Jack said.

The agent looked the passport up and down. The man was frail looking, very pale, with a thin mustache and large mole just to the left of his nose.

Jack figured he could take the agent out with one shot to the throat, crush his windpipe. Then he'd lift the table and use it to slam into the two military agents. He wouldn't, of course, just a little mental exercise to keep the mind sharp.

"Monsieur Howard Blair?" the agent asked as he dug through Jack's duffel bag.

"That's me," Jack replied.

"What business do you have in France this week?"

"My cousin called two nights ago. Aunt Josephine is very sick. They expect her to pass any day now. As a kid I spent a lot of time with her. Know her better than my own mother. Used up some of my vacation time at work and bought a ticket."

"My condolences, Monsieur Blair." He zipped the bag closed and slid it across the table to Jack, apparently happy with the contents. He then picked up the cell phone, spun it around a few times, pressed a couple buttons, placed it on the table and slid it across. "Enjoy your stay in France."

Jack threw his duffel bag over his shoulder, stuffed his phone in his pocket, looked up to say thank you, but the officer had already turned his attention to someone else.

"Monsieur, s'il vous plait."

Jack stepped to the curb and looked over the mile long line of taxis waiting to pick up tourists, business-people and locals, all of whom assimilated into a muddled line. Jack imagined that from above it looked like a flesh colored caterpillar writhing on the ground.

There were at least two dozen people ahead of him. He watched as a young woman tried to wrangle her three small children into the back of a taxi. A poke in his back interrupted his musings.

"Jack, right?"

"No, name's Blair. Howard Blair. You must have me mistaken." Jack heard the distinctive sound of a gun being cocked. He turned his head to glance over his shoulder and breathed a sigh of relief. "Pierre... Jesus Christ, I could have killed you seven ways to Sunday you dirty bastard."

This drew a considerable number of stares from the crowd around them.

"Come with me Jack, no need to wait in line for a taxi."

Jack looked around, making sure no one had followed him or Pierre. The area was clear as best he could tell. "All right, I'm staying at the Hotel de Crillon."

Pierre let out a long whistle. "Very nice my friend. Business must be good."

Jack laughed. "You have no idea, Pierre. No idea at all."

Pierre reached for Jack's bags, but Jack pulled back.

"Not a chance Pierre."

"Suit yourself. I was just being hospitable."

"I know your kind of hospitality and I'll gladly pass."

Pierre laughed and waved for Jack to follow him. "My car is in that lot there."

They walked in silence to the car. Jack glanced over his shoulder occasionally, making sure no one followed behind them.

"So this job, it's big, yeah?"

Jack nodded. "I'll tell you more at the hotel."

CHAPTER 2

"He's too much of a problem now. Why can't you see that?" Charles paced back and forth in the hotel room, his eyes focused on the old man.

"Mr. Charles," the old man said. "Just because you and Mr. Jack have a history together does not mean that I should just kill the best operator that I *don't* employ full-time."

Charles stopped, threw his arms in the air and clenched his large fists behind his head.

"When I have a job that requires a certain level of... separation... Mr. Jack is the man I go to." The old man stood up and jabbed a bony finger into Charles's chest. "You wouldn't even have this position if he had accepted the job."

Charles looked down at his boss, flared his nostrils and furrowed his brow, trying his best to intimidate the old man. But he knew any attempt to scare the old man was a lost cause. His boss feared no man.

The old man turned his back on Charles. "I have plans for Mr. Jack. You just have to accept that. No less than six assignments are planned for him, any one of which he might not survive. But I am quite confident that he is the only one who can handle them."

Charles nodded. "Boss, all I'm saying is..."

"All you are saying to me is rubbish," the old man yelled. "I have told you repeatedly to let this go, yet you continue to hound me with these suggestions that we take out Mr. Jack. If I hear this again, I will have you relieved of your position."

Charles took a step back. He knew exactly what his boss meant by those words. This was the first time that the old man had ever threatened him and it disturbed him. *Is he serious?* Charles decided not to push his luck too far. He took a few more steps back and sat down.

"I'm sorry, Boss," he said. "Sometimes I get a bit worked up. It's just the way he acted in the car, attacked me. I have a hard time not retaliating against that."

"One day you will understand, or you should hope to understand if you want to take over my empire, that there are times to retaliate and times when it is wiser to bite your tongue." The old man pulled a chair close to Charles and sat down. "If this were anyone else I would send a team to bring him back. I'd deliver him to you personally and let you have your way with him."

"Yeah, I know," Charles said.

"No, you don't know. If you did, we would not be having this conversation."

The old man had a temper but he had never acted this way with Charles before. Never talked down to him like this. Why would he choose Jack over him? Was there something that he didn't know? Nonsense, he knew every-thing that was going on. Nothing got to the old man unless it went through Charles. The old man didn't even carry his own cell phone for Christ's sake.

"I just gotta know," Charles said. "Why do you stand up for him? Choose his side over mine?"

The old man stood up and came toward Charles. He put his hands on the large man's shoulders, bent over and put his mouth next to Charles's left ear. "Listen to me. No one person is above the organization. No one. Not you, not Mr. Jack, not the guards that stand outside this hotel room."

Charles thought about what his boss just said to him. The frail old man was in a bad spot. One hit would be all it would take. One hit and he'd be out. He brought his hands together, cracked his knuckles one at a time. "Not even you?"

The old man straightened up and laughed. He started to turn away but instead pivoted on his heel and swung his open hand across Charles's face.

"How dare you speak to me like that, Mr. Charles."

Charles's head snapped to the side, not so much from force as from the shock that the old bastard had actually hit him. He righted his head and leaned forward, eyes narrow and lips curled. "I don't care who you are, you don't slap me."

His boss laughed at him. "What are you going to do?"

Charles reached out, grabbed fistfuls of his boss's shirt with both hands and pulled him forward. He pulled the old man's face close to his. "I can make it look like an accident. You know that no one would question me. I'd take over and soon after Jack would join you in hell."

The old man kissed Charles on the cheek and smiled.

What is with this old bastard?

"Oh, Mr. Charles," the old man said. "Now I know for sure. I know that you are ready to take over. You, like me, fear no man."

Charles let go of his boss's shirt and sat back in the chair. He rubbed his temples and traced the stitches on his large forehead, thought about what the old man just said to him. He opened his mouth to speak, but the old man beat him to it.

"Four more assignments and then Mr. Jack is yours. Fair?"

"The girl?" Charles asked nodding toward the room next door.

"I'm inclined to leave that to your discretion but you must keep in mind that she means a lot to Mr. Jack. She must be available on Thursday for the exchange. After that, and as long as she is not in his custody, you can do what you want."

Charles nodded.

"Keep it clean, Mr. Charles. It must not come back to me."

Charles stood up, pushing the old man back with his chest as he rose to his feet. He pointed a finger at the old man, opened his mouth to speak, thought better of it. He brushed the old man aside and left the room.

CHAPTER 3

"Would you like pancakes for breakfast, sweetheart?" Bear asked the little girl.

A mane of blond hair popped up from the edge of the dinette table followed by a pair of big blue eyes. "Mmm, pancakes. Yes, please."

"It must be your lucky day because they are serving pancakes downstairs right now." The hotel they were staying in was first class. No continental breakfast here. "But we gotta hurry before they stop making them."

Mandy jumped out of her chair and raced to the door, still dressed in her pajamas.

"You're not going to put on some clothes?"

She looked back at him like he was crazy. "Momma always said pancakes were s'posed to be eaten in your pj's, Bear."

He shrugged. Who was he to argue with that logic? "Sounds good to me, sweetheart. Let's go."

He opened the door and led Mandy down the hall to the elevator. It was a typical hotel hallway, drab paint, ugly wallpaper in spots, paisley carpet, ice, soda and vending machines at the halfway point. Nothing out of the ordinary, and that was exactly what Bear wanted. The quieter their stay in San Diego the better. He didn't know anyone in the city and no one knew him.

The elevator dinged and the doors opened up. Mandy stepped forward. Bear reached out and pulled her back, insisting on peeking in first.

"Why are you looking at the ceiling, Bear?"

He smiled. "Can't be too cautious, you know."

She giggled. Of course she didn't know. Or maybe she did after everything the little girl had gone through the past few days, lost in the middle of the city, rescued by Jack, abducted, orphaned when her mother was killed.

"Get in there, rascal." He nudged the little girl in the elevator. "Press the L button."

"L like Loretta. That's momma's name."

Did she realize her mother was dead? She was a hostage at the compound when it happened and Jack and Bear assumed that she had been a witness. Maybe she blocked it out and was in shock now, something like that, because she kept talking about her mother like she was going to be waiting for them at the airport when they went back home.

If they went back home.

Ding. The elevator doors opened. Bear held the little girl back, again, and checked to make sure it was safe to exit. He took her hand and led her to the dining room. The lobby was pretty empty and he was free to make note of more drab painting, terrible wallpaper and paisley carpeting.

"Smell that?" he asked.

"Yeah, smells yummy," Mandy replied.

"You bet it does."

The food was laid out in a buffet line. They grabbed their plates, filled them with pancakes, strawberries, butter and syrup. Bear led Mandy to a table in the corner, which gave him a full view of the dining room as well as the street in front of the hotel.

Mandy stuffed half a pancake in her mouth before she sat down. Bear smiled at her as she slowly worked her way through a mouthful of food.

His cell phone buzzed on the table. *Restricted number.* "Hello?"

"Hello Riley," A man's voice said.

"Who's this?"

"Who is not important, just know that I'm a friend of Jack's."

"Independent?"

"No," the man replied. "Government funded."

"What can I do for you?" He smiled at Mandy, who was staring at him, eyes wide. He motioned for her to keep eating.

"Just got word that someone sent a team out to California looking for you."

Bear covered his mouth with his hand, lowered his voice. "Did a certain Asian friend send them?"

"We believe they're his guys, but he didn't send them."

Charles, that bastard.

"I'm sure you can figure out who did," the man said.

"How long till they get here? You guys know?"

"Unfortunately our intelligence was skewed and we got this info late. They are already on the ground."

Bear pushed his chair back and stood up. Peeked through the window and scanned the dining room again. Nothing stood out.

"Riley? You there?"

"Call me back if you hear anything else." Bear hung up the phone. "Sorry sweetie, we gotta go."

"But I'm not done yet," Mandy protested.

He ignored her complaints, picked her up, threw her over his shoulder. "I'll get you more in a bit. But we gotta get out of here now."

He headed straight for the exit, leaving their belongings behind in the hotel room.

Bear turned left out of the hotel and hid behind a taco cart about a hundred feet from the entrance.

"Bear, what are we doing here?" Mandy asked.

"Shh, I need you to be quiet. OK?"

"But I'm hungry," she said. "Can I have a taco?"

He pulled out his wallet and handed her a five dollar bill. "Here, get however many tacos you can for five dollars." Now he had to watch two spots at once, the front of the taco stand and the entrance to the hotel, but at least she would be quiet and he could concentrate.

He repositioned himself so he had a view of Mandy, the street and the hotel entrance. Everything looked normal. Tourists walked around in shorts and t-shirts or colorful Hawaiian shirts, business people on their way to an early lunch, kids riding bikes. Nothing out of the ordinary.

Except for the four guys in dark suits crossing the street.

Bear ducked behind the cart, made his way to the other side and positioned his head to see the men as they approached the hotel. He did not recognize three of the men, but one was someone he knew, and that was a bad sign. Carlos Solano, a hitman who worked for the old man.

He took position behind the cart again, out of sight from the hotel. "Mandy," he said. "C'mon, we have to get going."

"One second," she said.

"C'mon kid," he said. "We don't have time to..."

Mandy yelled.

Bear froze. He feared the worst. He'd been spotted and now they had the girl. He took a deep breath, pulled the gun out of his waistband, spun around and crouched low, facing the front of the stand. He found himself face to face with Mandy, who was kneeling down, picking up the taco she had dropped.

"Jesus, girl," he said. "I thought... You scared me."

Mandy giggled. "You get scared?"

He smiled and forced himself to laugh, "Yeah, even I get scared."

Bear put away his gun, hoisted Mandy up and started down the street. The rental car was parked four blocks away.

"It's too bumpy," Mandy said. "I can't eat."

"I'll slow down in a few." He was walking fast enough that it could have been classified as jogging in some circles. They were now two blocks away and he was feeling better about their chances of making it out. He stopped and looked back.

"Shit," he said.

Mandy gave him a scolding look.

He frowned back. They were being followed by a man in a dark suit. He recognized the man. Not by name, but he knew his face, another one of the old man's crew. Bear looked around for a place to hide, turned his attention back to the hitman. He was gone. He must have made them and was now in stalking mode.

Bear started walking again, faster than before. The lot was less than two blocks away but he would have to make a detour. He turned right the first chance he had. They were at a major disadvantage here. He didn't know these streets at all and he didn't have time to stare at little maps on his phone. His sole thought was to find a place to hide. Only then would they have a chance. Halfway down the street was an alley. He turned there and hid behind a dumpster.

"What are we doing?" Mandy asked.

"Shhh," Bear said. He held his hand up to Mandy's mouth. "You need to be quiet as a mouse."

Mandy smiled. Bear reckoned she was trying to figure out just how quiet a mouse actually was.

Bear heard the sound of footsteps getting closer. They pounded on the pavement, running. Slowed as they got closer to the alley then stopped.

"Come out," a voice called. "I won't hurt you. We just need to escort you to the marina."

Mandy looked up at Bear, eyes wide, hand over her mouth.

Bear nodded at her and pointed her head away. He pulled out his gun and then crouched down.

The footsteps started again. They went past the alley, stopped. Came back and now were coming toward Bear's hiding spot.

Bear got ready. He would try to neutralize the man instead of shooting him but it wouldn't break his heart if he had to kill the guy.

The steps slowed. The man must have been close to the dumpster. His movements were cautious. Finally, a foot appeared.

Bear reached out, grabbed the foot and pulled. The man crashed with a thud. Bear pulled hard, slamming the man's body into the dumpster. He heard him let out a grunt and gasp for air. Bear got up, gun aimed down, stepped around the dumpster, stood over the man. The hitman dropped his gun when his head hit the ground. Bear kicked the gun to the other side of the alley then reached down and pulled the man up by his shirt. He lifted him in the air, walked him around the dumpster and slammed his back into the brick wall.

"What do you want?" Bear asked the man.

The man spit at Bear.

Bear elbowed him in the side hard enough to crack a rib or two. "Who sent you?"

"Little girl," he said. "She's dead."

Bear looked over at Mandy. She had scooted down to the end of the alley and hid in the corner, head at her knees, hands over her head. He turned his attention back to the man.

"I said, who sent you?"

The man puckered his lips to spit again, but Bear backhanded the man and dropped him. The man hit the ground with a thud, then scrambled to grab Bear's legs. Bear bent over and slammed his large fist into the man's head, collapsing him to the ground. Bear lifted him again, pinned him to the wall by his neck.

"Last chance," Bear said. "Who sent you?"

The man gasped and wheezed and swallowed hard. "And before we kill her, we are going to take turns raping her." He smiled.

Bear reached back and threw all of his weight behind a right hook that dislocated the man's jaw and knocked four teeth out. Bear didn't stop. He hit him again and again. His left hand squeezed the man's neck tighter with each blow. The man's body went limp. Bear let go and the man's body hit the ground and folded over itself.

He turned toward Mandy. The little girl stood there, mouth open, brow furrowed, eyes turned down. Tears streamed down her face. She gasped in between heavy sobs.

"Mandy," he said.

He held out his arms but Mandy backed up to the wall behind her. Bear's stomach knotted up. He walked up to her, knelt in front of her and placed his hands on her shoulder.

"He was going to hurt you, Mandy," he said. "I was protecting you from him. He wanted to do bad things to you. He left me with no choice."

The little girl cried harder and covered her eyes.

Bear looked over his shoulder at his reflection in a window. His face was spotted with blood, his hair, his beard, all covered with the man's blood. He took off his button up shirt and wiped the blood from his face and hands. Checked his undershirt and made sure it wasn't covered as well.

"Look at me Mandy."

She lowered her hands and opened her eyes, still crying.

"I won't hurt you. I'm here to protect you from anything and anyone." He opened his arms for her to hug him.

She buried herself into his chest, wrapped her fragile arms around his large torso and sobbed heavily.

Bear folded his arms around her and stood up, holding her tight to his chest. He started down the alley toward the street. Stopped at the dumpster and grabbed a few cardboard boxes, tossed them over the hitman, then went to the other side of the alley and grabbed the man's gun.

He took his time before stepping onto the main street again. Once he did though, he didn't look back. He made a line to the parking lot, got in the car and took off heading north on the highway.

CHAPTER 4

Pierre pulled up to the front of the Hotel de Crillon and motioned for Jack to get out. "You check in, I'll park the car."

Jack jumped out, grabbed his luggage and went inside the lavish hotel. The lobby resembled something out of an old film. Lit up, it had a golden glow. The checkerboard floor reflected the light of the chandeliers that hung gracefully from the ceiling. The huge marble columns were large enough for a man to hide behind.

Would be a good spot for a hit.

He went to the counter. "Howard Blair," he said to the concierge.

The concierge began typing on his keyboard with two fingers without looking up at Jack. He was an older man, thin, bald on the top and short gray hair on the side. The lines etched on the man's face led Jack to believe he was around sixty years old and had probably spent his whole life sucking up to the rich and famous who vacationed at the posh hotel.

"Monsieur Blair," he said. "There you are, room 314. How many cards will you require?"

"One," Jack said.

The man still hadn't looked up at him. It was for the better. Perhaps later he would be questioned about the man who checked into room 314, the man who left four bodies behind and skipped out without paying his telephone bill.

Jack smiled, playing the scenario out in his head. He imagined the look on the housekeeper's face when she pulled the duvet back, revealing four faces, each with a single bullet hole in their head. She'd scream of course, pass out most likely, then would come to with a crowd standing over her. The police would want to question her, she had to know something. They would question everyone who might have come into contact with Jack during his stay. Who was this man named Howard Blair and how did four people end up dead in his hotel room?

"Monsieur? Monsieur?" The concierge interrupted Jack's daydream. He held out a credit card sized plastic key card. "Your room card, monsieur Blair."

Jack grabbed the card, nodded his thanks and walked away, ignoring everything the concierge said after room card.

He stood on the sidewalk outside the building, waiting for Pierre. The street was busy, which was to be expected since the hotel sat in the heart of Paris. Tourists and locals passed by. This was the best place to stay. Here he was just another face. Any place less populated and someone might remember him.

Pierre walked up, slightly out of breath. He pulled out a cigarette, offered it to Jack.

"Thanks," Jack said.

Pierre lit it for him then retrieved one for himself. "Beautiful building. Really is."

Jack looked up at the archways and long columns that adorned the building's facade. He shrugged. He had seen plenty of beauty in his life. A building didn't really do anything for him. "It's ok."

"You really are quite the conversationalist. You know that, right?"

Jack rolled his eyes. He pulled out his phone. No messages. He wondered why Bear hadn't checked in yet and made a mental note to call him after Pierre left.

"So tell me more about this assignment."

Jack pressed his lips together and furrowed his brow at Pierre. "Not the right place."

Pierre shrugged and frowned. "Perhaps."

They walked in silence through the hotel lobby. Jack led the way to the elevator with Pierre right behind him.

"Three," Jack said.

Pierre pressed the button for the third floor and turned to Jack. "I have a few guys who can help if you need a team."

Jack nodded. "We'll know soon enough."

The elevator opened and they stopped in front of room 314. Jack stuck his key card into the door and looked at Pierre. Both men winced. Despite the alias, the old man knew Jack was coming to France and most likely knew that he was here now. Might even know where he was staying. It was possible that the old man arranged for Jack to stay in room three-fourteen. And if he did that, he just as easily could have rigged explosives to detonate as soon as the key card was inserted into the door, or arranged for someone to be waiting inside.

The door unlocked and Jack pushed it open. No explosion. No thugs waiting on the other side. It was just an empty room with a complimentary bottle of champagne. Despite the luxury rating of the hotel, the room was rather lackluster. Some people may have found it fancy, but to Jack it was just another boring hotel room in a long list of places he'd stayed.

Jack opened the closet and looked around. He felt up in the corners, slid the garment bags to the side, checked under the hanging rail, opened the garment bags. He closed the closet and turned over the chairs, lifted the table and turned it over on its side.

"So, Jack, tell me. Who is the target?"

Jack narrowed his eyes and looked at Pierre. He continued his search of the room without saying anything. He pulled the sheets off the bed, lifted the mattresses and crawled under to inspect the frame. He went on like this for fifteen minutes. Occasionally Pierre would say something and Jack would ignore him.

Finally satisfied, he said, "OK, room is clean."

Pierre smiled and pulled a small electronic device from his pocket. "You could have just used this, Jack." He held a bug sweeper up for Jack to see. "If the room was bugged it would have gone off as soon as I stepped through the door."

Jack clenched his mouth shut, working a muscle in his jaw. "You could have said something."

"You didn't seem like you wanted to talk, so I kept my mouth shut."

"You said every other thing that came to your mind," Jack said.

Pierre laughed. "You must learn to trust me."

Jack pulled out his cell phone, connected it to the TV and pulled up a picture of the target. "You want trust? Well then here you go."

Pierre studied the man. Dark complexion, shaved head, broad face speckled with four day old black and silver stubble. Both ears adorned with gold hoop earrings. Eyes covered with expensive sunglasses. A full mouth, partly open like he had a secret to tell and was just about to let them in on it.

"Is that who I think it is?" Pierre asked. "I know him. From the movies, right?"

"Yeah, Mitchell Foster. Started off in bit roles in the nineties, became a leading man toward the end of the decade. Used his big payday to start producing."

"What was his big payday?"

Jack rolled his eyes. "Some flick about a team of assassins. Garbage."

Pierre laughed.

"So why were you contracted to kill a movie producer?" Pierre asked. "I don't understand."

Jack sat down on the corner of the bed. Flicked the camera and put the next document up on the screen and nodded.

"Drugs, extortion, leading a criminal organization. Pretty basic stuff, Jack."

Jack nodded. "Read the last line."

Pierre raised an eyebrow. "Human trafficking? Intriguing."

"I'd say so," Jack said. "Rumor has it he is involved in kidnapping young children then shipping them off. The sex trade they call it."

Pierre curled his lips and pinched at his nose. "Sick bastard. What is he doing in France?"

"He was brought up on charges of tax evasion and wire fraud. Only charges they could get to stick." Jack ran his hands through his dark hair. "He got out on bail and fled. Spends his time between various countries. Right now they believe he is here, in Paris."

Pierre flipped over a chair and sat across from Jack. "So what do you need me here for? Certainly not to be the shooter."

Jack smiled. "No, I can handle that part. I need your intelligence network. Your people might be tracking him and know where he is and where he goes during the day."

"I see," Pierre said. "I can look into this for you. One thing though."

"Yeah?"

"I want to be there for the hit."

Jack studied the man for a minute before responding. He had to make sure that Pierre would not jeopardize the assignment. Failure to take out the target would lead to major problems for the government. But that wasn't what he cared so much about. He was more worried about the mess it could create. A mess he would need to clean up. A mess that could interfere with the exchange of the documents for Clarissa.

"OK, you can be there for the hit. You can even help me plan it."

"Excellent," Pierre said.

Pierre reached over and shook Jack's hand. He got up and stopped at the door. "I'll call you as soon as I have some information. I'll begin working on it as soon as I get back to my office."

With that, he left and Jack laid back, closed his eyes and drifted off to sleep.

Pierre stepped onto the street and whistled an old tune, one that his grandfather used to whistle when they went sailing when Pierre was a boy. He walked at a normal pace until he turned onto the side street that led to the lot where he had parked his car. Then he broke out into a run. He managed to keep his excitement over the case to a minimum in front of Jack, but now he let it out freely.

He got into his car and sped off toward his office. He kept replaying the scene in his head, remembering every detail about the once great Mitchell Foster. Ashamed to admit it in front of Jack, Pierre loved *A Dance with Assassins*, Foster's big hit, the one that propelled him to super-stardom. He could only recall a few other films made by the man. They were awful. Cash grabs, basically. Then he had lost sight of him and had forgotten all about him until today.

Lost in thought, Pierre didn't register that the car in front of him was stopped until it was almost too late. He hit the brakes, slammed on the horn and came within inches of hitting the vehicle. He buried his face in his hands, controlled his breathing and got his heart rate back to normal. When he opened his eyes he saw two large men standing on either side of his car at the front.

He held up his hands and made a sheepish face. Apparently that wasn't good enough.

The guy closest to him motioned with his finger for Pierre to get out of his car.

Pierre opened his door and acted like he was going to step out. Instead he threw the car into reverse and floored it. Before the men could react, Pierre whipped around a corner, just missing an old lady crossing the street. He spun the car around and stepped on the gas and kept his eyes on the rear view mirror and saw the car with the two large men turn the corner.

"Great, just what I need," he muttered.

The car closed the gap and rammed his bumper. He lost control of his vehicle briefly. He pulled over to the side of the road rather than trying to make another risky turn or get nudged off entirely by the maniacs behind him.

Pierre stepped out of the car, trying his best to remain calm. He moved to the front of his car, giving himself a shield should the man driving the Audi decide to run him over. He waited for the men to make a move.

The passenger stepped out first, carrying a bat. He walked around the back of the car, stood in front of the driver's door. The driver stepped out. It appeared that he had something in his hand, but Pierre couldn't make it out with the other guy blocking the view.

Pierre threw up his hands. "Guys, I'm not really sure what the problem is here?"

The driver stepped out from behind his massive friend, took a few steps toward Pierre and stopped. He was tall, over six feet and heavily muscled. Pierre estimated he was well over two hundred pounds. Both men had shaved heads. The man in the passenger seat was taller than the driver and had at least another hundred pounds on him. His big barrel chest gave way to an even bigger barrel stomach. It would be wise to avoid the bat should it come swinging Pierre's way.

"You really don't want to mess with me," Pierre said. "I'm just on my way to the office."

"Shut up," the driver said. "Turn around."

"Turn around? Afraid I'm going to have to respectfully decline." Pierre lowered his arms. "I will, however, place my hands behind my back."

The passenger started toward him. "Get your hands where I can see them."

Pierre sighed. "As you wish, monsieur."

He flung his right arm around faster than the passenger could react. Pierre aimed his nine millimeter at the man's head and pulled the trigger.

The large man stopped, almost suspended mid stride, when the bullet crashed through his skull and tore through his brain. Almost as soon as it happened, he collapsed.

Pierre turned his attention to the driver. "I did try to warn you that you didn't want to mess with me."

The driver stepped back and tried frantically to open his door.

Pierre closed the distance in a second and whipped the gun across the bridge of the man's nose. Blood sprayed and the driver covered his face with his hands and fell back against his car. Blood leaked through his fingers. His broken glasses dangled from his ears.

"Please," he said. "I'll do anything you want."

"I wanted you to leave me alone, but you ignored that request."

The man started to cry.

Some thug.

Pierre held the gun to the man's head and pulled the trigger. The driver's body jerked backwards and then slumped down the car and onto the ground.

A crowd had gathered. Not what Pierre wanted, but this wasn't the first time a crowd had gathered as he killed or beat somebody. Being one of the nation's top assassins had its benefits. One of those benefits being he had a virtual get-out-of-jail-free card. He was, in essence, a man who recognized no laws.

He shrugged at the crowd. "Street thugs." Then he got in his car and drove away.

CHAPTER 5

Clarissa stared out the window. She had a decent view of Paris, the Eiffel Tower in the distance. She'd be able to watch the sun set behind it. But she had no idea what hotel they were in. If it weren't for the view, she wouldn't even know which city she was in.

She remembered getting on the plane and being forced to have a drink. Then her memory of events simply stopped somewhere over the Atlantic and only picked back up Monday evening, when she woke up in the hotel room. There had been a tray beside the bed. It contained a decent meal, which she ate in five minutes. The old man came to see her that night, told her that they were here to make an exchange with Jack. Her for the documents, he told her. As long as Jack held up his end, she would be free to go. Clarissa asked him if Charles was at the hotel too. He said yes, Charles was in the hotel, his room across from hers. He must have sensed her apprehension, or perhaps he saw her crying, because he came back later and told her that he had moved Charles to another floor and stationed two guards outside her door.

That was pretty much it, as far as contact went. Every four hours one of the guards would knock on her door, she'd open it, and they'd slide a cart full of food into her room.

The room itself was fine, if not a bit boring. The windows were covered in frills and lace. The sheets on the bed were cream colored silk with a blue and pink floral pattern. The furniture appeared antique. Certainly not Clarissa's taste. But the view... She could get lost for hours in that view. And that was a good thing, because she had plenty of hours to kill.

She sat in a high back chair, staring out the window at the Eiffel Tower and wishing she had a pair of binoculars so she could check out the tourists clinging to the railing at the top, taking in the city from hundreds of feet in the air. On the window sill sat a foot long replica of the famous tower. She picked it up. It was heavy, made from silver, stamped .925 on the bottom. She twirled the mini tower in her hand while watching the line of people snake around the real one, waiting to see the monument.

A thump on her door shook her from her thoughts.

She hopped out of her chair, crept to the door, peered through the peephole. She saw the back of one of the guards and someone who looked like Charles in the middle of the hallway. She shuffled her feet to the wall so her toes couldn't be seen under the door and pressed her ear to the door in an attempt to listen in on their conversation.

"You can't go in," she heard the guard say.

"Like hell I can't," Charles said.

"Orders from the old man. No one enters this room."

"Get out of my way or," Charles paused and she heard the sound of cracking knuckles, "I'll break your friggin' neck."

"Maurice, go get the old man," the guard said to his partner.

"Like hell you will."

She heard a smacking sound followed by a thud on the wall. Clarissa rose up and put her eye to the peephole again. She could see Charles, one arm back ready to punch, the other arm attached to neck of the guard she knew as Jerry. She watched as Charles slammed his large fist into Jerry's face. The guard's head snapped back, blood splattered across the peephole.

Clarissa scrambled to barricade the door. She raced to the other end of the room and started to drag the chair she had been sitting in moments ago. Her plan was to pin the chair under the door handle, which would prevent Charles from getting in.

Click.

The distinctive sound of the door unlocking.

Clarissa froze. The door opened. Charles's large frame filled up most of the doorway. He smiled at her.

"Remember me?" he asked.

Clarissa backed into the corner between the nightstand and the window.

"Ah, now don't be like that," he said while holding his hand out to her.

She glanced around for something, anything that she could use to defend herself with. She still bore the wounds from their first meeting and would rather not add to the tally.

"We took out everything you could use to defend yourself. So don't bother."

Almost everything.

Clarissa shot a quick look toward the lamp on the nightstand.

Charles watched her and laughed. "What are you going to do with that?"

Clarissa inched closer to the lamp.

"You know what? You want to hit me with that lamp? I'm gonna give it to you." Charles bent over, dropped his head down. "Go ahead, take your best friggin' shot."

She thought it through. He'd be ready for the shot to the back of the head and it probably wouldn't even faze him. She looked over at the window, out at the Eiffel tower again. If this was it, she would at least go out with a beautiful memory. Her eyes shifted to the mini tower made of silver. He wouldn't be expecting that.

She stepped to the left, but angled her body to the right toward the window sill. Scooped up the replica Eiffel Tower and adjusted it in her right hand. She leaned left and let the momentum carry her through as she spun around on her heel. Her arm made a magnificent backward loop. Full circle it went as she stepped into a lunge. The point of the tower was the first thing to pass by her hip, her arm followed in an upward arc.

Charles had no idea what hit him as Clarissa buried the heavy silver Eiffel Tower replica into his face.

She didn't wait around to see how much damage she had done. His scream was enough to tell her that he would be permanently disfigured, more so than he already was. She leapt on the bed, used the spring of her step to propel her to the door, out into the hall, stepping over the bodies of the unconscious guards. A crowd of old people had gathered by the elevator. They pointed and whispered among themselves. For a moment Clarissa thought of running to them, begging them to hide her. But the elevator dinged, and the crowd disappeared behind the solid doors.

Clarissa banged on the old man's door. He took ages to open it. Meanwhile she could hear Charles getting closer. Judging by his grunts and the sound of his body crashing into the walls, he seemed to be stumbling around. She banged on the door again, urgently. This time the old man muttered something, but she couldn't make it out. She hit the door even harder and kicked at it.

"You twat," Charles said in a low, guttural voice.

She looked over and down. He was on his stomach, pulling himself through the doorway with his hands. He stopped and rolled over so he could look up at her. She put her hand to her mouth at the sight of him. Thought for a moment she might lose her lunch. She had hit him good all right. Directly under his left eye. All that was left of his cheek was a bloody hole.

He propped himself up on his elbows, got his knees under him and used the wall to slowly stand up.

"Please," she shouted at the door.

Charles staggered toward her. He had fifteen feet to close between the two of them.

Clarissa decided she would run when he got to five.

He stopped and leaned his body against the wall. "I'm...going to kill...you."

She made one last effort toward the door, banging, kicking and screaming.

The door popped open.

"What are you doing in the hall, girl?"

"Help," she said through tears.

The old man stuck his head out the door and saw Charles standing there, blood dripping from his face. "What the hell is going on?"

"He broke in, tried to attack me, I hit him."

The old man pulled Clarissa into the room and shut the door. "Go sit in the corner. I'll straighten this out."

He disappeared through the door. She picked her legs up off the floor, pulled her knees to her chest and buried her head between them. She knew he'd kill her when he came back in. Or worse, he'd let Charles take her back to his room to do whatever he wanted and *then* kill her.

Minutes passed. The door opened and the old man came in alone. He took his time walking toward her, sat down in the chair across from her. He held his hands up and interlaced his fingers in front of his chest.

"Mr. Charles will be ok," the old man said. "One of the guards had come to and informed me that he was attacked by Mr. Charles. We were able to revive the other guard. They have escorted Mr. Charles to the infirmary to have his face taken care of. As for you, I haven't decided what to do with you. I don't think you are safe here, so I'll need to find a place to store you for a few days."

Store her, like an old sweater. Is that really what he thought of her?

"If it were not for the fact that I need you as a bargaining chip with Mr. Jack, you would be dead right now. Do you understand?"

She nodded.

The old man leaned in, just inches from her face. "Further outbursts will not be tolerated." With that, he got up and left the room.

CHAPTER 6

Jack awoke to the sound of his cell phone ringing. The reddish light of the setting sun filtered through the window, turning the drab walls pink. He looked on the nightstand for his watch. How long had he been asleep? Unable to find his watch, he grabbed his cell and answered it.

"Yeah?"

"It's Pierre."

"Yeah, what do you have for me?"

"After an eventful afternoon, I have gathered some previous intelligence. It seems our friend enjoys casual dining. In fact he enjoys it so much he eats at the same place every day at the same time."

"You're kidding." Jack rotated his head in a circle trying to loosen up his neck.

"I know the place. We can scout it tomorrow."

"Sounds good to me."

"Do you have plans this evening?"

"Think I'm just going to stay in. No point in going out and getting into trouble."

"Ah, probably a good idea, Jack."

"Pierre?"

"Yes."

"You said eventful. What else happened today?" Jack asked.

"Ah," Pierre paused and cleared his throat. "Let's just say there are two less thugs in Paris tonight."

"Gotcha." Jack decided he didn't want to know any more. "Call me first thing in the morning."

He tossed his phone on the bed, stood up, stretched. He found himself a bit surprised he had slept so long. Not enough time between now and Thursday to waste hours like this. It would be a good idea to go out and start scouting some locations for the exchange. Besides, there had to be something to do on a Monday night in Paris. Right?

He went into the bathroom to wash up. He stared at his face in the mirror. When the hell did those lines start etching themselves into his forehead? And those crow's feet, where did they come from? Jack shook his head and splashed water on his face. Felt the sharpness of his three day old stubble and decided he would leave his face unshaven for a while. Maybe grow a beard. He smiled at his reflection. He had always been a master at distracting his mind with dumb thoughts like that in the middle of a crisis. Finally, he splashed a handful of water on his brown hair and combed it back.

The light on his phone flashed red. A message waiting.

"Jack, its Bear. Ran into some trouble in San Diego. Turns out our friend sent a welcoming party. Don't worry, Mandy is OK. I'm OK. Heading north. Watch your back."

Jack sat on the edge of the bed and thought about the message. He would have to watch his back. Things were coming to a head with Charles and the old man and the situation would play itself out soon. Hopefully not in Paris, though. Still, the news that the old man sent a team to San Diego troubled Jack. Wasting resources was not in the old man's bag of tricks. This reeked of an act ordered by Charles without the old man's permission. Jack feared that Charles was going to make a power play.

God help all of them if he did.

Jack stepped out of the elevator, walked through the elaborate lobby and nodded at the doorman as he stepped out into the cool night air. It felt good against his skin, but the smells of the city were a bit overwhelming, even for someone who had just come from New York City.

He pulled out his cell and dialed Pierre's number.

"Allo?"

"Pierre, its Jack. Look, I'm feeling a bit naked here. Think you can hook me up?"

"I presume you need some protection?"

"That's correct."

"There is a cafe not too far from your hotel. Get to the street, turn right, two blocks, a left and it will be the first building on the left."

"Got it."

"Good, see you in thirty minutes Jack."

The waitress rolled her eyes when Jack ordered a cafe Americano. No chance he'd order anything else. Why hadn't he trusted his instincts and suggested a bar instead of agreeing to meeting at a cafe? Whiskey is whiskey, no matter where you go.

He pulled out a cigarette and lit it. He looked around as he exhaled. No dirty looks from the non-smokers. One of the only good things about being in Paris, he figured. Half the city smoked. And the non-smokers didn't go around giving the smokers dirty looks or coughing loudly to make a point. Although he wanted to quit, he didn't feel like being judged for his vice.

He had asked for the table in the back corner on the terrace so he could see people as they came and left and could also get a good view of the street and the people passing by. He studied the crowd sitting outside the cafe with him. Two separate couples, one of which refused to make eye contact as they drank their coffee, were seated on either side of him. Two ladies sat near the entrance and were engrossed in a heavily animated conversation. They looked eerily alike, but he didn't think they were twins. Lastly, there were two individual men seated outside. One was reading a magazine, the other talking on his phone. More like groveling from what Jack and his limited French could understand.

"Hello, Jack."

Jack looked up and saw Pierre standing there. Instinctively he had grabbed the fork as soon as he heard his name.

"Sit," Jack said. "Scared me."

Pierre smiled. "You must be slipping, letting me sneak up like that when I should have been in full view."

Jack nodded. "Was trying to figure out what that guy on the phone was saying. Sounded to me like he was apologizing for cheating on his wife."

Pierre cocked his head and listened for a few seconds.

"I would agree with that assessment," he said.

Pierre raised his hand and signaled to the waitress.

She came over and said nothing while staring out at the street.

"Un cafe," Pierre said.

The waitress walked off without saying a word or acknowledging the men.

"Love the hospitality," Jack said.

Pierre laughed. "Takes some getting used to."

"Did you bring it?" Jack asked, his tone serious now.

Pierre grabbed a napkin off the table and wrapped it around something in his lap, placed the item on the table and slid it across to Jack.

Jack picked the item up, felt its weight and tucked it into the waistband behind him. He nodded approvingly. "This is just for protection. You'll be able to acquire an M40 for the hit, right?" The M40A3 rifle was Jack's preferred weapon for this kind of hit, where he would stake out and be making a distance shot. It's the weapon he grew up with in the Marines and he'd relied on it countless times.

"Yes," Pierre replied. "We select the location tomorrow and everything will be arranged for Wednesday."

Jack stood across the street from a small restaurant named *Sensationnel*. A green and white awning extended over a concrete patio. The patio was separated from the street by a three foot high black iron gate. About a dozen small bistro tables littered the patio. It was early, around ten a.m. Business was slow, just a few customers drinking coffee and checking emails on their phones or reading newspapers. One woman was talking loudly on her phone while her young daughter, maybe four years old, played on a tablet computer. The little girl kept looking up at her mother, opening her mouth to speak. Her mother just waved her off and continued with the conversation.

He saw Pierre walking up and gave him a nod. Pierre acknowledged him, turned and stepped into the building behind Jack. He followed the Frenchman inside. They climbed three flights of stairs.

"There," Pierre said while pointing at the apartment labeled C. "It's vacant. Has been for three months."

"Key?"

"Here you go," Pierre said as he handed the keys to Jack.

Jack pulled out the handgun Pierre had delivered the night before, unlocked the door and stepped inside the apartment. Dirt and dust greeted him. He pushed through cobwebs toward the window that looked onto the street and the cafe.

"Problem," he said. "If he's not at one of those first tables, the awning is going to block the view."

"They take the awning up at night. It's just there to keep it cool during the day."

Jack picked up a chair and set it down in front of the window. He grabbed a rag off the table and wiped the dust off the chair and window sill. "So what's his routine?"

"Twice a day he comes to eat here. Once around noon, stays for thirty minutes. Again he comes at five, and this time stays until eight or nine. Sometimes even later. Depends on who is with him."

"Think it's better to do this in the evening?"

"Probably. Will be hard to escape during the day, especially at noon. You will see shortly. Many people out. We'd be spotted for sure." Pierre walked to the window and looked down on the street. "You find this spot suitable?"

Jack nodded.

"Good." Pierre picked up a chair and sat it next to Jack's. He sat down and put his feet up on the window sill. "Now we wait."

Two hours passed and the men barely said a word. Jack was running different scenarios through his head. Every once in a while he would think about Clarissa. His thoughts drifted to Bear and Mandy. He wondered where they had gone. Bear didn't say in his message. Jack couldn't fault him for that. Someone fed Charles the flight information. That same someone might also be able to get information from Jack's mailbox.

"Foster," Pierre whispered.

"Where?"

Pierre pointed at the man dressed in black, flanked by three bodyguards.

Jack looked through a pair of binoculars to get a glimpse of Foster before he disappeared under the awning, managing to only see him from behind. The man had tanned skin, a shaved head with a day or two of growth on top, and a menacing tattoo on the back of his neck.

"Yeah, that's him," Jack said. "He stays about thirty minutes?"

"That's what our file says."

"I'm going to get a closer look." Jack stood up and pushed back the chair. "Need some coffee anyway."

"Be careful," Pierre said.

Jack nodded without looking back. "Will do. Cover me."

He jogged down the stairs, through the small lobby, through the door and into the street. He turned left, walked about two hundred feet and then crossed over. Turning right, he made his way back to the restaurant. He didn't want Foster's bodyguards to see him cross the street directly from the apartment building.

He took his time walking to the restaurant. He pushed through the gate and walked past Foster's table. Foster was sitting with his back to the road. That would make the hit easy if he sat like that for dinner tomorrow night. The table was to Jack's left. He turned his head to the right as he passed.

"Can I help you?" the waitress asked as Jack stepped inside the main building.

"I'd like a couple sandwiches and some coffee. Can I get that here?"

"Oui monsieur. Follow me."

She led him to a counter, ducked under and pulled out a menu for Jack. Her brown hair caught on the counter and pulled a good chunk of hair from the bands holding it in a ponytail. Her hair fell across her face, covering her blue eyes. She tucked her head and smiled at Jack, her large red glossy lips giving way to reveal white teeth as her lips parted. Jack smiled back. She brushed the hair from her face, regained her composure and took his order.

"On vacation?" she asked.

"That obvious?" he replied.

She shrugged. "You don't look like a tourist. That's a good thing."

He laughed. "I'm here on business for a few days."

"Perhaps you could come back tonight?" she said. "I get off around nine and would be happy to show you around the city?"

He thought it over. He didn't have any interest in the woman, but she might be able to provide him with some inside information on Foster. Things that even Pierre's sources didn't know.

She disappeared for a moment and returned with a bag and two cups of coffee. "Well?"

"Sure," he said. "Name's Jack."

"Corinne," she said. "Be here at nine sharp. I won't wait."

He stepped onto the covered patio and walked toward Foster's table.

"Mitchell Foster?" Jack said. "Is that really you? I'm a huge, huge fan."

Foster looked up at him with his dark eyes. True to form he had about a week's growth of hair on his face and wore a gold earring in his right ear. He was older looking than Jack imagined, though. He figured the man lived a tough lifestyle. Foster took a pull on his cigarette and nodded at Jack. This must have been routine for him. A fan walks up, says I loved you in such and such, asks for a picture and walks off. Jack figured Foster had been through this exact scenario thousands of times, but probably not so much in France.

"I loved you in *Assassins*." Jack smiled wide, really hamming it up. "But my favorite was *A Wind Swept Shot*. That had to be the most realistic hitman movie I ever saw."

Foster grinned. He seemed genuinely pleased by Jack's remarks. "Thank you. No one ever mentions that movie. Tell you the truth, I wish I had stayed on that track instead of going for the big payday."

"Ah, but the payday has merits right?"

Foster laughed. "Want to sit down?"

Jack pretended to look at his watch, then snuck a glance at the bodyguards who were all shaking their head slightly. The biggest one furrowed his brow and stuck out his lips.

"Perhaps some other time," Jack said. "I have to get back to the office."

Foster shrugged and nodded. "It was nice meeting you..."

"Where are my manners? Blair. Howard Blair."

"Nice meeting you, Mr. Blair."

Jack walked off, whistling, his mind going in twenty different directions. He caught himself at the last second about to step into the street. He swung his leg in the other direction, turned right and repeated his earlier path in reverse.

Back in the apartment, he set the food and coffee on the dusty table and gave Pierre the abridged version of events. He decided to leave out the bit about Corinne. He didn't want to be tailed when he left with her.

They ate in silence, like an old couple with nothing left to say to each other. They watched as Foster and his bodyguards left the restaurant. According to Pierre's information, it would be over four hours until Foster returned. Jack decided to use that time to familiarize himself with the area. He took a walk and got to know the street names, as well as the streets that intersected those. He scouted out a few possible places to hide for the night if it came down to it.

When he returned to the vacant apartment for the third time, Pierre was asleep. Jack decided to test his associate's skills. He had entered without a sound and crept up behind him. He took one of the cups from the table and pressed it into the back of Pierre's head.

"You would have been dead already, Jack," Pierre said.

Jack laughed. "Is that right?"

"Yes, that's right," a deep voice said from behind him.

Jack spun around, reaching for his gun, and came face to face with a large black man. "Who the hell are you?"

The large man smiled. Half his teeth were missing. The other half were discolored and chipped. He had a heavy beard, thick eyebrows and a bald or shaved head. Jack guessed shaved. The man's head was heavy with wax, the type you would use after shaving your scalp.

Pierre stood. "This is Gaston. He is going to set for us. I asked him here so that you could instruct him with what you need and where you need it. When we get here tomorrow, Gaston will have everything arranged for us."

Jack held out his hand. "Nice to meet you."

Gaston nodded and shook Jack's hand.

"You ever sneak up on me again," Jack said, "I'll kill you."

Gaston laughed, turned, and slipped past the door.

Jack gave Pierre a curious glance.

"Don't worry, he's trustworthy," Pierre said.

Another half hour passed without much activity. Jack had nearly dozed off when Pierre nudged him, pointing out the window at Foster and his entourage.

His party had grown considerably. There were the three bodyguards, but he was also accompanied by two men and three women.

"Is this typical?" Jack asked.

"Yes, he entertains at dinnertime. Always the bodyguards. Sometimes friends. Sometime his wife and kids. Sometime his mistress and their illegitimate child."

"Hopefully no kids tomorrow," Jack said.

Pierre nodded. "Yes, that would be messy."

The awning retracted and they saw Foster and his party. Four tables were adjoined. Two of the wait staff attended to him. One of them was Corinne. They'd have something to talk about tonight after all.

The remainder of the afternoon and evening went by with relatively little activity. The party shifted, a few people joined, a few people left. Occasionally someone would wander up and take a picture or get an autograph. Sometimes Foster would get up and hug a visitor. Jack figured this was when drugs or information were exchanged. Foster and his guests drank a lot. His bodyguards didn't. Quarter after eight, they got up and left.

"We'll do the hit at six," Jack said.

"Why six?" Pierre asked.

"It's arbitrary," Jack replied.

Pierre shrugged. "Good enough for me." He walked to the door and turned to Jack. "Coming? My neighbor Suzette is making a roast tonight."

"I'm going to watch for a bit. See if Foster or his bodyguards return. Never know."

"Suit yourself."

"Give Suzette my best."

The door closed. Jack sat back, pulled a flask from his pocket and took a good, long pull on the whiskey.

Just enough to calm his nerves.

CHAPTER 7

The street was dimly lit, perhaps enough so he could cross without being noticed. But Jack decided to play the same routine as earlier. He turned left, walked two hundred feet, crossed, turned back to the right and entered the restaurant through the patio.

Corinne sat at the bar. She looked about fifteen years younger than Jack. Why would she even be interested in him? Sure, he was a good looking guy and received his fair share of attention from the ladies. But why would a twenty one year old be interested?

She smiled and winked when she saw him. He smiled back and momentarily shoved the questions to the back of his mind.

"Shall we go?" she asked.

He glanced around the restaurant making a mental note of where the kitchen and restrooms were located.

"Yeah, let's get out of here," he said.

They stepped onto the front patio. He looked up at the strands of string lights woven above them.

"These on every night?" he asked.

She shrugged. "Most nights I suppose."

This would be something to consider if the hit went down after the sunset. The lights might offset his target. It would only be a bit, but it could be enough. The hit had to go down without a hitch.

"What time do they normally turn them on?"

Corinne faked a yawn. "Why are you asking me about stupid string lights?" She jumped in front of him and grabbed his hands. "C'mon, let's go have some fun."

He began to wonder if it had been a mistake to agree to go out with her.

She pulled him through the gate and they walked down the dimly lit street. She had her arm wrapped around his. He thought about pushing her aside, but truth was he didn't mind a beautiful woman hanging on him like this. His thoughts turned to Clarissa and for a moment he felt uneasy. They had always said that there was no attachment, each of them could come and go as they pleased. And they pretty much had over the last couple years. Jack wasn't really the type of guy who could commit to a long term relationship. He also wasn't the kind of guy who should be committed to. Anyone in his line of work only endangered the lives of their loved ones.

Corinne pulled him to the left, through another gate and into a bar. The room was dark. There were a few small pendant lights over the bar itself, and each table had a lantern on it. Jack felt like he had stepped back eighty years.

"What'll you have?" the bartender asked in French.

Corinne named a drink Jack had never heard of. He ordered himself a whiskey, figuring that wouldn't get lost in translation. The bartender nodded and walked to the other end of the bar to begin mixing Corinne's drink.

"Whiskey?" she said. "How boring. Why don't you try what I'm having?" She held the glass to her mouth and licked the rim.

Jack shrugged. "I stick with what works."

"Oh, I bet you wear the same white colored boxers every day and these boring Khaki pants all the time." She laughed.

The bartender returned with another round of drinks. Jack pointed at Corinne's green concoction.

"I'll take one of those too," he said.

The bartender nodded and disappeared again.

"So I saw a movie star at the restaurant today," Jack said, figuring this was a good a time as any to gather some intel.

Corinne scrunched her face. "Foster. I don't like that man."

Jack raised an eyebrow and didn't say a word.

"I think he is into some bad stuff."

"Why do you think that?"

"Something one of the other waitresses told me. She dated him for a while. His third mistress at the time. Anyway, there were always people showing up and his phone was always ringing. He would disappear for days at a time."

Days at a time? That wasn't mentioned in Pierre's reports.

"And he was always high," Corinne continued. "Finally, one day he beat her. No reason at all. He just beat her. She was in such bad shape that she was in the hospital for a week.

Jack acted surprised, but he figured Foster to be the type of man who would beat a woman. He didn't value women. That was obvious by his involvement in trafficking women for the sex trade.

"Anyway," Corinne said. "Let's change the subject."

The bartender returned with Jack's drink. Jack picked it up and held it to his mouth. He checked his reflection in the mirror, rolled his eyes to himself and turned toward Corinne. "Don't tell anyone."

She laughed.

He took a big pull from the glass, sat it down, made a face. "How can you drink that?"

Corinne continued laughing. She grabbed his hand. "C'mon Jack, let's get out of here. I want to go dancing."

Jack groaned. He threw back the rest of the green drink and followed her out the door.

She held his hand and guided him down the street. "It's not far."

They didn't get far before they were confronted by three men. They were young. Jack placed them around Corinne's age.

"What are you doing with this guy, Corinne?" the tall skinny one said. He had long hair, pulled back in a ponytail. He wore a checkered polo shirt and blue jeans. He had a patchy blond beard. "I said, what are you doing with this chump?"

The other two men positioned themselves on the side. The fat one was to the right of Jack, maybe three feet away. He was shorter than Jack, but had at least fifty pounds on him. All fat though. Jack figured he could drop the man in one hit. On the other side of Corinne was the third man. Jack didn't get a good look at him and wasn't going to take his eyes off the tall skinny one in front of him.

Corinne stuttered, "He...he's a friend of mine from America."

"A friend of yours?" the skinny man looked Jack up and down. "Or your mom's? I bet he screws your mom every night and you just had to have some, huh?"

"Don't talk to the girl like that," Jack said.

The man took a step to the side and lined himself up in front of Jack. "I'll talk to her however I want to." He reached behind and pulled out a black-jack, put the strap around his wrist and twirled it in front of him. He stopped and poked Jack in the chest with the weapon. "You got that, old man?"

Since when was thirty six old?

"Just leave him alone, will you?" Corinne said.

The skinny man looked cross. He leaned in to Jack, his face only six inches away.

"Oh, you want me to leave your lover alone?" The skinny man turned his head and gave Corinne a pouting look.

Jack didn't hesitate. He grabbed the man's wrist and elbow, pushed and pulled, separating the arm from the elbow joint. The blackjack was strapped to the wrist. Jack didn't even bother to remove it. Much to the skinny man's yelling objection, Jack smashed the fat man's voice box by jabbing the heavy weapon into it. Then he swung the blackjack in a circle. It hit the skinny man squarely in his testicles and the guy fell to the ground in a cradled position. The third man started to run. Jack pulled the blackjack off of the skinny man's wrist and threw it at the fleeing man. It hit him across the back of the head and he fell to the ground unconscious.

Corinne screamed, a much delayed reaction. She backed up against the wall. "Who are you?"

He approached her, arms out, trying to calm her down. "It's OK. It was us or them."

She looked at the three men on the ground. They were all injured but they were alive.

Jack heard a car approaching, turned and saw it was a taxi. He ran out into the street and flagged the taxi down. He pulled Corinne to the open door and put her inside. He leaned in and kissed her on the cheek. "Don't go to work tomorrow, OK?"

"What? Why?"

"Don't ask. Just call in sick." He shut the door and watched the taxi drive off.

When he turned around, he saw the tall skinny man had gotten up and picked the blackjack up off the ground. He was leaning back against the building in an effort to catch his breath. The fat man pulled himself up using a tree. The third man, who was much shorter than the other two, was still on the ground, although he appeared to have regained consciousness.

"You're dead old man," the skinny man said.

Jack shrugged. "What makes you think you can handle me?"

"You got lucky last time. A cheap shot."

Jack reached behind his back and retrieved his gun. He aimed it at the fat man, pulled the trigger. Two shots rang out and the fat man fell to the ground.

The skinny man raised the blackjack and took a step toward Jack. He stopped and looked down at his shirt. A bloodstain spread rapidly from the center of his chest. He dropped the blackjack and fell to his knees. Jack walked toward him and kicked him over. The man's head hit the ground with a thud.

Jack took a look around and noticed a few lights had switched on. He started down the street, making sure to put a bullet in the head of the third man who had finally managed to get to his knees.

At least these guys wouldn't bother Corinne again. Hopefully she wouldn't show up at work the next night. He'd have to find out how to get a hold of her though, if only to apologize for scaring her.

CHAPTER 8

"For Christ's sake."

"Is everything OK, Bear?" Mandy asked from the backseat.

"Yeah, everything's fine," he said. Only it wasn't fine. The blue sedan had been behind him for thirty minutes. It mirrored every move he made. If he sped up, so did the sedan. If he slowed down, the sedan did as well. He changed lanes and the sedan changed lanes too.

The bastards were following him. But how? There was no way they knew which car he was in. Besides, they had been on the road for three hours and he had constantly been looking for any sign of being followed. Until thirty minutes ago, he'd noticed no one following them.

He kept checking the mirror every ten seconds.

Mandy must have noticed. She leaned in between the front seats. "Are you sure you are OK?"

He ignored the girl, slowed down to about thirty miles per hour. The sedan slowed as well and was right on his tail. There were four men in the car. The two in the front seat were talking. It looked like the passenger was barking orders at the driver. The passenger pointed at the upcoming exit and the sedan swerved off the road.

Bear sighed loudly, leaned forward and hugged the steering wheel.

"Hey, what's that?"

"What, sweetheart?"

"That thing on your back."

He looked at Mandy sideways. "What thing?"

"I dunno, there's some metal thing stuck to your shirt."

Bear yelled as he swerved the car onto the emergency shoulder. Bear jumped out and pulled off his shirt. On the back he found a transmitter. He ripped the transmitter from the fabric, cursing at himself for allowing it to have been placed there.

The man in the alley must have planted it on him. They'd been tracking him for hours now. He pulled the transmitter off the shirt and put the shirt back on. He sat on the hood of his car and thought for a moment. They knew where he was. He could use this to his advantage, just had to hide the girl first.

Half an hour later Bear pulled into an alley lined with warehouses on both sides. He'd had the little rental car set at one hundred miles per hour on the highway, which should have provided him with at least ten minutes before they caught up. Mandy was safe at an arcade. The only one who could check her out of the place was Bear. If something happened to him she would end up in custody and a call would be placed to Jack. Now, Bear just had to trap the team sent to kill him.

He broke into one of the warehouses, they all had looked abandoned, and he planted the transmitter in an enclosed office. Solid walls, no windows, only one door in. Just like the warehouse itself. If the team was true to form, then three would go in and one would guard the door.

Bear took position in the abandoned building across the street and waited.

Eight minutes later the blue sedan drove by. It slowed as it passed the building then turned left at the next street. Bear assumed they were checking the back of the building, just as he had earlier. A few more minutes passed and the four men appeared on the street from the side of the warehouse. They were all dressed the same in dark suits and black shoes. All four had closely cut hair, three brown, one gray. None had facial hair. All were in pretty good shape. Bear would do his best to avoid a fight with these guys. They were the real deal. Trained assassins.

Three went inside. One stayed outside. He knew that it would take thirty seconds for the team to get to the office.

Bear timed it and at thirty seconds he fired a shot at the man positioned outside of the door to the warehouse. The shot hit the man in the forehead and he dropped to the ground. A half a minute later the door cracked open. Bear took aim and fired another shot between the crack of the door. A man fell out, onto the concrete, leaving the door wide open. A third man leaned out to pull him back in.

Bear didn't hesitate. He fired a third round into the top of the man's head. The guy collapsed on his partner's body.

Bear waited a few minutes, but the fourth man never came through the door. Now he was at a disadvantage. There was only one door in and no windows. Bear would be the one in danger of getting shot if he pushed through the door. He slipped out the side door of the building and started to make his way to his car. But curiosity got the better of him. He had to know who was behind this, confirm his suspicions. He doubled back and got to the side of the warehouse. He made his way to the door, back pressed tightly against the building. The door stood open, unable to close because of the dead bodies on the ground. Bear quickly poked his head around and saw the man sitting on the floor, knees pulled up, head buried between his knees.

Some professional.

Without hesitation, Bear leaned in and shot the man in the right shoulder.

The man screamed, fell backward and rolled onto his left side. The gun he was holding fell when the bullet tore through the flesh, muscle and bone in his upper arm.

Bear rushed in, kicked the gun and lifted the man, pinning him against the wall.

The man yelled out in pain.

"Who sent you?" Bear asked.

The man gritted his teeth. "Screw you."

Bear held the gun to the man's head. "You see your friends over there? Huh? You want to end up like them?"

The man squeezed his eyes tight and tried to spit at Bear, but it just dribbled out of his mouth and hung in strands from his chin.

Bear dropped the man and kicked him in the ribs. Then he grabbed him by the shoulder and dragged him to the front door.

"Look at them," Bear shouted. "Tell me what I want to know."

The man started to cry. "OK, I'll tell you. Just don't kill me."

Bear let go of the man and backed up a few steps.

"Charles sent us. Told me that the old man couldn't know."

Bear dropped his head and rubbed his eyes. He held the gun out in front of him. "You're telling me the truth?"

The man scooted back. "Honest to God, man. It's the truth."

Bear sighed and lowered the gun. "Thanks."

He walked toward the door. As he passed the man, he held the gun out and fired a single shot into the guy's head.

CHAPTER 9

Mitchell Foster opened his eyes, sat up and stretched his arms over his head. He rolled over and slid off of his custom made bed, which was four feet wider and two feet longer than a traditional king-size bed. Blue and pink custom-made satin sheets sat wrinkled on it. Foster made a trip to the bathroom and then went downstairs. His luxury apartment was filled with the smell of blueberry pancakes.

He stepped into the kitchen and greeted Gloria, his personal assistant, chef, maid and driver. She'd been with him since his high profile days as a famous actor.

"Hungry?" she asked.

He nodded and took a seat at the breakfast table. He stared out the window at the busy street below filled with people on their way to work and school, heading to the market or just sight-seeing.

Gloria placed a cup of coffee in front of him. "You have a lunch meeting today with Harstein."

"Great," he said. "Can't wait."

He and Jack Harstein had produced movies together nearly a decade ago. From what Foster had heard, Harstein was broke now and had more than likely spent his last two thousand dollars on a trip to Paris to visit Foster to beg for money to produce some crappy action movie.

Gloria looked over her shoulder at him. "You two used to be friends. What harm could come from pitching in on a new movie?"

"Past is the past, Gloria."

"Then why do you keep me around?"

He smiled. "You're the only one that understands me."

He heard the front door open. Little feet pounded the staircase.

"Daddy, daddy," Foster's six year old daughter said excitedly. Her pale face lit up at the sight of her father. Her two front teeth were missing, making her smile appear that much bigger but also giving her a slight speech impediment. She jumped onto his lap, her blond hair tickling his nose. "What's for breakfast?"

"Watch out for daddy's coffee, muffin," Foster said.

"Blueberry pancakes," Gloria said. "Don't they smell yummy, Anna?"

"Mmmhmmm," Anna said.

"Hello, Mitch." Foster's wife Sandra walked into the kitchen carrying their two other children, Jake their eighteen month old son and Jessie their three year old daughter. Both clung to their mother.

Gloria came to Sandra's aid and grabbed Jessie.

Foster sat Anna in the chair next to him and went to Sandra. He leaned in to kiss her lips. She turned her head to the side.

"Not yet," she said. "I still don't know."

"Just move back in," Foster said. "I miss you. I miss the kids."

"What about her?"

Sandra was referring to Lorraine, Foster's mistress with whom he had an illegitimate daughter named Sophie.

Foster turned away. "I told you that's over."

They all sat at the table and had breakfast together. Afterward, Sandra got the kids together and headed for the front door.

"Will I see you tonight, daddy?" Anna asked.

"Yes, of course," Foster replied. "Why don't you all come to dinner at the restaurant tonight?"

Sandra rolled her eyes. "Fine, we'll be there around six."

"Gloria," Foster yelled from the front door.

"Yeah," she said from the top of the stairs.

"I'm going to the restaurant for lunch."

She shrugged and made a gesture that said she expected as much.

"Do me a favor," Foster said. "Call Harstein and tell him to meet me there at four-thirty today. I got other business to take care of before then."

He stepped out and joined the stream of people walking the street. He passed through the market, stopping along the way to buy an apple. He chatted with several different vendors. Every day he made this walk and he enjoyed getting to know the everyday people of the city. People who had no clue that he had once been a major Hollywood player.

After he passed through the market, he turned right and stopped in front of a very old building. He knocked on the unassuming door. Red paint chips hung from the door in strips, and a few littered the ground. Underneath the paint was a door that had seen centuries of activity on the street before it. Foster stared at the street and wondered what the scene was like two hundred years ago.

The door cracked open. "Yeah?"

Foster turned around and nodded at the half hidden face.

"Sorry, Foster. Didn't realize it was you." The man opened the door.

Foster stepped in and tossed the man an apple. "No problem, Adrien. No problem at all."

Adrien led Foster to a small office. In the office was an antique desk covered with dust. There was a stack of papers close to a foot high at one end.

Foster cleared his throat. "Love what you've done with the place."

Adrien dropped his eyes. "Sorry, mate. Been really busy this month and haven't had much time to clean up."

"Just make sure anything that has my name isn't on this desk. Got it?"

"Sure thing."

"So what's the news? How are operations?"

"Well, not so good." Adrien fidgeted with a stapler and avoided looking at Foster.

Foster leaned forward and put his arm on the desk. "What do you mean, not so good?"

"Well, eh, we seem to have..." Adrien cleared his throat. "We've lost a shipment."

Foster stood up and pushed the papers off the desk.

"Lost a shipment?" Foster asked. He placed his hands on the desk and hovered over Adrien. "How do you lose a shipment of two dozen women?"

"We believe the shipment was intercepted."

Foster turned around, clasped his hands behind his head and started to laugh. From behind him Adrien let out a nervous laugh. Foster stopped laughing and looked at Adrien out of the corner of his eye. The man was back against the wall and he had something in his hands. Foster reached under his shirt and pulled a nine millimeter handgun from his waistband. He turned around and pointed the gun at Adrien, who was holding a golf club.

"What the hell are you gonna do with that?" Foster asked.

Adrien didn't respond. He stood there, eyes glassy, body shaking.

Foster stepped closer.

Adrien let out a high pitched humming noise.

Foster heard the sound of drops hitting the floor. He looked down and saw a growing wet spot on the front of Adrien's pants. He rolled his eyes.

"Fix it," Foster said. "Fix it by tomorrow or you're dead."

Foster stepped through the front gate, stopped under the awning, took his usual seat. He pulled out his phone and made a call to his bodyguard Terrance and told the team to meet him outside of Lorraine's house at one-thirty. He stopped a waitress, ordered a cup of coffee and a sandwich. He lit a cigarette and sat back, enjoying the unseasonably warm breeze in Paris that day.

The waitress delivered his coffee. "Your sandwich will be ready soon."

He nodded his thanks, put out his cigarette and took a sip of coffee.

"Hello, Mitchell."

He looked up and saw Lorraine, dressed in a white dress fitted firmly around her waist, flowing at her knees. He stood up, brushed her curly brown hair behind her ears and kissed her. He put a hand on her shoulder, pulled out a chair and motioned for her to sit.

"Where is Sophie?" he asked.

"She is with my mom," Lorraine told him.

He nodded. "Bring her by tonight?"

"Sure, I can do that."

"Just make sure it is after eight."

"Is she going to be here before then?"

Foster sighed. "Please don't start with me. She's moved out. Soon we'll be divorced and you and I can start our life together."

Lorraine looked away and snapped to get the waitress's attention. "Coffee and whatever he is having for lunch."

They sat quietly waiting for the food to arrive.

CHAPTER 10

Clarissa perched herself on the windowsill and stared out over the city. Seemed it was all she could do. The old man had moved her to another floor. She had two guards outside her room and one guard inside. found that odd. Why would they put an armed guard in the room with old man had to know she was capable of disarming a man and that 't think twice about taking a life to save her own. The only 'd come up with to comply was Jack. She had a feeling that if would get Jack into a whole lot of trouble.

attention to the city below and thought about her aw him she was sixteen years old. It was her birth- rty would be an overstatement. It was a gath- friends. Jack was there. She had met him lay her father made a point to introduce

anything ever happens to me, you the field with me. He saved my 'ect my little girl. You got

along. What would d protection? Why years old her father as well as any guy. She taken down two guys who

to

guard

table. "I took
down. We'll be
ten about the deal."
ughout this ordeal. I

Her father's last words to her on her sixteenth birthday, the last night she ever saw him alive, were, "If there is ever a day I am not around, you go to him." He pointed at Jack. She left with her friends after that. When she came back the next day she found a note he had left on the table saying he had to travel overseas. They spoke over the phone sporadically after that. A couple years later Jack showed up at her door, tears in his eyes. He didn't have to say anything, she knew the moment she saw him.

Jack held up his end of the bargain, despite Clarissa's initial resistance. Anytime he was home, he was with her. He reminded her of her father. Over time she grew to think of him as a big brother. When he left the service and moved to New York, she tagged along. He helped her get set up in an apartment and with an office job. The job didn't last long. It was too boring for her. He argued with her when she started dancing, but he couldn't do much to stop it. She didn't tell him about her freelance work, but she suspected he knew.

Then, about five years ago things changed. She was attacked on stage and ended up in the hospital. It wasn't anything serious, but Jack was there for her. How he had known, she wasn't sure. But he showed up and took care of her, stayed with her every night until she had healed enough to take care of herself. A few weeks later she saw the man's picture on the news. He had been brutally murdered. She asked Jack about it, but he just shrugge it off.

It was at that moment she knew Jack Noble was the man she wante spend the rest of her life with.

Clarissa stepped down from the windowsill and glared at the sitting at the other end of the room. He winked. She rolled her eyes.

His cell phone rang. "Yeah," he said. "Sure, I'll bring her down."

She leaned against the wall with her arms and legs crossed.

"Get dressed," he said. "Old man wants to see you."

"Hello," the old man said to Clarissa as she sat down at th the liberty of ordering for you. I hope you like Chinese."

She didn't say anything.

"Right," he said. "Tomorrow the exchange will g contacting Mr. Jack shortly to make sure he hasn't forgo He smiled. "I do thank you for being so patient thro hope you realize this is nothing personal."

She nodded and took a drink.

"I admire your toughness, Clarissa. I do wonder if you would consider taking a position in my organization."

A smile crossed Clarissa's lips and a laugh escaped her mouth.

The old man cocked his head. "Something funny?"

"You think I would work for a spineless insignificant pawn like you?"

The guard to her right grabbed the back of her hair and pulled her head back. "You watch your mouth," he said to her.

The old man held out his hands. "Calm down. There are people around."

Clarissa looked around. There were a few couples in the hotel restaurant. The couple closest to them stared at her. The man removed his wedding ring and gave her a look as if asking if she needed help. She smiled and shook her head at him, to which he eased back in his chair, not taking his eyes off of Clarissa's table.

"I appreciate your offer," Clarissa said. "But I decline."

"Very well," the old man said. "No hard feelings. Anyway, as I was saying, exchange takes place tomorrow. You will be free to leave as soon as Mr. Jack produces the documents. But I must prepare you for the other possibility too. If Mr. Jack does not show up or he fails to produce the documents, you will remain in my custody."

Clarissa fought the urge to jump up and run.

The old man produced a knife from under the table. He held it up and traced it along his fingers. "Every day that passes, you will lose a body part. A finger, then a hand. A toe, then a foot. These will be delivered to Mr. Jack until he upholds his end of the bargain."

"Why are you saying this?" she shouted. "You know he'll show." Tears streamed down her cheek.

The man at the table rushed over. "Are you OK, Miss?"

She nodded at him. "Go back, you shouldn't have..."

One of the guards stuck a gun to the side of the man's head. The man's wife gasped.

"Listen to the girl," the guard said. "Go back to your table and slurp up your soup."

The man backed up, hands in the air till he got to his table. He took his wife by the hand and ushered her out the door. The rest of the people in the restaurant followed their lead.

The old man continued when they were all alone. "I'm sure he will, my dear. I just wanted to prepare you for what might come."

Clarissa folded her arms and looked away. He was playing a game with her and she would play along.

CHAPTER 11

Jack arrived at the abandoned apartment before eight a.m. He didn't know Foster's routine well enough to establish whether or not Foster was the kind of guy who would have a bodyguard watch a regular location hours before Foster arrived.

Jack searched the apartment, slowly and deliberately. He checked the closets, behind drapes, under beds and tables. If a bug had been hidden he would find it. After twenty minutes he cleared the apartment, satisfied that Pierre and his associate weren't going to turn on him.

He returned to the kitchen and living area and finished his cup of coffee. As requested, an M40A3 rifle rested on the floor below the window he planned on making the shot from. A case sat open next to the rifle and inside the case were two nine millimeter handguns. Jack knelt in front of the case, took each gun out, inspected them carefully. They were ready for action.

Just in case.

There were plenty of scenarios where just in case would come into play. Jack grimaced as the worst possible scenarios played out in his mind. The absolute worst thing that could happen was the shot missed and someone spotted where it came from. Foster's bodyguards would find their way inside. He didn't know the men per se, but he knew their type. They were mercenaries. And considering the amount of money Foster had to spend, they would be some of the best in the business.

Across the street, chefs and wait staff started piling into the patio area of the restaurant. They pulled four tables together and sat down to smoke cigarettes and drink coffee and eat pastries before their work began. Jack studied the group and determined that Corinne was not among them.

In a few hours he would place a call to the restaurant and ask for her to verify that she had taken his instructions and stayed away.

Jack looked up and down the street.

Where the hell is Pierre?

He had asked him to be at the apartment by nine a.m. It was ten after and Pierre was a no-show.

Jack fidgeted with a subsonic bullet. The cartridge danced along the knuckles of his right hand.

He was pretty sure the old man had someone following him or at least reporting when he left the hotel. Could the old man have intercepted Pierre? That would be an unlikely move, even for someone as powerful as the old man. Pierre was a highly placed French government agent. Taking him out would be like taking out one of the top CIA operatives. It would be like the old man inviting himself to his own funeral.

Still, Jack couldn't shake the thought from his mind. What if Pierre was being tortured for information by the old man right now? Jack knew very well that Pierre was trained to not give in to torture. But would the French man risk his life for Jack? All Jack had to do was look at himself for the answer to that. There were only two people he'd die for, Clarissa and Bear. Well, make that three. He'd now give up his life to save Mandy.

There had to be a simpler explanation. Maybe Pierre had been arrested. No, a man like Pierre wouldn't stay in jail long, if he got put behind bars at all. One call and his employers would free him.

A mission? It's possible his employer needed him to take care of something. But wouldn't he find a way to notify Jack if that were the case?

Jack paced the room, checking the street from each window he passed. He slammed a fist against the wall. He was losing focus. His attention needed to be on the restaurant, not on the streets looking for Pierre.

Finally, Pierre appeared. He walked on the other side of the street, passed the restaurant and traveled an additional two blocks. Then he crossed the street and made his way to the apartment building.

Jack kept an eye on the people enjoying themselves before work on the patio. None of them seemed to notice or care that a man who had passed by them minutes earlier was now on the other side of the street.

Pierre disappeared from sight as he entered the building. Less than a minute later he stood in the apartment apologizing profusely to Jack.

"You're thirty minutes late," Jack scolded.

"I'm very sorry, Jack. Please accept my apology. I had something to take care of last night and I only finished up an hour ago."

Jack looked him up and down from his position near the rifle and two handguns. "What was it?"

Pierre scratched at the stubble on his face. "To tell you that would be a breach of my oath to the French government." He held out his hands apologetically.

Jack thought for a moment. "I understand." He turned back to the window. "What's in the bag?"

Pierre walked up next to him and opened the bag. "Tint," he said, "for the windows. Less chance of us being seen."

"You don't think that someone might notice the windows are suddenly dark?"

"Why would they care?" Pierre said. "It's not as if they know this apartment is vacant. And even if they do they'd assume the landlord did it to attract a new tenant."

Jack shrugged. It would be better for someone to notice the tint than it would for him or Pierre to be seen.

"I'll take care of it," Pierre told him.

"I'm going for coffee." Jack slipped out of the apartment, down the stairs and made a hard right onto the sidewalk.

Pierre pointed at the tan man with a shaved head walking alone, toward them, on the other side of the street.

"That's him," he said.

"Why's he alone?" Jack asked.

Pierre shrugged. "Nothing we have on him says he travels alone. Ever."

Jack slid down to the window at the end of the room, pressed against the corner where the walls met, and scouted the street behind Foster. *Maybe his guards are trailing?*

"Anything?" Pierre asked.

"No. No one is with him."

"Very out of character. Something must be going on."

Jack took his place next to Pierre again and pulled out a pair of binoculars. He studied Foster's face through the high powered lenses. He looked no different than the day before. In fact, he had a slight smile, and not the bored look that crossed his face the day before.

"Shall we take him out now?" Pierre asked.

Jack reached down and placed the rifle across his legs.

"Give it a moment," he said. "We don't know if his bodyguards are below us, in the restaurant, or in another building."

"OK," Pierre said. "We'll wait."

Pierre moved from window to window, pressing his face against each. "No one. I don't see anyone on the street."

Foster had taken his seat on the patio. The sky was overcast, and judging by the swaying of the trees, a comfortable breeze blew across the street. The awning was pulled tight against the building. Jack could get a shot off right now and be done with this job.

"I'm going to take the shot," he said.

Pierre sat up straight. "OK. Set up and I'll monitor."

Jack lifted the window, slowly. He reached into the bag next to where the M40A3 rifle had been resting and retrieved the tripod. Once erected, he placed the rifle on top, steadied himself and aimed at Foster's head.

"Head or heart?" Pierre asked.

"Head," Jack replied. "Why risk it."

It didn't matter though. Get near enough to either and this weapon would blow a hole through the body large enough to ensure death. Yes, it made a mess. But in a case like this, a mess was acceptable.

Jack leaned in and prepared to make the shot. "Steady," he whispered a few times. He hunched his shoulders, cracked his neck, exhaled loudly. "Here we go."

"Wait," Pierre said.

"What?" Jack asked.

"There, to the right."

Jack looked at his associate and followed the French man's outstretched arm.

"Holy Christ," Jack said. "Cops."

Three policemen entered the patio through the wrought iron gate and took a seat at the bistro table in front of Foster's table.

"We could always kill them too," Jack said. He looked over at Pierre with a smile.

The Frenchman was not amused. "Here in my country we don't accept collateral damage." His voice escalated as he turned toward Jack. "Especially not when the targets are members of the military or police force."

Jack held his hands up.

"Bad joke, Pierre. I apologize."

The men sat in silence for the next hour. Jack tried to apologize a few times, but Pierre refused to hear it. The sun beat down from overhead and the green and white awning now covered the patio. The policemen left ten minutes ago, but with the awning down, all Jack and Pierre could do was wait for Foster to leave. That would be a risky shot though. Foster might fall forward onto the sidewalk, perhaps onto the street. There would be a crowd. Someone from the crowd would surely see Jack and Pierre leaving the building.

A few minutes later Jack sat up. Foster stood at the edge of the awning, smoking a cigarette.

"What about now?" Jack asked.

Pierre sat up and looked out the window. "Do we know who else is under the awning?"

"A woman entered a bit ago. The policemen left about fifteen minutes ago."

"This could work then."

"Better than at the gate," Jack said.

He took position behind the rifle again, aimed and prepared himself to pull the trigger. Seconds felt like minutes as Jack steadied his hands and slowed his breathing. The tiniest movement could send the bullet off course. Not knowing the position of people under the awning could spell disaster. He could take out two or three people if the shot lined up right.

A woman dressed in a short white dress stood directly in the path of his shot. She was tall, her head nearly blocking Foster's.

"Collateral damage?" he asked.

"No," Pierre replied. "He'll be back. We'll make the shot tonight."

Jack got up and walked to the other side of the room. He put two holes in the wall, one for each fist.

"They're gone," Pierre said.

"Left?"

"Yeah."

Foster returned to the restaurant earlier than expected. Jack wouldn't have even noticed had he not lifted his eyes from the book in his lap at precisely the right time.

"He's back," Jack said.

Pierre opened his eyes, yawned. "He's out of character today, isn't he? It's only four p.m."

Foster's bodyguards flanked him. One of the wait staff nodded at the man as he entered and slipped under the awning.

Half an hour later one of Foster's bodyguards poked out from underneath the awning and greeted a man at the gate. Jack picked up the binoculars to get a look at the tall man with grey unkempt hair. He wore blue jeans and a blazer. He turned to look over his shoulder, and Jack got a solid look at his face. He looked familiar, but Jack couldn't place him. When it came to Foster, this guy could be anybody, a drug dealer, trafficker, actor, literally anybody.

The man disappeared under the canopy along with the bodyguard.

Another half hour passed and the sun had ducked behind the buildings across the street, casting a shadow over the urban canyon. A member of the wait staff appeared and unhooked the support lines for the canopy. A few minutes later it sat flat against the side of the building.

Foster sat in the corner, his back against the wall. Exactly the spot Jack would have chosen for himself. Two of Foster's bodyguards sat at the table on either side of him. The third stood near the door leading into the restaurant. The man with the wild grey hair sat with his back to Jack. He was talking rather animatedly. Foster shook his head at nearly everything the man said.

They watched the conversation play out for another thirty minutes.

"What I wouldn't give for a parabolic microphone right now," Jack said.

"A what?"

"It's a large dome shaped microphone. Great for picking up conversations, movements, things like that."

"Ah, I see," Pierre said.

The man in the blazer stood. Jack reached for the binoculars.

"Harstein," Jack said. "He's a movie producer. He and Foster did some flicks together a decade ago."

"You think he's involved with Foster's operations?"

Jack shrugged. It was possible, but judging by Harstein's body language, he looked like a man who had been rejected. "I don't think so, but you might want to follow up on that."

"You won't?"

Jack looked at Pierre. "Only if someone pays me to."

The standing bodyguard led Harstein to the gate then walked back to the table as the dejected movie producer slouched down the street.

"I think I'm going to go ask that man a question or two," Pierre said.

Jack nodded. "Not a bad idea."

Pierre left the apartment. Jack stood to get a better view of him leaving the building. As Pierre jogged down the street Jack alternated between watching Foster's party and Pierre. So far no one had paid him any notice.

Pierre caught up with Harstein and the two men rounded a corner and disappeared from sight.

It was nearly dark when Pierre returned to the apartment.

"You were right, Jack. He's not involved with Foster."

"What did he want?"

"Capital for a new film."

"Did Foster bite?"

Pierre cocked his head and raised an eyebrow. "Do you mean agree?"

Jack nodded.

"No. In fact, he told Harstein to go to hell."

Jack shrugged. He leaned over and pointed at Pierre's collar.

"Blood?" Jack asked.

Pierre smiled. "I couldn't have him returning to the restaurant asking why some strange but amazingly handsome Frenchman had followed him and asked him about their meeting."

Jack nodded, kicked his feet up on the windowsill.

"Getting close to time," Jack said.

"Agreed. Did I miss anything?"

Jack pointed. "Looks like his wife and kids have joined him."

"Shit."

"Agreed."

Jack shifted between his seat and taking position behind the rifle. He changed positions at least a dozen times since Pierre returned.

"I can't do it," he said. "At least not while the man's kids are around."

Pierre sighed. "It's my weakness too."

"You think she'll stay all night?"

"Normally I would say no. But everything Foster has done today is out of character according to my files. So who knows?"

"I'm going to get closer," Jack said. "Think you can cover me from up here?"

"I'm not quite the shot you are, Jack. My specialty is killing up close."

"Want to join me at the restaurant?"

Pierre picked up the binoculars. After a minute he shook his head.

"Unfortunately there are people eating down there that might recognize me if I walked past them."

Jack scratched at his head.

"Tell you what though," Pierre said. "He always exits and turns left. There is a cafe, not too far, just a few buildings down. I can station myself there."

Jack nodded in agreement.

"You go first," he said. "I'll cover you."

Pierre got up without a word and went to the door.

"Wait," Jack said. He walked across the room and handed Pierre a phone. "I'm the only one with the number. It rings, you answer."

"Got it," Pierre said.

"And see about getting a car dropped off. If you can, position it two blocks away."

"I'll see what I can do."

"Be safe."

"OK. You too, Jack."

Jack watched as Pierre walked down the street and out of sight under the tree cover. Across the street at the restaurant no one seemed to notice or care.

Fifteen minutes later Jack left and followed the same path. He walked to the cafe, made eye contact with Pierre and crossed the street before turning back and making his way to the restaurant.

Jack let himself through the iron gate and pushed through the crowd of people in front of the door that led inside the restaurant. He kept his head down and away from Foster.

He took a seat at the bar and asked the bartender for a whiskey. It was a different man from the night before. When the bartender returned with his drink, Jack asked if Corinne was in.

"She's home, sick."

Jack turned in his chair and found himself face to face with Foster.

"Mr. Blair," Foster said. "Great to see you again."

Jack fought through the shock and jumped into small talk.

"Hey, Mitchell Foster. Wow, what luck. You know, I've been to Hollywood three times and never once met a famous actor. Here I come to Paris and I run into one of my favorites twice."

A broad smile swept across Foster's face.

"Why don't you come sit with us?" Foster asked.

Dumb freaking luck.

"I'm meeting someone," Jack said with a shrug.

"They can join us." Foster motioned to one of the wait staff. "Set up another table."

"Oui, monsieur," the waiter said.

Jack turned his head so he wouldn't be recognized. That waiter had seen him leave with Corinne the night before. He'd rather Foster didn't know he had been there twice yesterday.

Foster led Jack to the patio and offered him a seat at the table.

"Who's that?" a woman said.

"Howard, I'd like you to meet my wife, Sandra." Foster pointed at the two of them. "Sandra, this is Howard Blair. He's from the States, here on business."

Sandra lit a cigarette. "You work with my husband?"

Jack shook his head. "Industrial sales."

She rolled her eyes and looked away as if she had decided he wasn't important enough to waste her time on.

Foster grabbed his arm. "Don't mind her, she's moody."

Sandra shot him a look and flicked him off.

A little girl jumped on Foster's lap.

"Anna," Foster said, "Say hi to Daddy's friend, Howard."

"Hello, Howard," the little girl said through missing teeth.

Jack smiled at the bubbly, blond haired girl. He watched and saw how gentle Foster was with her, the broad smile that appeared on his face every time she giggled. For a moment Foster seemed human. Not that he judged him for his criminal activities. Jack wasn't that big of a hypocrite. He was the one who killed for profit after all.

"You have kids?" Foster asked.

"No," Jack replied. "Don't even have a wife. Not enough time."

Foster nodded. "I know that feeling. When I was in the movie business I never had time. Ruined my first marriage."

Jack looked at Sandra. Her face tightened and she looked away.

"So what do you do now?" Jack asked. He was treading dangerous territory now.

"Don't have to do anything now," Foster replied. "One of the benefits of ripping off the American public with over-budget festering piles of dung for movies."

Jack laughed. Foster smiled and joined him.

They continued chatting for several minutes. Nothing of importance was said. Jack figured Foster wouldn't reveal anything of importance. Still, he couldn't quite figure out why Foster had invited him to sit with them.

Sandra pushed her chair back from the table and stood up.

"I'm leaving," she said. "Anna, come with mommy."

Foster stood and held his hands out to the side, palms up. "Do you have to go already?"

Sandra bit her lip and looked toward the street. "Yes, it's near her bedtime. Besides, I have to go pick up the babies from my mother's apartment."

Foster lowered his head. "I see." He lifted Anna up, hugged her tight. "And you my little princess, you take care of your baby brother and sister. You hear me?"

Anna giggled. Foster smiled. He kissed her cheeks a dozen times before handing the little girl to her mother. He leaned in to kiss her too, but she turned her head and he ended up with a mouthful of hair.

Sandra turned to leave. Foster nodded to one of his men who followed her out the gate and down the street.

The table was silent for a few minutes.

"There's a story there, you know," Foster said, inviting Jack into his life.

"There always is," Jack said.

Foster smiled and nodded. He waved to a waitress who promptly stepped up to the table. "Bottle of whiskey."

She smiled and disappeared into the restaurant. A few minutes later she returned with four glasses and an unlabeled bottle.

Foster filled each glass halfway, placed two in front of himself and two in front of Jack.

"Drink," Foster said. "Then I want to talk to you in private."

Jack dropped his hand below the table and squeezed the handle of one of the two pistols he had on him.

"Thanks," Jack said. He took his time sipping on the alcohol.

Foster laughed. "Be a man."

Jack rolled his eyes and threw back the drinks in rapid succession. He squinted and bit down hard. "Happy now?"

Foster laughed some more. "I think that deserves another round." He filled each glass to the top.

Jack got through the first one quickly. His strategy now was to finish these and get on to the talk before he felt the effects of the whiskey.

He picked up the second glass and held it to his lips. A hand squeezed his shoulder.

"Hello, Mitchell," a female voice with a French accent said from behind him.

Jack turned and saw the pretty brown haired woman in the white dress from earlier. She was holding a baby in her other hand.

"Lorraine," Foster said. "And my angel, Sophie."

Foster stood, kissed the woman and took the baby from her arms.

Jack stood and extended his hand to the woman. "Howard Blair."

She smiled and gave a quick nod. "Nice to meet you, Mr. Blair."

Jack offered her his seat.

"Are you an associate of my husband's?"

"No," Jack replied. "Just a fan that got lucky enough to have dinner with him."

Lorraine smiled at Jack and turned toward Foster. She cocked her head and rolled her eyes toward Jack.

"No, he doesn't work with me," Foster said. "At least he doesn't yet. I'm about to make a business proposal to my new friend."

Foster smiled at Jack.

Jack returned the gesture.

Foster leaned over to one bodyguard and whispered something to him, to which the bodyguard nodded. Then Foster motioned for the other bodyguard to follow him. The third had still not returned from escorting Sandra.

Foster stood, leaned over and kissed Lorraine. He handed her the baby then turned to Jack.

"Follow me, Mr. Blair," he said.

Jack got up and followed Foster through the restaurant. They pushed their way through the crowd around the bar and walked to the back. The bodyguard stood in front of the men's room. He opened the door for them and waited for them to pass before entering.

Jack heard a click as the bodyguard locked the door.

Foster checked each stall, verifying that they were empty.

The bodyguard coughed and rolled his eyes.

Foster smiled at him. "Just being careful, my friend. That's all." He walked to the other end of the bathroom and leaned against the light blue tiled wall. "How often would you say you are over here?"

"Paris?" Jack said. "I dunno, once every couple months. Sometimes more, sometimes less. Just depends on the numbers I want to hit."

"Do you go anywhere else?"

"Sure, other parts of Europe, China, Japan, occasionally South America."

Foster grinned and nodded. "What would you say to us establishing a strategic partnership?"

"Not sure I follow," Jack said.

"You see, Howard," Foster said, "I'm not actually retired. I run certain enterprises. If you helped me out in one of those enterprises, I could make you a very, very wealthy man."

"What would I need to do?"

"It's pretty simple," Foster said with a smile. "You would just have to escort one or two women from the U.S. to here. Or transport another kind of package."

Sick bastard.

"Sounds easy enough," Jack said. "What kind of pay are we talking?"

Foster gestured to his bodyguard and the large man stepped out of the bathroom.

As the door opened Jack could hear someone complaining about the locked door. The bodyguard yelled at the man. The door shut and it was silent again. Jack contemplated making a move now.

"Around six figures a month," Foster said.

Jack's mouth dropped. Maybe he was in the wrong business. He whistled with eyes wide.

"Should I take that as a yes?"

Jack nodded.

"Excellent. Knock on that door for me."

Jack knocked on the door and the large man pushed his way back in.

"If you'll excuse me, I hope you don't mind continuing this conversation between a stall door."

"Doesn't bother me," Jack said.

Foster disappeared into the stall. He continued talking about minor details of the arrangement.

The bodyguard stared at the wall, paying no attention.

Jack stepped up to the urinal throwing in an occasional "yes" or "I see" to keep the conversation going. He flushed the urinal and pulled the lever hard so it would stick. He turned his head and spotted the bodyguard out of the corner of his eye. He slipped his hand into his pocket and grabbed the handle of the blackjack he took away from the skinny man the night before.

"So you see, Howard, I can use a man like you." The toilet in the stall flushed.

Jack took a deep breath. Stepped his right foot out. Pivoted on his heel and pulled the blackjack from his pocket in one fluid movement. He slammed the weapon across the bodyguard's throat.

The guard fell back against the door, gagging and gasping for air.

Jack reached into his other pocket and pulled out a dinner napkin and stuffed it into the man's mouth.

The big man slid down the door, grasping at his throat. His eyes bugged out of his head as he slowly suffocated.

Jack pulled one of the nine millimeter handguns from his waistband, the one with the suppressor already attached. He stood near the door, the gun pointed at the stall.

Foster stepped out. "I see us building a long..." His eyes dropped to the sight of his bodyguard on the floor, lifeless. He looked up at Jack in horror. Frantically, he reached behind his back.

Jack pulled the trigger. The bullet slammed into Foster's forehead, an inch above his eyebrows. Foster staggered for a second. There was no life left, just a few stray electrical impulses guiding his body. He fell to the ground.

Jack exhaled, turned on the faucet and splashed cold water on his face. He had to move fast. He grabbed a towel off the wall and covered the gun and his wrist. If anyone got in his way he would shoot. Simple as that. He pulled out his phone and called Pierre.

"I'm leaving." He hung up.

He unlocked the bathroom door and pushed through, leaving the bodyguard where he lay. The crowd around the bar had dispersed. Jack walked through the restaurant with his head down. He hit the patio and kept walking.

Lorraine was standing near the gate, smoking a cigarette. "Mr. Blair, before you go..."

He walked past her.

"Hey," she shouted.

He looked back and saw the other bodyguard moving toward the gate.

"Mr. Blair," he called out. "Come back here."

Jack stopped, turned, raised his arm, shot the bodyguard in the chest. Lorraine screamed and dropped to the ground.

Had the bullet gone through the guard and hit her too? There was no time to check. Jack turned and sprinted two blocks to the cafe where Pierre had gone. He heard a honk, looked over and saw Pierre in a silver coupe. Jack jumped in. The car made a u-turn in the middle of the street and sped off.

CHAPTER 12

J ack took a shower as soon as he got back to his hotel room. He debated over whether or not to stay. Only two people knew that Jack Noble was staying there. Pierre, who had just assisted with the hit on Foster, wasn't going to say anything. The old man knew, Jack was sure of that, but until the old man received the documents, he would stay out of Jack's way. Only then did Jack realize that the old man still hadn't gotten in touch with him about the spot for the switch. Last minute surprises pissed Jack off.

He got out of the shower, put on a pair of shorts and fell into bed. He replayed the hit over and over in his mind. He had started to like Foster and for a moment felt bad about having had to kill him. He thought about the four kids now without a father. Two of those kids would have no memory of him when they grew up. Even little Anna would barely remember the man in five or six years.

Then again, perhaps Jack had done them all a favor.

He reached into the antique nightstand and pulled out an unopened bottle of whiskey. He contemplated whether or not it was a good time to drink. The pros outweighed the cons. He retrieved a glass from kitchenette table and filled it halfway, sat down in a chair, took a small sip. He clicked on the TV and found a local news station. Jack fumbled with the remote until he enabled subtitles.

A small reporting team was positioned outside the restaurant. The camera focused on a gurney being pulled through the door and onto the patio. Judging by the large lump on top of the gurney, they were pulling out the bodyguard. Two more bodies lay on the ground, covered in sheets. They flashed a picture of Foster on the screen and then showed amateur cell phone camera footage of a man leaving the restaurant.

Jack held his breath the length of the segment. They had film of him leaving the restaurant. The shaky footage continued long enough to see Jack turn and fire. The darkness concealed his face, and his body. When the station zoomed in on the footage there was no way to identify his face from the blurred and distorted picture.

Jack exhaled, sat back. He read the subtitles on the screen as eyewitnesses recounted the ordeal. Not a one had a good look at him. And as it turned out, Lorraine had been hit by the bullet. The wound left her unconscious and they feared she would die during the night.

Then they displayed a composite sketch of the shooter.

Jack grinned. No way was anyone going to figure Jack as the shooter.

He picked up his cell phone and placed a call to Bear.

"Hey, Jack," Bear said.

"How are you two doing?"

"Everything's a mess, Jack. A total mess."

Jack sensed something was wrong. "Mandy OK?"

"Yeah, she's fine now."

"Now?"

"The guy in the alley, he bugged me. They followed us. Mandy actually spotted the transmitter on my shirt."

"What did you do?" Jack poured himself another drink.

"I let them know I spotted them following me. They pulled off the highway and I took off like a bat outta hell. Pushed over a hundred for thirty minutes. Dropped Mandy off at one of those protected arcade places and then found a place to set them up."

"I take it everything went fine?" Jack asked.

"Yeah, killed all four." There was a pause. "Jack, you won't like this."

"What?"

"It was one of the old man's teams."

"I have to meet with him tomorrow."

"Yeah, I know. But they weren't sent by him. He might not even know about it."

"What are you saying, Bear?"

"Before I killed the last guy, he confessed that Charles had sent them."

Jack rubbed his temples. "OK. I'll call you after the exchange tomorrow."

He hung up and thought for a minute, then dialed the old man.

"Mr. Jack," the old man said.

"How do you know it's me?"

"I know all of your numbers, Mr. Jack."

He decided against pressing the phone number issue. "What the hell is going on? Why did you send a team after Bear and the girl?"

"I'm sorry?"

Was he being condescending?

"You know what I'm talking about. They went to San Diego and were greeted by a hit team."

"Ah, I see," the old man said. A long pause ensued. "I seem to have a loose cannon in my organization. I take it the team was not successful?"

"All five are dead."

Muffled voices filled the ear piece of Jack's phone.

"Hello?" he said.

The old man cleared his throat. "One minute, Mr. Jack."

Jack tried to make sense of what the muffled voices were saying but it was pointless. He couldn't make out a single word.

"Mr. Jack, my apologies. That team, which was one of my better ones, was not sent by me. I didn't order a hit on Mr. Bear and I wouldn't dare harm a hair on the little girl's head."

Jack didn't believe the last part, but he did believe the information Bear had coerced out of one of the hit men was correct.

He changed the subject. "Where are we going to do the exchange?"

"I've got a spot selected, Mr. Jack."

"Yeah, where is it?"

"I will tell you that tomorrow morning at ten o'clock. You should be waiting outside your hotel."

"Why?" Jack asked.

"It will take you fifteen minutes to reach the location by foot," the old man said, ignoring Jack's question. "You are to travel only by foot. Do not attempt to drive."

Jack looked up at the ceiling, clenched his fist, took a deep breath.

"OK," Jack said. "Anything else?"

"Yes, come alone. Do not attempt to bring your friend from the French government with you."

So he did know about the hit.

"Do not bring anyone. If you do, the girl dies. Understand?"

"Yeah, I got it."

The old man started to talk, but Jack hung up the phone. He had wasted enough time on the phone tonight.

Jack stood up and looked at the door. He thought about going out for a few hours but decided against it. Instead, he collapsed onto the bed and fell asleep.

CHAPTER 13

Jack stood outside the hotel and looked at his watch. Ten a.m. He held his cell phone in the opposite hand. It rang.

"Yeah," he answered.

"Le Pont Alexander III," the old man said. "Meet us on that bridge."

"Got it."

"And remember, Mr. Jack..."

"Yeah, yeah, come alone."

The old man hung up. Jack flipped the GPS on his phone on, and after a short walk down Cours la Reine, turned left on Avenue Winston Churchill. He could see the bridge in the distance. It took him just seven minutes to reach this point and he had time to spare, so he sat next to an older woman sitting on a bench smoking a cigarette. He bummed a smoke from her and scouted the area.

Right away he spotted two men positioned on either side of the road, standing against the large fifty foot high columns at the end of the bridge. He figured there would be two more on the other end, and anywhere from one to four along the bridge.

The bridge was busy, a combination of cars and pedestrians. Locals, businessmen and tourists all made their way along the century old bridge that spanned the width of the Seine River

He saw a luxury car stop in the middle. An old Asian man and a woman got out.

Clarissa.

Jack leaned his shoulder toward the older woman, thanked her for the cigarette and asked if he could have another for his walk. She handed him two and a book of matches. He thanked her again and made his way to the bridge.

The two men at the end stood motionless. Jack nodded at each. They didn't respond. Jack took comfort in the fact that they knew that he *knew* they were there. He walked down the side of the bridge, along the edge. He stopped to take pictures with his cell phone for no reason other than he wanted to drag this out and piss off the old man's bodyguards.

He got closer. The old man nodded to him. Clarissa spun, smiled and dropped her head.

Jack stopped ten feet away.

"Send her over," he said.

"Give me the documents," the old man said.

Jack reached into his pocket, pulled out a cell phone and placed it on the ground. He backed up another ten feet.

The old man took Clarissa by the arm and stepped forward. He reached down and picked up the phone.

Jack was surprised the old man was so bold. What if he had planted an explosive instead of a real phone? But he wouldn't take that chance with Clarissa's life and the old man knew it.

"What's this?" the old man asked.

"The documents. I had to get rid of the originals in case customs stopped me. They're stored on the phone."

The old man frowned and shook his head.

"What did you expect me to do? France was your idea, not mine."

"What else is on there?" the old man asked.

"Nothing," Jack said. "I wiped everything else off."

He pulled another phone from his pocket, showed it to the old man then put it away.

The old man raised his left arm and waved. One of his men crossed the street, dodging cars along the way, and approached Jack.

Jack reached behind his back, grabbed the butt of his gun.

"Now, now Mr. Jack," the old man said. "There's no need for that."

The old man looked through the phone and nodded at the man standing next to Jack. The man walked over to Clarissa, took her hand and led her to Jack.

Jack reached for Clarissa's hand, held it tightly. He watched the old man turn to walk away, then stop abruptly.

"Mr. Jack," the old man said. "If you happen to see Mr. Charles, please do let me know."

With that, he walked another twenty feet. The luxury car pulled up next to him and he got in.

Jack waited until the car disappeared. He turned to Clarissa and hugged her tight to his body.

"Oh, Jack," she said through muffled sobs.

"Shh, take it easy. We still need to get off this bridge."

Clarissa looked at him wide-eyed.

"He's got what he wants. He might think of me as dispensable now." Jack brushed her windblown red hair out of her face.

She reached up and cupped his hands with hers.

"We are going to turn around and walk. Don't look back. Don't look to the side." He slid his hands behind her head, pulled her face close to his. He pressed his lips firmly against hers and kissed her. "Take my hand, let's go."

They walked back the way Jack came. As they neared the large columns, Jack leaned over and whispered, "Don't look to the side. Keep your eyes straight ahead."

She squeezed his hand tight, dropped her head a few inches and kept her stride.

Jack led her by the bench where the older woman still sat smoking a cigarette.

"Need another?" she asked.

Jack smiled at her. "In fact, I do." He didn't, but what the hell. They were safe now. The crowd was thicker here. No way would the old man chance firing at them now.

"Take these dear," the old woman said. She handed Clarissa a pair of large sunglasses and shook her head at Jack.

He frowned at her. "Wasn't me."

"Well I hope you take care of the one that did it."

"I have every intention of doing just that," he said.

Clarissa tugged at his hand. He looked over at her. She bit her lip and raised an eyebrow at him and she looked around at the crowd.

Jack nodded. "You take care, dear."

CHAPTER 14

C harles paced the living area of the hotel room. *Where is that old bastard?* The dark haired man on the floor started to move. Charles hit him over the head three times with his gun. The man had been guarding the old man's door and refused to let Charles in.

Big mistake.

The door handle jiggled, gave way. The door pushed open and the old man stepped in, followed by two guards. The first guard moved past the old man and ran up to the motionless man on the floor.

He looked up at Charles. "You are a dead man," he said.

Charles grinned at him.

The man stood and pulled a handgun from inside his sports coat.

"There will be none of that," the old man said. "Take him and leave me and Mr. Charles alone."

Charles crossed his arms and raised an eyebrow. He didn't take his eyes off the old man. He knew well enough that his boss was as capable of taking a life as Charles himself was.

"How did the meeting go?" he asked.

The old man shook his head. "Fine, no thanks to you." He took off his coat and hung it in the closet.

Charles shrugged. "Wasn't no point in me being there."

"There was every point in you being there," the old man yelled.

"Why?" Charles asked. "Not like you would have let me take care of Jack like I've been asking."

"Why this fascination for killing Mr. Jack?" the old man asked.

Charles moved toward the old man and stooped over so they were face to face.

"Look at my face," he said. "Look what he has done to me." He pointed at the long scar on his cheek and the wound on his forehead. "He's attacked me not once, but twice and I can't do anything about it."

"He was defending himself," the old man said.

Charles turned his back on the old man and walked to the window. He stared out at the city, his eyes sweeping side to side. He caught a reflection of the old man in the window. Charles narrowed his eyes and honed in on his boss's figure, holding a knife.

"You know," said Charles, "I've never actually been in the Eiffel Tower."

"We should go later this afternoon," the old man said. "I'll arrange it after a nap."

Charles watched as the old man crept closer. He sighed, feigning tiredness.

That's it you old bastard, just a little bit closer.

He took a deep breath and spun to his right, his outstretched right arm connecting with the old man's chin in a vicious backhand.

The old man was lifted from his feet and flew more than eight feet in the air. Probably would have gone farther if the wall wasn't there to break his flight path. His motionless body lay on the bed. Blood trickled from the back of his head.

Charles ignored the old man's groans. He moved to the door and looked out. Only one of the guards remained. Charles armed himself and pushed the door open.

"Back up Briggs," he said.

Briggs looked at the gun in Charles's right hand. The man was half the size of Charles and eight years younger. His dirty blond hair was cut short. His blue eyes were wide with fear. He backed up to the wall.

Charles moved slowly, never turning his back to Briggs. The little man might not look it, but he was more than capable of taking Charles down in a hand fight. Charles would make sure he never got close enough for that to happen. He pushed the button with the down arrow in the elevator lobby. When the door opened he stepped in sideways, keeping an eye on Briggs until the final second when the doors shut.

The nudge to his ribs jarred Jack from his sleep. He sat up, fists out, ready to take on an attacker. Clarissa jumped back. She was holding his phone.

"It's ringing," she said.

Jack opened his hands and reached for the phone. He didn't recognize the number.

"Yeah?" he said.

"Good work on Foster," a man's voice said.

Jack stayed silent while placing the voice.

"It's Frank."

"Yeah, Frank, you saw it?"

"The whole country did. Doing the hit in a restaurant? That was a nice touch, Jack."

Jack laughed. "Didn't intend to."

"Whatever, it got the job done. We opened an account in Switzerland under Howard Blair. Your money is there."

"Appreciated," Jack paused. "Not setting me up are you?"

"We're not dumb enough to do that."

Jack hung up, got to his knees, pulled Clarissa close. He caressed her face then shook his head.

"I'm so sorry for letting them do this to you," he said.

She shrugged. "I didn't make it easy for them."

He leaned in and kissed her neck, pulled her close until her breasts brushed against his chest. She moaned in his ear. He rubbed her back as his hand slipped down toward her waist.

The phone rang again.

"Jesus," said Jack. He picked up the phone. "It's the old man."

Clarissa shuddered and slipped over to the other side of the room.

Jack answered the phone.

"Mr. Jack, thank you for taking my call. I'll make this brief. My associate Mr. Charles, you know him, has become something of a nuisance to me. I'd like to offer you a job."

Jack stood and looked out the window. "What kind of job? A position?"

The old man laughed. "Oh dear no. I learned long ago that a tiger cannot be caged and still be effective. I need you to take care of Mr. Charles."

Jack almost dropped the phone. Did the old man really just ask him to kill Charles?

"Hang on," Jack said while he locked himself in the bathroom.

"Why do you need me? You've got guys that can handle this assignment."

"Two things," the old man said. "For one, I don't know where certain people's loyalties lie."

"The rogue team that tried to take out Bear and Mandy," Jack said.

"Exactly," the old man said. "And in addition to that, I don't have people that can move in and out of countries like you can. At least, no one other than Mr. Charles."

"What happened?"

"Excuse me, Mr. Jack?"

"What happened that you are on the phone asking me to take care of your right hand man?"

"We had an argument. It escalated and came to a head this afternoon after the exchange."

"This sounds like a family thing and I don't like to get involved in family messes," Jack said.

"Please consider it. I'll pay you five hundred thousand dollars."

The number kept going through Jack's head. He could disappear for a while on that kind of money while he contemplated his future. Take Clarissa and go. Set Mandy up in a boarding school far away from all of this.

"I'll think about it." He hung up the phone.

A knock on the door jarred him from his thoughts. He cracked it open.

"Everything OK?" Clarissa asked.

"Yeah, yeah. I'm going to get a shower."

Clarissa jumped on the bed and rolled over onto her back. The sound of the shower provided the right amount of white noise and she felt her eyelids getting heavy. She forced herself to sit up, knowing that if she fell asleep now it would be hours before she awoke.

She and Jack had some business to attend to and it didn't include sleeping.

She didn't have much of a wardrobe, so she opted for a simple white button up shirt that belonged to Jack. She took off her clothes and slipped into the shirt. She smelled the collar. It had the faint smell of Jack. She closed her eyes and wrapped her arms around her chest.

Clarissa sat down at the table and poured whiskey into a glass until it was half full. She took a few sips and let the alcohol warm her.

She went to the mirror and stared at her beaten body. Her chest and back were bruised. Her face was lined with cuts. One eye was still partially swollen. What a screwed up week. Never in her life had she endured so much pain and torture. But she made it through it and was stronger for it.

Clarissa was startled by a knock at the door. She hesitated to answer it.

"Who is it?" she called out.

"Room service," a female voice said back.

Did Jack order something?

She had been in and out of sleep the past hour and couldn't remember anything clearly.

"One moment," Clarissa said.

She knocked on the bathroom door. "Jack?"

He didn't respond. Probably couldn't hear her over the sound of the shower.

She tried the door, but it was locked. She dropped her head and sighed. Clarissa looked through the peephole, saw the young blond haired woman on the other side dressed in the hotel's standard uniform. The woman had a cart with trays and a bottle of wine. Clarissa shrugged, unlocked the door, opened it.

The woman stepped through the doorway, looked at Clarissa head to toe and smiled. "Looks to be a fun evening, eh?"

Clarissa blushed and looked away.

"Where should I put this?"

Clarissa pointed at the table. "That should be fine." She walked over to the window hoping to avoid any further contact with the pretty attendant.

"Do you two have plans tonight?" the woman asked.

Clarissa shook her head. "Just staying in."

"If you are up for a short walk you should see the Le pont Alexander III at night. Much better than in the day time."

Clarissa straightened up.

Why had the woman said that?

"And maybe this time you won't have to leave so quickly," the woman said.

Clarissa searched the windowsill for something, anything she could use. Finding no options readily available, she turned to face the woman.

"Who are you?" Clarissa asked.

"Nobody," she said.

The woman lifted the lid off a silver tray and pulled out a gun with a suppressor attached to the end.

"Oh, God. Please no," Clarissa said.

The woman smiled at her. "It won't hurt for long."

The shower cut off. The woman looked toward the bathroom and frowned. She backed up to the door, fired a single shot at Clarissa and left the room.

Clarissa stumbled, nearly falling over. She caught and steadied herself on the back of a chair. She managed to get to the bed and fell backwards onto it. Crimson blood bloomed across the white shirt. Her right hand pressed tight against the wound.

"Jack," she whispered.

"What the hell was that?" Jack said.

He turned off the water, grabbed a towel, got out of the shower, pressed his ear against the door. He heard his name being called faintly. He pushed the door open and saw Clarissa lying on the bed, bleeding.

"Oh dear God," Jack said. "Clarissa, what happened?"

The wounded woman opened her eyes and pointed toward the door.

Jack ran to the open door and looked out in the hall. Two old ladies stood by the elevator.

"Someone call a doctor," he yelled.

He didn't wait for a response. He grabbed a towel from the closet and returned to Clarissa. He held the towel to her chest, keeping pressure on the wound. On the table next to the bed sat the room service tray. A white piece of paper had a simple message on it:

PAY BACK, JACK. PAY BACK.

-Charles

"Bastard," Jack said.

"What?" Clarissa whispered.

"Don't speak, Clarissa. Just breathe."

A deep voice from behind him said, "What's going on in here?"

Jack turned and saw a man holding a medical bag. He was older, maybe in his mid-sixties, with grey hair and a grey goatee and moustache. He wore thick black rimmed glasses. His eyes widened when Jack moved to the side and the doctor got a view of a blood soaked towel covering Clarissa's chest.

"Can you help her?" Jack asked.

Behind the doctor stood his assistant. He turned to her. "Call an ambulance."

Jack grabbed the old man. "Help her," he pleaded.

The old man grabbed Jack by the shoulders and shook him. "Calm down and do what I say."

Jack stared back at him. His breathing was rapid and shallow. He felt lightheaded. He felt the old man slap him across the face. Jack shook his head and stepped to the corner of the room. He grabbed a pair of khakis from his bag and put them on. He tucked his nine millimeter into the back of his waistband. He threw a blue button up shirt on over his still wet upper body.

"Fix her," he said to the doctor.

Jack ran out into the hall, to the stairwell, back to the other side of the floor. Guests lined the hall, everyone pointing at him or his hotel room. Frustrated, he fell to his knees and let out a yell.

The elevator doors opened. He looked over his shoulder and saw the gurney being wheeled out by two paramedics.

"Down here," Jack called to them.

The medics followed him to the room and assisted the doctor.

The next few minutes went by in a blur for Jack. The doctor, his assistant and the two medics all worked feverishly on Clarissa. They wheeled her out. One of the medics grabbed Jack.

"Come with us," he said to Jack.

"I'll be down in a second," Jack said.

He grabbed his cell phone and stuffed it into his pocket. Threw a few items into his bag, zipped it up and threw it over his shoulder. He took the stairs to the lobby and met the doctor, his assistant and the medics at the ambulance. One of the medics held the door open and gestured for Jack to get in. He jumped into the back of the ambulance, sat near Clarissa's head, held her hand in his and stroked her hair.

CHAPTER 15

"Monsieur Blair," a woman's voice said.

Jack looked up, saw the petite nurse with short brown hair motioning for him to come to the door.

"Is she ok?" he asked.

"Come with me," the nurse said.

Jack followed the petite woman down the corridor.

"Where are we going?" he asked.

"The doctor wants to speak with you about your wife."

He didn't bother to correct her.

The nurse stopped in front of a room, opened the door and nodded for Jack to enter.

The room was full of medical gadgets, which he presumed were intended to keep Clarissa alive. Machines whirred and beeped. The doctor smiled at him and offered Jack a seat. He shook his head at the doctor. Jack's eyes pleaded for good news from the grey haired man.

"She's stable now," the doctor said.

"Thank you," Jack said.

"No thanks yet. We aren't out of the woods. We lost her once during surgery. Dead for five minutes. And almost lost her another two times. She's in a coma and might not wake from it."

Jack bit his lip to keep from crying.

"When will you know?" Jack asked.

The doctor shrugged and pointed his clipboard upwards. "No telling. It's up to Him."

Jack collapsed into the chair nearest Clarissa's head, took her hand between his and kissed it.

"I'll leave you be," the doctor said.

Jack didn't respond, nor did he watch the man leave the room.

"I'm sorry, so sorry," he whispered in Clarissa's ear.

She squeezed his hand. He sat up and watched as her eyes fluttered open.

"Clarissa," he said.

She smiled for a moment, then her grip weakened and her smile faded and her eyes shut again.

"I'm sorry about your woman, Jack."

He stood up and saw Pierre flanked by two men. They were standing in the room. With a deep breath, Jack steadied himself.

"Christ, Pierre. Knock first."

Pierre smiled. "These are my best guys. They will not leave her side until you return."

Jack raised an eyebrow. "Return from where?"

"Walk with me, Jack."

"Cigarette?" Pierre asked.

Jack nodded and took the lit cigarette from Pierre's hand. He drew the smoke into his lungs and held it in. Looked up at the starry sky and exhaled the smoke, watching it drift above their heads.

"Southern France," said Pierre. "That's where I need you to go."

"Why?"

"We have a target that needs to be neutralized." He lowered his head slightly and raised his eyebrows. "My people cannot be involved."

"Who is it?"

"It's on here." Pierre handed him a USB thumb drive. "The rest will be provided by a contact in Nice."

Jack grimaced.

"Pay?" he asked.

"Two hundred thousand US dollars."

Jack shrugged.

"Can I think about it?" he asked.

"Sure," Pierre smiled. "I'll give you thirty seconds."

Jack turned his back on Pierre and took another drag on the cigarette.

"If it helps," said Pierre, "we believe that the old man's associate has fled to the target city."

Jack tossed the cigarette into the parking lot. Tiny red embers exploded like fireworks as the cigarette landed on the asphalt. He looked up at the sky and clasped his hands behind his head. He'd find Charles no matter what, might as well make some money along the way.

"Give me the contact info," Jack said.

Pierre placed a hand on Jack's shoulder. "They will find you when you arrive in Nice. You are on the six thirty a.m. train."

Jack turned his head slightly and looked at Pierre out of the corner of his eye. "So sure I'd accept?"

"Yes. And why don't you call the old man and accept his job as well."

Jack laughed. He planned to do that as soon as he was alone. He pulled the cell phone from his pocket and dialed the old man's number.

"Yes," the old man answered.

"I'm in," Jack said.

"Excellent, I will send a car at..."

Jack hung up.

"Bastard," he said.

"The old man or Charles?"

"Both of them. All of them." He pulled his gun from his waistband and aimed it at an orange street lamp. "Every last one of them is going to die."

EPISODE 3

CHAPTER 1

A ct. React.
Jack Noble considered himself a man of action. Put him in the worst possible situation and force him to make a decision. He'd act, deliberately.

Reacting was saved for moments of ultimate duress, moments where he didn't have time to contemplate his next action. Times when primal instincts take over and lives are saved.

Gun pointed to his head? Act.

Knife swinging at his head? React.

A death threat on his family? Act.

A kid hanging from the edge of the roof by one hand, about to fall? React.

That's how Jack's mind worked. It's not hard to understand, then, why he was so troubled by the situation he found himself in. He *reacted* to Clarissa's comatose body and accepted two jobs.

Jobs he wanted nothing to do with.

First assignment, the job in Southern France for Pierre. Good pay, bad setup. The job would keep him in Europe longer. Not an idea he was particularly fond of. Pierre provided him with no physical details, only a thumb drive. Jack wasn't the most high-tech of guys. He knew what to do with a thumb drive, but he had no device with which to use it. He planned on buying a laptop computer after he departed the train in Nice.

More time wasted, more opportunity for his face to be captured on camera.

There was also the possibility that this job could be a setup. Jack could link Pierre to the death of Foster if Jack were pinched by the local cops. Hell, Jack could blame the whole thing on Pierre and say he was there to *save* Foster's life from the French government, and it wouldn't matter. They'd do nothing to Pierre.

Jack had a bad taste in his mouth over this.

Second assignment, find and kill Charles for the old man. There was a problem with this job. Charles had the loyalty of half the men in the old man's organization. If Charles got wind that Jack had orders to terminate him, Charles would have over one hundred men at his disposal to fight back. Maybe the old man was setting Jack up? Christ, Jack hadn't even thought it through. His initial response was a simple no. The old man and Charles were like family to each other and getting involved in a family dispute was always a bad idea. But standing outside the hospital where Clarissa lay lifeless, he dialed the old man's number without giving it second thought.

Jack hadn't acted deliberately.

He'd reacted.

He pulled at his hair with both hands as he went over it time and again in his head. He needed a distraction. The monotonous scenery visible through the train window bored him. Beautiful, yes. Boring, doubly so.

Two people sat across from him. A couple, perhaps. Both had wedding rings on, but different designs. She wore white gold or platinum. He wore yellow gold. Both had newspapers. The man read his. The woman didn't.

He caught the woman's eye.

"Can I borrow your paper?" Jack asked the woman in French.

She smiled, nodded and handed the paper across to him.

"Thanks," Jack said.

He flipped through the pages of the paper. He spoke French well enough to get by. Sure, he sounded like an American, but some people appreciated that he'd tried. However, when it came to reading French, his skills were shaky at best.

There wasn't much of interest to him in the paper. He skipped the section on French politics. Soccer bored him to tears. And then he saw it. A blurred image from the concrete patio of *Sensationnel*. A photo of him leaving the scene. Below the large photo was a close up of the face, his face. A blurry photo, but it looked enough like him that it could cause a problem. Could he tell because he knew, or did it really look that much like him?

He looked across at the woman who now sat with her arms and legs crossed, head cocked sideways, resting on the wall, eyes closed. He shifted his gaze to the man. The man still held the newspaper in front of him. If he turned the page he would see Jack's picture.

He had two choices. Kill the man or leave and hope the guy didn't remember his face. Killing on a moving train didn't appeal to Jack. Who knows how many people he'd have to take out to keep it quiet? Jack and the man had not spoken a word to each other. Chances were he'd never remember what Jack looked like

Best bet was to leave.

Jack slid the compartment door open and stepped out into the hallway. He walked toward the front of the train until he found an unoccupied compartment where he stayed until the train arrived in Nice.

The train arrived at the Gare de Nice Ville, Nice's main train station, around noon. The journey had taken six hours. He spent the last two alone. He half expected to step off the train and find a welcoming party of French police waiting for him. In the end there were no cops, no government officials. Nobody waited for him.

He stepped off the train and onto the platform. He looked up through the high arched windows on the ceiling. Sunlight filtered in. The air was warm. He looked back at the train as it moved ahead another hundred feet or so. Between the rails was a median. Palm trees sat at either end, welcoming new arrivals, saying goodbye to those who were on their way to some destination not as nice or hip as the famous French city.

Jack exited through the front of the train station. The taxi line was empty. No taxis, either. He stood at the curb, looked right, then left. His instincts told him to go left, so he turned to the right and began walking. He didn't trust himself today.

A few blocks away he saw a sign in a window indicating he could purchase a cell phone and SIM card inside. He could just use his current phone and get a new SIM card, but the technophobe in Jack wouldn't allow that. He walked into the store and nodded at the old French man behind the counter. The old French man nodded back. He was bald on top. A thick mustache adorned his upper lip. He wore a brown shirt that made Jack think the man was going bowling. Wide collar, button up, two inch wide white stripes on either side of the buttons. Perhaps this was his store. Perhaps it wasn't. Jack didn't care.

He pointed at a cell phone on the wall. The old French man nodded again. He turned, pulled the phone down, opened a drawer and reached in

162 / L.T. RYAN

and retrieved a tiny piece of plastic. He held the phone and tiny piece of plastic up in the air for Jack to inspect. Jack looked at it for a second. Nodded his approval. The old French man inserted the card into the phone, connected it to his computer and punched at his keyboard with two short stubby fingers. Five minutes passed. Jack didn't move. The old French man barely moved. He handed the phone to Jack.

"Thirty-nine," he said in English.

Jack smiled. The man figured him for an American even though he hadn't said a single word. He reached into his wallet and pulled out forty euros. Handed the money to the man with his right hand, grabbed the phone with his left. He nodded at the old French man and left the store.

Thirty-nine.

The only words spoken during the entire eight minutes he was in the store.

He walked a few more blocks and stopped in front of an electronics store. A brand new laptop was on display in the window. Jack walked in and a sales associate came up to him. He wore a red vest over a light pink polo shirt. He had blue jeans on, the cuffs rolled too high. Black socks showed under the high cuffs, and blue sneakers finished off his outfit. He was probably close to Jack's age judging by the light dusting of silver hair on his temples.

"How can I help you, sir?" the sales associate said in English with a heavy French accent.

I really need to get a change of clothes.

"I need a laptop," Jack said.

The sales associate's eyes lit up. "Great, I have several choices. Follow me."

Jack followed him.

"Over here we have our most popular model. It's --"

Jack tuned him out. Nothing the man said would make sense, so there was no point listening to him. He looked at the price tag. Nine hundred ninety nine euros. Over twelve hundred dollars US.

"Next," Jack said.

The sales associate frowned and stepped to the right one pace.

Eight hundred ninety nine euros. Jack frowned. The sales associate did not say a word. He held up a hand, turned, and motioned with his finger for Jack to follow. He did.

"Here we are, sir," the sales associate said. "Perfect for a man like you."

Jack smirked. Four hundred ninety nine euros. "I'll take it."

"Excellent," the sales associate said. "And let me tell you about our warranty program--"

Jack held up his right hand.

"No warranty. I understand, sir." He led Jack to the counter.

Jack pulled out a credit card with the name Sherman Harrod. He pulled out an ID card with the same name then handed them both to the sales associate.

The sales associate smiled, ran the card and placed a receipt for Jack to sign. The associate stuck the receipt under the money tray in the drawer, then he placed the box the laptop was packaged in into a bag labeled with the store's name.

The men smiled at each other. There was a hint of contempt behind Jack's smile and he felt positive that the sales associate's smile contained the same emotion. Jack turned and exited the store.

He continued in the same direction and stopped in front of the first hotel he saw, the Hotel Azurea. It sat at an angle on the corner of Rue de Belgique and Rue Paganini. The front of the building was only twelve feet wide with two doors in the middle. As the building rose, balconies stretched out from similar doors that stretched up the facade. Two longer sides stretched out along the streets in a window-balcony-balcony-window pattern, repeated twice on each side.

He crossed the street and entered the Hotel Azurea. A young woman stood at the counter. She wore her blond hair in a bun. Her light brown eyebrows framed her light blue eyes perfectly. Her face was thin and narrow. Her nose and lips matched her face. Still, Jack found her attractive enough. She wore a black button up shirt, long-sleeve, and matching black pants. A nameplate pinned to her shirt said Celeste. Jack walked up to the counter.

"How may I help you?" she asked in French.

Jack smiled.

"I'd like a room. Cheapest one you have," he replied in French.

"I'm sorry," she said. "Check in isn't until two-thirty in the afternoon."

Jack looked at his watch. One-thirty.

He nodded. "I'll be back in an hour."

"I'll be here," she said. Her lips parted and curled at the ends in a smile.

He exited through the same door he entered through, turned to the right and walked down Rue Paganini. He stopped at a small cafe, went inside, ordered a double espresso.

He sat at a table and noticed the plug in the center. He looked around and saw that half the patrons of the cafe had their laptops plugged in to the middle of their tables. He pulled out his new computer, plugged it in and hit the power button.

"What the hell is this crap?" he muttered. A splash screen wanted him to enter all kinds of details and personal information. He could find no way to skip the steps.

The barista set his double espresso down out of arm's reach. "Just select that." She reached across his body and pointed at the screen.

Jack looked back at her. Dark hair, dark eyes, tanned skin. He hadn't noticed her at the counter.

"What?"

She smiled, pulled a chair close and sat down next to him.

"Here," she said. "Let me help you."

Jack lifted his arms as she reached over and grabbed the laptop. She set it in front of herself and Jack could no longer see the screen.

"Name?" she asked.

"Jack," he replied.

"Jack what?"

"Just Jack."

"Ok."

Jack heard a button pressed, held, and then released. Then he counted nine quick strikes on the keyboard.

"There you go, *Just Jack*, as requested." She smiled at him.

He grinned back. "Cute."

"Thanks." She winked, stood up and walked back to the counter. She turned toward him. "Give it five minutes to finish and then you can use it." She ducked behind the lift-up entrance and disappeared behind a beaded door.

He watched the curtain for a few minutes. She didn't step back out. He sighed and returned to his new piece of technology. A welcome screen greeted him. He reached in his pocket and pulled out the thumb drive. Lifted and turned the laptop until he figured out where the thumb drive was supposed to go. He heard a few snickers. He set the laptop down and looked around. The younger crowd apparently got a kick out of the thirty-six year old Jack trying to figure out what to do with his new computer.

"It don't work like that old man," one of them said.

Jack frowned, closed the lid and unplugged the laptop. He stuffed it in his bag and walked to the counter.

"I'll take another," he said. "To go."

He leaned against the counter, hoping that the woman would step back through. She didn't. The girl at the counter took his money, handed him his drink and said nothing to him. Jack picked it up and took a sip. *Last chance.* He turned, walked to the entrance, pushed the door open.

"Goodbye, Just Jack," the sexy barista said from behind the beaded door.

He smiled, slipped outside and walked back to the hotel.

Celeste still sat behind the counter. "How can I help you, sir?" she asked in French.

"Me again."

"Oh, yes. It's only two in the afternoon, sir."

"Can't you make an exception? I traveled all night by plane. All morning by train. I'm tired and just want to go to sleep."

She sighed, smiled and said, "For you, I will make an exception."

Jack handed her the credit card with the name Sherman Harrod on it and the matching ID card.

She took the credit card and the ID card, punched some keys on her keyboard and swiped the credit card on her machine. She handed both back along with a receipt for him to sign. He returned the receipt and she unlocked a drawer below her computer and dropped the receipt inside. She pulled out two cards from the same drawer, swiped them through a different machine and punched a few more keys on her keyboard.

"Room 402," she said. "Enjoy."

Jack took the keys from her outstretched hand, picked up his bags and headed for the elevator. He pressed the up button. It took two minutes for the lift to arrive. He stepped in, pressed the button labeled four, rested with his back against the mirrored wall.

The ride didn't take as long as he expected, maybe twenty seconds or so.

He stepped out into the hall and found his room. Plain and simple, just the way he liked it. A bed, dresser, TV, and bathroom. Small table in the corner. Red checkered curtains hanging over the window. He closed the curtains, turned on the TV and laid down on the bed.

He hadn't lied when he told Celeste he just wanted to go to sleep. Within five minutes of his head hitting the pillow Jack was out, despite his second double espresso, which sat half empty on the dresser, under the TV.

CHAPTER 2

"**B**ear?" Mandy asked.

"Yeah, sweetie," Bear said without taking his eyes off the road.

"Is momma dead?"

Bear slowed down. He had prepared himself for this question for a week. He thought he had the perfect answer. Now the words seemed wrong.

"Yeah," he said.

"I thought so."

He looked over at the little blond haired girl. Her blue eyes glassed over with tears. One started down her cheek leaving a deep track in its wake. She sniffed then wiped her nose with her sleeve.

"I miss her," she said.

"I know, Mandy. I know."

The little girl fiddled with her seat until it slipped backward. She leaned back and closed her eyes. She bit at her lip trying to keep from sobbing.

Bear pulled the car over, got out. He walked around and opened Mandy's door.

The little girl unclicked her seat belt and jumped into his arms. She buried her face into his shoulder and sobbed.

Bear held her tight. He released his grip when he felt her pull back. Her eyes were bloodshot, making the blue stand out even more. Tears stained her pale cheeks. Thin strands of blond hair stuck to one of them. Her lips trembled.

"Will they kill me too?" she asked.

"No," Bear said. "Never. Me and Jack won't let that happen."

She wrapped her arms around his thick neck, squeezed tight.

He hugged her back.

"A real live bear hug," he said and then he growled.

Mandy giggled, sniffed, coughed. She let go and climbed back in the car.

Bear shut her door and walked back to the driver's side, stepped in and started the engine.

"Where are we going?" she asked.

"Montana."

"What's in Montana?"

"Someone who can keep you safe while I go deal with bad guys." He looked over at her before pulling the car back into traffic. She nodded without saying a word. He hoped she wouldn't be scared when he left. He had to get overseas. Things were a mess in France and Jack needed his help.

"Who?" Mandy asked.

"His name's Scott Brayton. He's my brother."

"You have a brother?"

"Step-brother. My mom was married to his dad for six months when we were eleven. We didn't live together, but we spent two months in the mountains that summer. Always kept in touch."

"OK," Mandy said.

"I know, too much information."

"Huh?"

Bear laughed. "The important thing is that no one will find you there. No one knows about Scott. Not even Jack."

"But," Mandy paused.

"What if something happens to me?" Bear finished her question.

"Yeah," she said.

"Don't worry. I'll make sure that Jack will know what to do. Ms. Clarissa, too." He reached over and patted her head. "You will always be safe, Mandy."

They sat in silence the next few minutes. He looked over at the little girl, now asleep, her head resting against the window.

The car crossed the Montana state line and Bear pushed hard on the gas pedal. It was still daytime. Speed limit, reasonable and prudent. In other words, no speed limit. Bear looked at the speedometer. One hundred ten. Seemed reasonable enough.

Three hours passed. The mile posts flew by two per minute. They were close to Scott's cabin. Bear slowed down.

Scott lived north of Billings, outside of a small place called

Roundup on Highway 12. Although he hadn't visited in five years, Bear had been there enough times to know the way without a map. He turned onto the cracked paved driveway. Holes had been left by the previous winter and were filled with dirt and gravel. The sedan bounced up and down as he drove too fast on the half-mile long driveway.

Mandy sat up. "Where are we?"

"Here."

"Where's here?"

"Roundup."

"Huh?"

Bear laughed. "Hang on, sweetie." He pointed at the house that appeared as they pulled into a clearing.

A stocky man came through the door with a rifle at his side. His dark hair was sprinkled with grey. He had short sideburns and a matching mustache. Three small children, all blond, pressed their tiny faces against the screen door. A tall blond haired woman stood behind them.

Bear stopped.

The man lifted his rifle.

Bear waved.

"Scott," he yelled.

Scott lowered the rifle, smiled at Bear, and then turned around and motioned his wife and kids out of the house.

Bear walked around the car and scooped Mandy out of the seat. He lifted her to his hip and walked toward the house.

Scott stepped down from the porch. He held out his hands, pointed one at Mandy. "Yours?"

"Guess she is now."

Scott raised an eyebrow but didn't ask anything else. He gave Bear a half hug and turned to Mandy. "What's your name?"

"Mandy," she said.

"How old are you?"

"Nine."

"My daughter Bernie is nine, too."

"Her name is Bernie?" Mandy's face twisted.

Scott laughed. "Yes, short for Bernice."

Mandy puckered her face. "Can I meet her?"

"Sure." He reached out and took Mandy from Bear's arm and set her down. "She's on the porch."

Bear watched Mandy run up to the porch. He imagined she was quite anxious to play with someone her own age.

"Walk with me?" Scott said.

Bear nodded.

"What's this all about?" Scott asked.

"Girl's in trouble. Mother was killed. Got mixed up in something she shouldn't have been. Jack saved her."

"Noble? Your friend from the Marines?"

"Yeah, we're business partners." He raised an eyebrow.

Scott nodded and frowned. "I wish you would come out here. Go into business with me."

"Love the area, the scenery, but sitting in an office dealing with contractors isn't for me." He put a hand on Scott's shoulder. "You know that."

Scott shrugged. "Yeah, I do." He turned away from Bear. "How long do you need us to look out for her?"

Bear took a few steps and stood next to Scott. He stared at the mountains in the distance. They had to be a hundred miles away, maybe more. It felt like you could reach out and touch them. The sun was setting behind them. The sky above the mountains turned a shade of pink, a reflection from the atmosphere.

"A few weeks at least," Bear said.

"Know anything about her schooling?"

"I assume she went to school. You'd have to ask her that."

"Cathy can home school her with the kids."

Bear nodded. Scott was strict in some ways. This would be a good place for Mandy until the situation with Charles and the old man was cleaned up.

"Let's go inside. Cathy's got dinner ready by now."

Bear followed Scott back to the house. Climbed the wooden steps and went inside. The kids were sitting around the kitchen table. Mandy played with Bernie. They had dolls on the table. Bear wasn't sure about the brand or even who the dolls were. He didn't spend much time around kids. He watched Mandy interact with Bernie and the two younger children. Her face glowed. She didn't look as pale. Definitely not as sullen.

Cathy brought dinner to the table, a hefty pot roast. Scott rubbed his hands together and made some noises. The kids laughed. Bear smiled and nodded. Dinner took over an hour. Eating intermingled with conversation. Afterward Bear led Mandy to the door. Scott stood a few feet behind her.

"Mandy, listen," Bear said. "I'm leaving now."

Mandy's eyes watered. She bit her lip. Sniffed.

"I'll be back. Don't you worry."

She forced a smile. She exhaled deeply. "Bear hug?"

He wrapped her up in his over-sized arms, dwarfing her little body. She sobbed a couple of times and then giggled. She leaned back and grabbed his shirt. "You be careful, mister."

Bear laughed. He stood up and stepped outside. Scott followed him.

"Take good care of her," Bear said.

Scott nodded. "Will do."

Bear walked to the sedan and opened the door. He stood there for a second. Looked up at the sky. It was clear, beautiful and full of stars.

"Where you going?" Scott asked.

"North."

Bear got in the car, started the engine and left without saying another word.

Bear made his way northwest and picked up Interstate 15 in Great Falls. At night the speed limit was reduced from whatever you deem reasonable and prudent to sixty-five miles per hour. He did eighty. Two hours after passing through Great falls he arrived at the Canadian border.

The Mountie approached the car. He was tall and heavy. His cheeks were red. Possibly from the cold, possibly from his high blood pressure. He stood tall and stiff. Kept his pudgy hand on the butt of the gun secured in a holster attached to his belt. He kept a watchful blue eye on Bear. He stepped up to the car. "ID, sir?"

Bear pulled out a Michigan license that had the name Marvin Schlater. Handed it to the Mountie.

"What's your business in Canada, Mr. Schlater?"

"Fishing."

"Tackle in back?"

"No sir, this is a rental. My guide is supposed to supply everything."

"What's your guide's name?"

"Gibson. Only name I got for him."

"Where you fishing, eh?"

"Coastal tributaries. Meeting Gibson up at Tweedsmuir."

"Ah, beautiful park." The Mountie turned and made his way around the car. Walked around it with a mirror attached to a stick. He came back two minutes later and handed Bear his ID. "Have yourself a great trip, Mr. Schlater. Catch lots."

Bear grabbed his ID and nodded. Stepped on the gas and took off onto

Canadian highway 501. After that he had a twisting and winding eight hour drive to Vancouver.

The trip to the airport took six and half hours. He arrived at four in the morning. Good time to enter the airport. Two more hours and the place would be a madhouse. He ditched the car in long term parking and made his way into the airport's main building. Found a young Japanese woman behind a counter labeled EVA Airlines. Her dark hair was pulled up, held in place with pins. She wore a traditional airline outfit. Nothing out of the ordinary here. No direct flights to Tokyo that night. He bought a ticket to Taipei, Taiwan with a connecting flight to Tokyo. The flight left in an hour. Dumb luck, he figured. He would take it, though. He could use some extra luck on this trip.

Bear took his time walking to the international terminal, gate D. He arrived during boarding. Showed his passport and ticket. Followed the nice lady's instructions and made his way down the tunnel. Stepped into the plane and found his first class seat. He couldn't sit in coach. Too large of a man. He slid into his window seat, buckled up and asked the flight attendant for a drink. Two, actually. She returned with a drink in each hand. She was older than the woman at the ticketing counter. A bit heavier. Her hair was pulled up as well. She smiled and handed him his drink without saying a word.

Bear sat back in his seat, checked his phone. No messages. He drank his first drink while the plane taxied. Drank the second when the pilot announced they would take off soon.

By the time the plane reached cruising altitude Bear was asleep. He stayed that way all the entire flight to Taipei.

He had a six hour layover in Taipei. Perfect time to call Jack. He pulled out his global phone and powered it on. One message waiting. He dialed the voicemail access code and listened to the message.

"Bear," said Jack's voice. "Go to Paris. Clarissa is there. I'm not. French spooks are watching her, but I don't fully trust them. I want you there by her side."

The message stopped. Simple enough.

Bear found an Air France counter. "Ticket to Paris, first class."

A thin, shaved head Taiwanese man looked up at him with empty eyes and a dull expression. "When would you like to depart?"

"As soon as possible."

The man frowned as he played around with his computer. "You are in luck. One more seat, first class, leaves in an hour. About twenty hours trip time. Layovers in Xiamen and Amsterdam."

"How long in Amsterdam?"

"Just two hours."

Just was right. Two hours was not enough time to blow off steam in Amsterdam. "I'll take it." He handed the thin man his credit card. Less than five minutes later he had his ticket and was on his way to the gate. Headed for Paris.

CHAPTER 3

The pounding on the door startled Jack from his nap. He tiptoed to the door, gun in hand, and checked the peephole. No one there. He turned around. Another bang. He cracked the door open with his left hand, gun tucked behind his back in his right, and stuck his head out the door.

A short, stocky, brown haired man stood at the door next to Jack's. He had a thin brown beard. His eyes were covered with amber tinted sunglasses. He wore a blue sport coat, white pants and white deck shoes. He turned toward Jack and raised his hands.

"What the hell do you want?" he said with a New York accent.

Jack didn't respond.

The man stepped wide, facing Jack. "You gotta hearing problem? I said, what the hell do you want?"

"Stop banging on the door."

The man laughed. He grabbed his pants by the waistband, shuffling them side to side. He made a clicking sound with his mouth. "So, you a tough guy, huh?"

Jack tucked the gun in the back of his pants, opened the door and stepped out. Jack towered over the man. He stepped forward. They stood chest to chest, mostly.

"I said stop banging on the door," Jack said.

"Or what?"

"Do you really want to find out?"

The door opened. "What's going on out here?" a female voice said.

Jack didn't take his eyes off the brown haired man.

"Nothing, Marla," the brown haired man said. "Just getting to know your neighbor." The man backed into the room. Shut the door.

Jack heard the double lock click against the door. He grinned and shook his head. *Tough guys.* He went back into his room and picked up his phone. Placed a call to Bear. No answer. He left a message instructing Bear to call him at a new number when he arrived in Paris. Then he dialed Pierre's private number.

"Allo?"

"It's Jack."

"Jack, everything going ok?"

"Yeah, about to review the info."

"You haven't yet?"

"Had to get settled in first. And listen, before I do..."

"Yeah?"

"Before I do I need you to get my face out of the papers and off TV. Can you do that?"

"Yes, Jack. I am sorry for that. We had measures in place to prevent it, but someone acted independently. We've made sure it won't happen again."

"What's your plan?"

"It's already in action, on the news. We put up dummy footage and a fake photo. The new photo goes in tomorrow's paper."

Jack exhaled. "Sounds good. OK, give me any details not on this thumb drive."

"Your contact is Oscar. You are to meet him in Cap-d'Ail in thirty-six hours."

"Where at?"

"When you arrive in Cap-d'Ail you are to contact me and I will provide you the details."

"Is there a train station?" Jack asked.

"Yes, but the town's not that far. You could rent a motorbike and get there inside half an hour."

Jack stood and looked out the window, toward the coast. "Yeah, I think I might do that."

"Then at least you'll have some transport."

"OK, I'm going to review now." Jack hung up without waiting for input from Pierre.

He placed his laptop on the table and turned it on. He twirled the thumb drive between his fingers while he waited for the computer to boot up. When it finished, he inserted the thumb drive and navigated to a folder with its contents. There were three files. The first was labeled *1 - Grigori*. He opened that file first. It contained a picture of a man with thinning grey hair and a cropped grey mustache. He wore round thin-rimmed glasses. They sat atop a wide nose, a stark contrast to his thin lips. He had a wide jaw and matching chin. He looked to be around fifty-five or sixty years old. Under the picture was a name. *Grigori Dorofeyev*. Below that were several labels.

Primary target.

Birthdate: August 23, 1954

Threat Level: Red

Member of the Russian Government Defense Ministry, part of the "Presidential Bloc"

Intelligence confirms that Dorofeyev is planning an overthrow of the Russian government in the next five years. He has the support of several members of the government who want to return to the old ways. He also has support within the military. Those who have been exiled fully support him. Anyone that has been approached and refused to support him has been killed or imprisoned falsely. Threat must be neutralized.

The list went on in a what's what of Dorofeyev's accomplishments.

Jack closed the document and opened the next one. It started with a name. *Fyodr Olkhovsky, General of the Army*. A picture of Olkhovsky followed. He looked older than Dorofeyev. He was bald on the top of his head with grey hair closely cropped to the sides. His face was stretched long and sullen. Dark eyebrows sat over his dark eyes. He wore a green military dress uniform. His shoulders adorned with a dark patch, red stripes on the outside, four gold stars in a line on the inside.

Below his picture was a list of accomplishments.

4 star General - General of the Army. Reports only to the Marshal of the Russian Federation.

Formerly the Commander of the Western Military District - Western Operational Strategic Command. AKA the "Gateway to Europe"

Now commands all four districts, strategic commands.

Promoted friends to both the Western and Southern District commands.

The list continued with his entire military record including his involvement in the Chechen Wars.

Below Olkhovsky's list was another name. *Mikhail Korzhakov*. Judging by his picture he was much younger than the other two men. He had a full head of black hair. His face was free of wrinkles and facial hair. He had dark eyebrows and eyes, a heavy brow, and a square jaw. There wasn't much information about him. He was a politician and appeared to be Dorofeyev's right hand man.

Jack closed the second file and opened the third. It contained a vacation itinerary. The men were due to arrive in Paris today. Tomorrow they would take the train to Cap-d'Ail and presumably spend some time in Monte Carlo. Monday a fishing trip. Depart eight in the morning on the *Danseur du Vent,* or Wind Dancer, for an all-day fishing trip. The page said one more thing. *Oscar.*

Jack closed the program, unplugged the thumb drive and closed the lid of the laptop. He lay down on his bed and stared at the ceiling, mentally reviewing the information from the folder. It didn't take him long to piece it together.

Dorofeyev had considerable power in the Russian Federation government. He knew all the players and likely had strong ties to them. He knew who he could count on and who he would have to kill. He had served in the Army alongside Olkhovsky in their younger days. The days before communism fell. The two weren't happy about the fall of Mother Russia, but didn't have much choice in the matter. They chose two separate, but important paths in their careers. Now Olkhovsky controlled the Army and had trusted friends in place on the Western fronts. They could attack Europe and the Middle East at will. These guys were old school and could care less if their attack sparked a nuclear war with Iran or another nation.

Korzhakov would be their link with the younger members of government. The guys who were teenagers or in their early twenties when communism fell. These were the guys who you saw on TV, smiling, happy that Gorbachev dissolved the Soviet Union. But not all of them felt that same sentiment these days and had a longing for the way things used to be. Korzhakov was one of those guys and he would know the other young politicians who shared the same sentiment.

Jack had the full picture now. These three men were the head of a new Russian Revolution. Jack's assignment? Make sure they failed. Why him though? Why didn't Pierre put together his own team for this? Maybe Jack would ask. Or maybe he'd just do the job, collect his money and disappear for a while.

Jack stepped out of the elevator and made his way through the hotel lobby. Again he turned to the right and walked down Rue Paganini. Stopped in front of the little cafe. The lights were on inside. He went in and saw a different crew working than the one from earlier. He stepped up to the counter and ordered a double espresso. He found a table with a view of the street and checked his phone. No messages. He dialed an access number to check another line. No messages. He fidgeted with his phone while waiting for his double espresso.

"Nice to see you again, Just Jack."

He looked up. The dark haired woman stood there, holding his espresso, a smile spread across her face. She sat the drink down in front of him.

"May I?" she asked, her hand holding the back of the chair next to him.

Jack scrambled to his feet. "Please," he said.

She sat down and ran her hand through her hair. "What business do you have in Nice?"

"Only here for a day or two, then I'm going fishing."

She nodded. "Want to get out of here?"

Jack sipped on his espresso. "Where do you want to go?"

She shrugged. "Dinner?"

"My favorite meal."

"My name's Vivienne. Call me Viv." She stood up. "I'll be right back."

Jack watched as she disappeared behind the beaded curtain that hung in the doorway between the back of the cafe and the front. He finished his double espresso and waited by the door for her to return. She emerged from the back, now dressed in a short yellow sundress. The dress stopped mid-thigh and exposed her long tan legs. Her hair spilled across exposed shoulders. She looked gorgeous. All Jack could do was smile and hold the door open for her.

She took his hand and led him through the door into a maze of streets. They made small talk along the way. She told him about growing up in rural southern France. He made up a story about a business he ran in the U.S. that brought him to France two or three times a year to negotiate contracts. She didn't question anything he said, just nodded silently.

"Here we are," she said.

Jack looked up at the plain plaster building. No sign hung over the door to indicate where they were.

"What's this?" he asked. His hand instinctively rested near his concealed Beretta nine millimeter.

Viv smiled and pulled on his arm. "It's a place for locals. No sign means the tourists just walk on by. They have no clue the best cuisine in southern France is inside."

He pulled back at first and then followed her inside. They entered a dimly lit room. The overhead lights were sparse. Each table had a single lit candle placed dead center. The dark red walls served to make the room look even darker. The woodwork appeared to be handcrafted and stained dark. An ornate bar covered the entire back wall of the restaurant.

"Let's sit at the bar," Viv said.

"OK."

They took a seat at the far end of the bar. Jack angled his seat to the corner so he could watch the patrons, staff and the entrance.

"What will you have?" the bartender asked.

"Martini," Jack said.

"Armagnac," Viv said.

Jack raised an eyebrow at her.

"Brandy," she said. "From Gascony, about three hundred miles from here."

Jack shrugged.

The bartender placed their drinks in front of them. She held hers out.

"Try it," she said.

He took a sip and sat it down in front of her. "Too sweet for me."

She rolled her eyes. "That's the problem with you American men."

He shrugged and turned his head to survey the crowd of diners. The place was busy. A local's secret. Funny how people who lived in an area supported by tourism often hated tourists.

"Hey," she said. She reached out and gently guided his face toward hers. Their eyes met. She smiled and leaned back on her stool slightly. "Hungry?"

He thought for a moment about how to answer. Hungry could have many connotations. But the bartender standing in front of him with a pen in one hand and a pad in the other told him how to answer.

"Steak," he said. "Rare."

"Cut?" the bartender asked.

"Whatever the chef recommends."

"I'll have the same," Viv said.

They stepped outside the unmarked restaurant. The cool air felt good on Jack's face after two and a half hours inside the warm, stuffy restaurant.

"Where to?" Viv asked.

"Should probably head back to the hotel."

She pouted and took both his hands in hers. "Are you sure?"

"What do you recommend?" he asked.

"The beach is nice," she said. "And my apartment is only a block away." She blinked slowly and lowered her head a notch, engaging his stare.

Jack stared into her eyes. He thought about how the rest of the night would go. The buzz they had from the alcohol would last another hour or two. Long enough for them to walk to the beach, hand in hand. Once under the cover of the night sky and out of the way of the city lights he would kiss her. She would kiss him back. She'd lead him to her apartment where they would drink a bottle or two of wine. Somewhere during the course of drinking the wine her sundress would slip off, as would his shirt and pants. Maybe they'd go to the bedroom. Maybe they'd just drop to the floor.

"Well?" she asked.

He leaned in to kiss her. "Clarissa," he whispered.

She turned her face. His lips grazed her cheek. "Who is Clarissa?"

Jack dropped his head. "I'm sorry. I should just go back to the hotel."

She took his hand and led him through the dark streets of Nice. They walked in silence, passing through pools of light left behind by the evenly spaced streetlights. Fifteen minutes later they arrived at the hotel.

"I don't care who Clarissa is," she said. "I'm yours tonight. If you want me."

"It's not a matter of wanting you," he said. "I do care who Clarissa is. That's all that matters."

She shifted her eyes to the side and gave him a forced smile. "Look me up if you are ever in Nice again, Just Jack." She stood on her toes, leaned in and kissed his cheek.

Jack watched her walk away until she turned right and disappeared from sight. He sighed. Made his way through the hotel lobby and into the elevator. The lift dinged when he reached his floor. The doors opened and the brown haired man from earlier stood outside, leaning back against the far wall.

"Well look who it is," the brown haired man said. "Nice's number one tough guy."

Jack stepped out and avoided looking at the man. He started toward his room.

The man stepped in front of him, blocking his path. "Where you think you're going?"

"To my room."

"Like hell you are."

Jack cocked his head to the side, rotated his shoulders and cracked his neck.

"Now apologize to me," the man said.

Jack narrowed his eyes. "What?"

"You heard me motherfu--"

The men were barely twelve inches apart. Jack struck fast. He struck hard. The blow landed just under the man's sternum. The man collapsed in a ball on the floor, gasping for breath. Jack stepped over him, catching the man in the groin with his foot on the way to his room.

CHAPTER 4

Pierre stepped out of the cab and walked into the hospital. He passed by the information desk. He knew where he was going. He promised Jack he'd look after Clarissa and he intended to uphold that promise. He was flanked by two of his men. They would relieve the two that had stood by her bed for the past twenty four hours.

They rode in the elevator, got out on her floor and walked to her room without saying a word. He nodded at the two men standing by her door. They nodded back and walked off. The two men flanking Pierre stepped in front of him and took their places on either side of the door to Clarissa's room.

"I don't need to tell you what's at stake here, do I?"

"No, sir," they said in unison.

Pierre nodded and stepped into the room. Her unconscious body lay still. She breathed on her own.

A doctor entered the room. "Good evening."

Pierre smiled at him. "Any update?"

"She's fine. Just needs to wake up now." The doctor gestured toward the door. "I need you to step out for a few minutes so we can examine her."

"OK," Pierre said.

"Any chance your men can--"

"No."

Pierre stepped out into the hall. "Stay put until I relieve you." He continued down the hall, looking into each room as he passed. No one seemed to notice. At this time of night the staff on this floor consisted of a

184 / L.T. RYAN

skeleton crew. He took notice of a brown haired woman sleeping. He lifted the chart from the door. Lorraine Laurent.

He looked both ways down the hall. Empty. He stepped into the room and let the door close behind him. He nudged the sleeping woman.

She opened her eyes. "What?"

"Lorraine Laurent?"

"Yes," she replied.

Pierre flashed a badge. "I need to ask you a few questions."

"I don't know anything about Mitchell's businesses," she said.

"I'm not here for Foster. Do you remember the man who shot you?"

She nodded.

"Think you can pick him out of a photo lineup?"

She nodded.

He leaned over and helped her sit up. Placed a folder on her lap. He opened the folder and spread out the pictures of six men. "Please point to the man you believe shot you."

"Him." She pointed at Jack's picture.

"Thank you," Pierre said. "Study the pictures a few moments longer just to make sure."

He turned around and reached into his bag. He pulled out a needle and a vial full of liquid. He drew the liquid into the needle, turned to face her with the needle behind his back.

"Now," he said, "are you still certain that is the man who shot you?"

"Yes, absolutely. He was having dinner with Mitchell."

"I see. You've been very helpful Ms. Laurent." He leaned in to grab the folder. He stuck the needle into her neck and injected the liquid into her bloodstream.

Her eyes fluttered. She reached out for him, but quickly lost her balance and fell back in her bed where she slipped into unconsciousness.

Pierre slipped out of her room. Already the sounds of her body failing could be heard on the machines surrounding her bed. He figured it would be just a few more minutes before the skeleton crew gathered around her and fought to save her life. It would be a losing battle.

Pierre sat down in the chair next to Clarissa's bed. He looked around the room. Just like every other hospital room he had ever been in. Gadgets littered the room. He had no idea what most did. Why would he? He had medical training, but in field medicine. He never had a need to learn any more than that. If a man went down they did everything they could to save him. If they couldn't save him, then they did everything they could to save the body. If they couldn't save the body, they moved on.

He watched Clarissa. Her chest rose and fell with each breath she took. He thought about his own daughter, who was eighteen now. She decided to forgo her education for two years and join the Peace Corp. He shuddered at the thought. Some of the places the Peace Corps operated were the same places he did, both during his time in the service and now. He worried that she'd end up in the middle of a gun fight, or worse, taken hostage by a band of rebels or a guerrilla force.

"What kind of man is Jack?" he asked the sleeping woman.

She didn't respond.

"Is he a man of nobility, as his name suggests?" Pierre snickered. He doubted that was an original joke, but he said it anyways.

"Why does he care about you so much? You're not related, at least not by the case jacket we have on him."

She still didn't respond.

He sighed, stood, and leaned over her. "Whatever it is, we better make sure to keep you safe. I don't need Jack Noble taking out half my team."

Her eyes fluttered and opened. "Jack?"

"No," he said. "Save your strength."

He saw fear in her eyes. Her mouth opened to scream, but all she could manage was a whisper.

"It's OK. My name is Pierre. I am a friend of Jack's."

She settled back and tried to smile.

"Welcome back, Clarissa." Pierre sat back in the chair. He pulled out his phone. He typed a simple message. *She's awake.* He sent the message to Jack as he left the room.

CHAPTER 5

C harles walked slowly down the narrow road. A few mopeds passed by. The road was too narrow for cars. The coastal Italian town of Ameglia suited him fine. Located halfway between Genoa and Pisa, Ameglia was often neglected by tourists. Those who made the trip found a town made up of a cluster of seaside buildings set between the hills and the Mediterranean. The locals totaled fewer than five thousand. Charles didn't exactly blend in, but the locals didn't pay him much attention.

Seven men accompanied Charles. Two in front and two behind him. Another man stayed about a hundred yards ahead. The sixth man stayed around a hundred yards behind. A dark haired man named Alonso walked with Charles. Alonso stood around six feet tall and weighed an athletic two hundred pounds. Charles dwarfed him. They were engaged in light conversation. Alonso had become Charles's right hand man and stayed by his side.

Charles pulled a vibrating phone from his pocket. He called to the four men nearest him. They all walked away, giving him some space. Alonso stayed by his side.

Charles answered the phone.

"Mr. Charles," the old man said. "How are you today?"

"I'd be better if you were dead."

Alonso pulled out a cigarette, lit it and offered it to Charles.

Charles drew on the filterless cigarette. "What do you want?"

"Is that any way to talk to your boss, Mr. Charles?"

"You ain't my boss anymore."

"Do you have any idea who you are talking to? You should hold your tongue."

"You should hold yours," Charles said.

"I could have a team of ten men to that little town inside fourteen hours, Mr. Charles. Do you understand that?"

"Better choose the right ten, Feng."

Alonso tapped Charles on the shoulder. He mouthed the word *Feng*.

Charles nodded and covered the phone with his large palm. "Yeah, that's his name."

"Last name?" Alonso asked.

Charles shook his head and returned his attention to the phone. "Listen, I'm not taking this from you anymore. We are through. If you want to make a big deal out of it then let's go."

"Mr. Charles," the old man said. "We don't have to go down this route. Let bygones be bygones."

"Screw you."

"What do you want? More power? More men? Tell me what you need to make you happy."

"I already told you, Feng. I want Jack dead. You wouldn't give me the satisfaction."

"Just let me use him a few more times and then I'm done with him," the old man said.

"Screw that and screw you."

"You had better watch your back, Mr. Charles."

"You had better watch yours, Feng."

Charles hung up and chuckled. He turned to Alonso. "Old bastard has no idea what's about to happen."

"You know he's going to come after you, right?" Alonso said.

"Yup," Charles said. "I know that."

"What will you do?"

Charles shrugged. "Pay them off. Hell, he might make the mistake of sending guys we already own."

Alonso nodded. "I'll keep an ear open."

The only people who knew that Alonso defected were Charles and the team of six men with him in Ameglia. Alonso knew which men were already in Charles's pocket, so he spent his time talking with the higher ups that weren't.

"When will we take action?" Alonso asked.

"After he tries to take me out."

"Risky, isn't it?"

"We should have a lead on when it goes down. If we do it sooner we run the risk of losing the guys on the fence. The more internal dissension there is the more risk we run that one of the families tries to take over our territory."

"Makes sense. So we wait then?"

"Yeah," Charles said. "We wait."

CHAPTER 6

The pounding in Jack's head woke him up early Saturday morning. Sunlight filtered in through the sheer curtains hanging in front of the large windows. He rolled over, grabbed his watch off the nightstand. Six a.m. Not a good start to what promised to be an eventful few days. He rubbed his eyes with his palms, sat up and stretched his arms over his head. He picked up the telephone receiver and dialed 0 for the front desk.

"Bonjour," the cheerful female voice said.

"Coffee," Jack said. "Make that two coffees."

"Oui, yes sir. Right away."

He placed the receiver on the cradle and grabbed the TV remote. He flipped through a few stations and stopped when he saw footage of the hit on Foster from three days ago. His eyebrows raised in unison. The footage had been altered. The shot of him leaving was darker and grainier now, making it impossible to pick him out. They showed an altered photo of the suspect. Long hair, glasses, and thick around the midsection. No one would mistake the photo for Jack.

Jack exhaled loudly and stood up. He opened the door to the small balcony. Before he could step outside he heard a knock at the door. He grabbed his nine millimeter off the nightstand, went to the door and checked through the peephole. A young woman in a hotel uniform stood on the other side. He cracked the door to make sure she was alone.

"Good morning, sir."

"Morning," he said. He opened the door and let her in.

She carried the coffees on a tray. A silver cup with a spout contained more than enough cream. Around a dozen sugar cubes sat in a plastic bowl.

Jack stepped around her and grabbed his wallet off the nightstand. He pulled out five euros and handed it to her for a tip.

"Thank you, sir."

He nodded and showed her out of the room. The obnoxious New Yorker walked by and made an obscene gesture at Jack. Jack rolled his eyes at the man. *Let's meet one more time.*

Jack fixed his coffee with cream and one sugar. He stepped out onto the small balcony. The city hadn't yet come to life. The serene atmosphere lulled him into a false state of comfort. He knew it wouldn't last, but decided to enjoy the feeling. At least for one cup of coffee.

He looked out toward the sea and planned his day. No longer a suspect, he didn't have to hitch a ride or take the train. He decided to rent a moped for the short trip. The town was barely thirty miles away. The coastal highway would get him there in under an hour.

Pierre told him to wait until Sunday morning to make the trip. Jack decided to leave earlier than that. He wanted as much time in the little town as possible before making the hit. He still didn't know when the hit would go down, though. He pulled out his cell phone and called Pierre.

No answer.

He tossed the phone on the bed and got dressed. He stepped out of the room, down the hall and into the elevator. The elevator stopped on the second floor and an elderly woman with a small fluffy white dog stepped on. He nodded. She smiled. They rode to the lobby in silence. Jack waited for the elderly woman to step out. She did. He followed. Walked through the lobby and stopped at the front desk.

"Bonjour!" the young woman with the name tag Olivia said.

He guessed she was the same cheerful voice that greeted him on the phone a few hours earlier.

"I'd like to extend my stay another week," he told her.

"Excellent. What name is the room under?"

"Harrod."

"Yes, OK. All set. Anything else?"

"Yeah, where can I rent a moped for a few days?"

She smiled and gestured with her hands. "Out through the doors and turn right on Rue de Belgique. Three blocks down there is a shop where you can rent mopeds and bikes. A bike might be easier."

"Thank you," Jack said.

He walked out through the doors and turned right on Rue de Belgique. Passed the small cafe. He turned his head and looked in. Viv stood close to the window. She was talking to a young couple. Looked to be Americans. Probably here on vacation. He wanted to go in. He wanted to apologize to her. He walked past the cafe and continued on.

He reached the shop and walked through the frosted glass door. The shop was empty. Bells that hung from the glass door chimed and alerted the store to Jack's presence. A young man stepped through the open door behind the sales counter. He had short blond hair and blue eyes. His head looked large on his slight frame. He smiled at Jack.

"How can I help you?" the man asked in French.

"I'd like to rent a Moped for a week," Jack replied in English.

The man nodded, smiled and then ducked behind the counter. He popped back up moments later with a large binder. He sat the binder on the counter and opened it.

"You have ID with you, yes?" he asked.

Jack nodded and placed his Sherman Harrod picture ID on the counter.

"Excellent," the man said. "How much do you weigh?"

"Two-twenty, maybe two-twenty-five."

"Do you plan on traveling far? A Vespa might not be the best option if so." He looked Jack up and down. "Wouldn't be comfortable for a man your size on a long drive."

"No, not far at all. Just around town."

Jack didn't care. He'd once spent a week in a muddy field without leaving his spot. An hour on a Vespa wasn't going to bother him.

The man spun the binder around and held out a pen to Jack. "Sign right here, please."

The man retrieved a set of keys and stepped out from behind the counter. "Follow me, sir." He led Jack outside and unlocked the chain that secured a black Vespa to the building. He handed the keys to Jack. "You've ridden one before, yes?"

Jack nodded. "Yeah. I've got a motorcycle collection back in the States."

The young man smiled. "You're all set then. Return it by eleven in the morning, next Saturday."

Jack got on the moped, started it and rode back to the hotel. He stopped on the curb and jogged into the lobby. He snapped to get Olivia's attention. She looked up from her magazine and smiled at him.

"My moped is parked right outside. I'm just going up to the room to get something. Should be back in ten minutes at the most. Don't let anyone move it."

"Yes, sir," she said.

She pointed at the doorman. "Stand outside and make sure no one touches Mr. Harrod's moped."

The elevator doors opened. New York and his wife were in it.

"You go ahead, hon. I'm gonna talk to my new friend here," New York said.

Jack smiled at the woman as she exited. After she passed he stepped into the elevator. He stood next to New York, uneven shoulder to shoulder.

New York spoke first. "You ever pull a stunt like last night again, I'll have you killed."

Jack said nothing.

"Got it?"

Jack still said nothing.

"You got a hearing problem?"

"Screw you," Jack replied.

"Don't you know who I am?"

"Do I care who you are?"

The elevator dinged to signal they reached the fourth floor. Jack stepped out.

"Might be best if you are gone when we get back," New York said.

The elevator doors started to close. New York smiled at Jack.

Jack stuck his foot in front of the doors. They stopped and retracted. Jack reached in, grabbed the man by his collar and dragged him out of the elevator. He placed his arm around the man's head, securing him in a tight headlock. He dragged the guy down the hall, banging his head into the wall wherever a door frame stuck out. They reached Jack's room. He opened the door and threw the man inside.

New York stumbled and fell to the ground. He crawled to the far side of the room. Using the wall to stand up, he turned.

Jack waited a few feet away. He kicked the man in the middle of his stomach. New York doubled over, but didn't fall to the floor. Jack stepped forward, grabbed the man by the back of his head and delivered a bone crushing knee to New York's face.

New York screamed out in pain. He fell back against the back door. The door gave way and the man spilled out onto the small balcony.

Jack followed him out. He pulled the man to his feet. Slapped him across the face three times, backhand-openhand-backhand.

"Do you know who I am?" Jack yelled.

The dazed man didn't answer.

"Hey, jackass, I'm talking to you. Do you know who I am?"

The man shook his head.

"I'm the guy you hope never gets sent to your house. All of this, this beating, wouldn't happen if I were. It'd just be a bullet between your eyes. Got it?"

The man didn't respond.

Jack pulled his gun from his waistband and stuck it under the man's chin. "Got it?"

The man shook his head again.

Jack tucked the gun away and then lifted New York up and let him hang back over the balcony. "This what you want?"

"No," the man shouted.

"Then get out of my way." Jack pulled the man down, spun him and threw him inside the apartment.

The man crawled toward the door. Jack stayed a foot behind, kicking him in the butt with the heel of his shoe. The man reached the door. Jack reached over him and pulled it open hard. It thumped as it slammed into New York's head. New York dropped to the floor and groaned. Jack stepped over him and dragged him into the hall. Jack pulled him by the back of his head and sat him up against the door to the man's room.

Jack went back to his room, grabbed a second Beretta nine millimeter and a duffel bag packed with a few pairs of clothes, his computer and a few other supplies. He slipped out of his room and checked the hall to make sure no one had gathered around New York. Made his way to the stairwell. He reached the lobby and walked by Mrs. New York.

"Your husband isn't feeling too well. He said to go on without him."

He smiled at Olivia, stepped through the door, handed the doorman five euros. He hopped on his Vespa and drove away from the hotel.

CHAPTER 7

J ack followed the curved highway that stretched along the coast of Southern France from Nice to Cap-d'Ail. Cap-d'Ail, a quaint seaside resort town, butts up to the border of Monaco. The small town of five thousand people was overrun nearly every day by daytrippers from Nice and Monaco who flock there for the scenery, serenity, and the happening shopping district.

Jack's reason for visiting was slightly more sinister.

He drove through town slowly and pulled over on the side of Sentier du Bord de Mer, Seaside Trail. He stepped off his moped and stood looking over the short cliff, out at the sea. He looked to the left and saw the city marina. He recalled the map from earlier. On the other side of the marina sat the border to Monaco, which occupied a two mile long, quarter mile deep stretch of shoreline. Another six miles past Monaco's sliver of the French Riviera was the French border with Italy.

Jack pulled out his phone and called Pierre.

"Hello?" Pierre said.

"I'm here."

"Already? I told you not to go until Sunday."

"What can I say? I got restless legs."

"You'll have to wait until tomorrow to speak with Oscar."

"Why can't I talk to him now?"

"Why didn't you wait till Sunday, like I instructed?"

Jack sighed. He looked at his watch. Barely two in the afternoon. He looked around. Fixed his eyes on the land behind the marina. Monte Carlo.

"OK, I'm going into Monaco for the night then."

"Be careful," Pierre said.

"How's Clarissa?"

"Still have my men guarding her. She'll be well enough to move in a day or two. We can relocate her to a safe place then."

"Keep me informed."

Jack hung up, stuffed his phone into his pocket and crossed the border. He drove through the resort city of Monte Carlo until he found Av. De Monte-Carlo. He pulled off the road and entered the circular drive in front of Hotel de Paris. The four story front of the hotel stood out any time of day and especially at night. At night the hotel lit up as if it were built with gold. The first story of the building stood close to thirty feet high. Behind the main building, to the left, sat another section of the building. It was round, like a turret, and towered over the main building.

Jack parked his moped between a 700 series BMW and a 500 series Mercedes. He admired the cars for a moment. He mulled over the idea of getting one when he returned to the States. After completing this job for Pierre and taking out Charles for the old man, he'd have netted over three hundred thousand dollars this trip. A new car might be a nice reward for his hard work. Jack smiled and shook the thought out of his head. Too fancy.

He walked into the expansive lobby. A statue of a man on a horse greeted him. He didn't know who it was or why he was important, and he didn't bother to read the inscription to find out why. It didn't matter. He looked up at the priceless ornate chandelier suspended from a gold chain. He followed the chain upward where it hung from a huge blue and yellow stained glass window over thirty feet from the ground. Light poured through the window and lit up the entire lobby.

He continued through the lobby, veering to the left in front of the wide marble staircase. He walked up to the concierge who glanced at Jack and then returned to writing in his book.

"I'd like to book a room for three nights," Jack said.

"Nothing available for three nights," the concierge said.

"What do you have available?"

The concierge lifted his head and looked Jack up and down. "I have a two bedroom suite available. Four night minimum. Thirty-five hundred Euros a night." He returned his attention to the book on the counter.

"I'll take it."

A smile swept across the concierge's face.

Jack realized he fell for the man's ploy.

"How will you be paying?" the concierge asked.

Jack didn't answer. He slid a Visa card across the deep rich wooden counter.

The concierge picked it up and looked at it. "Very well Mr. Harrod." He turned his attention to a slim computer monitor and punched at the keys on a small keyboard. A few minutes later he handed Jack a key card for his room. "Fourth floor, room 410. Dial 0 for the concierge on duty. Exit through the front and turn left, and the Le Grand Casino de Monte Carlo is a short walk." He dipped his head and leaned forward. He gestured with his hand to Jack.

Jack leaned forward.

They were inches apart.

The concierge reached into his jacket and pulled out a card. He placed the card in Jack's hand. "You give them this card and you'll get a twenty-five percent bonus on your deposit."

"Thank you," Jack said.

The man nodded and raised an eyebrow. "I only give one or two of those away each month."

Jack nodded his thanks again and stepped away from the desk. He made his way up the wide marble stairs, past the glass walled fitness center and stopped in the elevator lobby. He stepped in the open elevator and pressed the button for the fourth floor. When the doors reopened he walked down the hall and stopped in front of room 410. He unlocked the door and stepped into the hallway. He walked past corridors on either side that led to the bedrooms and bathrooms. He pushed open a set of double doors that opened up to the living room. On the far side of the living room another set of double doors led to a balcony that looked out over the sea. He backed out of the living room, turned left and stepped into a bedroom. The suite was huge, over one thousand square feet. Larger than some of the apartments he and Bear owned in New York and other areas.

Jack dropped his bag at the foot of the bed and fell back on the soft mattress. He closed his eyes and drifted off to sleep.

B ear's flight landed at Charles de Gaulle airport, Paris mid-afternoon. He stood out among the crowd of tourists and businesspeople. Hell, he stood out everywhere he went. Customs stopped him. He handed them a passport with his picture and the name Marvin Schlater. They searched through his bag, but didn't question him. The customs agent waved him through without ever making eye contact.

Thirty minutes later Bear sat in the backseat of a cramped taxi on his way to the American Hospital of Paris on Boulevard Victor Hugo. The taxi driver was an older man wearing a blue ball cap. Tufts of grey hair stuck out from the bottom of the hat. White stubble littered his face.

The driver tried to engage Bear in conversation.

Bear ignored him.

"Do you not know how to speak?" the taxi driver said in a gruff tone.

"Leave me alone," Bear replied. He kept his eyes fixed on the road, avoiding the taxi driver's stare in the rear view mirror.

The taxi driver started yelling in French.

Though not fluent in French, Bear picked up a few choice curse words during the driver's tirade. Bear smiled when the old man stopped yelling.

"I like you," Bear said.

The driver looked up at the rear view mirror.

Bear caught his gaze. "You're a crazy SOB, aren't you?"

The driver laughed and shook his head. "You Americans, you got it all wrong."

"How so?"

"Always so self-absorbed and thinking ahead, making plans. You miss the moments that matter."

Bear nodded and sat back in his seat. He stared up at the dome light on the ceiling. His thoughts turned to Mandy. How was she getting along with the family? Was she scared? He pulled out his cell phone and started to dial, but stopped half way through. He needed to focus right now. He might be walking into a dangerous situation at the hospital.

The taxi stopped.

"We're here," the driver said.

Bear looked out the window at the large red brick and white plaster building. It stood six stories tall. The first two floors were taller than average. A retro looking glass enclosed entrance stuck out from the building, a chrome roof circled the entrance and had *American Hospital of Paris* engraved in it.

Bear handed the driver twenty euros, opened the door and stepped out. He walked through the rotating door hidden in the glass capsule and made his way through the hospital. He stopped at the information desk. A thin man with a long nose, brown glasses, and a receding hairline looked up at him.

"Clarissa Abbot's room?" Bear asked.

The man typed her name on his keyboard, waited a few seconds, and then tore off a piece of paper and handed it to Bear.

Bear looked down at the paper. It simply said, *Third floor ICU.* He walked away without acknowledging the man behind the desk. He found the elevator lobby and rode up to the third floor. The doors opened and a sign told him to turn left for the ICU. He rounded a corner and saw a large sign labeled ICU hung over closed doors. He pushed through the door on the right and walked up to the nurse's station.

"Clarissa Abbot?" he asked.

"*Ami ou un parent?*" the nurse replied.

Bear held up his hands and scrunched his face up at her.

"Friend or family?" she said in English.

"Both," Bear replied.

The nurse pursed her lips. "Follow me."

She got up from her seat and led Bear to Clarissa's room. The two men at the door moved close together to block entrance when they saw Bear.

"Move," Bear said.

"We can't do that," the one on the left said. He was tall, thin and wore his brown hair high and tight like a Marine.

"Who are you?" the man on the right asked.

Bear turned his attention to the man on the right. He was tall as well, but with a heavier build than his partner. He had a similar hairstyle. Both men wore tinted glasses and Bear couldn't tell if they were looking at him or past him.

Bear leaned in to the man and spoke in a hushed tone. "Riley Bear Logan. Friend of Jack's, and I'm responsible for the safety of this woman."

"Didn't do such a good job, did you?" the thin man said.

Bear grinned and looked down at the floor. He stepped forward and brought both his hands up at the same time. He wrapped his large hands around both men of their necks and pushed them backwards into the room.

"Oh my God," the nurse called out as the heavier man reached out and grabbed her shirt, pulling her into the room too.

Bear threw both men on the ground and closed the door.

"I don't know who the hell you think you are," Bear said. He reached behind his back and pulled out a gun. Pointed it at the thin man. "Don't you ever talk to me like that again."

Both men pushed themselves back to the far wall and held their hands out.

"Who's your boss?" Bear asked.

"Pierre," the thin man said.

"Get her up," Bear said to the nurse. He motioned toward Clarissa.

"What?" she said. "She can't leave. She was only shot two days ago. It's not safe."

The heavier man stood up. "I think we just had a misunderstanding here, that's all."

"Is that what you think?" Bear pointed the gun at the man.

"Let me call Pierre and get this straightened out," he replied.

Bear nodded. He kept his back against the door and his gun aimed toward the two men. The nurse paced the length of the bed.

"Pierre," the heavier man said. "We are in the room right now with a man named Riley."

"Bear," Bear corrected him.

"Sorry, he says his name is Bear," the man said. He paused. "OK." Another pause. "OK, will do." He hung up the phone, placed it in his pocket and held his hands up. "I am deeply sorry, Mr. Logan. We had orders to allow no one into the room. Pierre says you can stay and he will visit you later today."

CHAPTER 9

The ringing phone woke Jack. He looked out the window. Dark. He picked up the phone's receiver.

"Yeah," he said.

"Good evening, Mr. Harrod. This is a courtesy call to let you know we are having a wine tasting in the lobby followed by a courtesy dinner."

"No thanks." Jack hung up.

He sat on the edge of the bed and contemplated his plans for the evening. A night at the casino. Find a table, play cards and remain anonymous. He showered, shaved, and dressed in his best clothes. Best was an overstatement, but they'd have to do. They were all he had.

The walk to the casino took no more than five minutes. He stopped in front of the building and gazed up. Jack wasn't one for architecture, but he couldn't help admiring the design and the way the light danced against the facade. Palm trees lined the manicured grass in front of the building. He followed a path that led to the casino's entrance. He pushed his way inside and found the change counter. He placed ten thousand euros on the counter and set the card the concierge gave him on top of the pile of bills. The lady behind the bulletproof glass smiled at him and pulled a lever. His money disappeared from sight. A minute later, the woman pushed the lever and a pile of chips appeared in front of Jack. He grabbed the tray from the deposit box and found a hundred euro minimum bid blackjack table.

He took a seat at the table between two other players. To his right was a heavy man with a shaved head and a dark goatee. Thick black rimmed glasses covered his eyes and wrapped around his ears. He wore a light pink polo shirt with dark tan dress pants. A thin gold chain wrapped around his wide neck, gold bracelets on each wrist, but he didn't have any rings on.

To Jack's left sat an older woman. Her grey hair was pulled up in a bun. She wore a minimal amount of makeup. A short, sleeveless black dress revealed her toned arms and legs. He considered her attractive, albeit too old for him. She had a way about her that told him she had money.

"Is this seat taken?" Jack asked.

The heavy man didn't acknowledge him.

"No. Please sit," the woman said with a British accent. She smiled.

Jack nodded. "Thank you, ma'am."

Jack sat down. He waited for the current hand to finish and then he placed two hundred Euro chips on the table. The dealer signaled the pit boss and then nodded at Jack.

Jack found the dealer to be a stunningly beautiful woman. Her dark eyes turned slightly upward. Her long ringed hair fell across her shoulders. Her mocha skin was smooth. He wondered why she was dealing cards instead of working in the casino's show. She dealt two cards to everyone at the table, including herself. Her top card faced up. Five of spades.

Jack looked at his hand. Eight of clubs and six of hearts. Fourteen. Smart money said stand. The woman next to Jack showed fifteen. She waved her hand across her cards to indicate stand to the dealer. Jack's turn. He tapped his cards. The dealer flipped another card over and placed it next to the six of hearts. Three of diamonds this time. Seventeen. He should stand. He tapped his cards again. Five of clubs. Bust.

The man next to Jack snorted. Jack looked at the heavy man's cards. King and queen of hearts. He waved his hand over his cards. Jack would have split.

The dealer finished with the table. She flipped over her second card. Jack of clubs for a total of fifteen. She dealt herself another card, this time the queen of diamonds. Bust. Everyone won but Jack.

"You're not very good at this," the woman said.

Jack shrugged.

"Maybe you should go play at a five Euro table, pal," the heavy man said with an eastern European accent.

An hour passed. Jack lost half his money. Most of the table got up when the dealer stepped back and a man stepped forward to take her place. The woman next to Jack gathered up her chips.

"Buy you a drink?" Jack asked the woman.

She laughed. "I'm old enough to be your mother."

"Just one drink."

"I suppose."

Jack followed her to the bar. They took a seat.

"What can I get for you?" the bartender asked.

"Martini," Jack said.

"You?" the bartender asked the woman.

"Sidecar."

Jack exhaled. "Glad we aren't in Paris at the Bar Hemingway." At the Bar Hemingway at the Ritz-Paris, the Sidecar is served with a Cognac that is considered one of the finest in the world, bottled between 1830 and 1870.

The woman smiled. "That's the first place I had a sidecar. Back then it didn't cost over a thousand Euros, though."

"I know. I was there Dottie."

The woman kept looking over Jack's shoulder. He turned to look. Jack figured the man was close to her age. He had a full head of grey hair, cut short, with a grey beard to match. He wore a custom tailored blue pinstripe suit. A Breitling chronograph watch wrapped around his left wrist. A platinum bracelet around his right.

"Who is he?" Jack asked.

"Thornton Walloway," she said. "One of the most powerful men in England. A billionaire."

"Your husband?"

She nodded.

"What are you worried about?" Jack asked.

"He'll beat me if he sees me with you." She took a sip of her cocktail.

"When did you get mixed up with him?"

"Shortly after the last time we worked together," she said. "Here he comes."

The man walked toward them.

"Dottie," he said. "Who's this?"

Jack held out his hand. "Sherman Harrod, sir. Nice to meet you."

Thornton didn't reach for Jack's hand. He grabbed his wife's arm. She winced.

Jack stood and moved close.

Thornton raised his other arm and snapped. Two large men appeared. They said *yes sir* in unison. Their accents were Irish. They walked over and stood next to Jack. They were both taller than Jack by a few inches and wore dark suits.

"Who the hell are you?" Thornton asked.

"Nobody," Jack said.

"Dottie," he said. "Why are you talking to this nobody?"

"We were at the same blackjack table," she replied. "I got up and came over here to get a drink. He followed me. What do I know of who he is?"

"That's right," Jack said. "I just came over to talk, that's all. My wife is back in Paris. Just wanted some friendly conversation."

Thornton nodded and the man on Jack's left grabbed Jack's left arm and held it out.

"Where is your wedding ring then?" Thornton asked.

"Lost it a long time ago. Never replaced it."

Thornton held his hand up, palm facing Jack. "So you take a trip to Monte Carlo. You have enough money to piss it away in this casino, but you can't replace your wedding ring?"

Jack smiled. "You got me. I struck out with a younger woman at the bar. I spotted your wife and could tell she was a sure thing."

Thornton's face turned beet red. His breathing quickened. His eyes widened and his nostrils flared.

"Take him outside," Thornton said. "Escort him to the sea and wait for me."

"Thornton, no," Dottie said.

He didn't listen.

Jack winked at her as the two men placed their hands inside his elbows and escorted him out of the casino. Jack didn't resist.

Outside the casino one of the men dropped back behind Jack and jammed the barrel of a gun into his ribcage.

"No funny business," he said. "Got it?"

"Yeah," Jack said.

They led him down past the casino and hotel, across a street and around a large building. They stopped at the entrance to a long pier.

The man behind him stepped back around. "Hope you can swim."

The other man laughed. "Gonna be hard to do with a bullet in your gut."

Jack smiled. He pictured the surroundings in his mind. The long concrete pier extended in front of him. Concrete and sand backed up behind him into the wall of a building. The concrete gave way to a parking lot to his left. A steep, sand embankment dropped down ten feet or so into the sea on his right.

Jack jumped and swung his right elbow out and up. He struck the pale bald man across the bridge of the nose. He landed and kicked the darker man in the stomach. The darker man keeled over. Jack kicked again, his foot smashed into the man's face. The man straightened up for a second and then fell backwards.

Jack turned around. The pale man was bent over, holding his face. Blood dripped through his cupped hands and spilled onto the ground. Jack lunged toward him and delivered a knee into the man's stomach from the side. The pale man collapsed face first onto the concrete. Jack leaned over, picked him up by his pants and shirt and dragged him over to the embankment. He dropped him on the ground and kicked him in the face. Then he pushed him over the side. He didn't stay to watch him hit the water. The sound of the splash confirmed it, though.

Jack walked back over to the darker man, who was now on his feet. He held a gun in his shaky right hand. Jack stepped to the side. The man's aim couldn't keep up. Jack slid his left leg behind the man and delivered a crushing blow to the man's throat with his elbow. The man fell back hard, tripping over Jack's outstretched leg. His head hit the ground with a thud. Jack reached down and tore at the thug's sleeve until a piece ripped free. He grabbed the gun off the ground with the sleeve, being careful not to get his fingerprints on it. He grabbed a rock off the ground and held it in his other hand. He slipped into the shadows and waited.

He didn't have to wait long. Thornton and another man dressed in a dark suit stepped into the light from behind the building a few moments later. They stopped. The man in the dark suit held his gun up and extended an arm, keeping Thornton back. The man approached. He looked shorter than Jack, slighter too. Probably ex-Special Forces. The big guys didn't scare Jack. They were typically meatheads. The men he worried about were the smaller, wiry guys. Experience told him those guys usually had training in covert operations and knew how to handle themselves.

Jack tossed the rock to the other side of the landing area. The man turned and fired at the area where the rock landed. That was all Jack needed to see. He lifted his arm, aimed the gun and shot. The bullet hit the man on the side of the head. He collapsed.

"Jesus Christ," Thornton said. He backed up to the wall of the building behind him. His eyes darted wildly side to side.

Jack stepped out of the shadows.

"You," Thornton said. "What have you done?"

"Same thing you were going to do to me."

"No, no, no. I was just going to have them rough you up. Teach you a lesson."

"Like the lessons you teach Dottie?"

Thornton looked down. He sidestepped along the wall.

"Don't move." Jack pointed the gun at him. "You screwed up, Thornton. Ten of these guys couldn't take me out. Should have listened to Dottie. She wasn't pleading with you. She was warning you." Jack stopped a few feet from the older man and pointed the gun at his head.

"I'll give you whatever you want. Anything. Name it, it's yours."

"Give Dottie her freedom," Jack said.

"What?"

Jack slapped the barrel of the gun across the man's face.

"OK, OK!" Thornton yelled.

"Thing is, I don't believe you." Jack stepped closer. Pressed the gun into Thornton's forehead.

Thornton whimpered. Begged for his life.

"Drop your weapon," a deep voice called from Jack's right.

He looked over, but couldn't see anything because of the powerful flashlight pointing in his direction. He looked back at Thornton, who now had a bloody smile on his face. Jack jerked his arm to the left and fired toward the deep voice. The light from the flashlight disappeared. He kneed Thornton in the groin and took off. He slipped around the corner of the building and disappeared into the darkness. He stayed hidden for a while, waiting to see if the police ever arrived. They didn't. The man with the flashlight was private security, probably employed by Thornton.

An hour passed and his watch said it was just after midnight. He made his way back to the hotel, through the lobby, into the ornate elevator and up to the fourth floor. He took a shower once back in his room and fell asleep before his head hit the pillow.

CHAPTER 10

Jack stood on the balcony and drank his coffee. He looked out at the sea and watched the sun rise. From the balcony he could see the pier where he took out Thornton's men the night before. No cops. No crime scene tape. Perfect.

He threw on a pair of shorts and a polo shirt, packed his bags and left his room. He took the stairs down to the lobby. He pushed through the lobby and saw four police cars and an ambulance outside. He slipped around the marble staircase to the dark wooden counter where the concierge sat. This morning's concierge was the same man he spoke with yesterday.

"What's going on?" Jack asked.

"Woman found beaten outside her room. Older lady. Husband's a billionaire." He glanced at Jack's bag. "Checking out?"

Jack shook his head. "Going hiking with friends. Do they know who did it?"

The concierge shrugged. "I think we are about to find out." He pointed at the line of police officers making their way through the lobby toward the entrance. In the middle of the group of cops was an older man in handcuffs.

Thornton.

"Looks like that old bastard did it," the concierge said. He leaned in and lifted an eyebrow. "They say he runs one of England's most powerful criminal organizations."

"Can I get out through the side?"

"Up the stairs and make a left. Where are you headed to?"

Jack didn't answer. Jack took the stairs two at a time and made a left turn

212 / L.T. RYAN

at the top. He walked quickly down the hall, pushed through the exit door and made a roundabout loop to his moped. He hopped on, started it and drove back to France and the seaside resort of Cap-d'Ail. He kept checking over his shoulder the entire ride through Monte Carlo, making sure no one had followed him.

He rode until he found a store that sold cell phones. He went in and purchased a new phone and SIM card. Back outside in the parking lot he placed a call to Bear.

"Hello?" Bear said.

"It's Jack."

"What the hell number is this?"

"The one I'm calling from. How are things there?"

"Good. Clarissa's good."

"Can I talk to her?"

"Nah, she's asleep."

"Pierre or his guys give you any trouble?"

"A bit. They're straight now."

"OK, Bear. I've got to arrange a meeting. Call you later."

Jack hung up, pulled out his other phone and called Pierre.

"Good morning, Jack."

"Where am I going?"

"Rue Grimaldi. A place called All Day Charters. Go inside and only speak to the young blond haired woman with brown eyes. Ask for Oscar."

"Does he know my name?"

"No. I told him to address you as Howard."

Jack closed the phone and followed the GPS route to Rue Grimaldi. He turned onto an alley next to All Day Charter's office and parked the moped on a curb. He walked back through the alley, stepped onto the sidewalk and stopped in front of the double glass doors that led into the office.

What if he was being set up? The idea certainly wasn't out of the realm of possibility. He had a good working relationship with Pierre, but he didn't know this Oscar guy from Adam. Jack hated working with people he didn't know. Why the hell did he accept this job to begin with? He had no control from the outset. Now he had no idea what to expect or anticipate from this guy.

Screw it. He pulled the door open and stepped into the office. An older brown haired woman smiled at him. He ignored her and walked up to the young, blond haired woman with brown eyes.

She held a cell phone to her head and raised a finger toward Jack without making eye contact.

"I can help you over here," the other woman said.

Jack ignored her.

Finally the blond haired woman put away her cell phone.

"I need to see Oscar."

"Your name?" she asked.

"Howard."

"Follow me," she said.

Jack followed her through a door, into a break room.

"Wait here," she said.

Jack poured a cup of coffee and drank it while he waited.

The woman poked her head into the break room. "Oscar can see you now."

He followed her down a hall. She stopped and opened the door. He smiled as he passed by. She looked away.

Oscar sat behind a large antique wooden desk. He was a heavy man, with deep set blue eyes. His reddish brown hair was sparse on top, thick on the sides. He had long sideburns that were speckled with grey. He pushed his chair back to the wall, lifted his legs and placed two heavy combat boots on the desk. He crossed his thick, muscular arms.

"This is how it's gonna go down," he said in thick Irish accent. "Monday morning, tomorrow, seven o'clock, you board the *Danseur du Vent*. She's my ship. The regular captain has been given the day off. I've borrowed two deck-hands from another company. You are going to pilot the vessel. You've sailed before?"

Jack nodded.

"Good. There is a course plotted. Stick to the course. There will be five of them. Three targets you are aware of already. They'll be traveling with two bodyguards. Dorofeyev cannot live. You know which one is Dorofeyev, correct?"

Jack nodded.

"We prefer the other two die as well. Do what you want with the body-guards. Try to spare the deckhands."

"No deal," Jack said. "That's a recipe for disaster. A confined space. Five men, two of whom will be armed. On top of that you want me to spare witnesses."

Oscar glared at him, but said nothing.

"Let me do this my way."

"Hold on." Oscar lifted his phone from the cradle and dialed. He stared at Jack while waiting for someone to answer. His eyes shifted. "Your man is flaking on us."

Jack sat back, trying to fill in the blanks.

"Yes, I see."

Jack leaned forward and adjusted the gun in his waistband.

"OK, I'll tell him." Oscar hung up and looked at Jack again. "Pierre says if you want your money then you do it our way."

"I don't care about the money."

"He said you'd say that." Oscar smiled. He opened a drawer and fumbled around.

Jack tensed. His hand reached for the handle of his weapon.

Oscar pulled out a pack of cigars, offered one to Jack.

Jack declined.

"Pierre says that if you want to see the girl alive, then you do the hit on our terms."

Jack narrowed his eyes. "Is that what he said?"

"Yeah." Oscar's eyes narrowed to slits. "That's what he said."

Jack's grip on the chair's arm rails tightened. He took a deep breath. "What time should I be here tomorrow?"

"Don't come here. Go to the marina. The deckhands will meet you and take you to the boat."

Jack left the office and set out to find a cheap room for the night. Best not to go back to Monte Carlo after last night's events. He drove through the streets of the little town and stopped in front of an unassuming house with a small sign in the window that read *Vacancy*. It looked promising.

He walked up a carefully laid brick sidewalk and knocked on the weathered wooden door. An elderly woman answered.

"I'd like to rent a room for a week," he said.

She lowered her eyebrows and cocked her head to the side. Shrugged her shoulders at him.

He repeated himself in French.

She smiled. "Two hundred euros."

"Per night?" he asked in French.

She nodded. He reached into his bag, retrieved five two-hundred euro bills and handed them to her. "Five nights." He held up his hand, all five fingers extended.

She held her hand in the air and opened and closed it a few times to acknowledge. Then she turned and walked away, one arm in the air, waving Jack inside.

He liked this. No questions, no ID, just a simple transaction.

She pulled two key rings from her pocket and opened a narrow door. She ushered Jack inside the room as she took two keys off of the second key ring. She held the first up in the air, pointed at the narrow door and handed him the key. She held the second key up and pointed out the hall. He assumed it was for the front door. She handed him the key and walked away.

He threw his bag on the bed and looked around the room. Small bed, one dresser and no TV. At least he had his own bathroom.

Jack opened the door and checked the hallway. Empty. He pulled out his cell and started to dial Bear's number. He stopped and walked out the front door and down to the street where he finished dialing.

"Jack," Bear said.

"We got a problem."

"What?"

"I don't know if it's a legit problem or not, Bear."

"What is it?"

"Have you met with Pierre yet?"

"Yeah, he came by yesterday and again this morning."

"Any issues? He seem tense or anything like that?"

"No. What's this about?"

"I met with the contact down here. Don't like the setup. Told him I want to do it my way. He didn't like that. Called Pierre and said Pierre insisted I follow the plan or Clarissa might not make it out of the hospital alive."

"When was this?"

"An hour ago."

"Wasn't Pierre on the phone then. He's been with me for the last two."

Jack didn't say anything.

"You're being set up," Bear said.

"Yeah. But by who?"

"Want me to come down there?"

"No, stay there. Maybe Pierre set this up in advance. If that's the case then you be ready to do whatever it takes to get Clarissa out of that hospital."

"OK," Bear said. "You sure you're gonna be OK, Jack?"

"Yeah," Jack said. "But you can be sure I'm the only one getting off that boat alive tomorrow."

CHAPTER 11

J ack arrived at the marina before six in the morning. The sun peeked over the horizon and provided enough light for him to find the boat. He admired the white craft. It looked to be over fifty feet long. Blue trim swirled down the side. *Dansuer du Vent* was painted in bold blue letters on the back. The deck was open with a hard top covering the wheel. Special fishing seats were mounted in the front and back of the boat. A grey 100 gallon cooler nestled up to the back of the boat. The deck was spacious, but it would be a tight fit for seven men plus him.

He stepped on board and got to work. He pulled a roll of duct tape from his bag and crawled under the wheel. He placed a loaded gun underneath and secured it with the tape. Then he began searching the boat for any scuba gear. He found none.

He stepped back on the dock and investigated the boats nearby. Two slips down was a boat with a sign labeled *Adventure Scuba*. He boarded the vessel and broke the lock of one of the bins on board. He lifted the lid and found everything he needed; a vest, regulator, all instrumentation, and even an alternate air source. He grabbed the gear and two air tanks from the boat and returned to his vessel.

He lifted the bench seat to the right of the wheel and placed his scuba gear inside. He checked inside the opposite bench seat. A twelve gauge shotgun and box of ammunition rested there. He pulled the weapon out, inspected it and found it to be loaded. He carefully placed the weapon back and closed the seat. He stood at the wheel and acclimated himself to the controls. A navigation chart sat open behind the wheel. He studied it and decided that the second wreck would be the spot for the hit.

He sat down and relaxed while watching the sun come up. The lights were on in the main building. He made his way to the general store where he purchased four cases of beer and five bags of ice. The supplies were loaded on a cart. He stocked the grey cooler with the beer and ice. The job would be easier if his targets were drunk.

The two deck hands showed up half an hour later. If they were working with Oscar they sure fooled Jack. Neither of them appeared to be over twenty years old. The first deckhand on the boat introduced himself as Marcel. He pulled his stringy blond hair back in a ponytail and then extended an arm toward Jack. Jack reached out and shook Marcel's bony hand. He wore a white t-shirt and tan cargo shorts. His legs poked out of the shorts like toothpicks.

The second deckhand stepped on board. He was taller and thicker than Marcel. "Guy," he said in a deep voice when Jack asked him his name. Guy wore a blue and white striped button up shirt with pockets on both sides of his chest. He twisted his long brown hair and tucked it under a wide brimmed khaki hat. Several fishing lures adorned the green strap wrapped around the hat. He wore camouflage cargo pants that tucked into black combat boots.

"I'm Captain Conway," Jack said. "Nice to have you two on board."

"Nice to be on board," Marcel said.

Guy shrugged and started pulling fishing rods from the boat's lock boxes. "How many passengers, Captain?"

"Five, but only three will be fishing," Jack said.

Guy set up six rods and unlocked another box at the front of the boat. He pulled out six reels and attached one to each rod. Afterward he turned to Jack. "Going to get bait." He held out his hand.

Jack reached into his pocket and handed the young man a hundred euros. He watched Guy as he walked up the dock toward the bait shop in the marina.

"Don't mind him," Marcel said. "He's hungover."

"You two work together often?" Jack asked.

"Most days, yeah."

Jack smiled, nodded and pretended to work on his chart. Good info to have. He'd try to spare their lives as long as they didn't get in the way.

Guy returned a short while later carrying large white buckets. He boarded the boat without saying a word.

Jack checked his watch. Five minutes till eight o'clock. He looked over the dock toward the marina. Five men made their way toward the boat. Jack immediately recognized the three men in the middle as Dorofeyev, Olkhovsky, and the younger Korzhakov. The men were flanked by two others around Jack's age. They were dressed in dark fatigues. One wore a hat, the other had short black hair. Both were lean and looked to be in shape. Jack figured them for ex-military, maybe even Special Forces. They boarded the boat first.

The guard wearing the hat started checking bins and crates. The other walked up to Jack.

"My name is Aleksandr," he said. The man had a chiseled face with a square jaw and a thin nose and lips. He took off his sunglasses and revealed a set of eyes so dark they were as black as his hair. He was a little shorter than Jack, but built the same.

Jack nodded. "Conway."

"We must perform a routine check, Conway," Aleksandr said. "I'm sure you understand."

"What's your partner's name?" Jack nodded toward the thin, pale man rifling through the ship's containers. He was shorter and thinner than his partner.

"You can call him Viktor." Aleksandr walked to the wheel and flipped up the cushions. He reached in and pulled out the twelve gauge shotgun. Pointed it at Jack. "What's this?"

Jack didn't flinch. "In case we catch something we can't handle."

Aleksandr looked over his shoulder at Dorofeyev and yelled something in Russian.

Dorofeyev nodded.

Aleksandr removed the ammunition from the weapon as well as a few rounds from the box of ammunition and put them in his pocket. He threw the rest of the bullets overboard and placed the gun back in the compartment. "You can keep the gun. I'll hold the ammunition. You know, in case we catch something we can't handle."

Jack nodded and didn't say anything. He took a quick look at the three targets and then returned to his charts.

Aleksandr said something else in Russian. Dorofeyev, Olkhovsky, and Korzhakov boarded the *Wind Dancer*.

"We can leave now, Conway," Aleksandr said.

Jack stood up. Looked at the men on the boat. Two deckhands, three

Russian criminals, two private contractors, and him. How many would die today?

"Everyone take a seat," Jack said.

Marcel and Guy sat at the back of the boat. Viktor sat near them. Dorofeyev, Olkhovsky, and Korzhakov sat at the front, in the fishing chairs. They had found the grey cooler stocked with beer. The three men held a beer in each hand. Aleksandr stood next to Jack.

"Let's go," Aleksandr said.

Jack purposefully overshot the first wreck by a quarter mile. Less chance the men would catch anything here. He figured that would make them more willing to move to the next spot that much sooner.

"Captain," Dorofeyev shouted almost on cue. "Take us to another spot."

"Restock your beer," Jack said. "It'll take us about an hour to get there."

All three men turned to him and smiled.

Jack motioned to Marcel. Handed him a bucket. "Take this, fill it with ice and put a dozen or so beers in it, then take it to them. OK?"

"Sure," Marcel said.

Marcel did as Jack asked. He started toward the front of the boat.

Viktor stopped him. "What are you doing?" His spoke with a heavy accent.

"C-c-captain's orders. Just bringing them some beer," Marcel said.

Viktor took the bucket and looked at Aleksandr.

Aleksandr motioned with his head and Viktor brought the bucket of ice and beer to the three men.

Drink up, bastards.

Jack put the boat in gear and adjusted his course to make up for his previous overcorrection.

Jack started planning the hit in his head. By this point he had got past his anger over the job. Now he needed a plan, his own plan, to get this job done. The guards were armed, no doubt about that. How armed was hard to say. They carried at least one handgun each, most likely a semi-automatic nine millimeter like the Beretta he had on the boat. What about Dorofeyev, Olkhovsky, and Korzhakov, though? Would they be armed? Olkhovsky was a career military man. Good chance he had a personal firearm with him. The other two, maybe, maybe not. The guards had to be taken out first. Taken out fast. Olkhovsky had to be next. Then it would be a tossup between Dorofeyev and Korzhakov.

So how to make it work? A diversion. He needed a diversion. Three miles off the southern coast of France.

Jack slowed the boat and dropped the anchor. The sea was choppy and the boat rocked side to side.

"Best spot in the Med," he said as he walked toward the front of the boat. "You gents ready for the catch of your life?"

All three men shouted. They were drunk.

Perfect.

Jack gestured to Marcel to move up and help the men get their bait in the water. Marcel did as instructed and both guards followed him to the front.

Jack pointed at Guy, who sat in the back corner of the boat. Guy stood up, arms crossed, as Jack approached. Jack took a quick look over his shoulder. No one was looking back. He leaned in and shoved Guy overboard. The push was enough to knock the young man off balance. He flipped backwards over the short rail, arms and legs flailing, and hit the water. The current pulled hard and no matter how hard he tried to swim against it, the water pulled Guy further away from the boat.

"Man overboard," Jack shouted. He rushed to the wheel and put the boat in gear. Disconnected the anchor.

"Help," Guy's shouts were barely audible over the roar of the engine.

Jack moved the boat toward Guy.

Aleksandr and Viktor moved to the back of the boat. Aleksandr found a rope and tossed it toward Guy, but the man was too busy trying to keep afloat to grab the rope. Aleksandr shouted in Russian.

Jack looked back and saw Viktor nod and lift his arms. Aleksandr tied one end of the rope around his wrist, and the other end around Viktor. He pulled the mesh gate off the back of the boat. Both men stood at the edge. Viktor jumped in.

Aleksandr looked at Jack. "Get us closer."

Jack nodded and smiled when Aleksandr looked away. The current pulled Viktor, drawing the rope tight. Aleksandr strained to keep his footing and stay on board. He had one arm outstretched, the other held tight to the railing. He let go of the rail and reached forward, grabbing the rope with both hands. He squatted low, sitting back to balance.

The three men at the front of the boat watched from their seats. Marcel clung to the side of the boat, his face drawn.

Jack reversed the boat. He waited for Aleksandr to straighten up. The moment the man rose up Jack lurched the boat forward. Aleksandr fell face first off the boat. His right arm outstretched, attached to the rope. His left arm reached back and grasped at air.

Jack left the wheel and moved to the back of the boat, while the vessel continued forward.

By this point the three men, Dorofeyev, Olkhovsky, and Korzhakov, had left their seats and moved to the side of the open wheelhouse.

"Help them," Dorofeyev shouted.

Jack turned around, walked back to the wheel. He motioned the three men toward the back of the boat.

"Get ready to help pull them up," Jack said.

Marcel sat next to the wheel. He stared at the back of the boat. His face was frozen. Eyes didn't blink. Jack patted him on the head to reassure him.

He put the boat in reverse, figuring that would distract the men and keep them from looking toward him while he removed the gun from under the wheel. He ducked under the wheel and removed the layer of duct tape holding the gun to the column. He turned around, took aim and fired a round into Olkhovsky's back. The man stood up straight at the moment of impact, then his body fell forward into the sea.

Dorofeyev and Korzhakov spun around. Jack held the gun out and alternated pointing it at each man. They both raised their hands. Jack looked beyond them and saw Aleksandr and Viktor fighting the current and getting close to the boat. Jack reached behind and put the boat in forward gear and slowly moved away from the distressed men.

"Who's first?" Jack asked.

"What are you doing?" Dorofeyev asked. "Don't you know who I am?"

"Grigori Dorofeyev, member of the Russian government Defense Ministry. You are planning an overthrow of the government within the next five years. You have the support of some powerful people. Anyone who refuses to support you is imprisoned on false charges. Or killed."

Jack took two steps closer to the men.

"And you," he pointed to Korzhakov. "You're an up and comer in the party. You are the man they'll use to convince the younger generation that Grigori's plan is the right one."

The men looked at each other.

"What do you want?" Dorofeyev pleaded.

"Nothing," Jack said.

"Who sent you? How much are they paying you?" Dorofeyev asked.

"The French government and they are paying me a lot."

"I'll give you one million dollars to stop this now."

Jack shrugged, nodded and lowered his weapon.

Dorofeyev smiled, lowered his hands and stepped toward Jack. "I can have the money to you tomorrow."

"Not good enough." Jack raised his arm and shot Korzhakov in the chest. The man stumbled backwards. One foot slipped off the back of the boat causing his body to give way and plunge into the ocean. Within seconds he disappeared from view.

Dorofeyev clenched his teeth, his face, and his fists. He shouted something in Russian that Jack didn't understand.

"Anything you want me to tell them? For you?" Jack asked.

Dorofeyev straightened himself up. He dropped his arms to his side. "Yes. Tell them that I, Grigori Dorofeyev, was strong until the last--"

Jack pulled the trigger and fired a bullet into Dorofeyev's chest. The man's body recoiled, staggered a step forward, a step backward, but he kept his footing and stood tall. Jack pulled the trigger again, hitting him in the stomach. Dorofeyev leaned forward, but stayed in place, his head held high. Jack took two steps forward. Fired a shot between the man's eyes. Dorofeyev's head snapped back then slowly rolled forward. His body stood still. Finally it collapsed backwards into a heap on the deck.

Jack took a deep breath and pulled his phone from his pocket. He snapped a picture of Dorofeyev's body and sent it to a number that would store the picture on a secure server that only he had access to. He took a few steps forward, leaned over and shoved the lifeless body into the sea. He stood and watched as the body was pulled out and under by the heavy current.

Jack turned and saw Marcel standing there, holding a shotgun. Jack looked past him and noticed the radio was on and the receiver lying on the counter behind the wheel.

"What did you do, Marcel?"

Marcel raised the barrel of the shotgun.

"Don't move," Marcel shouted. "Stay right there."

Jack took two steps forward. He didn't want to get caught close to the back of the boat.

"Put the gun down," Jack said.

Marcel stomped his foot. "I said don't move."

Jack took two more steps forward. He had watched Aleksandr remove the shells from the gun. Was there a chance there were more? It didn't matter. He stepped closer to Marcel until he was inches from the barrel of the gun.

"You saw what I just did," Jack said. "Do you want me to kill you too?"

Marcel didn't say anything.

"Who did you call?"

Marcel looked away.

Jack reached out and yanked the gun from his hands. He stuck the Beretta to Marcel's forehead. "You dumb bastard. All you had to do was keep quiet. Dammit."

"Please don't kill me," Marcel said.

"Shut up."

"Please don't kill me," Marcel said again.

Jack tucked the handgun in his pants and picked up the shotgun. He slammed the butt of the shotgun into the side of Marcel's head. The deckhand fell to the floor, unconscious. Jack secured the rear of the boat and moved Marcel out of the way. He checked his charts and set the boat on a course to the northwest. He locked the wheel and pulled out the stolen scuba gear. He prepped the gear in the event he needed to use it.

He looked up and spotted a plane. It flew low, passed overhead, circled around and passed by again.

Jack cursed under his breath. He took position at the wheel and increased throttle. The boat sped up. The roar of the plane diminished. He checked over his shoulder and watched the plane drop back. He lowered his eyes. Marcel was waking up. Jack locked the wheel and knelt in front of Marcel.

"Who did you call?"

"No one." Marcel held the side of his head. He pulled his hand out and stared at the blood on his palm.

"Then why is that plane following us?"

Marcel shrugged. "I'm telling you Conway, I didn't call anyone."

Jack reached for the handgun tucked in his pants. He aimed it at Marcel's head.

"You never saw me, got that?" Jack said.

"I-I never saw you," Marcel repeated.

"You don't want to screw with me, Marcel. I'll find you, find your family. Kill all of you. Got it?"

"Yeah, I got it," Marcel said.

"OK, this is how this is going to go down. When we get closer to shore I'm gone. Jumping off the boat."

Marcel nodded without saying a word.

"When they board, you tell them you knocked me overboard," Jack said.

Marcel nodded.

"I find out you told them anything other than that, I'm coming after you."

Jack went back to the wheel. He checked the GPS and compared it to his charts. Close enough. He put on the scuba equipment and slowed the boat. The roar of the engines diminished. The plane approached. Jack kept himself hidden under the canopy over the wheel. In the distance he heard another boat approaching.

"There," Marcel said, his arm outstretched pointing to a dot on the horizon. "Police boat."

"Ship's yours," Jack said. He leaned back against the rail and fell backwards into the sea.

CHAPTER 12

Jack ditched his gear a couple hundred yards from shore and swam above water the rest of the way. He treaded water and stared at the deserted landscape in front of him. He could make out no discernible landmarks. A compass kept him on track, but the strong current pulled him further to the east than anticipated. He expected to be slightly east of Monte Carlo, but could tell that wasn't the case.

He carefully pulled himself up on the slippery rocks along the edge of the water. Stripped off his clothes and wrung the water out. He put his pants back on and started walking to his right. Just beyond the trees was a clearing. He'd get a better idea of the area from there. He hoped.

From the clearing he saw a sliver of black pavement. He jogged through the clearing and made his way through a group of trees. Stopped at the edge of the road where it curved sharply. Jack closed his eyes and listened. The sound of an old engine filled the air. A rusted pickup truck appeared from around the corner. It slowed down as it approached the curve. An old man with glasses and a short white beard peered at Jack through the windshield. The truck came to a stop.

"You in trouble?" the man asked in Italian.

"Yes," Jack answered in English. "Do you speak English?"

Jack could understand basic Italian phrases, but couldn't speak it very well.

The old man nodded. "Hop in."

Jack stepped into the cab of the truck and sat down on the passenger side of the blue cracked vinyl bench seat.

"Where you headed?" the man asked.

"Nearest train station," Jack said.

"Well, I'm not going that far. But I can help you get there."

"OK."

"What's your name?"

"Jack."

It didn't matter what name he used.

"I'm Sal." He pushed in the cigarette lighter on the dash, reached into his pocket and pulled out a pack of filterless cigarettes. He handed one to Jack. "How come you're soaking wet?"

The cigarette lighter made a popping sound. Jack grabbed it, lit his cigarette and handed the lighter to Sal. He drew on the cigarette and exhaled slowly, blowing the smoke out through the window.

"Boating accident," Jack said.

"Alone?"

"Yeah."

Sal nodded. "Sorry about your boat."

Neither man spoke for the next fifteen minutes. They passed a sign that said *Levanto*. Sal pointed at the sign then up ahead toward a cluster of shops. "That's your stop."

Sal pulled over a couple hundred yards from town. He reached in his shirt pocket and pulled out the pack of cigarettes. He handed them to Jack. "Figure you might need those after the day you've had."

"Know where I can buy a phone around here?"

Sal threw back his head and laughed.

Of course he doesn't. Old bastard has no need for a phone.

Jack watched as Sal dropped the shifter into drive and pulled away, leaving Jack standing on the side of the road.

He walked into town with his head turned to the west, eyes fixed on the setting sun. Most of the shops were closed. A drugstore still had its lights on. Jack went in to see about a phone.

A woman stood behind the counter.

"You sell mobile phones?" Jack asked in English.

She looked up from her magazine, brushed her blond hair out of her face and smiled. "Sure do." Her smile faded, but the thin lines next to her eyes and lips didn't. The rest of her face was smooth. He figured she was in her mid-thirties, maybe forty.

Jack reached into his pocket and pulled out his wallet. It was soaked through with water despite being in a plastic bag. He pulled out forty euros and placed the money on the counter. "Sorry, the money's wet."

The woman shrugged. "No matter to me." She returned to her computer and programmed the phone.

"I'll be right back."

Jack went to the back of the store. Found the restroom and washed up. On his way back to the front of the store he grabbed a generic t-shirt and a pair of shorts. He changed his clothes in the middle of the store. He turned around and saw the woman looking at him, smiling.

He waved.

She blushed.

He returned to the front, placed his damp clothes on the counter.

"Don't see that every day." She peeked at him through her dangling hair.

Jack laughed. "Sorry, had to get out of those clothes. Getting a chill."

"Your phone is ready." She slid the cell across the counter.

"Across the street," Jack said. "They serve food?"

"You asking me out?"

Jack winked, picked up his phone and walked out of the store. Crossed the street. He pulled open the door to the dimly lit bar and took a seat near the bartender.

"What will you have?" the man asked in English with a heavy Italian accent.

"A shot. Make it a double."

"Of what?"

"Something that will knock me on my ass."

The bartender laughed. "You got it."

Jack pulled out the pack of cigarettes and reached for a clean ashtray with a pack of matches sitting on top.

The bartender placed a tall shot glass in front of Jack.

"Can't do this in New York anymore. You know that?"

The bartender shrugged.

Jack threw back the drink, grimaced and exhaled loudly.

"One more," he said. "And a beer."

Two more shots and six beers later, Jack felt relaxed for the first time in over a week.

The crowd in the bar grew. A mix of tourists and locals intermingled, sharing stories and jokes. Jack had become friendly with the other patrons. Anytime someone asked him his name, he'd ask them theirs. Whatever they said, he told them that was his name too.

He chatted with a couple from Long Island, talking about all things New York. He felt a tap on his shoulder. He turned and saw the blond woman from the drug store. She greeted him with a smile.

"Buy me a drink?" she asked.

"What's your name?" he replied.

"I'll take whatever you're having," she said.

"I'm Jack."

Again, it didn't really matter.

She smiled. "Gianna."

They continued to talk. Jack continued to drink. Gianna continued to move closer.

Hours passed and the bartender started shutting down.

"Where are you staying?" Gianna asked. "I'll give you a ride."

Jack looked at his watch. Eleven at night. "Where's the nearest hotel?"

Her eyebrows rose high into her forehead. "You won't be able to get a room now."

Jack stuck his hands in his pockets and hunched his shoulders. "I'll be OK."

"Nonsense, you come stay with me tonight."

CHAPTER 13

G ianna's small car sped through the country road leading away from town. Jack barely fit in the passenger seat. His knees pressed into the dash and his feet were standing up on the tips of his toes.

"How much further?" he asked.

"Not enjoying my company?" she asked. "Almost there," she added.

Jack followed her outstretched finger and spotted a small light. As they got closer he recognized it as a porch light.

Gianna pulled the car onto a gravel driveway and stopped next to the house.

Jack followed her inside.

"Hungry?" she asked.

"Always," Jack said.

She led him into her small kitchen. An old fashioned fridge took up one corner. A bare countertop with a sink in the middle ran the length of the wall. At the end of the counter was a small two-burner stove. Jack sat down at a narrow wooden kitchen table.

Gianna grabbed two glasses and placed them on the table. She reached into a cabinet and pulled out a bottle of red wine. She opened the bottle and poured a glass for herself and a glass for Jack.

"It's homemade," she said.

Jack sniffed the wine. Strong. He took a sip. The taste matched the smell. He fought to hold back his reaction. "That code for smelly feet wine?"

She placed an assortment of meat and a roll on a plate in front of him. "Eat," she said.

She talked. Jack listened. He ate. They both drank.

"I need to make a phone call," Jack said after finishing his sandwich. "Is there anywhere I can get some privacy?"

"Checking in with the wife?" Gianna asked.

Jack smiled and said nothing.

Gianna frowned and pointed at a white door just past the kitchen.

Jack stepped outside. Looked around. Completely deserted. He took out his new cell phone and called Pierre.

Pierre answered the phone. "Who's this?"

"Jack."

"Jesus Christ, Jack. What the hell happened today?"

"You tell me, Pierre."

"What do you mean?"

"The police showed up. How do you explain that?"

"I can't."

"Wait a minute. Pierre, why'd you ask me what happened?"

"Your face is on TV. Again. But this time in conjunction with three missing politicians from Russia."

"Two politicians, one General," Jack said.

"Whatever."

"So who's behind this?"

"Hold on, the deckhand is talking."

Jack could hear the sound of the TV in the background, but the voice was muffled.

"What's he saying?" Jack asked.

"Said he doesn't know what happened. He bumped his head and when he came to, everyone, including you, was gone."

"Good," Jack said. "I threatened his family's life."

"Not very nice."

"Sue me."

"So if it wasn't me," Pierre said, "and it wasn't him, that only leaves Oscar."

"How well do you know Oscar?" Jack asked.

"We've used him many times. But, there is always a risk--"

"Don't tell me about risks. Just tell me what you are going to do to clean this up."

"It's a touchy situation, Jack. We can control the media to a point, but this took place at sea. That's why our operatives didn't get involved. It adds a whole other dynamic."

The door opened. Jack looked up and saw Gianna standing in the doorway.

"Everything OK?" she asked. "You were yelling."

Jack covered the phone. "Yeah, I'll be right in." He put the phone back to his ear. "I gotta go."

"I heard," Pierre said.

"It's not what you think," Jack said.

"I'm sure."

"Screw you. Fix this."

Jack hung up the phone and lit a cigarette. He stared at dark night sky littered with sparkling stars. *Missing.* That's all they had at this point.

Jack walked through the doorway into an empty kitchen.

"Hello?" he called out.

"In here."

He left the kitchen and made his way into the main living room. Gianna sat in a chair wearing a black and red shimmering robe. On the table in front of her sat another bottle of wine and two half-full glasses.

"Have a drink," she said.

Jack sat down across from her. He picked up his wineglass and finished it off.

"What's the rush?" she asked. She rose to her feet. The robe slipped open from her neck to just under her belly button. She made no attempt to close it. She leaned over the table and picked up the bottle of wine. Jack watched as her ample breasts fought against the robe, forcing it open a bit more. She leaned forward and refilled his glass. She stood up, one hand on the bottle, the other on the red drawstring that kept her robe closed from her waist down.

Jack slammed his drink.

Gianna pulled the drawstring. The knot untied and her robe fell open.

Jack sat back in his chair.

She placed one knee next to his leg and leaned over him. Lifted her other leg and sat her knee outside of his other leg.

Jack leaned his head back and closed his eyes. He felt her lips brush against his and then he drifted away into unconsciousness.

Jack opened his eyes and checked his watch. It read four in the morning. He sat on the couch alone and fully clothed. A folded piece of paper with his

234 / L.T. RYAN

name on it sat on the table. He opened it. It read, "Sorry you passed out so soon. Coffee is in the pot, just hit start. -G."

He got up and looked down the hallway. The door to her room was closed. He turned and went to the kitchen. Started the coffee pot. He checked the fridge and grabbed a pear. He recalled the map on the wall in the bar. Brugnato. The town had a train station and was only ten miles away. He didn't know the location of Gianna's house, though. He remembered a GPS unit on the dash of her car. He stepped through the back door into the chilly morning air and opened the car door. The GPS sat on the dash, just as he remembered. He turned on the device and panned the display out. The town was a little less than ten miles away.

He checked his watch again. Four-thirty. Only ten thirty at night in New York. He dialed fast and from memory.

"Hello?" the old man answered.

"It's Jack."

"Mr. Jack, how are you this evening?"

"Cut the crap. Where is he?"

"Italy," the old man said. "A town called Ameglia."

Jack said nothing. He punched the town name into the GPS. He smiled at the result. Ameglia was barely twenty miles from his location.

"Thanks," Jack said. "I'll be in touch."

He hung up the phone and went back inside, taking the GPS with him. He poured a cup of coffee, sat at the table and began sketching a map. He was roughly six or seven miles from La Spezia, a city about halfway between him and Charles. He'd travel there. Get a room and wait for Bear.

Jack grabbed a travel mug from a cabinet and another pear from the fridge. He stepped through the back door once again, and walked down the gravel driveway to the road.

Jack passed a tiny sign that read La Spezia. Checked his watch. Seven-thirty in the morning. He kept his head down as he stepped out of the woods and into town. He followed Via Sauro for half a mile, then made a right on Via Roma and walked another quarter mile. He stopped in front of the Hotel Astoria, a cream colored four story brick building that occupied about half a block.

Two hanging lanterns marked the entrance. He stepped through the door and walked up to the woman behind the desk. Her gold plated name tag said Jemma. Short brown hair framed her narrow face. Her nose looked a tad too wide. She had wide set brown eyes and a thin upper lip.

"*Ciao, posso aiutarti?*" Jemma said.

"Sorry," Jack said. "My Italian is very rusty. I know you said hello--"

Jemma smiled. "Yes sir, no problem. How may I help you?"

"I'd like a room for a week." He looked at the sign over the desk. It stated check-in time began at two-thirty. "Do you have a room I can check into now?"

Jemma looked down at her computer. "I do have a room available for a week, and it is unoccupied right now." She typed some more, then leaned over the counter. "They really don't allow early check-in, sir."

Jack placed fifty euros on the counter and looked back over his shoulder at the door.

"Of course, what are rules for if not to break them?" she said.

He turned his head and the money was gone. He smiled.

"Do you have ID?" she asked.

"Stolen," Jack said.

Jemma sat up straight and lifted an eyebrow at him. "Name?"

"Smith. Mitch Smith."

It didn't matter.

"How will you be paying Mr. Smith?"

He pulled out a wad of euros.

"The total for the week is one thousand euros."

Jack counted out the money and laid it on the counter.

Jemma took it and tucked it into an envelope. She opened a drawer and pulled out two plastic cards, ran them through a machine and handed them to Jack. "Fourth floor, room 412. We have an indoor pool and exercise facilities on the first floor. You would walk past the elevators and turn right at the first hallway. Did you travel by car?"

"No." He tucked the green key cards into his pocket and walked to the elevator lobby.

He called Bear from his room.

"Jack?"

"Yeah. How's Clarissa?"

"Should be out of here in a couple days."

"Can you move her sooner?"

"Why?" Bear asked.

"Seen the news? Apparently my face is all over it."

"Yeah, I heard. You think our friend is behind it?"

"I dunno what to think right now. He says he isn't, but you know."

"What does he have to gain by setting you up?"

"Money?"

Bear laughed. "Risky gamble there."

"Find out when she can leave. Pay someone extra to bump the date up. I'm in Italy. La Spezia."

"Train run through there?"

"Yeah."

Jack hung up and placed the phone on the nightstand next to the bed. He stepped out onto a narrow balcony that overlooked the small town toward the sea. He reached into his pocket and pulled out the pack of cigarettes Sal gave him.

I really need to quit smoking.

CHAPTER 14

C larissa stared out the window as the train pulled away from the Aulla station.

"Almost there," Bear said.

She smiled through the pain. Her chest hurt like hell. The stitches pulled every time she moved. But she was alive. Very lucky, the doctors told her, that the bullet missed her lung and all major arteries. It passed right through. Her head hitting the wall caused a concussion and was the reason she didn't wake up for nearly five days. None of that mattered today, though. She'd see Jack soon. She'd feel his arms wrap around her and hold her tight.

Bear briefed her on the situation during the ride through France. Jack had to lay low and it would be for the best if they all did.

"How long will we stay here?" she asked.

"A week, maybe longer," Bear said.

"What's special about this place? Wouldn't it be safer to head to Corsica or Sicily, maybe even southern Italy?"

"Probably." Bear paused and scratched at the growth of hair on his face. "But we got something to take care of near here."

Clarissa nodded and turned back toward the window. The lush, mountainous terrain kept her mind off of the pain in her chest. The scenery soon gave way to the outskirts of La Spezia.

"We're here," Bear said.

She lifted her head from the glass window and turned to face him.

"You know where we need to go?" she asked.

Bear pulled out his phone and punched at the front of it. He held it up, facing her. "Just need to follow that red line and we'll be at the hotel in about half an hour."

The train came to a stop. A voice came over the speaker, first in Italian, then in French, and finally in English. Time to depart.

Clarissa stood and reached for her bag. Bear snatched it before she had a chance to grab it.

"No way are you carrying this," Bear said.

She nudged against him. Who needed family with guys like Bear and Jack around?

They entered the Hotel Astoria from the street and walked up to the front counter. Clarissa smiled at the woman and turned to face the door.

Bear did all the talking.

"Room for a week, please," he said to the woman.

"Yes sir," she said. "ID?"

Bear bumped against Clarissa as he reached into his pocket. She heard something hit the counter and assumed it was his ID.

"Mr. Schlater, I have a room on the fourth floor for you. The charge will be one thousand euros. How will you be paying?"

Clarissa looked over at Bear and watched as he placed a credit card on the counter. The woman tapped on her keyboard and clicked on her mouse. A few moments later Bear handed Clarissa a green key card to their room.

"Room 422," the woman said.

Clarissa walked to the elevator as the woman gave Bear the rest of the speech. She tuned it out and pressed the up button. The elevator doors opened. She stepped in, turned, and pressed the button labeled four. She looked at her reflection in the gold tinted mirrored elevator door. She quickly brushed her hair with her fingers, tucking one side of her long auburn hair behind her ear. She straightened out her clothes.

The doors opened. Clarissa stepped into the hall and found her way to Jack's room. She bit her bottom lip, took a deep breath and knocked on the door. She heard footsteps approaching. Her stomach turned to knots as the door latch clicked.

Jack turned the handle and pulled the door open. His lips broadened into a smile at the sight of Clarissa. He stepped into the doorway and took her in his arms. Pulled her close. Held her tight.

She winced.

"Am I hurting you?" he asked.

"It's OK," she replied.

He placed both hands on her hips and stared into her blue eyes.

They said nothing.

He slid a hand up her side, around her back and settled it on the side of her face. He leaned in. Their lips met. Her hands wrapped around his broad shoulders and ran through his hair. Her nails scratched lightly on his neck.

"Break it up," Bear called from outside the room.

The two separated, smiling at one another.

"I've been waiting so long for that," Clarissa said softly.

Jack winked, led her inside and returned to the door to wait for Bear.

"Look like garbage, Jack," Bear said.

Jack laughed and followed Bear into the room. Clarissa sat on the edge of the bed watching TV. Jack and Bear sat at the small table in the corner.

"What's the plan?" Bear asked.

"Lay low a few more days. Then we take down Charles."

Clarissa turned toward them. "I want to be there."

Jack shook his head. "No."

"Like hell no," she said. "You know he's the reason I was in the hospital. The reason my face still has these bruises."

Jack lowered his head. Rubbed his temples. He looked to Bear for guidance.

The big man shrugged.

Who are we to stop her?

"OK," Jack said. "You do exactly as we say."

"When are we gonna do this?" Bear asked.

"Friday night."

"Where?"

"Close to here."

"C'mon Jack."

"Sorry. Everything has gone wrong this week. No point in screwing this up too."

CHAPTER 15

Jack unfolded a small map of northwest Italy on the small table in his hotel room. He pointed to Ameglia.

"There," he said. "That's where Charles is."

"Not far from here," Bear said. "Taking the train?"

"I want you to find where to rent a car and get one big enough for the three of us. I'll call the old man and get the latest on Charles."

"Got it." Bear left the room.

"You going to be OK?" Jack asked Clarissa.

"Is there some reason I wouldn't be?"

"You know, I just --"

"You need to stop babying me," she said. "I can handle myself."

Jack threw his arms up. "It's just been a rough couple weeks. I don't want anything else to happen to you."

"You can't worry about that. It'll screw everything up."

He nodded. He would screw everything up if he constantly worried about her safety.

Shut it down, Jack. Just shut it down.

Clarissa stepped in front of him. Put her arms around his shoulders. She stared into his eyes. "We've got a while before Bear gets back, you know."

Jack lifted her arms and gently pushed her away. "I have to make some calls."

He slipped through the door at the end of the room and stepped onto the balcony. He pulled out his cell phone and dialed a number in the US.

"Hello?" a tired voice said.

"It's Jack. This you?"

"Mr. Jack, why are you calling me at five-thirty in the morning?"

"It's not five-thirty here. Almost noon. What's the latest on our friend?"

"He's in the same place. He eats dinner every night at a little place called Rosalita's. Gets there around six in the evening, stays until ten or eleven."

"How do you know this?" Jack asked.

"His right hand man, Alonso. He's still loyal to me. He has orders to let you through."

Jack said, "How do you know this guy isn't double crossing you?"

The old man laughed. "After all these years, you still underestimate me Mr. Jack." The old man paused. "I have his wife and daughter. They are being held. Safely. Here at my place."

"Got it." Jack stared out over the town, into the sea. "This is it. I'm done after this one."

The old man didn't say anything.

"I'm serious," Jack said.

The old man laughed. "Mr. Jack, if I call, you will answer."

"Don't think so, old man."

The old man continued. "If you don't, there will be a price to pay."

"Go to hell."

"I'm sure the little girl enjoys Montana. Perhaps enough to make it her final resting place."

Anger clawed through Jack.

"I'll be in touch, Mr. Jack."

The line went dead. Jack stood on the balcony, leaning over the wrought iron black railing. He watched a small car pull up to the curb in front of the hotel. A door opened and Bear stumbled out of the little vehicle. Jack turned and went back inside. He put his hand on Clarissa's shoulder. "Let's go."

The drive to Ameglia took less than twenty minutes. No one talked. Jack assumed he had pissed off Clarissa. She hadn't looked at him since they left the hotel. Jack couldn't look at Bear. The old man's words ate at him.

Her final resting place.

Old bastard might do it too. Bear would freak the moment Jack told him. Better to wait until they finished the job rather than getting Bear upset now.

"Rosalita's." Jack broke the silence as they passed a small stand-alone red brick building. "That's the place. Eats there every night. Stays there from six till ten."

"Let's scout around," Bear said.

They drove around the small town for the next couple hours until they knew every possible escape route and had every street name memorized.

They left town and headed to the coast to relax for a while. Jack found a path that led through some trees to an opening on a cliff that overlooked the sea.

He sat there for half an hour, staring out at the Mediterranean. He wondered if any of the bodies had been found yet. It wouldn't take long for them to figure out what happened after they found one of the Russians he shot.

He heard footsteps behind him, light and quick. They stopped a foot or so from him.

"Did I do something wrong?" Clarissa asked.

"No," Jack replied.

"Then why are you shutting down on me?"

"To protect you."

"I don't need protection," she said.

"If I'm worrying about you then I might screw up. If I screw up then one of us might end up dead." He stood up and took both her hands in his. "If you end up dead I won't be able to live with myself. Got it?"

"You're too good to mess up that bad, Jack."

"Explain the last two weeks then."

Bear stepped into the clearing. "It's six. We need to head back."

Jack let go of Clarissa's hands and followed Bear back to the car. They all got in and drove back to Ameglia in silence.

"That's a guard," Jack said. "Definitely one of Charles's men."

Bear stopped the car next to the curb a hundred or so yards away.

"You sure, Jack?" he asked.

"Yeah, I recognize him."

"How many you think he's got with him?" Bear asked.

"Not sure," Jack said. "I know he has a man named Alonso with him. He's working for the old man, against his will from what I gather. So we need to be on high alert. This could be a setup."

Jack looked back at Clarissa. "You recognize that man?"

She leaned forward between the two front seats and narrowed her eyes. Her lips shifted back and forth. She shook her head. "No. Never saw him before."

"Good." Jack handed her a pair of large dark sunglasses. "Put those on." He got out of the car and pulled the seat forward. "Go down there and distinct him. Try to get him over to the corner of the restaurant."

"How?" she asked.

"Use your assets." He winked.

She smiled.

Jack got back in the car. "When she reaches the building start moving slowly."

"OK," Bear said.

"Now," Jack said.

Bear started the small car and approached the building.

"Stop here," Jack said.

They watched as Clarissa walked past the guard. She turned her head toward the bald man wearing sunglasses and a black suit. Jack figured she smiled at him. As she walked past the far end, she fell to the ground and clutched at her ankle.

"Wait," Jack said.

The guard turned and walked over to her. Knelt down and reached for her leg.

"Now," Jack said.

Bear stepped on the gas and stopped in front of where Clarissa lay on the ground.

Jack opened the door, hit the pavement and lunged at the man. Jack's outstretched left arm caught the man on the neck. Jack wrapped tight and pulled him to the side of the building. Jack sat back, leaning against the building, choking the guard.

Bear appeared a moment later. He leaned over and delivered two bone crushing shots across the man's face.

The guard went limp in Jack's arm.

Bear pulled him off of Jack and carried him behind the building. He returned a moment later. "He's out."

Jack turned to Clarissa. "How do I look? Any blood?"

She shook her head as she straightened out her clothes.

"OK," Jack said. "Here's the plan. Clarissa you go in and talk to the hostess. Tell her to hang on, come back out and tell us what you see."

She nodded and stepped around the corner of the building. Jack watched her slip in through the front door.

Two minutes later she stepped outside and returned to the side of the building.

"There's another man," she said. "Dressed like the one out here. He is standing in front of a closed off room."

The door opened. Jack looked around the corner. He saw a tall, well-built dark haired man step onto the sidewalk. The man held a cell phone to his ear and fumbled with a cigarette with his other hand.

"Alonso," Jack said as he ducked behind the building again.

"I'll take him out," Bear said.

"OK," Jack said. He pointed at Clarissa. "You distract the guard. Get him away from that room."

"How?" she asked.

"You go inside and tell the hostess to seat you. See the table and then change course. Walk up to him and whisper in his ear. Tell him to follow you to the ladies room."

She smiled.

"And then beat the hell out of him in there," Jack said.

"OK," Clarissa said.

She stepped around the corner. Jack held his breath until he heard the door close behind. He nodded at Bear.

Bear stepped around the corner and Jack heard two thuds. Bear's fist hitting Alonso's face and Alonso's face hitting the ground.

Jack moved to the door. "Good work, Bear. Wait thirty seconds and then come in."

Jack pushed through the door. He looked around. Saw Clarissa leading the guard by his tie toward the restrooms. Jack smiled. He ignored the hostess and moved through the restaurant toward the back corner and the room with a curtain drawn shut. He stopped outside the curtain and listened.

No one said anything.

He peeked through a tiny slit.

Charles was the only one in there.

Jack opened the curtain and sat down at the table, gun drawn and pointed at Charles's head.

"Hello Jack," Charles said calmly. He placed his hands flat on the table in front of him

"Charles," Jack said with a nod of his head.

"What brings you to Italy?"

"Your boss," Jack said. "He wants me to kill you."

Charles smiled.

"Something funny?" Jack asked.

"It's a death sentence, Jack."

"What is? Working for the old man?"

"No." Charles lifted his hand and reached for his jacket.

"That's enough of that." Jack straightened his arm for emphasis.

"Relax," Charles said. "I'm just getting my smokes."

Jack kept his arm tight and his finger resting on the trigger. He watched Charles pull back his coat and produce a pack of cigarettes.

"Want one?" Charles asked.

"Trying to quit," Jack said.

Charles shrugged.

"What's a death sentence?" Jack asked.

"Killing me." He lit his cigarette and let the smoke slowly escape his mouth.

"For you."

Charles smiled. "Half the old man's organization is behind me. Ready for a change, so to speak. They are tired of his leadership. Things are a mess. Jobs are botched. We are losing our grip."

"The whole organization can go to hell for all I care," Jack said.

"You get the point, though, Jack? You do something to me and they'll know who did it. A hundred guys will be after you, ready to take you down."

Jack shrugged.

"How'd you know where to find me?" Charles asked.

Jack smiled. "Your followers aren't as loyal as you think." He sat back in his chair, but kept the gun pointed at Charles.

Bear pushed through the curtain, dragging Alonso with him. Blood poured from the dark-haired man's nose.

"Why don't you ask him?" Jack said, pointing at Alonso.

Charles shook his head. "You ratted me out to the old man?"

Alonso gritted his teeth and cleared his throat. He spit blood on the floor. "He's got my kid, Charles. Left me no choice."

Charles pushed his chair back.

"Don't move," Jack said. He shot a look at Bear and ticked his head to the side.

Bear stepped back and pulled Alonso out of the room.

"Let's cut the crap, Jack. How much is he paying you?"

"Curious how much your life is worth?" Jack asked.

"I couldn't care less. I just want to make you an offer."

"I'm listening."

"It really doesn't matter what you do here, Jack. You kill me and it's next man up. A lot of guys want change within the organization. You can kill the next guy and someone else will take his place. Understand?"

Jack nodded and said nothing.

"The old man is going down. You do this job for him, and you are going down too."

Jack thought about Mandy for a moment, pushed the thought from his head and nodded again.

"Help me take him down, Jack."

Jack raised an eyebrow and opened his mouth to speak.

"I'm willing to let bygones be bygones, Jack. You cracked my skull, left me with a few scars. Screw it, it's in the past. I beat on your lady a bit, she beat on me. Screw it, it's in the past."

Jack nodded.

"Leave now, let me live and you and I have no problems anymore," Charles said.

Jack stood up. His gun still aimed at Charles's head.

"If you agree to help me take down the old man, I'll triple whatever he offered you. Are you in?"

Jack shrugged. He lowered his weapon. "You can live. I'll think about the rest."

He slipped through the opening in the curtain.

"I'm serious, Jack," Charles called from the enclosed room. "I'll triple it."

Jack saw Bear and Clarissa standing near the room. Bear lifted his arms, hunched his shoulders.

"Let's go," Jack said.

"You're not completing the job?" Bear asked.

"No," Jack said. "You and I need to talk about that."

They left the restaurant quickly and piled into the little car.

CHAPTER 16

T hump, thump, thump.

Jack sat up in bed.

"C'mon Jack, open up." Bear said from the hall.

Jack took a deep breath. Leaned back. He looked over at the tuft of dark red hair covering the pillow next to his. He rubbed Clarissa's back with his hand and brushed her hair to the side. Kissed her neck.

He got up and threw on a pair of shorts. He opened the door and stepped into the hall.

"What do we need to talk about, Jack?"

"The old man," Jack said. "He told me if I don't do what he wants he'll go after Mandy."

"She's being taken care of."

"He knows she's in Montana."

Bear looked up at the ceiling and wrapped his massive hands around the back of his head. "I need to leave."

"I know."

"What about you?" Bear asked.

Jack shrugged and leaned back against the floral printed wall. "My face is all over the news. I'm missing. I can't risk getting caught. I'll transfer some funds. You'll need to wire me some cash."

"There's something else, Jack."

Jack raised an eyebrow.

"A body washed up. One of the Russians."

Jack said, "The kid say anything?"

"They didn't show him. But who knows what he's saying to the police."

"I'll call Pierre. Find out what he knows."

Bear took a step back and leaned up against the wall opposite Jack. "What about Clarissa?"

"I don't know if she can fly. This isn't a safe place for her, though."

"I'll take her to Rome, get her on a transAtlantic."

Jack nodded. "That's probably best."

Bear turned and walked to his room.

Jack stepped back in his. Closed the door. Turned around and saw Clarissa sitting on the edge of the bed with a sheet barely covering her body.

She smiled.

He frowned.

"What's wrong?" she asked.

"You have to go," he said.

"Where?"

"Back to the States."

"Aren't you going too?" she asked.

"Can't," he said. "At least not yet."

"Why?"

"I'm supposed to be missing."

"So, you've been found." She stood up and wrapped the sheet around her body, covering her chest down.

"One of the other men from the boat washed ashore."

"I'm guessing that's a bad thing."

"Yeah," he said. "It's not good."

"One thing before I go?"

"Anything."

She dropped the sheet and grabbed him by the waistband of his shorts. Pulled him onto the bed. They held each other in passion. An hour later they fell asleep with the morning sunlight filtering in through the window.

Bear drove and Clarissa sat in the passenger seat. He focused on the road and she stared out the window. They didn't say much. She thought about Jack and wondered how long until she would see him again. Finally, she spoke.

"What's on your mind, Bear?"

Bear cleared his throat. "Mandy."

"She OK?"

"Yeah, but," Bear paused, "I need to get her to a safe place."

"Where am I going?"

"Putting you on a cruise ship, transAtlantic. You'll dock in Cape Canaveral. Once docked you have four hours to find and board another ship. That one is going to the Virgin Islands. You are going to get off in the Virgin Islands and not get back on the ship." He reached into his pocket and pulled out a piece of paper. Handed it to her. "That's the number of an old friend of mine. He lives in the islands. He's going to meet you at the pier."

Clarissa took the paper from Bear and looked at the phone number. She went to work memorizing the ten digits.

Bear continued, "I'm going to be down there a few weeks after you get there. Me and Mandy."

"OK," Clarissa said.

They didn't speak the rest of the trip. When they reached the dock, Bear got out and told her to wait. He returned with a ticket and a duffel bag. He handed both to her along with a stack of bills.

"That's five thousand euros and five thousand dollars. Go shopping, get some clothes. Fill the bag. Your ship leaves in eight hours. You can board an hour from now. Spend the next hour or so in the mall right there."

She looked over his shoulder at the collection of stores. She leaned in and gave the large man a hug and kiss on the cheek.

"You be careful," she said.

"You too." Bear got in the car and drove away.

Clarissa followed his advice and spent as much of the money as she could on new clothes. Two hours later she boarded the cruise ship and locked herself in her cabin.

CHAPTER 17

Sergei Ivanov sat back in his oversized leather chair. His heavy black boots rested on the antique dark wood desk. He held a typed letter in his thick hands and read it intently.

Across from him two men fidgeted in their seats.

"What is the meaning of this?" Sergei asked in Russian.

"Murdered," one of the men said. "Dorofeyev was murdered. It was no accident."

Sergei dropped his legs. Leaned in. "Who did this?"

"We think it is a man called Noble." The other man reached into a briefcase, retrieved a photo and handed it to Sergei.

"Jack Noble." Sergei stood and walked across the room. He looked at his reflection in the silver rimmed mirror. His brown hair was parted on the side, thinning a bit. Made sense considering his age. At least he hadn't gone grey. He scratched at the silver speckled scruff on his face and turned back toward the men. "What do we know about Jack Noble?"

"He's an American," one of the men said.

"Did he act alone?"

"We think he was working with the French."

"You think or you know?" Sergei asked.

"We can't say for certain." The man turned to his associate. "Bring him in."

The other man got up and went to the door. He knocked three times and opened it. "Come with me."

Sergei stared at the heavy set man with reddish-brown hair on the side of his head. "Who are you?" he said in English

"Oscar," the man said.

"You have information for me?" Sergei asked.

Oscar nodded. "For a price."

Sergei smiled. "Name it and you shall have it Mr. ...?"

"Oscar is all you need to know. And the price is five hundred thousand."

"Euros I presume?"

"Yeah," Oscar replied.

"Deal." Sergei snapped his fingers and one of the men disappeared. "Now, tell me what I need to know."

"The man who killed your men is an independent contractor named Jack Noble. He gave me an alias, but I knew who he was. He's working with a French operator named Pierre." Oscar reached into his shirt pocket, pulled out a cigarette.

Sergei nodded at the man. "Continue."

"The French government, or at least some part of it, is onto your plans."

"What do you know of my plans?" Sergei asked.

Oscar leaned back in his seat and crossed his arms. "Me? Nothing."

"This Pierre, what more can you tell me of him?"

"Not much," Oscar replied. "Based in Paris. Leads a team. He's covert."

"Can you pick him out of a lineup?"

"With my eyes closed," Oscar said.

Sergei pointed at his man standing behind Oscar. "You find everything we have on France. Find me all operators named Pierre." He returned his attention to Oscar. "So this man, Jack Noble, the reports say he is missing too. What do you think of that?"

"It's made up. They just don't know where he is."

"Do you?"

"Italy. Near La Spezia or Genoa."

"How do you know this?"

Oscar smiled. Held out his hands. "I can't give up all my sources."

"You sure about that?"

"Yeah, I'm sure."

Sergei nodded at the man standing behind Oscar. He dropped his eyes and smiled as his man slammed a blackjack into the back of Oscar's skull.

Oscar fell forward onto the desk. Blood leaked from his head onto the antique wood.

"Get him out of here," Sergei said. "And get a team to Genoa."

"Yes sir," the man said.

"I want this Jack Noble, and I want him alive. We will break him and make him our own. Or he'll die." Sergei turned and looked out his window at the empty compound behind the building. "Commence Operation Black Dolphin."

EPISODE 4

CHAPTER 1

"Tag," Mandy said. "You're it."

"You always tag me," Bernie said.

Mandy giggled. "You're too slow."

"Let's play hide and seek now," Bernie said.

"What do the little kids think?" Mandy put her hands on Bernie's little brother and sister and winked at their friend Mac.

"They do whatever I say." Bernie scrunched up her face and glared at the little kids. "Right?"

The three younger kids nodded in unison.

"Hide and seek sounds fun," her little brother said.

"Not it," Mandy said.

The three little kids took off running.

"Fine," Bernie said. "I'll go first. One, two, three..."

Mandy turned and ran toward the corner of the house. No way would Bernie find her today. She had already scouted the property for the best hiding spot, and today she would use it. She ducked around the side of the house and peeked back around the corner. Bernie stood against the tree, face first, counting out loud.

"Twenty-one, twenty-two, twenty-three..."

Mandy had until fifty to hide. The little kids were already out of sight, although she was positive she could find them with ease if she needed to.

Mandy slid along the side of the house and bolted for the cover of the trees. She ran through the woods along the first line of trees then cut back into the open area between the woods and the shed. A quick sprint and she was behind the big shed, out of view. She fiddled with the wood block that held the crawl access door closed. It came loose and she opened the little door. Mandy slipped under the shed, head first, and reached back to close the access door.

She crawled under the shed, belly scraping on the ground as she slid under the sagging floorboards. A cutout at the front end provided her access to the area under the stairs. She slid through the opening and found a small piece of plywood that she secured against the opening. She exhaled loudly and took her place under the stairs.

They'll never find me here.

She giggled and peered through the narrow opening between the stairs.

"Fifty. Ready or not here I come."

Oh, I'm ready.

Bernie walked toward Mandy, stopped at the corner of the house and peeked around the corner. Bernie crouched low, either trying to stay out of sight or making herself ready to sprint off at a moment's notice.

One of the little kids yelled something in the distance. Mandy couldn't decipher what was said, but it seemed to catch Bernie's attention because she took off running across the front of the house, yelling.

Mandy sat back against the wall. Her thoughts turned to her mother. She wished she could see her again, even if just for five minutes, one last time to say goodbye. She never saw enough of her mom. And now she'd never see her again. Her eyes watered and a tear streamed down her face. Mandy sniffed and shook her head. Not today. No tears today. This was play time. Time to have fun. She diverted her thoughts to the good time she'd been having since Bear left her here over a week ago.

The kids played together rather than watching TV during the day. She got to see a few programs, but no more than one hour a day. That was Ms. Cathy's rule and all the kids had to follow it. Mandy didn't mind. These kids were fun. Not like the stuffy kids back home that wanted to sit on their computers all day long or watch boring TV shows. Here they played games, hiked through the woods near the house, and did creative things inside if it rained.

Ms. Cathy taught her things, interesting things. Not like school where she had to sit all day and would end up daydreaming out of boredom.

She couldn't wait to see Bear again and maybe Ms. Clarissa and Jack, but she wasn't sure that she wanted to leave her new family.

A family. A real one, too.

This was the first time in Mandy's life that she felt like part of a real family.

"C'mon Mandy," Bernie called. "Where are you?"

Mandy covered her mouth and giggled. She'd make them wait it out a bit. When no one was looking, she'd get out. No way would she give up a hiding spot this sweet.

The group of kids approached. Mandy scooted back to the wall and made herself small. The kids stopped and turned toward the house. Mandy heard the roar of a car engine coming up the driveway. The kids ran toward the sound of an approaching vehicle. When the black car came into view, Mandy didn't recognize it. The other kids must not have either, because they all turned and disappeared from view as they went toward the porch stairs.

The sun was going down and the car had its lights on. The vehicle swung around and the bright lights blinded Mandy temporarily. Finally, the car stopped.

Mandy scooted forward to the stairs so she could get a better view of the car and whoever was inside of it.

The door opened. A man in a dark suit stepped out. He looked at the kids and then over both his shoulders. He leaned back into the car for a second and then emerged again.

Mandy gasped.

The man raised a long gun and fired.

Tat-tat-tat-tat-tat.

Mandy screamed, her eyes widened, her mouth dropped open. She put her hand over her face and scooted back against the wall. She could still see the car and the man. Two more men got out. They walked toward the porch. One of them, a big fat guy, looked her way but didn't seem to notice her.

Ms. Cathy burst outside and began yelling at the men.

"What have you done?" Ms. Cathy shook her hands in the air. She leapt from the porch and ran toward the men. One of them, a tall skinny man, raised his arm and shot her.

Mandy gasped. She fought back another scream.

Ms. Cathy fell to the ground and cried out in pain.

The man who drove the car barked orders at the other two. They lifted Ms. Cathy's body and brought her inside. The third man, the one who shot at the kids, got into the car and drove it toward Mandy. He turned right at the corner of the house and parked behind it. Mandy dug at the ground and lay as flat as she could. The man walked back around the house. He passed by the shed, close to her. She held her breath. It didn't look like he saw her.

262 / L.T. RYAN

262 / L . T . RYAN

It got quiet. Mandy passed the time by counting the beats of her heart. The sky grew dark. She found the courage to sit up and change positions and look through the slits between the stairs. She could see the porch now. One man sat in Mr. Scott's rocking chair. He had a long gun across his knees.

Mandy heard the roar of Mr. Scott's pickup truck approaching. She heard the tires kicking up gravel as the truck wound its way along the path to the house. The truck appeared and the lights flicked off as it neared the house. She wanted to run out there and warn Mr. Scott, but she was frozen in place.

Mr. Scott jumped out. "Who the hell are you?"

"Where's the girl?" the man on the porch asked.

"Who the hell are you?" Mr. Scott said again.

The man motioned with his hand. "Perhaps you didn't hear me the first time." The louder he got the more he sounded like the men from New York. "Where is the little girl?"

"Don't know what you're talking about," Mr. Scott said. "What are you doing on my property?"

The screen door opened and the skinny man backed out. He had Ms. Cathy's arms in his hands. The fat man had her feet. She didn't seem to be moving.

"What the hell is going on here?" Mr. Scott's face twisted and his jaw went slack. "Cathy?"

They dropped her body on the porch.

"You want that to be you?" the man in the chair asked.

Mr. Scott jumped into his truck and emerged with a long gun of his own.

The man in the chair stood and fired.

Tat-tat-tat.

Mr. Scott fell to the ground, clutching his leg. The shotgun lay a few feet away.

Mandy watched, her hand covering her mouth, afraid she'd scream again.

The three men stepped off the porch and walked over to Mr. Scott. They stood over him. The man with the long gun pointed it at Mr. Scott. He spoke, but it was too quiet for Mandy to hear what he said.

She did hear Mr. Scott scream out some curse words. Then she heard one more shot. She closed her eyes and made herself as small as possible against the wall. The sound of footsteps on the gravel path that led to the shed grew louder. They approached slowly and deliberately, one at a time. She opened her eyes to get a peek. Two legs in dark pants blocked out the light from the porch. A smaller light scanned the ground. It flicked through the openings in the staircase. She buried her head under her arms.

The wooden stairs creaked as he climbed them. She prayed it wasn't the fat man. He might actually fall through. She heard the door handle jiggle and then click. The sound of the man's footsteps echoed under the shed as he walked through the empty room. Moments later the door opened and she heard him directly above her. The slits in between the stairs lit up. First the top step, then the lower ones with every step he took. He stopped at the bottom step.

Mandy held her breath and counted the seconds.

"It's clear, Russ."

Russ.

"Let's get out of here. We'll call the old man on the way and let him know."

"What are we going to tell him?"

"The girl's dead."

Mandy heard the car start and then the sounds of the wheels sliding through the gravel. She moved forward to get a better view. The car turned. She watched the lights flicker through the trees as the men drove toward the road.

Mandy curled into a ball and cried herself to sleep.

CHAPTER 2

Sergei Ivanov sat behind his desk and stared at the two men sitting across from him. His elbows rested on the arms of his chair. His hands folded together in front of his chest. He stared at Julij and ignored the younger man to Julij's right who was several ranks lower than both of them.

"What do you have for me?" Sergei asked.

Julij stretched his arm across the wide desk, a folder in his hand. The contents spilled from the folder onto the desk. "Sorry." He fumbled with the photos and documents.

"Leave them," Sergei said. "Just tell me."

"Jack Noble," Julij said, "enlisted in the Marines at the age of eighteen. An athlete. He was supposed to play American football in college."

Sergei scooped up the mess of papers on his desk and organized them into a stack. He scanned them one at a time as Julij spoke.

"He decided not to go," Julij continued. "Enlisted as military intelligence but never got that far. Went to sniper school right after basic training."

Sergei looked up. "Scout Sniper?"

"Yeah."

"Snipers aren't close range killers. How's that put him on a boat where he can kill three of our men along with two bodyguards?"

"Sir, we believe —" the younger man said.

"I'm not talking to you." Sergei held his hand up toward the younger man and kept his eyes focused on Julij. "What's he doing here, anyways?"

"Sir, he compiled the data I have here."

Sergei nodded. "Continue, Julij."

"Noble did eight years, we believe, in the Marines. Then we lose him for a couple years."

"Lose him?"

"Yes, sir. He just disappears."

"FBI?"

"We'd have a listing on him."

"CIA then?"

"Possible. Maybe NSA. We aren't sure. Our men are working on it, though."

Sergei frowned. "We can just assume he has advanced training."

Julij nodded. "Two years later he shows up again. Went into business for himself."

"What kind of business?"

"Independent contractor. Assassin for hire. Recon work."

"U.S.?"

The younger man raised his hand to speak. Sergei shook his head and shifted his gaze back to Julij.

"Global, it seems," Julij said. "Takes government work. Works a lot for Feng Chou in New York. Others as well. Seems he did quite a few jobs for a lady we only know as codename Blue Willow, formerly of British Military Intelligence."

"Anything recent?"

Julij nodded. "We believe he is responsible for stealing documents from a group of radicals."

"Do we care?"

"You know the documents I speak of, sir. And yes, we care. We care if the plans are in the hands of anyone but the radicals. The information could damage our cause."

"Make sure we press him on that." Sergei stared at a picture of Jack. "What were you doing in France, Mr. Noble?"

"There was a hit on a film producer, Foster or something like that. He was into a few criminal activities. We think that a U.S. agency was behind the hit. They contracted Mr. Noble to handle it."

"We think? Or we know?"

Julij's lips thinned. "Think, at this time. We can question him on it. We also believe the French spy was in on it."

"Do we have a lead on him?" Sergei asked.

"Yes," Julij responded. "We are working on that now."

"Excellent." Sergei stood and walked to the window. "There was a time when an act like this would have given us every right to go to war. But now, with these pansies running our government?"

"I know, sir."

Sergei returned to his desk, opened a drawer and pulled out two cigars. He handed one to Julij. "So where is Jack Noble now?"

Julij lit his cigar, puffed on it a few times and leaned back in his chair. "Our team turned up nothing in Genoa. But we've been able to persuade Oscar to give up a bit more information. He's been able to place him in a small town called Levanto. We doubt he is there now, but perhaps he made a friend while in town."

"When will our men be there?" Sergei asked.

"Within an hour or two."

"Excellent." Sergei stood and saluted Julij. "Dismissed."

Julij stood, saluted and started toward the door.

"One more thing," Sergei said.

Julij stopped and turned to his partner. "Leave us."

Once the other man left, Sergie continued. "How are our relations with the gangster you mentioned?"

"Feng Chou? Neutral, I'd say."

"Maybe we should reach out to him. Perhaps he could be persuaded to help."

"Yes, sir," Julij said as he left the room.

Sergei leafed through the documents on his desk. He found himself impressed by Jack's body of work. He picked up the picture again.

"Mr. Noble," he said to the picture. "Will you come to work for me and help restore Russia to its rightful place in the world? Will I have to break you first? Or maybe I should just kill you..."

CHAPTER 3

Jack flipped through the TV channels. Twenty-two stations, not a thing on. Some things were the same no matter where you hid out. The hotel bored him. All the hotels bored him. He couldn't remember the last time he spent this much time in a hotel doing next to nothing. He'd hit the gym in the morning and late at night. Swim laps a couple times. Other than that he found himself confined to the room and the tiny balcony.

He found a commercial with two scantily clad Italian women tossing an orange back and forth. He stopped and watched. Decided it'd be a good opportunity to brush up on his Italian.

His cell phone vibrated against the wooden nightstand. He answered without checking the caller ID. It didn't matter. Only a handful of people had the number and he'd talk to any of them right now.

"This is Jack."

"It's Pierre."

"How's my favorite Frenchman?"

"You need to move, Jack."

"Am I blocking the view?"

Pierre paused. "I appreciate your sense of humor, Jack, but this is serious. You are in trouble."

"Thought you said this was serious."

"Jack, listen to me. The Russians, they are after you."

Jack sat up. "Explain?"

"I don't have much time."

"Then get to it."

"My source tells me that they apprehended our friend Oscar."

"He's your friend."

"Whatever. They apprehended him and he gave your location to them."

"Who is this source?"

"Someone I know inside the Russian government. Young guy. Our paths crossed once five years ago."

"Where did Oscar tell them I am?"

"I don't know specifically, but I know they have multiple teams in Genoa right now." Pierre paused. "They know you were in Levanto. Jack, did you make any friends there?"

Jack stood and walked to the balcony. He stepped outside.

"Jack?"

"Yeah, I'm here. Got any friends nearby?"

"No one I can trust."

"Is there anyone you can trust now, Pierre?"

Pierre chuckled. "Afraid not."

"Saying I'm alone on this one?"

"For now, yes. Get to Naples. I think I can help you there."

"Think? I'm not driving six hundred miles for 'think.' Christ, you know I can't fly or take the train with my picture all over the place for the boat incident."

"Best I got right now, Jack."

Jack sighed. "Damn you, Pierre."

"Damn you too, Jack."

Jack hung up, walked to the bathroom, closed the door behind him. He stared at his reflection in the mirror. He ran his hands through his hair and scratched at the stubble on his face. He traced the thin lines extending from the corners of his eyes. When had he started to age? Feeling young was what was important. At least that was what he told himself. He reached under the sink and pulled out the complimentary grooming kit. He unzipped it and left it sitting open on the counter. He turned on the shower faucet, took a deep breath and stuck his head under the stream of water to wet his hair.

He placed a towel over the sink and pulled the scissors from the grooming bag. He went to work on his hair, cutting it short and uneven, letting the clippings fall onto the towel. He bundled up the towel and placed it in the trash. He reached into the bag and pulled out a razor and shaving cream. He wet his head again. He put shaving cream on his face and head, ran the razor under water and proceeded to shave off everything but his eyebrows.

He washed the remaining shaving cream from his face and dried off. He laughed at his reflection in the mirror, remembering why he didn't keep his hair close cut after leaving the Marines. The bald look did not suit him.

Jack stepped out of the elevator and into the lobby. He walked to the front desk and smiled at the woman with the nametag that said Jemma.

"How may I help you sir?" she asked.

Jack frowned. "Don't recognize me?"

She peered at him through narrowed eyes. Her thin upper lip disappeared as she pressed her lips tight. "Mr. Smith? Is that you?"

Jack laughed. "I know, looks horrible."

"No," she said. "I think it's an improvement."

Jack shrugged and shook his head. "Everyone's got an opinion, I guess."

She smiled. "Well, mine is the one that counts."

"Look," Jack said. "I need a car. Problem is, with no ID I can't rent one. Any way you can help me out?"

"How long do you need to borrow it for?"

"Couple days. Four at the most."

"Where are you going?"

"Rome."

She whistled. "That's a long drive."

Jack placed five hundred euros on the desk.

"And as long as you have it back to me in four days it shouldn't be a problem." She grabbed the money and handed Jack her keys. "Blue car, around back. Can't miss it."

Jack lifted an eyebrow but didn't question her. "Thank you. Hold my room another week?"

"Yes, Mr. Smith. Will do."

Jack exited through the hotel's rear door. It didn't take him long to find the car. Small. Blue. *Jemma* written across the side in sparkly gold letters.

"For Christ's sake."

Jack opened the car door, sighed and packed his body into the cramped space. He started the car and checked his fuel. The gauge read full. He felt confident he could get far on a single tank of gas in the little car. He pulled out of the lot and followed signs to the highway.

It had only been a day since Bear and Clarissa left. He hadn't spoken to either of them since. Clarissa was getting close. Too close. Being close to a woman wasn't something Jack was used to. In his world, romantic relationships caused problems. He ended relationships the moment he felt them going somewhere.

The past two weeks spiraled out of control because of a commitment he had made years ago to protect Clarissa. Jack laughed. He knew he was lying to himself. It went beyond the commitment to her dad. His feelings for Clarissa had grown into something more than that of a protector. Maybe he'd retire from the business. Money wouldn't be an issue. He had enough stored up to last a lifetime. He thought about where they could go. The islands were nice. He always enjoyed his time in the Keys and the Caribbean. Hell, they could go to South America or even better, Australia. He'd never set foot on the Australian continent before. If there was one place Jack Noble could hide, Australia was it.

Would Clarissa go for it? Jack had no idea, but he decided he would ask next time he talked to her.

Jack merged onto the highway. The chatter in his mind settled down as he focused on the traffic around him. One wrong move in a tin can like Jemma's car and he'd be dead. The thought held a sliver of appeal. At least then he wouldn't have to worry about Charles, the old man, or the Russians.

CHAPTER 4

"What do you think?" Charles leaned back in his chair, strategically placed in the corner of the room. He could see the front door, the back door and the street through the front window. He had men positioned outside and kept two plus Alonso with him at all times.

"About what?" Alonso cocked his head to the side.

"Should I go to war with him?"

"Jack? Or the old man?"

Charles shrugged. "We'll worry about Jack later."

"Is there any way to work it out with him?"

Charles stared at his dark haired associate. "He just tried to have me killed. You tell me?"

"I'd say if you can work it out, then work it out."

"Why do you say that?"

"You can accomplish more if you make amends. You want to take on our boss, take on the world? Who's going to back you up when it's all done? You say you have half the organization in your pocket. What about the other half? Fifty percent of *those* men are sure to leave. Of the remaining, who can you really trust? How do you know someone else might not take a stab at offing you? Hell, I could do that, Charles."

Charles sat back in his seat. His large thumbs massaged his temples. He shifted his eyes toward Alonso. "You might be right."

"I am right. You know it." He picked up Charles's phone and placed it in front of him. "Call him."

"Leave the room." Charles picked up the phone and nodded toward the door. "Oh, and you better be kidding about offing me."

Alonso smiled, got up from the table and closed the door behind him.

Charles thought for a moment. What did he want to accomplish with this call? He didn't plan to suck up to the old man. Hell with that. He had to be strong. If they were going to co-exist it needed to be in a capacity of equals. He'd had enough of taking care of Feng's castoffs and dirty work. He'd proven himself a loyal soldier and a great leader. If the old man knew how many of his own men were ready to defect, the bastard would probably disappear. Or go on a killing spree. Charles figured it would be the latter.

He poured a drink and slammed it in a single gulp. He pushed the tiny buttons on the phone with his large hands. The phone rang.

"Mr. Charles, how are you?" the old man answered.

"Let's get right to it, Boss." He figured it was better to use his usual greeting rather than the old man's first name. "Why'd you do it?"

"You gave me every reason to do it."

"Maybe so. But to send Jack. What the hell was that?"

"I had a feeling Mr. Jack would not complete the job."

"A feeling? You risked my life because of a feeling?"

"No, Mr. Charles. At the time I contracted Mr. Jack, I wanted you dead. You know better than to mess with me, yet you did."

Charles didn't say anything.

"After I thought it over, I hoped that you would fight back. I figured if one of you were out of the picture, things might be better for me."

"Is that right?"

"But I've had a change of heart. I believe we can maintain our relationship. Don't you?"

Charles laughed. "Crazy S.O.B."

"How do you like Europe?"

"Food's good," Charles responded.

"How'd you like to stay there, Mr. Charles?"

"I'm not following."

"It has come to my attention that there is a void to fill with the recent demise of one Mr. Foster."

"Go on," Charles said.

"He was moving quite a bit of product through Paris. Now his organization has split into five factions, all of which compete with other Parisian organizations."

Charles moved to the front of the room and stared out at the quiet street.

"I believe that you have a loyal following within our organization, Mr. Charles."

Our?

"And I believe that relocating part of that following to Europe could lead to quite a bit of expansions for us."

"What is this 'our' and 'us' talk?"

"When you first came to me, you were incompetent. No argument there, right Mr. Charles?"

Charles said nothing.

"Hell, I had to give you directions when you first started driving for me. But I saw something in you. And over time you grew into the kind of leader I thought you would. But I never anticipated how powerful you would become."

Charles still said nothing.

"I understand the dynamics here. A lot of my men are loyal to you, Mr. Charles."

"Don't do anything to those men," Charles said.

The old man laughed. "Why would I? Well, at first I was going to. But then I realized something. You know what I realized?"

"You were losing control?" Charles said.

"Just the opposite," the old man said. "You see, we are in a unique position here. We can expand. I have you, and that means I don't have to worry about how things will be run if I'm not around."

"What took you so long?"

"Let's get one thing clear though," the old man said. "Do not for a minute think that you would still be alive if I wanted you dead. Jack was not the only one there who could have killed you that night."

Who else did he send? Charles sat down and rubbed his forehead. "So put this to me in simple terms. What are you saying?"

"I want you to relocate to Paris at once. I have purchased a place for you there. You will head up our European operations until I am ready to retire, at which point you will move back to New York and take over the organization."

Charles sat back, said nothing.

"Mr. Charles," the old man said. "Do you accept this offer?"

"What about Jack?"

"Why are you so difficult?"

"He let me live. He had me, Feng. He could have killed me and he didn't."

"So you want him dead now?"

"I want his respect," Charles said. "Or I want him dead."

"Let's forget about Mr. Jack. As I understand it, he is in a lot of trouble and we might not have to worry about him again."

Charles grinned.

"As to him not killing you and you wanting him dead," the old man said. "A life had to be taken, Mr. Charles. And a life has been taken."

"Who?"

"Not to worry. Get to Paris."

"Ok, Boss."

"Please, call me Feng from now on."

Charles grinned.

The old man hung up the phone and sat back in his chair. "So difficult, I don't understand him. When did he become like this?"

"No idea, Boss," Miguel said.

The old man looked at his new second in command. Barely thirty, Miguel had not a speckle of silver in his dark hair, nor a line on his face. His dark eyes gave nothing away, and his good looks charmed the ladies that willingly came through the compound. The old man had taken notice of Miguel a few years earlier and had watched his progress since. He worked well with all of the other captains in the organization and seemed a natural fit to back up operations here. Maybe he'd even be a candidate for west coast operations if they decided to expand into new territory.

"Do you have the documents prepared?"

"Yes," Miguel said. "Pretty difficult. We had to decipher the code."

"How did you manage that?"

"Hayward," Miguel said. "Turns out he has a background in code rigging."

The old man shrugged. "Whatever."

"Well, anyway, here it is."

"What's it say?" the old man asked. "Have you looked?"

"Why don't you take a look yourself?"

Feng opened the folder and scanned through the documents. He lifted his eyebrows and smiled.

He looked up from the papers. "This name here," he pointed at the documents, "why does that sound so familiar?"

Miguel straightened up and leaned forward. "Korzhakov?"

"Yes, Korzhakov. I recognize that name."

"Our friend, Jack Noble."

"Oh yes, the thing on the boat." Feng straightened and read over the documents again. "Tell me, Miguel, why would a high ranking Russian official be communicating with a radical group intent on overthrowing the U.S. government?"

Miguel lifted an eyebrow and read through the documents. "How did we get these?"

"The same friend you mentioned a moment ago. He secured them for us while they were in transport."

"On your orders?"

"Yes, that is correct, Mr. Miguel."

"How did you know about them?"

Feng stood up and walked around the table, behind Miguel. He placed his hands on Miguel's shoulders. "Why so many questions, my young companion?"

Miguel shrugged. "Just curious."

"First thing you need to realize is that you are not privy to all my information."

Miguel nodded and said nothing.

"I have my hands in many pots and I have many sources. That is all you need to know. Now back to my question. Why?"

"I guess because they are planning something together."

"Very good, Mr. Miguel," the old man said. "They are planning something together. Or were planning, I should say. What do you think of this?"

"Risky," Miguel said. "Very risky."

The old man sat down and smiled at his associate. "You look worried."

"I'm not that into government overthrows," Miguel said.

Feng laughed. "Overthrows? Mr. Miguel, me neither. And quite frankly I think it's a fool's plan. These fanatics, they have a lot of followers and might be able to do some damage locally. But they are no competition for the U.S. military."

Miguel shrugged. "So why do you care about these documents?"

"Money," Feng said. "I'll sell them to the highest bidder."

CHAPTER 5

The closest flight Bear could get took him to Salt Lake City. He rented a car and drove north toward Billings. He'd been driving nine hours straight. He pushed the little car to 120 miles per hour. The signs on Highway 12 flew by in a blur. He slowed as he neared the turn for Scott's place. The small car bounced along the driveway as gravel kicked up against the undercarriage. He pulled into the clearing, turned off the car and got out.

He stood at the base of the porch stairs and listened. Complete silence. He gripped his pistol tight. He inspected the stairs and the porch. And there he saw it.

Blood.

He reached down to see if the puddle of blood was fresh. It barely smeared. He stood up, held his gun out and went to the door. He peered through the windows and saw an empty house. The door sat cracked open about two inches. He pushed. The door opened further. Bear slipped through the opening and walked into the house.

"Oh, Jesus Christ," he said.

Scott lay on the floor, eyes wide open.

Cathy lay on the couch, her shirt soaked in blood, her chest heaving slightly. He went to her side and felt her pulse, it was weak but steady.

He glanced around the room, saw four children on the floor behind the dining room table. Bear rushed over to them. Their hands and feet were bound, their mouths gagged. Three were asleep, but Bernie was awake. Her wide eyes watered over when she saw Bear. He nodded at her, brought a finger to his mouth, and turned away. He'd get to her after he found Mandy.

He crept through the house, stopped at the base of the stairs. He heard crying from upstairs. Bear rushed up the steps, three and four at a time. He broke down the door the crying came from.

"Stop!" The little girl held a shotgun in her tiny hands. "I'll shoot."

"Mandy," Bear said. "It's me, Bear."

Mandy looked up, set the shotgun down, wiped the tears from her eyes. "Oh, Bear." She leapt into Bear's outstretched arms and sobbed and shook uncontrollably. He stroked her hair. She calmed down after a few minutes. "The men, they pulled up in a car and just started shooting."

"Shhh," Bear tried to quiet her.

"And they killed Bernie and the other kids, and then Ms. Cathy, and then Mr. Scott. They killed them all." She started sobbing.

"The kids are OK, Mandy," Bear said. "Cathy is hurt, but she's alive."

"Mr. Scott?"

Bear shook his head.

Mandy clenched her mouth and eyes tight and cried some more. Finally, she composed herself and said, "One of the men was named Russ."

"Russ?"

"Yeah, I heard them call him Russ."

"Did you see him?"

She shook her head. "Not very well."

Bear took a deep breath. He knew a Russ that worked for the old man. He knew him well, in fact. Bear would have to pay a visit to Russ in the near future.

"I want to get out of here, Bear."

"Ok, Mandy. Let's go." He carried the girl downstairs, held her head tight against him so she wouldn't see Scott's body.

She cried when they passed him.

He set her down by the front door and instructed her to not turn around. Bear walked back to Bernie, untied her, told her to call the police at once.

"Please stay, Uncle Riley."

"I can't."

"Why not?"

"Cops will slow me down."

Bernie said nothing. She clutched the phone tight in her hands.

"And don't tell them I was here."

Bernie nodded, wiped her face with her sleeve, and pressed *nine-one-one* and brought the phone to her head.

Bear got up, went to the front, grabbed Mandy and brought her outside. He put her in the front seat of the car and buckled her seat belt. He got in on the other side.

She turned to look at him. Tear tracks stained her pale cheeks. "Ms. Cathy says I'm supposed to sit in the back seat."

"Do you want to sit in back?"

"No," she said. "Where are we going?"

"Florida," said Bear.

"What's in Florida?"

"We're going to pick up a friend."

"In Florida?"

"Well, an island nearby," Bear said.

Mandy shook her head. "How far is it?"

"Pretty far, kid. Going to be a long drive."

"Can't we just fly?"

Bear thought this over on the way to Montana. Too risky to fly right now. The old man had many people on his payroll, and most likely had someone who could notify him the minute Bear and Mandy showed up on a computer screen. Hell, he probably already had a team on their way to Salt Lake City.

"It's not a good idea, sweetie. We'll just have to drive."

She sighed. "I'm going to need some books, markers, and an MP3 player."

Bear laughed. "An MP3 player? You don't like talking to me?"

"No, I don't like that rocker roller music you play."

"Don't even think I'm going to put on some teenie bop music, kid."

"What's teenie bop?" Mandy asked.

Bear laughed. "We'll stop in Billings."

He pulled out on the road and pressed the gas pedal down as far as it would go. An ambulance flew by in the opposite direction, followed by three sheriff vehicles. He watched them in the rear-view mirror until they disappeared from sight.

Bear pulled the car into an empty spot in the parking lot, got out and led Mandy into the superstore. "Let's get you some clothes first."

"OK." She pulled his hand and led him toward the girl's section.

"Know your size?"

"Mmhmm, yes I do," she said.

"Go ahead and grab what you want. Fill this cart."

Mandy's eyes widened and she smiled for the first time since he'd taken her from the house. She went to work picking out outfits.

Bear watched with a smile on his face.

"OK, done."

"That's all you're getting?" Bear asked.

Mandy nodded.

"OK, what else did you want?"

Mandy led him to the electronics department. She stopped at the MP3 players.

Bear shook his head.

"Please?" Mandy said.

"Fine, which one you want?"

"This one," she said.

"Put it in the cart."

She did.

"What else?"

Mandy led him down the main aisle until they came to the book section. She grabbed a couple books to read as well as a couple activity books. She threw a box of markers into the cart.

"OK, let's get out of here," Bear said.

He headed toward the front of the store. Mandy followed. They found an empty line and put everything on the belt. Bear looked around the store. His eyes settled on a tall man with black and silver hair. He looked familiar.

"What's wrong?" Mandy asked.

Bear didn't realize that he hunched over the cart and was squinting. "Nothing. Stay behind me."

Mandy grabbed onto Bear and stood behind him.

"Sir?" the cashier said. "Sir? How will you be paying?"

Bear looked over his shoulder and handed the cashier a credit card.

"We have a machine for that," the cashier said.

"Just run it," Bear said.

"Fine."

Bear finally recognized the man as James Reston. The last time he saw James, the man had partnered with Russ. Bear turned back to face the register.

"Sign the machine," the cashier said.

Bear signed, grabbed the bags and picked up Mandy. He left the cart at the register, headed for the door, taking one last look back over his shoulder. James was gone and he didn't see Russ.

"What's going on, Bear?"

"Nothing," Bear said. "We need to get out of here."

Bear bolted for the car. He put Mandy in the car and told her to buckle up. He threw the bags in the backseat.

"Hey," she said. "What about my stuff?"

"Get it in a bit," Bear said as he got in the car. "We need to go."

What the hell were they doing this close? Did they think he might come this way?

Bear rationalized the situation. They weren't following him. No way would they be standing in the middle of the store like that if they were. More than likely they were waiting for further instructions from the old man or Charles. They'd camped out in Billings, closest thing to a big city for hundreds of miles. Seeing them was just a coincidence and a reminder that Bear needed to put as much distance between themselves and Montana as possible tonight. There would be a time and place to deal with the men, but not now and not here.

He started the car, left the parking lot and merged onto the highway a few miles down the road.

CHAPTER 6

C larissa slipped through the door and onto the deck of the cruise ship. She leaned against the rail, stared out across the Atlantic Ocean, watched the sun rise. Miles of blue and orange watery desert spread out before her.

She thought about the day ahead. Yesterday she had spent the majority of the day walking on the track that wrapped around the sixth deck. The more ambitious passengers jogged by her, but none of them spent six hours circling the ship like she had. A few of the joggers acknowledged her. Most passed by without a word or a smile. Felt like home.

She couldn't help but be bored by the floating city. She had no interest in gambling, just a waste of money as far she was concerned. Drinks were free, but she didn't want to be caught in a situation where her instincts weren't intact. She could see a show, but then she'd just feel bad about dropping out of Juilliard and giving up her real performing career.

The food was good, too good, in fact. After two weeks of hospital and hotel food she could barely stop herself from sampling everything the ship's chefs had prepared. And for that reason, she'd spend another six hours or so walking around deck six today. Probably every day of the cruise, for that matter.

Thinking about food made her stomach growl. She stepped back inside and took the elevator up to the tenth deck to grab breakfast.

She picked her way through the buffet and found an empty table in the corner of the dining room. She sat with her back to the wall so she could watch everyone.

A man walked up. She guessed he was older than her, maybe forty judging by the strands of grey mixed in with his light brown hair. Expensive sunglasses sat atop his head. He had tan skin with distinguishing lines etched into his forehead.

"This seat taken?" he asked.

"Yes," Clarissa replied.

The man sat down.

Clarissa blinked at him. "I said it's—"

"I love these transAtlantic cruises. Know what I mean?"

"No," Clarissa said. She took a bite of her eggs.

"Seven days at sea, crossing the mighty Atlantic. Such a rush."

"Yeah," Clarissa said. "It's a real hoot."

"What's your name?"

"Sam," replied Clarissa.

"I'm Mike."

"I didn't ask."

Mike laughed. "Feisty, aren't you?"

"Don't you have a wife to get back to, Mike?"

He smiled. "Single."

"Well, I'm not. And if my very tall, very strong, very jealous boyfriend sees you sitting here talking to me, he'll probably beat your old ass."

Mike laughed. "You're not here with anyone. I saw the big guy drop you off. You didn't board with anyone. You haven't dined with anyone."

Clarissa stopped chewing her food. Her eyes narrowed as she sized up the man.

"Well, I better get going. Busy day at sea and all that." He rose. "Maybe see you on the shuffleboard deck?" He turned and walked away.

What the hell was that?

A wave of panic washed over her. She scanned the room. No one seemed to be paying attention to her. She lost sight of Mike. She searched her memory, but he didn't seem to fit. His accent wasn't local to her, either. In fact it was pretty neutral. Still, Charles and the old man had quite a reach. Had Mike followed her and Bear from La Spieza?

Clarissa folded a napkin around the knife on the table and slipped it into her pocketbook. She took a deep breath, steadied herself. If Mike was going to do something, he already would have. He no longer had the element of surprise. Surely the old man or Charles would have warned him about her. That warning would have been enough to keep him from revealing himself the way he just did.

Probably just a psycho stalker.

Clarissa smiled. She looked at the food on the table, picked up a slice of bacon, folded it once and stuffed it in her mouth.

No point in letting this go to waste.

After breakfast, Clarissa took a three hour walk around the sixth deck, and then ate lunch. She followed up lunch with a four hour walk. Walking was the only thing that cleared her mind. She'd always been able to get into a rhythm and just go. She'd heard it called moving meditation on a TV program. Whatever it was, it worked for her. She finished her walk and went to her room and took a quick shower and a nap.

She woke and looked at her watch and frowned when she realized that she didn't know which time zone she was in.

Clarissa threw on a pair of shorts and a collared shirt then left her room. The hall was similar to a hotel hallway, with the exception that it was narrower and it rocked side to side. By this point she had become used to the persistent rocking. She knew that once she got back on dry land she'd continue to sway for a few hours, maybe a few days.

"What time is it?" she asked the first ship employee she found. He was young with blond hair poking out from the edges of the silly hat the cruise line made him wear. "Better yet, how long until dinner?"

"Dinner will be available according to your dining schedule, ma'am."

"I can't wait that long." She smiled, wondering if he'd picked up on the fact that if she didn't know what time it was, she wouldn't know when she was to eat.

"Top deck has a twenty-four hour buffet," he said. "I suggest that."

Clarissa winked at the man and jogged to the elevator. The door opened. Mike stood inside.

"For Christ's sake," Clarissa said. She stepped in without acknowledging him and pressed the button for the top deck.

"What a coincidence. I was just thinking about you, Sam."

"Lame."

The elevator stopped and the doors opened. Neither of them moved.

"Your stop, right?" she said.

"No, I'm going wherever you are," Mike said.

She took a deep breath. *Just a psycho stalker. That's all.*

"I'm going to jump overboard from the top deck. You go first. I'll meet you in the ocean."

Mike laughed.

She looked at him in the gold plated mirrored doors. His mouth formed a smile, but his eyes didn't match. His brows were furrowed and his eyelids narrowed over his brown eyes. She looked away.

The doors opened and she stepped through. "Leave me alone, Mike."

Clarissa pushed her way through the afternoon crowd and checked over her shoulder. He was gone. She turned around. He stood in front of her.

"Who the hell are you?" she asked.

"I told you before. My name is Mike."

"Get away from me." Her voice rose. "I'm serious."

"I'm just getting in line for dinner."

A muscular bald man in a yellow tank top walked up to Clarissa. "Is this guy bothering you, miss?"

"Yes," Clarissa said.

The muscular man got in between Mike and Clarissa. The men were the same height, but the guy in the tank top was twice as wide.

"I think you should leave the lady alone," Muscles said.

"I was just leaving." Mike winked at Clarissa and pushed past the muscled man.

"You know that guy?" Muscles asked.

"No," Clarissa replied.

"Why don't you come eat with the family?"

"I'm getting something to go." She turned and walked to the buffet, loaded her plate and found a seat at the back of the sectioned off open air dining room. She scanned the deck as she ate. It didn't take her long to spot Mike sitting on a lounge chair at the edge of the deck near one of the pools. He stared in her direction. She lifted her hand and pressed her middle finger against her cheek.

He smiled, nodded and rose. She lost sight of him as he pushed his way through the crowd around the pool.

She returned to the track on the sixth deck after dinner. Had no choice. Three slices of cheesecake was two and a half too many. She figured it would take at least thirty laps to work her indulgences off.

The ship had a concert going on that night and the track was empty as a result. It didn't bother her. It was easier to clear her mind with fewer people around. She made her way around the rear of the boat and along the other side. She came to the tunnel that wrapped through the bow of the ship. Lights in milky colored glass fixtures adorned the ceiling every ten feet or so. Heavy machinery lined the passage, exhibits of parts of the ship's engine. Although not working, the replicas were interesting nonetheless. She had stopped and read the plaques next to each piece her first day on the ship.

"Hello, lovely," a voice said as she approached.

She slowed down and craned her neck to get a glimpse of who the voice belonged to, although she already had a pretty good idea.

Mike stepped out from the shadows, smiled at her.

"Christ," Clarissa said. "Why don't you drop dead already, scumbag."

He laughed. "Funny, I was going to say the same thing to you." He took two steps toward Clarissa and pointed a gun at her.

She gasped.

"Got anymore smart remarks, Sam?"

"Who the hell are you?"

"If you don't shut the hell up I'll be the last person you ever see."

Clarissa took a step back. She figured she was fifty feet from the tunnel exit. Thirty of which gave Mike a clear shot at her. No way would she make it.

"Stop," he said.

Clarissa froze in place.

He walked toward her. "Turn around."

She turned.

He stuck the gun in her back. "You are going to walk forward. Not too fast, not too slow. Turn at the first door and step inside. Find the elevators and press the down button. When we get inside the elevator, press three."

He stood inches from her, his breath hot on her neck and foul in her nose.

"Understand?" he said.

She nodded and started walking.

Please someone walk by.

No one did.

Clarissa felt her heart pounding in her chest. She managed to keep her breathing at a regular pace and kept her muscles loose. No time to panic. She needed her wits. With everything she'd been through the past three weeks, there was no way this psycho stalker was going to take her out.

She came to the first door leading inside.

"Here," he said.

She grabbed the handle, opened the door and stepped inside. She held her breath as she scanned the hallway and elevator lobby, looking for help.

Not a soul in sight.

She stopped in front of the elevator doors and pressed the down button, as instructed. They waited for the elevator to arrive. He pressed the gun to her back again, perhaps as a subtle reminder.

A chime sounded and the elevator doors opened. She stepped in and he followed close to her heels. She reached down and pressed the button labeled three.

The doors closed and she stared at herself in the mirror. Her dark red hair matted against the side of her face. Sweat covered her brow. Eyeliner streaked down her cheek. She couldn't make herself any less desirable. However, judging by the hard bulge pressing against her hip, Mike didn't agree.

His grip on her tightened.

She closed her eyes and took a deep breath while waiting for the elevator to stop and the doors to open.

CHAPTER 7

Clarissa felt the elevator slow to a stop. She knew she had to act. She pressed back against Mike and moaned. His grip around her stomach loosened and his hand clawed at her skin. The gun pulled away from her back.

The elevator door opened.

"Get out," he said.

Clarissa stepped into the hall.

"Wait a sec," Mike said.

She turned her head and saw him tuck his gun in his pants. She scanned the open lobby. Empty. Everyone was busy with other activities, not hanging around below deck.

Mike stepped into the lobby. He pointed down the hall. "That way."

"We're on the same floor," Clarissa said. "I have a balcony. It's private."

"Wait a minute." Mike eyed her and tapped at his chin with his index finger. "What gives? Ten minutes ago you wanted nothing to do with me."

"Danger excites me." Clarissa grabbed his shirt and leaned in and licked his neck. She felt his hands squeeze her waist. One slid up her side and moved toward her breast. She grabbed his hand. "Not yet." She led him to her door.

An elderly couple approached from the other end of the hall. They walked slowly, feet shuffling. The old man looked straight ahead. The old woman made eye contact with Clarissa. They both smiled. The old woman nodded. Clarissa broke eye contact and tried to stay in front of Mike. She hoped the couple wouldn't remember him.

"Here it is." Clarissa slid her card through the magnetic lock and opened the door. She extended her arm.

"You first," Mike said.

She stepped into the room and mentally inventoried everything that wasn't nailed down. It didn't leave much, but then again, she didn't need much. Still, a blunt weapon of some sort would make this easier, perhaps more humane. The room was barely twenty feet long and it didn't take Clarissa long to reach the far side of the room. Nothing stood out to use as a weapon. She sighed and reached for the balcony door. She cracked it, turned her head. Mike stood at the other end of the room wearing nothing but his boxer shorts.

"You coming out here?" she asked.

He smiled. "No compliments?"

She shrugged. Nothing special as far as she was concerned. She stepped onto the balcony. A glass vase sat on the small table. She knew from trying to pick it up earlier that it was glued down. She ripped it free and tucked it behind her back.

Mike stepped out. "Why don't you lean up against that rail and let me—"

Clarissa slammed the vase down across the top of his head. The glass was thick and the vase heavy, despite its small size. The vase shattered over his head.

Mike fell to his knees. Blood flowed freely and profusely from the wound to his scalp. He scrambled to the corner of the balcony and turned to face Clarissa. "What are you doing?" He held his hand on the top of his head. The blood continued to pour from the wound.

"You screwed with the wrong woman," Clarissa said.

He used the railing to get to his feet, stuck his hands out in front of him, beckoning her forward. "Bring it."

Judging by the amount of blood on his face, Clarissa doubted he could see her. She winked anyway, then she took a step forward and whipped her leg around, catching him in the chest.

He fell back against the rail. His head snapped back, but his hands grabbed the rail and stopped his backward momentum. He straightened up and took two steps forward, swung his fists blindly.

Clarissa avoided the first two swings and caught the back end of the third with her hand. A slight tap of her hand against his arm is all it took to send Mike reeling head first into the metal railing.

He collapsed. For a few moments he lay still.

She wondered if he broke his neck.

Finally, he got to his knees.

She looked around. The deck was a mess, covered in his blood.

Time to end this.

Mike pulled himself up using the railing.

Clarissa waited for him to turn.

He did.

She delivered a jump kick that caught him in the chest.

He fell backwards over the railing, hanging on with one hand.

Clarissa still held the sharp jagged remains of the vase in her hand. She lifted it high in the air and slammed it down, severing his middle finger.

Mike screamed. Let go. Fell.

She leaned over the railing and watched as the rolling Atlantic Ocean swallowed him alive. She rested her elbows on the railing, placed her head in her hands and took a few deep breaths and steadied herself.

Clarissa went back inside and grabbed all but one towel from the bathroom and linen closet. She soaked three of them in water then went back outside. She cleaned the blood from the deck, the railing, and anywhere else she could find it. Once satisfied, she threw the soiled towels overboard. Watched again as the ocean swallowed the bloody evidence.

Her mind raced. Was he here alone? If not, how long till his friends noticed he was gone? She assumed that the ship had cameras placed everywhere. If they reviewed the footage they'd see the two of them. She'd be questioned. Although, she figured for the most part she blocked his face from view since they were about the same height.

Don't panic until you have to. That's how you get through this.

She had a drink, relaxed. Got a shower, dressed and went inside the first bar she could find.

CHAPTER 8

Dimitri pulled the sedan into the first parking lot he found inside the small town of Levanto. He brushed his short brown hair forward and covered his blue eyes with dark sunglasses.

"Get out," he said to the three men in the car.

All four exited the vehicle. Dimitri worried they would attract attention. After all, a little town like this probably wasn't used to four Russians walking around in custom tailored suits.

"That's it," Kostya said. "The drug store."

Dimitri nodded at his short, stocky partner. He motioned for the two other men to go in first. "To the back of the store. Call me and give me a count."

"Yes, sir," one of the men said.

Dimitri turned to Kostya. "Think he's close?"

"A man like Noble?" Kostya said. "No way."

"You know him?" Dimitri asked.

"Know of him," Kostya replied. "Before I took employment with Ivanov, I was associated with an associate of Noble's."

"Ever work with him?"

"No," Kostya said. "But I heard stories."

"How's he compare with us?"

"He's better."

Dimitri squared up to Kostya and lifted an eyebrow. "Than who?"

"All of us."

"Not me."

"Yes. You, me, all four of us combined."

Dimitri leaned back against the car, didn't say anything.

"Shoot to kill would be my recommendation."

"Can't," Dimitri said. "Ivanov specifically stated he wanted Noble alive."

"What's the deal with the store?"

"Girl inside. Last known point of contact."

Kostya shook his head. "I figured the spy would be. The French one."

"Probably right. But she'll be a hell of a lot easier to catch and question than the Frenchman."

Kostya nodded.

Dimitri's phone rang. "Yes?" he answered in Russian.

"It's clear," Vlad told him over the phone.

"OK, we'll be right in. Tell Rolan to stay at the back of the store. You come to the entrance."

"What's the plan?" Kostya asked.

Dimitri shrugged and smiled. "Get her to talk."

They pushed open the single glass door that led in and out of the small store. Dimitri nodded at Vlad who stood against the wall, hands crossed at his waist with a gun in his right hand. Dimitri scanned down the aisles until he saw Rolan positioned at the back of the store. Dimitri raised his fist. Rolan did the same.

"Let me do the talking," he said to Kostya.

Kostya nodded.

They walked up to the counter where the blond woman stood.

"Can I help you?" she asked them in Italian.

"Gianna?" Dimitri said.

"Yes," she replied.

Dimitri placed a picture of Jack on the counter. He looked at the woman and nodded toward the picture. "Know this man?"

"Jack," she said. "Is he OK?"

"When was the last time you saw Jack?"

"It's been a week. He came through town, needed a place to stay."

"Do you know where he stayed?" Dimitri asked.

"With me. But he left before the sun came up."

Dimitri leaned in, lifted his hand and motioned Gianna closer.

She leaned in.

Dimitri struck her across the face.

She fell to the floor.

He hopped over the counter and threw her over his shoulder.

"Check outside," Kostya said to Vlad.

Vlad disappeared and returned a few moments later. "It's clear."

"Here," Dimitri said. "Take the keys and bring the car close."

He tossed the keys to Kostya and yelled for Rolan to follow them out. Dimitri carried the semi-conscious woman outside. Vlad slid into the back seat. Dimitri put Gianna in after him. Rolan followed, sandwiching her between him and Vlad.

"Move over," Dimitri said to Kostya.

Dimitri sat down behind the wheel and took off. He noticed two men outside the bar across the street. The men pointed at the Russians. One of them pulled out his car keys and disappeared around the side of the building.

Dimitri groaned.

"What's wrong?" Kostya asked.

"We might have followers."

Kostya shrugged. "Couple of locals. Rolan can handle them."

Laughter erupted from the back of the car.

Dimitri didn't laugh, though. His eyes shifted from the road to the rear view mirror. It didn't take long before a small gray car appeared behind them. Flickering headlights reflected off the mirror and the sound of the gray car's horn filled the air. Soon enough the car was a few feet behind them.

"Pull over," Kostya said. "I'll take care of them."

Kostya reached into his coat and pulled out a Yarygin PYa 9 mm pistol.

Gianna screamed.

Dimitri waved his hand at Kostya. "Not yet." He drove on, keeping his speed steady while the car behind him swerved side to side and continued honking.

A few miles down the road Dimitri spotted a dirt road. He slowed down and turned right onto the road. The car bounced along another mile before Dimitri stopped.

The men in the grey car quickly got out.

Dimitri took his time getting out.

"What are you doing with Gianna?" asked one of the men as he pulled his brown hair back and tucked it under a hat.

Dimitri smiled at the man. "Gentlemen, please relax."

The other man, a tall heavyset guy, kicked the back of Dimitri's car, shattering the brake light.

"Let me kill him," Kostya said in Russian.

"In a minute," Dimitri said. "Let's have some fun."

Kostya smiled. He pushed his door open and jumped out then walked around the front of the car.

The brown haired man turned to face Kostya.

Dimitri stepped out from behind the car door and made a hand gesture to Vlad, who in turn cracked his door open. Dimitri turned his attention to the heavyset man.

The large man pulled a blackjack from his pants and taunted Dimitri. "You want some of this?" He bounced from foot to foot.

Dimitri held up his hands and smiled. "No, can't say that I do."

The big man took a failed swing at Dimitri.

Dimitri jumped back. "That was uncalled for. Now I'm going to give you one warning. Put the weapon away."

The big man swung the blackjack and smashed in the rear window.

Gianna screamed and the two men in the backseat cursed. Vlad's door swung open.

The heavy man shifted his gaze to the open door.

Dimitri reached into his jacket and retrieved his Makarov 9 mm and fired a round into the big man's shoulder. The blackjack dropped to the ground and the man fell against the car. Dimitri nodded to Vlad, who emerged from the car and grabbed the big man from behind after kicking his legs out from under him.

The man at the front of the car froze at the sound of the gunshot. He looked back and gasped at the sight of his friend leaning against the rear fender, a puddle of blood pooling below him.

"What the hell did you do?"

"This." Dimitri fired a single shot into the man's head.

Gianna screamed and fled from the car.

Dimitri said, "Get her."

Kostya took off after Gianna and tackled her about fifty yards away. He dragged her back to the car by the back of her head, scraping her bare legs across the dirt road, bloodying her knees.

Dimitri knelt in front of the woman. "Why did you run?"

She didn't answer him.

"Only a guilty person would run."

She still didn't answer him.

Dimitri smiled at her. He lifted his arm behind him and fired a shot into the large man who'd come to her rescue.

The man fell over and his blood leaked from the side of his head and mixed with the light brown dirt.

Gianna screamed. "You monster!"

"No more so than your friend Jack."

She shook her head.

"Now tell me, where did he go?"

"I don't know."

Dimitri slapped her. "Please don't make me do that."

"I'm telling you, I don't know. I got up and he was gone."

"Where was he going?"

"He never told me."

Dimitri looked up at Kostya and nodded. Kostya took off his belt and handed it to Dimitri.

"Tell me what I want to know."

Gianna clenched her teeth and released a guttural scream. "I don't know."

Dimitri whipped the heavy leather belt across Gianna's face.

Her head snapped sideways, her body followed. She crashed into the ground. Her cheek was split open and her blood mixed with the dirt.

Kostya leaned over and picked her up. Mud caked the side of her face. Blood flowed from her broken nose.

"You have to tell me something," Dimitri said. He cocked his arm back again.

"GPS," Gianna said.

Dimitri lowered his arm. "What about GPS?"

"He took my GPS unit from my car."

"Was any part of it left behind?"

"Yeah," she said breathlessly. "A mount. Still attached to the wind vents."

"Where is your car?"

"Behind the store. And the box is still in the glove compartment."

Dimitri stood, stepped over the woman and took Kostya by the arm.

"What are you thinking, Dimitri?"

"Most commercial GPS units have some sort of unit ID," he said. "If we can get that ID we might be able to track Noble."

Kostya nodded. "Put her in the car or "

"Kill her here," Dimitri said.

Gianna sobbed.

"Wait." Dimitri turned and held out his hand to stop Kostya.

Gianna wiped her face off and looked up at him, eyes wide, lips trembling.

"Find her keys first," Dimitri said.

Gianna started crying and screaming.

Kostya ripped at her clothes until he found her keys.

Dimitri opened his car door and slid into the seat. Started the car and turned the radio up. It wasn't loud enough to drown out the sound of the shot that ended Gianna's life.

Half an hour later they pulled into the parking lot behind the small store where they abducted Gianna. Dimitri scanned the area. Empty but for the small car butted up against the back of the store. The lot was closed in on three sides. One way in, one way out. He hoped they weren't spotted. Didn't really feel like another fight today.

"Guess that's her car." Kostya pointed at the sole car in the parking lot.

Dimitri pulled up next to the small car. He looked at the men in the back seat. "Get out. Watch our backs. Anyone enters the lot, stop them."

"Yes, sir," the men said in unison.

"How do you want us to stop them?" Vlad asked.

"Use your imagination," Dimitri replied.

Dimitri and Kostya got out of the car. Kostya unlocked Gianna's car with the keys he took from the woman before executing her.

"Grab the mount." Dimitri said as he made his way to the other side of the car and waited for Kostya to unlock his door. The lock clicked up. Dimitri opened the passenger door and sat down in the seat. He opened the glove box and pulled out the flattened, folded box that once held the GPS unit. He opened the box and looked inside. The corners of his mouth turned upward as a smile swept across his face.

"Look," Dimitri said. "A sticker."

He pulled the box apart at one of the corners. Unfolded it and held it out for Kostya to inspect.

"It's a unit ID number," Kostya said.

"Excellent."

"I'll call it in."

"Let's get out of here first," Dimitri said.

Dimitri started their vehicle and left the parking lot, making sure not to drive by the bar this time.

Kostya pulled out his cell phone and started dialing.

"Yeah, we need to see if you can track a GPS unit ID." Kostya paused. "You can, that's great." He read off the unit ID and waited.

"What are they doing?" Dimitri asked.

Kostya shrugged.

"OK, yeah you can reach me at this number anytime." He hung up.

"Well?" Dimitri held one hand up.

"They are tracing the ID through a few satellites. Once they get a lock with one satellite, they'll triangulate and call us back with a location."

Dimitri smiled as they left the town limits. "Excellent."

CHAPTER 9

Jack fiddled with the buttons of the GPS unit he borrowed from Gianna. He'd mounted it on the dash of the *Jemma-mobile* prior to leaving the hotel parking lot.

Almost to Rome.

He decided to bypass the city rather than go through the middle. The extra miles would add time, but so would traffic in Rome. Not to mention that there would be people who might have seen his picture. Getting stopped at every light in the city would ultimately lead to him being spotted. He fumbled with the GPS unit again while avoiding the lines of cars stacked around him.

The GPS estimated three and a half hours until he reached Naples. He checked the gas gauge. Almost empty. He would need to stop for gas. Last thing Jack wanted to do on this drive was get off the highway near Rome. But he had no choice. He sighed and took the next exit, searched for a gas station. Five minutes later he found one.

Jack pulled up to the pump, grabbed the nozzle and stuck it in the side of the car. He leaned back and stared at the little store.

A couple of nearby teens pointed and laughed at him.

"Nice car, Jemma," one yelled.

Jack nodded and waved. "Jackwagons," he muttered.

Two minutes later the tank was full. He restarted the car and parked in front of the store. He went in and followed the signs for the restroom.

Jack leaned over the sink, washed his face with cold water. He looked at

304 / L.T. RYAN

his reflection, ran his hand over his bald cranium. He dropped his head and shook it. He hardly recognized himself.

The door burst open.

Jack looked up.

A dark haired man with a thick beard stood behind him. The man's outstretched arm reached behind Jack.

Jack straightened up.

"Don't move," the man said in English with an Italian accent.

Jack turned around. A small caliber pistol greeted him. The man was an amateur. Jack smiled.

"You are that man, Jack Noble. Right?"

Jack shrugged. "That man has a head full of thick brown hair. Quite a handsome fellow if I recall correctly. I'm bald. Have been since I was twenty-two. Still handsome, though."

"Lies," the man said. "You are him. I've seen you on TV."

"Maybe I am," Jack said. "What are you going to do about it?"

The man said nothing.

Jack narrowed his eyes and placed his hands firmly on the sink.

The man looked toward the door.

"Who's over there?" Jack asked.

The man said nothing.

Jack turned his head. He looked out of the corner of his eye and saw the man turn his head too. That was all Jack needed. He pushed himself into the man. Jack's arm knocked the gun loose while his knee slammed into the man's groin.

The guy fell forward.

Jack leaned over and pulled the man's leather jacket over his head, blinding him. He picked the guy up by the belt loops on the back of his pants and flung him into the rear stall. The man collapsed on the floor and then got to his knees. Jack rushed him and kicked him in the ribs. He grabbed the gun off the floor and stepped inside the oversized stall and locked the door behind him.

"Never, ever screw with someone accused of killing five Russians on a boat," Jack said. "What are you? An idiot?"

The man moaned, covered his bloodied face with his hands.

Jack picked the guy up and sat him on the toilet. He pulled the jacket off the man. Rolls of toilet paper were stacked on top of the dispenser. Jack grabbed a roll. He placed it inside the jacket, stuck the barrel of the gun against the roll, wrapped the jacket around the toilet paper and the gun.

The man sat with his mouth open and eyes wide. He tried to talk but could only gurgle. Blood trickled from his mouth and broken nose.

Jack jammed the coat covered toilet paper roll against the man's head. "At least you won't make that mistake again."

He fired two shots. The homemade suppressor did a good enough job keeping things quiet. He checked the man's pulse. None. Good.

He opened the stall as another man burst into the bathroom.

"Christ, what do you want?"

"What did you do?" the man said. "Antonio."

The man rushed past Jack and into the stall.

Jack followed. He walked up behind the man and fired one shot into the side of the guy's head then dropped the gun.

Jack walked through the store, grabbed a soda and didn't pay for it. The clerk didn't appear to notice. Less than thirty seconds later Jack was merging onto the highway again.

Great start to this trip, Jack.

CHAPTER 10

Charles pulled his Cadillac up to the security gate at the rear entrance of the compound. He pushed a button on the side of the door and the window rolled down automatically.

The man in the guard house straightened up when Charles leaned out of the car.

"Evening, sir," the guard said. "Nice to see you again."

Charles nodded.

The gate opened. Charles drove through and parked his car outside the garage. He didn't know if he'd be staying the night. He stepped out of the car and walked to a black door equipped with an electric lock. He ran a card through a machine mounted next to the door. Only five men had access to this door. The old man called it his "special friends" door.

"Special my ass," Charles muttered as he stepped inside.

He made his way through the familiar maze of halls and rooms. He stopped outside the old man's study. Two men guarded the door. Charles nodded. They didn't. He really didn't expect them to after what he did to them in France.

"Step aside, boys. Boss is expecting me."

One guard didn't move. The other knocked on the door and opened it a crack. "Charles is here, sir."

"Send him in," the old man said from the room.

Charles pushed past the guards, winked at the one of the left. The door closed behind him.

"Mr. Charles, so good to see you." The old man got up and crossed the room. He held out his hands.

Charles reached for the old man's hand. "Good to see you too, Boss." He knew he'd have to work the old man a bit. If he acted like a jerk in here he might not make it out of the compound alive.

"How was your flight?"

Charles waved him off. "Let's talk about Europe."

"I want you to choose your team. You'll need at least twenty men. You can have another captain accompany you. And of course, Alonso too."

Charles shook his head. "I don't want him working for me."

"Oh," the old man said as he turned away from Charles. "Why is that?"

"You know," Charles said. "If he wasn't married to my cousin he'd be dead right now."

"I'm sorry to hear that."

"I'm sure you are."

"We should leave this in the past, Mr. Charles." The old man stood up and walked to a drink cart. He filled two shot glasses. "Things had to be done. You understand this. It's just business."

"Yeah," Charles said. "Business."

The old man handed Charles a drink and sat down. "We've worked through our differences. You should work through yours with Alonso. He only acted the way he did because I held something precious to him. If he didn't do as I said then he'd never see those precious items again. Wouldn't you do the same if I held your wife and daughter, Mr. Charles?"

"What do you know about that thing? With the Russians?" Charles asked, changing the subject.

"The boat? I believe our friend Mr. Jack was involved with that."

Charles nodded. "Makes sense now."

"How's that?"

"Nothing."

"Speaking of the Russians," the old man said, "I'd like to show you something."

Feng got up and unlocked a drawer, pulled out a folder. He sat the folder on the table and opened it. He motioned to Charles to join him.

"What's this?" Charles asked.

"The documents."

"Jack's?"

The old man nodded.

"Dumb freaking luck," Charles said. "He axed the guy. Think that's why he did it?"

"Doubtful. The documents were encrypted."

"You think—"

"I am not wasting my time speculating, Mr. Charles. You should not either."

"So what are you going to do with this information?"

"Sell it. I'm not interested in their plans. But you know certain groups are."

"To who? The Russians? Radicals?"

"Maybe the government," the old man said. "Really depends on who gives me the best price."

"You approach the feds with this and you're toast," Charles said.

The old man sighed. "You still underestimate me."

Charles laughed. "Guess so."

"Forget you saw these unless I say otherwise."

"Done."

The old man put the documents away and pulled out another folder. He handed it to Charles.

"What's this?"

"Open it."

Charles did. "Deed and keys?"

"To your new residence in Paris."

Charles nodded.

"Pick your men and get over there, Mr. Charles. We've got work to do."

CHAPTER 11

Pierre sat at his desk located in the dimly lit concrete-walled room that had no windows. He referred to the space as his home away from home. He stared at a computer screen, monitoring security streams and reviewing information relayed by field agents around the globe. Nothing exciting today. True, the press would have a field day with some of this information if they got their hands on it. But to Pierre it was boring, routine stuff.

He pulled up the local investigation on Foster's murder, scanned through the information. Two things stood out. *Random act. No suspects.* Pierre smiled. Wouldn't be long till they moved it to unsolved murders and the case would be filed away along with thousands of other murders never solved in Paris, the City of Light.

Pierre's smile faded. He thought about his mother, once a vibrant woman who'd give the shirt off her back to help a stranger. She'd been strangled under a bridge in the middle of the night. The police worked her case for the requisite forty-eight hours and then filed her away. The only one who remembered was Pierre. To anyone else, she was now what was commonly referred to as a cold case.

He reached into his shirt pocket and pulled out a cigarette. Lit it and exhaled loudly. The brass didn't allow smoking in the building and under normal circumstances he'd agree with them. Then they stuck him in this concrete hell of an office. Screw them.

His cell phone lit up. He picked it up off the desk and answered.

"Pierre?"

"Yeah," he said. "What do you want?"

"We have something that just popped up on our radar."

Pierre jiggled his mouse and waited for his computer monitor to turn back on. "Continue."

"Your, uh, acquaintance," the man said. "Mr. Noble. You know him, yes?"

"Yeah. What's this about?"

"Two things." The man paused. "We believe he had an incident outside of Rome. At a gas stop. Looks like two guys tried to jump him, but they weren't successful."

"OK." Pierre started reading football news.

"Well, we don't care about that. But, one of our satellites was hijacked."

Pierre chuckled and then composed himself. "You think Jack did this?"

"No," the man said. "Someone tracking him."

"I don't follow."

"We broke into security footage and saw Mr. Noble leaving the gas station in a small car. The satellite was tracking a GPS unit that matched—"

"You can do that?" Pierre asked.

"Yes," the man replied. "It's not public knowledge."

Pierre didn't say anything.

"So anyway, we backtracked the times on the satellite tracking and matched time and location to the car Jack drove off in."

Pierre felt his stomach drop.

"We think it's the —"

"Russians," Pierre said.

"Yes, sir."

Pierre took a deep breath and ran his free hand through his hair.

"We can only assume it's related to that thing off the coast last weekend."

Pierre nodded. "Yeah." Pierre paused a beat. "What's his location now?"

"He's been moving, but has stopped in Naples."

"Who else knows this? Do the Russians still have control over our satellite?"

"No, sir. We cut them off and continued tracking on our own."

Pierre figured that didn't matter. The Russians likely had multiple satellites tracking Jack.

"How long till you can get a team to him?" Pierre asked.

"Inside six hours."

"Probably not good enough, but get on it."

"Yes, sir."

"One more thing," Pierre said. "Tell them that they are not to approach Mr. Noble until you have my confirmation."

"This team can handle themselves, sir."

Pierre laughed. "And Jack Noble can handle them. Trust me on this."

Pierre hung up his phone and flung it across the room. It hit the concrete wall and bounced across the floor. He cursed under his breath.

He couldn't shake the feeling that he'd taken advantage of Jack when he asked him to do the job. The poor man had just seen Clarissa nearly die from a gunshot wound and Pierre sent him on a mission doomed from the start. Why? Because he couldn't have done it himself. None of his men could.

He picked up his cell and searched through his contacts until he found Jack's number. He pressed a button and put the phone to his ear.

"Come on, Jack. Pick up."

CHAPTER 12

J ack squeezed himself in the car and started the engine. His phone
vibrated on the dash. He looked at the display. It read "Pierre." He sent
the call to voicemail and then turned off the phone. He'd call him back
from the hotel later. Maybe tomorrow. For now he wanted to stay off the
phone in case anyone was tracking him through it. He had thought about
ditching the phone in the street, but figured switching it off was good
enough.

He drove back to the cheap motel he found just outside the city. It
looked out over the sea from the back window. Other than that he considered it a dump. He had to walk up two flights of stairs to get to his room.
Not a bad thing though, not after his recent experiences in elevators. Jack
chuckled at the thought of the jackwagon from New York.

He stopped and parked in an unmetered parking spot on the street two
blocks from the motel. Even at that distance he didn't feel safe. He would
have ditched the car, but he felt compelled to get it back to Jemma in one
piece. Of course, he could just wire her the money. He looked back at the car
and shook his head.

He walked the two blocks to the motel while carrying a bag of groceries.
He scanned the area. Saw things that most people would ignore. Two bums
talking, heads down looking at something in one of the bum's hand. One
looked up at him, eyes flicked wildly, then returned to the prize in his palm.
A woman passed by with a stroller. Jack eyed her the entire way. She looked
at him out of the corner of her eye as he passed. Jack altered his course and
stepped behind a building. Waited a minute and then peered around the

corner. She was gone. He took a deep breath and double timed it the rest of the way to the motel.

Inside the room Jack sat the grocery bag on the table and laid out his phone and the two Beretta 9 mm pistols on the bed. He sat at the table and turned on his laptop. He waited for the machine to find a wireless signal. It didn't. He sighed, sat on the bed and turned on his phone. An icon indicated he had new messages. He dialed in and listened.

"Jack, its Pierre."

He skipped the message.

"Call me," Bear said in the next message.

He ended the voicemail call and dialed Bear's number.

"Jack," Bear answered. "How you holding up?"

"Sitting in a fleabag motel outside Naples, Italy. Couldn't be better."

Bear laughed.

"You find the girl?" Jack asked.

"Yeah," Bear said. "She's here with me. Sleeping."

"Where you headed?"

"Someplace warm."

"Hope I can join you soon," Jack said.

"You got a lead out of there yet?"

"No," Jack said. "I need to get a hold of my contact."

"Anything from our friends here?"

"Nah," Jack said. "Tell you the truth, I haven't bothered. I wasn't helping them when I got into this mess. I'm sure they're pissed. You know someone is going to point the finger at certain groups over this."

"True."

"Let me know when you get down there, Bear. And watch your back."

"Trust me, I am."

Jack hung up. He took a few bites of the bread and cheese he bought in town. Picked up his phone again and called Pierre back.

Pierre answered.

"It's Jack."

"Jesus, Jack. You are up against something the likes of which you've never faced."

"Tell me something new," Jack said.

"I'm not kidding. The Russians are on to you."

"What do you mean?"

"The car you took. It has a GPS unit, yeah? They've been tracking you."

"I've had the GPS since before I got this car."

"Then they found the source car and got the unit's ID somehow."

Jack thought about Gianna. He shook his head. "The girl?"

"Dead," Pierre said.

Another innocent life taken because of him.

"Jack?"

"Yeah, I'm here. Thinking."

Pierre didn't say anything.

"Give me your contact's info."

"Jack, I-I'm afraid I can't do that."

Jack squeezed the phone. "What the frig, Pierre?"

"They could be watching you right now, Jack. I can't risk my man's life."

Jack said nothing.

"Listen, stay put. We're trying to get a team down there."

Jack said nothing.

"Jack?"

"What?"

"Just stay put."

Jack leaned against the wall next to the window. He squinted against the light and scanned the street back to the car. Two men in dark suits stood on either side of the little vehicle.

"Don't have a choice now," Jack said.

"Jack, I'll do what I can to—"

Jack tossed the phone on the bed, placed his hands behind his head and took a deep breath. Only two men, so far. That put the odds in his favor. He returned to the window and checked the street. Same two bums still sitting on a stoop getting excited over God knows what. Other than that, nothing. Except, there, across the street and to the right. Two more men. Both wearing dark suits.

Jack grabbed the only chair in the room, an old wooden chair with no padding, and placed it next to the window. He sat down, leaned against the window sill, keeping as much of his head covered as he could. He watched the four men, alternating between the two at the car and the two across the street.

CHAPTER 13

"Da," Dimitri said into the cell phone. "The GPS unit is a perfect match. He's around here somewhere." He listened, nodded at Kostya. "Excellent, sir. We'll stay here until they arrive."

"Good news?" Kostya asked.

Dimitri nodded again, turned and waved his arms to get Vlad or Rolan's attention.

Vlad waved back.

Dimitri gave a *thumbs up* signal.

"What did he say?" Kostya asked.

"The other team has been working the east coast and cut over to Rome. They are going to come here. Should be here in three or four hours."

"How many men?"

"Eight."

"Eight?" Kostya asked.

Dimitri nodded. "We'll need them."

Kostya frowned. "You and I could take this guy."

"Sure, if we could use these." Dimitri pulled his jacket open and pointed at the gun holstered on his side. "But we have orders to bring him in alive. We can't shoot to kill. He can."

Kostya shrugged and said nothing.

"I don't know about you, but I want as many people in between me and him when he does."

Kostya shrugged again, said nothing.

"It's not a slight against you, comrade. It will be a great honor to catch this creep and turn him over."

"What if he shows up before the team arrives?"

"Then we try to take him. Think about it like this. If he shows up now, then he's not aware of us."

"You believe that?"

"No," Dimitri said. "I believe he's probably watching us right now. Figuring out how to take us down."

"So why doesn't he?"

"He doesn't know we have orders to take him alive."

Kostya shrugged. "Where do you think he is?"

Dimitri turned his back to the motel across the street. "My guess would be in that motel behind us."

"Why?"

"Just a hunch."

"I'll go in and show a picture to the manager."

"No," Dimitri said. "He sees you go in there, you're a dead man."

"So, what do you want to do now?"

Dimitri paced on the sidewalk in front of the motel for a few minutes thinking the question over. He didn't want to risk leaving the hotel and missing Jack if he slipped out. Then again, what if his hunch was wrong and Jack wasn't here.

"Dimitri?" Kostya said.

"Thinking." He continued pacing. "Let's get the car and wait here."

CHAPTER 14

J ack watched the two men as they left their position across the street. They walked toward the Jemma-mobile, passed it with a nod at the two men standing there. They turned left and rounded the corner, disappearing from sight. The two men by the car stayed put and kept their focus down the road, toward the motel.

Jack waited a beat and then moved to the back of the room. He looked through the window at the alley behind the building. He had planned to scope it out today, but his new visitors threw a wrench in that plan. From the single window he could see approximately fifty feet in either direction. Unfortunately, that didn't offer him much.

He watched the back alley for five minutes. It looked to be about twenty feet wide. Cracked black asphalt. Not much else. And no action. Jack returned to the front window and scanned the street. No change. Had they already returned and took position closer to the motel? Jack looked over the parking lot and saw eight cars, one less than before. No signs of movement in any of them. Stepping outside to get a look directly below was tempting, but it was also risky.

A car stopped across the street and parked where the men had been standing. He didn't get a good look at the faces of the two men in the car, but the dark suits told him all he needed to know. It would be a long night. A dozen scenarios raced through Jack's mind, none of which had a pleasant ending. Of course, he could try the alley. He just had no idea where it went, if it went anywhere at all.

He called Pierre.

322 / L.T. RYAN

"Get a team here," Jack said.

"Jack," Pierre paused. "I'm sorry. Those plans fell through. We've got no one near there."

"Got friends in Italy?"

"I do," Pierre said. "But you have to understand. You have created quite a bit of negative press. They aren't likely to help."

"Dammit, Pierre," Jack said. "If I get out of here—when I get out of here — you're a dead man. You got that?"

"Jack," Pierre paused again, seemingly trying to find the right words to calm Jack down, "I'd come myself, but its eight to ten hours for me to get there."

Jack banged his head against the window. "Give me an idea then. I'm fresh out."

"Don't think you can take them down?"

"Four men, sure. But they have tactical advantage over me, Pierre. Two down the street about two blocks away. Two directly across the street." Jack checked the other end of the road just to make sure he didn't miss anything new. "I can take out the first two, but then the others can get a drop on me."

"I'll make some calls, Jack. Keep your phone switched on."

Jack hung up.

He opened the back window and stuck his head out, looked left, then right. The alley opened to a street at both ends. About four feet to his right a drain pipe offered his best chance of escape. Jack shook his head. It would have to do. About a mile behind the building sat a marina with hundreds of boats. If he could make it out of the alley he could take cover for the night at the marina and find a boat to steal. Solid plan, assuming he made it out of the alley.

Jack returned to the front window, sat down in the hard wooden chair, watched the street again. The blue sky started to give way to the orange glow of sunset. He checked his watch. An hour till dark and his best opportunity to slip out undetected.

Thirty minutes passed. Jack noticed a car approaching just as he prepared to abandon his position. It wasn't the car that caught his attention as much as the reaction of the men guarding Jemma's car. One of the men stood tall, appeared to yell at his associate, and pointed at the approaching vehicle. The car slowed as it approached the front of the building. Another vehicle, same make and model, pulled up behind the first. Three men got out of each, then the drivers pulled into the motel's parking lot and got out.

They jogged across the street and joined the other six men. Five minutes later the eight men were joined by the original four.

All of them across the street.

All of them stared at the motel.

All of them had their hands on their pistols.

You gotta be kidding me.

CHAPTER 15

"Comrades," Dimitri said. "Let me explain what we have here."

"This better be good," the man Dimitri knew as Demyan said.

Demyan, like Dimitri, had been one of Russia's top agents. Now they were the most sought after independent contractors in the country. Together, the two of them could take down any man, any normal man that is.

"Jack Noble is not a normal man," Dimitri continued. "Not a normal target. Truth is he's better than any five of us combined. When governments have a job that requires precision, accuracy, and secrecy—something they themselves have to distance themselves from—Jack Noble is the man they hire when they cannot fail. You know why we were sent. He took out three officials, and two of our own men. All on a boat less than fifty feet long. How does a man do this?"

No one said anything.

"He's a trained sniper. He could take three of us out right now before we could make a move."

"Then why are we standing here?"

Dimitri smiled. "I welcome him to do it. Then we'd know which room he's in. I'd give any of your lives for that information."

The men laughed.

"How do we know he's in the hotel?"

"I just do," Dimitri said. "You two." He pointed at two men from the other team. "I want you to go in and give this picture of Noble to the manager. Get his room number."

326 / L.T. RYAN

Kostya took the picture from Dimitri and nodded. He motioned to Vlad and the two slipped across the street.

"Now we wait."

"If he's up there," Demyan said, "he's probably watching us. We should move now."

Dimitri shrugged. "I'm in charge here. We wait."

Demyan squared off with Dimitri. His eyes were wide, brows furrowed, nostrils flared.

Dimitri smiled. "Relax, Demyan."

Kostya emerged from the office and ran across the street.

"Where's Vlad?" Dimitri asked.

"Taking care of the body," Kostya said.

Dimitri arched an eyebrow. "Did we get what we wanted?"

Kostya smiled and held out a key.

Dimitri took the key and looked at the tag. "Room 322." He looked up and pointed at the third floor. "Let's go. You know the plan."

The eleven men crossed the street in a group and fanned out once they hit the parking lot.

CHAPTER 16

The only thought that crossed Jack's mind as he watched the eleven men cross the street was run.

Run as fast as you can.

The men hit the parking lot and split up. He knew it would only be a minute at the most before two of them blocked his escape route at each end of the building.

He grabbed the bag off the bed and tossed it out the back window. Jack pulled himself through the window and reached for the drainage pipe. His right hand slipped on the pipe at first, but he managed to get a grip with his left and he steadied himself. He dragged his left foot around the outside wall and placed the sole of his shoe against it. He did the same with his right. He scaled the wall slowly and deliberately. Ten feet from the ground he pushed off from the wall and let gravity take over. Pain seared through his right knee when he landed. Jack brushed it off. He straightened up, looked right then left. Both directions were deserted. He chose left. It looked shorter.

Jack sprinted through the alley in a race against the clock. He was a sitting duck back there. He needed to get to the open street to have a chance. He rounded the corner and kept his sprinter's pace.

"You," a heavily accented voice yelled from behind. "Stop."

Jack didn't stop.

"Ivan, Makar," the voice yelled. "This way."

Jack looked back over his shoulder and saw three men chasing him on foot. He spotted another alley up ahead. He turned at the alley and looked back, only two men now. The other one must have gone back for a car.

328 / L.T. RYAN

Jack pushed through empty boxes and trash that clogged the narrow alley.

"Stop," the voice called.

Jack looked back. They were at the entrance to the alley now. He knocked over a stack of boxes and pushed through an old wooden door. The room was dark, musty and cluttered with junk. He got low and went to the darkest part of the room.

The men stopped outside the door. Jack heard their heavy breathing. One wheezed. They spoke in Russian. Only one man talked. The other said nothing during the pauses. Jack knew it wouldn't be long until the rest of the men showed up.

Cornered like a rat.

He looked behind him, but couldn't make out any discernible exit. He got low and found the back wall. Felt along the wall until he came to a door frame. He searched for a knob, found one.

"Mr. Noble," a different voice said with the same thick accent. "We are not here to hurt you. We need to talk to you."

Jack said nothing.

"Our government," the voice continued, "wants to thank you for your service. You took care of some very bad men. Saved us a lot of time and money."

Jack bit his lip to keep from laughing. They had to know better than that. He leaned back against the door, one hand on the doorknob, the other on his Beretta. He slowed his breathing and prepared for his escape, or a gunfight.

The footsteps got closer, only one set, though. The other man must have remained near the door waiting to signal the others when they arrived. Jack thought he could hear the sound of hard soled shoes hitting the pavement in the distance.

The sliver of light the front door provided disappeared. Jack made out the shape of a man. A light flicked on and pointed at Jack. Jack fired just above the source of the light. The flashlight fell to the ground and so did the man who had been holding it.

"Ivan," the other man yelled. He appeared above the dead body of his associate.

Jack fired again.

The man collapsed.

Jack stood, reached for the door handle. It didn't turn. Locked.

"In there," a voice said.

Jack kicked the door. It bent, but didn't give.

Lights flooded the room.

He kicked the door again. It burst open.

Shots rang out behind Jack.

He ducked and slipped through the door. Wide open space greeted him. He turned to his left, sprinted about twenty feet and then set off diagonally for the next set of buildings. He didn't look back, but he heard the men as they emerged from the dark room. Shots rang out. He braced to be hit.

He hit the sidewalk at full speed. Felt the pain in his knee again, ignored it. He followed the sidewalk along the wide building. Tires squealed in the background. Jack dug deep down and went into an all-out sprint. The end of the building was just ahead.

More shots rang out.

A bullet slammed into the building above his head. The wall crumbled. A cloud of plaster dust enveloped the air around him. He didn't stop. His knees pumped and his feet hit the ground in a fast rhythm.

C'mon, Jack. Run.

He grabbed the corner of the building and propelled his body around it. The alley cut clear through to the next street. Halfway down the alley he heard brakes squeal.

"Stop," a man yelled.

Gunshots rang out, missed him again. He didn't look back. He knew he had to make it to the next street. Anything could be waiting there, but it was better than what he had behind him at that moment. He pushed harder. His muscles screamed. His lungs burned.

I really gotta quit smoking.

He emerged from the alley, turned right, stopped, leaned against the wall. He took a moment to catch his breath while waiting.

The man popped through the opening. Jack caught him with an outstretched arm. The man's legs kept going, his torso didn't. He flipped in the air and landed on his head. Jack kicked him in the side.

He looked around. Across the street, to the right, he made out the entrance to the marina he saw earlier from his motel room. He took a deep breath, scanned the street. Empty. He dashed across the street and took cover behind a stretch of thick, unkempt bushes. He waited and watched. Ten feet of open grass stretched out behind him. He peeked over the bushes. Five more men gathered around the guy on the ground. A car stood by with no one in the front seat.

Now or never, Jack.

He crouched low and ran as fast as he could. It didn't take long, a second, maybe two, to reach the relative safety of the wall, out of sight. He stayed close to the plaster wall until he reached the six foot fence. Jack scaled the fence then sprinted to the first building he saw, a concrete restroom and vending facility.

He opened the door to the ladies room and yelled. No response. He stepped in, cut the lights and slipped into a stall to catch his breath.

Only another twenty minutes or so until dark, then he'd find a boat.

Jack cleared his mind and mentally went over every possible scenario. Three men down. That meant there were nine left. Had any of them seen him cross the street? Run away from the bushes? Climb the fence? Every move he made he'd had to check behind him to make sure no one else was following. What about all the missed shots? If he was dealing with who he thought he was dealing with, there was no way would they have missed that many shots.

He got up and cracked the restroom door open an inch, heard nothing but silence. He slipped through the door and picked his way across the grassy area to the concrete walkway that led to the piers. The walkway butted up to the water. During the day you could probably see the bottom of the sea. Now it was nothing more than dark glass that reflected the lights.

Jack scanned the area. The place was deserted. He chose a pier at random and looked for a boat, trying to find one that could stand up to heavy seas and appeared to have been sitting for a while. The pier was long and Jack took his time checking each vessel. Every once in a while he'd check over his shoulder to make sure that no one followed him.

Then he saw it. It took over an hour, but there it was, a forty foot Flybridge motor cruiser. Perfect. He hopped on deck and checked the wheel house. Broke open a lock box and found the keys. Jack smiled, sighed. He searched the ship for extra gas cans. Found a couple, but they were empty. He grabbed the twenty-gallon containers, stepped back onto the pier and took the empty cans back to the end of the pier to the gas pump. He set the containers down and scanned the area for movement.

Jack took a deep breath. Perhaps he was in the clear now. He crossed the concrete walkway and leaned up against a building where he lit a cigarette. He'd been saving it for a while. It tasted—well it tasted like the street. But that didn't matter. The rush of nicotine coursed through his body and steadied his nerves. He closed his eyes and listened to the sounds of the sea. The small waves gently lapped against the bulkhead. A small plane passed by overhead. A gentle breeze blew in from the sea. The smell of salt filled

Jack's nose and reminded him of being a kid at the beach. He smiled, probably for the first time all day.

Every scent, sound, and taste felt like one thing. Escape. And escape was close. He could ride that boat across the Med if he wanted. He'd likely take it around the boot of Italy and settle in somewhere along the coast of Croatia or Albania or Greece. He had friends in those places that could help him get back to the States. He scratched at the stubble on the top of his head, chuckled. God, he hated being bald.

Jack dropped the cigarette on the ground and crushed it with his foot. He walked toward the gas cans. He didn't hear the footsteps behind him until it was too late. The gun pressed into his back. The barrel felt cold through his sweat soaked shirt.

"Don't move, Mr. Noble," the man said. "My name is Dimitri. As long as you cooperate, I'll treat you like a friend, and we'll have a nice trip back to Russia."

Jack didn't say anything. He remained still. Then felt the man's breath against the back of his head, which meant he was probably as tall as Jack, if not taller.

Roll to the right, elbow up. Follow through with a left, across his nose.

Jack shifted.

"Don't think about it, Noble," Dimitri said. He whistled.

Jack heard several more footsteps hit the concrete. He looked side to side, saw three men on each side, all with their guns drawn.

"Nowhere to go, Jack," Dimitri said. "Even if you can get to me, these men will be on you in two seconds."

The men stepped forward, slowly and deliberately.

Jack took a deep breath. Ten feet to the edge of the walkway. Ten feet to the water. He didn't know how deep it was and didn't care. He squatted slightly, right leg back, left leg planted in front. He started to sprint. He felt Dimitri's free hand wrap around his shoulder. Jack shrugged it off, but not fast enough. Dimitri's grip altered Jack's path. His leg twisted. Pain shot through his knee again. He tried to ignore it, couldn't this time. He only made it a few steps before one of the men tackled him. Jack twisted and flung his elbows. He caught the man in the neck, twisted some more and put the man in a choke hold.

"Back off," Jack said. "Back off or I'll break his neck."

No one said anything. No one backed off.

Jack grunted, squeezed tighter. The man tried to talk but nothing came out of his mouth, then he went limp in Jack's arms. Jack pushed at the dead weight and struggled to free himself. He caught sight of Dimitri and saw the Russian nod toward one of the other men. Jack looked up in time to see the blackjack swinging toward his face, slamming across his forehead. The pain started above his eyebrows and spread throughout his face and wrapped around the back of his head. The edge of his vision darkened. The blackness swallowed up the night and he slipped into unconsciousness.

CHAPTER 17

Pierre stepped out of the agency building and onto the sidewalk. Perfect night. Just like the TV weatherman predicted. Clear and cool. He'd walk home tonight. His apartment was only a few miles away. Perhaps he'd even stop and get some dinner on the way home. Anything to keep his mind off of Jack and the situation Pierre put him in.

He pulled out his phone. No missed calls and no messages. He called Jack's phone. It rang a half dozen times and then went to a generic voice-mail. "C'mon, Jack," he said. "Answer." He dialed again, still no answer.

Pierre put his phone in his pocket and started down the street toward home. Quieter than normal tonight, especially for such a lovely evening. It didn't bother Pierre. Sometimes the crowds of Paris got to him. He longed for the days when he was on assignment. He never partnered with more than one other person, and often he worked alone. He preferred to work alone. Another person meant more opportunities for screw ups. Screw ups he had no control over.

A young couple approached. They walked arm in arm. The man nodded at Pierre. The woman smiled.

Pierre nodded back.

He stopped, leaned up against a building and lit a cigarette. He watched the couple pass. Had they any idea, he wondered, how close they had been to a killer? And if he had orders to kill them he wouldn't give one iota of concern about their love, their past or their future. Nor would he care about the number of family and friends who would be devastated by the lost lives.

Pierre smiled. Perhaps it was a bit demented how he amused himself, but at least he let his mind go there. He figured most people could have the same thoughts if they allowed themselves.

There's a bit of psycho in all of us.

He and Jack—and people like them—were the real heroes of the world. They did the dirty laundry of nations, kept the peace. Everyone else was a pussy in Pierre's eyes.

The couple turned down the street and was out of sight. Pierre flicked his cigarette onto the asphalt and continued on his way. He approached his favorite cafe, aptly named *Le Café*. He opened the wrought iron gate and took a seat in the corner against the wall.

A young, attractive waitress named Katrina walked up to the table. Her brown hair was pulled back, save for a long strand that framed the right side of her face. She wore dark rimmed glasses that dulled her blue eyes. She parted her red lips and asked him what he wanted to eat. He barely heard her, for his focus was on her exposed cleavage.

"Monsieur," she said in a sing-song tone.

Pierre looked up.

She smiled at him.

He returned the smile.

"Quiche," he said. It was his favorite dish.

"*Oui, immédiatement,*" she said. *Yes, right away.*

He couldn't take his eyes off of her as she walked to another table set at the other end of the patio. She faced away from him, placed her hands on an empty chair and leaned over. Her tan pants clung tight to her buttocks and thighs. She turned and caught him staring. He felt his face burn red. He had no idea why.

She winked and smiled as she passed him on the way to the door that led to the main dining room.

Pierre smiled and took a sip of water.

A moment later the waitress reappeared with a bottle of wine. She set it on the table.

"Oh, no thanks," Pierre said. "I just want the meal."

"Please," she said. "It's on me."

Pierre smiled.

"And," she continued, "if you can wait an hour or so, you can have it with me."

Pierre cocked his head to the side. "Who put you up to this?"

"Sorry?" she said.

"Come on now," he said. "I've been eating here for years. You've waited on me several times and never before now have you asked me anything other than what I'd have."

She shrugged.

"What's different? Why tonight?"

She said nothing.

"You sure no one put you up to this?"

She smiled and leaned forward. She put her face next to his, her lips next to his ear. "Does this convince you?" She licked his neck and bit his earlobe lightly.

Pierre grinned. "Suppose so."

She left the bottle on the table and disappeared inside.

He sat back in the chair, bristling with confidence.

The waitress appeared with his dinner. He dropped his cigarette into the ashtray and crushed it out.

"Can you sit?" he asked.

She shook her head. "Not till I'm off."

Pierre nodded and took a bite of his food.

The waitress gasped and flew across the table.

Pierre pushed back in his chair in an attempt to reach for his holstered weapon.

Two large men, one with a colorful tattoo covering half his head, stood before him. Both wore dark suits with t-shirts under their jackets. Both held Russian-made 9 mm pistols in their hands. Both pointed the pistols at Pierre's head.

"Don't move," the tattooed man said with a Russian accent.

The waitress rolled off the table and scrambled to her feet. "What the hell is going on here?"

"Shut up," the other Russian said.

"Just back up slowly, Kat," Pierre said.

"Pierre, what the hell is going on?" she said.

Tattoo Head pointed his gun at her. He kept his eyes on Pierre. "Tell her if she wants to live she needs to shut that hole in her face now."

"Shut up, Kat," Pierre said.

She backed up against the railing that separated the cafe terrace from the property next door. She slid down the railing and wrapped her arms around her knees.

"That's good, Kat," Pierre said. "Just keep quiet."

"Get up," the bald Russian said.

Pierre smiled, put his hands in the air and rose. The other man leaned in and pulled Pierre's gun from his holster.

"Any more weapons?"

Pierre nodded. He placed his right foot on the table and looked at his ankle. The man lifted Pierre's pant leg and pulled the knife from its sheath.

"That all?"

Pierre nodded. He didn't take his eyes off of the Russian. However, he could feel the stares of everyone on the patio.

"Shall we go?" Pierre asked.

The bald Russian stood behind Pierre, keeping his gun pressed tight into Pierre's back. The other man led him across the patio, through the gate and down the sidewalk. They stopped in front of a black sedan. The man opened the door and motioned Pierre in. He slipped in and the bald man got in next to him. The other man ran around front and started the car. They sped off.

"Where are we going?" Pierre asked.

"Shut your mouth," the man next to him said.

"I came peacefully," Pierre said. "The least you can do is tell me."

The Russian sighed. "You are coming with us to Russia."

"For?"

"To answer for your crimes."

"What crimes are those?"

"The murder of Dorofeyev and his party."

Pierre said nothing.

Double crossed. But by who? Jack? Oscar? Someone in the agency?

"Anything else?" the man asked.

"Why me?"

The Russian turned and looked at him. "You trying to tell me you are innocent?"

Pierre shrugged. "Well, I didn't pull a trig—"

The Russian's large elbow slammed into Pierre's head. It caught him under his left eye and on the end of his nose. Pierre's head snapped back and then forward. He brought his hands to his face and felt blood pool in the bottom of his palms.

"Anything else?" the Russian asked again.

"No," Pierre said. "I'm good."

He cleared the tears from his eyes then stared out the window, watching the streetlights as they flickered by. They drove through the city, past the *Boulevard Périphérique*, and through the suburbs.

The panic didn't really set in until he realized they were too far from the city to be heading toward the airport. He cleared his throat and parted his lips to speak.

"Don't say a word," the Russian next to him said.

Pierre sighed and slumped back in his seat.

Less than half an hour later the car slowed and turned. Now he knew. They turned into a private airport that he himself used from time to time. They were taking him to Russia. First class all the way. He laughed at the thought.

"Something funny, Pierre?"

Pierre shook his head.

The car stopped. The man in front got out, circled around the car and opened the door.

Pierre stuck a foot on the soft ground. The man in the backseat pushed him and the man at the door pulled him by his hair. Pierre stumbled out and fell to his knees. The man at the door kicked him in his ribs. Pain ripped through Pierre's side. He forced a deep breath and winced.

"Let him get up," the bald Russian said.

The other man laughed and yanked Pierre to his feet by his hair.

"Thank you," Pierre said through gritted teeth. "Ever so gracious."

"The French," the man said. He spit at Pierre.

Pierre looked down at his shirt and frowned at the wet spots. He shook his head.

"That's enough," the bald man said. He grabbed Pierre by the elbow and led him to the plane. Three other men greeted them.

"Gentlemen," Pierre said.

One laughed at him.

Pierre smiled back. They could beat him, but they wouldn't break him.

"Get on board," the bald man said. "Try to enjoy the last flight of your life."

CHAPTER 18

Clarissa leaned against the balcony railing. The rolling waves of the Atlantic finally gave way and they were passing through the Gulf Stream. She leaned over and looked forward, but couldn't make land out yet. She knew they were close, though. She should have several hours before the next ship left. She assumed she could catch a shuttle somewhere, but ditched the idea. Best thing to do would be to get on the next ship as soon as possible.

A knock on the door startled her from her thoughts. Her mind raced. A couple days had passed and not a word had been uttered about Mike in any of conversations she eavesdropped on. She even convinced one of the ship's security officers to give up the details on the passengers they were watching. According to him, there were two men on board that they suspected of transporting heroin. They planned on taking them down as they left the ship, after they settled their bill, of course.

Mike was nothing but a ghost. Maybe someone would be waiting on shore or in another state. But it would be days before they traced him back to Clarissa, if they traced him back to her at all.

Another knock.

She got up and checked the peephole. A young woman stood on the other side wearing the ship's uniform.

Been there, done that.

She cracked the door. "Yes?"

"Ma'am, we have a letter for you, from shore."

Clarissa put her fingers up to the crack in the door and the woman slid the envelope through.

"Thank you," Clarissa said. She shut the door and returned to the balcony. Opened the envelope and read the letter.

Clarissa,

Skip the next boat. My associate is meeting you at this stop. He'll drive you to Miami and put you up there. I'll meet you there and we'll discuss where to go next.

-Bear

She took a deep breath. She told people she hated when plans changed, but that wasn't the truth. She didn't mind at all.

Clarissa stuffed as much as she could into a backpack and threw everything else overboard. She watched as the ocean swept away half her wardrobe.

An hour passed and the ship docked. She pushed her way through the crowds, off the boat. Once on shore, she switched her cell phone on and found a place to sit. The phone rang and she answered.

"Clarissa?"

"Yeah, that's me," she said.

"OK, I'm here to get you. Look for a black Lincoln stretched Towncar."

She stood up and scanned the long line of cars. "I see at least ten."

"I'm waving."

"Don't see you."

"Wearing a black cap, black suit, have a thick brown beard."

"Oh, there you are," she said as she stood up on the bench. "I'm waving back."

"Got you," he said. "I'll be right over to help with your luggage."

"Don't bother," she said. "Just have my backpack."

She hung up and stuffed the phone in her pocket. She weaved through the line of people waiting for their buses and shuttles then crossed the street.

The bearded man met her at the back of the car. He popped the trunk.

"Go ahead and put your bag in there."

She clung to the bag. "I prefer to hold it."

"I insist," he said. "You'll be more comfortable."

She sighed and handed over the bag.

"You're Bear's friend?" she asked.

He shrugged. "Don't know who Bear is. Guessing that guy's his friend." He pointed at the tinted rear window.

Clarissa squinted and leaned forward but couldn't see anything.

"Whatever," she said.

The driver stepped around her and opened the back door. "Beautiful day, you know. But we'll hit showers on our way to Tampa."

She put one foot in the car and turned toward him. "Tampa? I thought we were going to Miami?"

He smiled and pushed her in the car, shut the door. The locks clicked.

Clarissa pulled on the handle but the door wouldn't move. She slid across the black leather bench seat and pulled on the opposite door handle. The door didn't move. She screamed and threw her head back, slammed her hands into the leather seat. Finally she looked up and noticed the man sitting at the other end of the car. He wore a wide brimmed hat and leaned forward. The hat blocked his face.

"Who the hell are you?" she said.

The man looked up and smiled.

Clarissa felt her stomach drop. Her pulse and breath quickened. Her hands tingled. Images of the burning hot ice pick filled her head. "No, not you."

"Hello, child," the man said with a smile. "Remember me?"

"Sinclair," she whispered. "What? Your friends—Bear? I—"

"I'm touched you remember me. I certainly have not forgotten about you."

Clarissa felt sick. Her face felt flushed, her hands clammy. Her muscles cramped. Panic overcame her and she felt the world closing in on her.

He pulled a needle from his black bag and slid across the back and sat down next to her. "Now relax. This won't hurt a bit."

Clarissa wanted to fight back, but the panic hit her hard and fast and she couldn't move fast enough. She felt the needle plunge into her arm and her senses dulled at once. She slumped in her seat. Half awake, half passed out. She tried to fight the drug, but it was pointless. However, this drug was different from their first meeting. Even in her current state she could tell that.

"Don't worry, Clarissa," he said. "I'm going to take real good care of you."

She shook her head, or at least thought she did. She tried to speak but nothing came out.

He laughed.

She passed out.

CHAPTER 19

Bear leaned against the rental car and watched the traffic on I-75 fly by. They'd been at the rural rest stop in southern Georgia for about half an hour now. Mandy didn't feel well. He wanted to give her a chance to recoup. She'd been sick most of the week. He figured it had to do with the scene she witnessed in Montana. Though she only told him a little, it was enough for him to figure out she saw too much.

He paced along the cracked sidewalk, keeping his eye on the little girl in the car. He pressed his cell phone tight to his ear.

"Answer, Jack," he said.

No answer.

He ended the call and dialed Clarissa's number. It rang eight times and then went to her voicemail.

"Where the hell is everyone?" he said.

Mandy gave him a funny look from inside the car.

He smiled and waved. "Don't mind me."

She giggled.

He winked at her and turned around. Dialed Clarissa's phone again and then Jack's. He tried the Frenchman, Pierre. No answer. Finally he left Jack a message.

"Jack, it's me. Don't know what's going on. Can't reach anyone. Not you, Clarissa or Pierre. What the hell is going on? Call me."

He hung up. Scanned through his phone and dialed Brandon, one of their contacts in the agency.

"Hello?" Brandon answered.

"Thank God," Bear said.

"Who the hell is this?"

"It's Bear, Jack's associate."

"Noble?"

"Yeah, man," Bear said. "Have you heard anything?"

"About what? Jack?"

"Jesus," Bear muttered. "Yeah, Jack. The old man, Charles, whoever, I don't care. Have you heard anything?"

"Yeah," Brandon said. "You might want to sit down."

"I'm sitting." He wasn't.

"We picked up some chatter, man. Some bad dudes after Jack."

"Who?"

"Russian agents."

Bear said, "When did you get the last update?"

"Few hours at least."

"You know the French guy, Pierre?"

"Yeah, I know who you're talking about."

"Anything on him?"

"Nah."

"What about, " Bear paused a beat, "Can you pull TSA records?"

"Sure can. Who you looking for?"

"Abbot, Clarissa Abbot."

"Let's see here."

Bear heard Brandon's fingers working the keyboard as his stubble grated against the mouthpiece of his phone.

"Ok, here's what we got. Departed her ship around ten this morning."

"That's it?"

"Yup."

"She'd be in there if she got on another ship, right?"

"Sure would."

"Then where is she?"

"Florida would be my guess."

"Ass," Bear said. "Give me something I can use."

Brandon didn't say anything.

"If I give you cruise info can you tell me if it's departed?"

"Don't have to give me anything if she's leaving from the same pier," Brandon replied. "I can tell you that all ships that are departing today from that location have already departed. Your friend didn't get on any of them."

"Take down my number, Brandon. If you get wind of anything out of the ordinary down there, let me know."

"OK," Brandon said. "Who'm I looking for? Spooks?"

"Yeah, them or anyone in the old man's organization, and any contractors."

"You got it, man."

Bear hung up and got back behind the wheel of the rental car. He growled and slammed his hands on the wheel.

Mandy turned to him. "What's wrong?"

He closed his eyes and took a deep breath. He didn't want to scare the girl. "Nothing, sweetie. I lost something out there and couldn't find it."

"Did you trace your steps?" she asked. "That's what I do when I lose something."

"Yeah," Bear said. "I traced my steps."

He checked his map and altered their course. They'd cut across Florida at I-10 and pick up I-95 in Jacksonville, then south to Cape Canaveral.

CHAPTER 20

Charles leaned against the railing on the balcony of his new place. He had a clear view of the Eiffel Tower. Not one to call himself a romantic, Charles was surprised to find out how charming he found the view.

"It's something else, isn't it?" Alonso asked.

"Sure is," Charles said.

"Charles, we never talked about —"

"Shut up," Charles said. "Don't ever mention it. I know you did what you had to do. Just swear that you are loyal to me now."

"I am," Alonso said.

Charles turned and stared him in the eye. "Swear it."

"I swear it, Charles. I swear I am loyal to you. I'll die for you, if necessary."

Charles nodded and turned back around.

"Good," he said, "That's exactly what I need to hear. We're going to take over this entire city starting tomorrow. Anyone that doesn't get in line is going to end up in the ground."

Alonso moved next to Charles. "I've got meetings set up with those men as you requested."

"Excellent," Charles said. "Be ready, OK?"

"For what?"

"If they don't agree, we'll have to take action right there."

"I'm ready."

Charles scanned the horizon. "Beautiful, isn't it?"

"City of Light," Alonso said.

"And soon it will all be mine." He looked at Alonso and extended his hand. "Ours."

Alonso straightened up and grabbed Charles's hand. "Yes, ours."

CHAPTER 21

The shackles dug into Jack's wrist. The heavy chains connected to the shackles were anchored to the wall with thick iron plates. The room was damp and dark, with a sliver of light coming in from the end of the narrow hall. The sound of dripping water echoed through the chamber every twenty to thirty seconds.

He wasn't sure how long he'd been in there. Could have been hours, could have been days. They'd fed him a couple times. Beat him a few times more than they fed him. He drifted in and out of consciousness. Somehow he'd managed to not say a word.

The gate at the other end of the room opened and slammed into the wall. Metal against metal clanked and the sound ripped the air. Jack's muscles tightened as he prepared himself for what might come. He pushed back against the wall and got to his feet, which was sure to piss them off even more. Why do it? Because screw them, that's why.

Footsteps echoed through the cell. Jack preferred the water drops.

He heard two voices speaking in Russian, followed by laughter. Then he heard the distinct thud of a fist against flesh.

"Get up," a Russian accented voice called out.

One of the men entered the cell. "We've brought you a friend, Noble."

Jack said nothing.

The man walked up to Jack.

Jack pressed back against the wall, every muscle in his body flexed, ready for the beating to come.

The man smiled. "Not today, Noble. You've had enough. For now." He turned. "Besides, we've had a good time with your friend here."

The other Russian pushed the new prisoner on the ground. Stood over him and pulled him up by his hair. "Say hello to your friend, Pierre."

Jack closed his eyes. At least now he knew it wasn't Pierre that set him up. Or, at least if he did, he got hauled in too.

They chained Pierre to the adjoining wall a few feet away from Jack.

"You two enjoy your stay," one of the Russian men said.

The guards laughed.

Jack waited until he heard the second door click before saying anything.

"What the hell, Pierre?"

Pierre breathed fast and shallow. "I—Jack I had nothing to do with it."

Jack shook his head. It didn't matter. They were both in here now. And from here, who knew where they'd go.

"We're screwed, Jack."

"Just figuring that out?"

"I heard them mention—"

"Don't ever ask me to do another job, Pierre. Got that?" Jack spit at the opposite wall. "Don't even ask me to help you get out of this nasty hole."

"—Black Dolphin, Jack. I heard them mention Black Dolphin."

"What the hell is a black dolphin?" Jack said.

"It's—" Pierre went quiet. His breathing remained fast and shallow. "I can't talk right now, Jack."

"Great," Jack said. "So now it's just you, me, and a pod of black friggin' dolphins."

He angled his body to the right and reached into a shirt pocket. Pulled out a cigarette and matches. They might not feed him, but they kept him stocked with smokes. He lit the cigarette and sat in silence with his new cellmate.

EPISODE 5

CHAPTER 1

"Jack?"

Jack said nothing. He had shared the dark, damp cell with Pierre for the past twenty-four hours. Pierre had talked for twenty of those hours.

"Jack? You awake?"

Jack lifted his chin off his chest and glanced over at Pierre. Even in the dark he could see that Pierre's face was long and drawn. "Yeah?"

"Got a smoke?"

"Got a lighter?"

"Don't you?" Pierre held his arms out as far as his restraints allowed.

"I'll throw you a smoke," Jack said. "But not my lighter."

"Why not?"

"You drop a smoke and I'm only out one cigarette. Drop my lighter and I can't smoke." Jack lit a cigarette. Inhaled deep. "Maybe the guards can give you a lighter." He pointed toward the empty corridor outside their cell.

Pierre sighed. "Screw you, Jack."

Jack laughed. Tossed the lit cigarette at Pierre. It hit the French spy in the stomach. Pierre cursed and twisted his body until he lifted the cigarette from the floor.

"Thanks, Jack."

Jack nodded and said nothing. He stared out past the rusted iron bars that kept them from getting out. A rat sniffed around his foot. He kicked at it, sending it scrambling into a hole in the side of the cell. Why couldn't they block the holes with smaller rusted iron bars and keep the frigging rats out?

"What do you think they'll do with us?" Pierre asked.

Jack sighed. He wondered the same thing. A dozen scenarios played out in his head and none of them had a happy ending. "You're the government agent, Pierre. You tell me."

"In France, and I'm sure the U.S. as well, there would be a special military tribunal for this kind of thing."

"What kind of thing is that?" Jack knew what kind of thing.

"I assume they are bringing us in as terrorists." Pierre paused a beat. "Threats to national security. Something of that nature."

"Tribunal," Jack said the word aloud while mulling it over. "How's that work here?"

"Not sure," Pierre said. "Haven't encountered it before."

Jack said nothing. He lowered his head and rested his chin on his chest again. Crossed his legs at the ankles and put his hands on his thighs.

Pierre took one last long draw on the cigarette and stubbed it out on the wall behind him. Flicked it toward the bars that confined them.

"I would expect," Pierre said, "that one man is going to play judge, jury, and executioner."

Jack sighed and said nothing.

"And that," Pierre continued, "you and I are already guilty."

Jack looked up again. "How do they execute people over here?"

"They won't operate under any civilized governmental rule." Pierre looked up at the ceiling. "I can assure you of that."

"Where do you think we are?"

Pierre shrugged and shook his head.

Jack chuckled. How the hell did Pierre drag him into this conversation? Jack would have been happy to just wait it out and be surprised when whatever fraud of a judge ruled against him. Too late now. Pierre pricked his curiosity.

"Best guess?" Jack asked.

Pierre shrugged again. "They blindfolded me when the plane landed. The drive here took quite a while. If I had to guess I'd say at some military base or possibly somewhere that our governments have no information on."

Jack reached into his shirt pocket and pulled out his cigarettes. "Another?"

Pierre nodded.

Jack lit two and tossed one at Pierre. "Wish they'd unchain us. Friggin ridiculous."

Pierre laughed. "Surely they know who we are."

Jack shrugged and said nothing.

"That or the bars," he nodded at the rusted iron bars at the front of the cell, "are garbage and we'd be able to break out." He leaned back and thought for a moment. "Most likely they are afraid of us."

Jack smiled. He stared down the corridor. A faint light flickered at the far end of the dark hall and then disappeared. A moment later the sound of metal grating against metal echoed through the corridor and into their cell. The door opened and four men stepped through.

They were about to get a visit from the guards.

Jack stiffened.

"Pierre," Jack said. "In case we get separated—"

"That won't happen, Jack. Not yet."

"Hear me out," Jack said. "You had nothing to do with it. OK? This was all my idea. I freelanced and took the Russians out on my own."

"They've got Oscar. I'm almost one hundred percent certain of that."

"I set that up, then. I stole your contacts last time we worked together and got Oscar's information."

"Jack—"

"Shut up, Pierre. Don't try to talk me out of this. I'm a dead man no matter what." Jack pressed back against the wall and worked his feet under him. "There's no reason for both of us to die."

"Jack?"

"Yeah," Jack replied.

"Got any family?"

Jack thought about Bear and Clarissa. About the little girl. They were his family. But no one could know that.

"No," Jack said.

Laughter erupted from the other end of the corridor. Jack made out the shapes of four men walking toward them, one considerably stockier than the others.

"Four of them," he whispered.

"Christ," Pierre said with a nod.

A high beam flashlight blinded them. Both men tried to shield their eyes.

"Hello, cupcakes," the stocky Russian said. He took off his hat and tucked it behind him. He pulled a gun from his belt and pointed it at Jack.

Another man stepped in the cell and pulled a gun from his belt. Pointed it at Pierre. The two remaining guards stepped into the cell and approached the prisoners slowly.

"Hands out," the stocky Russian said.

Pierre stuck his hands out. Jack didn't.

The stocky Russian lifted his gun. "Hands out," he said again, this time much louder. His words echoed through the cell.

Jack took a deep drag on his cigarette and brought a hand to his mouth. He pulled the cigarette out and flicked it at the stocky Russian. Dropped his hands to his side.

"Jack," Pierre said.

The stocky Russian kept his eyes on Jack and nodded at the young guard. The guard stepped up and punched Jack in the stomach.

Jack knew it was coming. He had tightened his stomach as tight as possible. His muscles absorbed some of the impact, but not all of it. He coughed and struggled to fill his lungs with air, but managed to keep his body tall and upright. He forced a smile.

The young Russian moved closer to Jack. He grabbed Jack's wrists. "Sir," he said. "Please put your hands up."

Jack stood still for a moment, defiant. He thought of everything he could do to the young man in the space of ten seconds. The man knew it, too. Jack could see it in his eyes. They wavered back and forth. The Russian's nostrils flared and the pace of his breathing increased. He felt the man's heart racing through the fingertips that gripped Jack's wrists. Yes, Jack could kill him. Right here and now. But what would that gain? The stocky Russian would shoot him on the spot.

"Sir," the man said again with a thick accent. "Please."

Jack lifted his arms.

The guard placed the handcuffs around Jack's wrists. He unlocked the chains. They fell to the floor with a crash.

"Out," the stocky Russian said with a nod of his head. "You need to get ready."

"Ready for what?" Jack asked.

The Russians said nothing.

Pierre shot him a glance.

Jack understood the silence. He said nothing else. Followed the guards into the corridor and walked toward the light.

CHAPTER 2

S ilence. Clarissa had forgotten how deafening silence could be. She laid still, eyes closed, struggling to remember where she was. The events leading up to this moment played out in her head. The cruise ship. The man who tried to attack her, Mike. Her heart raced. She opened her eyes. The glare of the lights on the stainless steel walls and ceiling blinded her.

Where the hell am I?

She jumped from her bed and backed into a corner. She slid to the floor and clutched her knees to her chest. For a moment, the fear that she was being held in the mental ward of a prison swept through her head. No, that couldn't be right. She got off the boat. Found her ride. The memory was still fresh. Then it hit her. Sinclair.

Clarissa dropped her head and buried her face in her hands. After everything she'd gone through, to come back full circle to this was nothing short of life draining. She shook her head and fought back the urge to cry.

She stood and felt along the wall. The cold steel bit at her fingers and palms. She knocked around the fabricated seams. Solid. No hollow spots. She returned to her bed and looked around the room. Aside from the bed, the room included a stainless steel toilet and sink combo. Nothing else. No chairs, no table, no books. Nothing. The door appeared to be made from the same material as the rest of the room. She moved to the door and stared at her reflection in the small nine-by-nine inch mirrored glass window. She pressed her face to it, her hands blocking out the light. She thought she saw the outline of a person just on the other side of the door.

Clarissa backed up and slammed her fists on the door. She screamed for them to let her out.

No one responded.

She kicked at the door.

Still, there was no response.

She backed up and fell on her bed. Stared up at her distorted reflection on the stainless steel ceiling. Why the ceiling? To keep people from escaping? A dark glass pane covered a single square foot section in the corner of the room. She stood on the end of her bed and peered at the corner The vague outline of a camera hid behind the smoky glass. She turned her head toward the toilet-sink combo. No privacy. She steadied herself against the wall and extended her right hand toward the camera. She greeted whoever watched her with an extended middle finger.

"Perverts," she muttered.

Clarissa fell back into her bed, placed her hands behind her head and continued staring at the ceiling.

What now? The old man has the documents. What the hell does Sinclair want with me?

She closed her eyes, sighed and ran a hand down her body. It was only then that she realized they had changed her clothes. She lifted her head and curled her lip at the sight of the drab grey cotton shorts and tank top they dressed her in. She didn't recall seeing her backpack either. So much for the Italian designer clothes she bought before boarding the cruise ship. She sighed and closed her eyes again.

Her thoughts turned to Jack. She wasn't one to wish for a knight in shining armor to come save her, but right about now she found herself wishing Jack would show up and rescue her from this cell.

A rap at the door jarred Clarissa from her thoughts. She sat up and put her feet on the floor. A clicking sound filled the room. The door cracked open. Clarissa stood and positioned herself against the wall, next to the door.

"Present yourself," a male voice said.

Clarissa said nothing.

"Now," the voice said.

Clarissa stood motionless. The door opened a bit more and she saw a white canister appear.

"I'll gas you," the man said.

Clarissa pressed back against the wall. She took a deep breath and jumped toward the door, lunging into it with her shoulder. She pushed against it with all her weight. The door didn't budge. The sound of the gas being sprayed hit her just a moment before the gas itself. Her throat tightened and she fell to her knees. She crawled toward the back of the cell, toward the sink. It felt like swimming through wet cement. By the time she reached the sink she could barely lift her hand an inch off the ground. She forced herself back on her heels and managed to get one arm up on the sink. She fumbled for the handle, turned it and placed her hand under the faucet. A stream of water trickled over the sink and onto her face. She opened her mouth and let the water slide down her throat. The muscles of her throat relaxed and she fell to the floor, gasping to fill her burning lungs with oxygen.

Footsteps approached. "Ready to go peacefully now?"

Clarissa propped herself up on her elbow. The blond haired man stood over her. Tall and lean. She figured she could take him. She sat back on her heels, facing him. Smiled.

He reached into his pocket and pulled a stun gun out. "Don't try it, doll."

Doll?

Clarissa lunged, managing to wrap her hand around his testicles before he fired the stun gun at her. Fifty thousand volts of electricity coursed through her body. She shook violently. Her hand, still wrapped around his groin, squeezed even tighter, allowing the electricity to flow through him as well.

The man screamed as they both collapsed to the floor.

Clarissa smiled through the pain.

The burst of electricity only lasted a few seconds, but it was enough to render both of them useless piles of flesh on the floor of her cell.

Clarissa shook the effects off. She lifted her head and saw the door wide open. She dragged herself over the incapacitated guard and made it to her knees. She tried to get to her feet and stumbled. The after effects of being tased hit her every few seconds and she convulsed uncontrollably. It seemed to take forever to reach the door.

She stuck her head out and checked the hall. Empty. Dumb luck, she figured. Inch by inch she crawled through the doorway, pulled herself up on the wall.

"Stop," the guard said from inside her cell.

Clarissa threw her body forward, grabbed the door and pulled it tight. From the other side, the guard railed his knuckles against the door. She smiled at the sight of his twisted face pressed up against the mirrored window.

"Now what?" she muttered while trying to figure out which direction offered her the best chance for escape. She shrugged and turned right, keeping her left hand against the wall, leaning in for support while her muscles still spasmed.

She reached the end of the hall. Looked left. Dead end. Looked right and saw that there was an adjoining hallway at the end. She moved faster now, regaining control of her limbs. Her pace quickened. Occasionally she touched the wall for balance. She heard voices. Turned around and saw no one. Kept pushing forward. The cold air made the sweat that clung to her body feel like ice. Her fingers and lips tingled. Paranoia swept over her and she couldn't shake the feeling that her every move was being watched. She brushed it aside and kept moving. "Just get out" became her mantra.

She reached the end of the hall and stopped before the corner. Pressed her back tight to the wall, closed her eyes and listened. Silence. It didn't make sense. She recalled the camera in her room. If there was a camera, then there should have been someone watching. If someone was watching, then they would have alerted everyone that she escaped. Yet, there were no alarms and no one seemed to be following her.

Satisfied with the silence, Clarissa rounded the corner. Three men stood twenty feet or so from her, blocking the hall. All three were armed, two with pistols and one with a rifle.

Clarissa stopped. Gasped. Backed up and dove for the corner. She hit the floor with a thud, the wind knocked from her lungs. She got to her knees and pulled her body up using the wall again. Clarissa ran, clutching her stomach, down the hall. She looked over her shoulder at the empty hall behind her. The men weren't following. She slowed down and inched closer to the hall she'd run through moments before. The hall remained quiet. She peeked around the corner. Three different men blocked this hall.

They moved toward her.

She backed up and screamed.

A light filled the dark end of the hallway as a door opened. A man stepped out, working his way through the shadows.

Clarissa slid to the ground. Trapped. The first three men stood mere feet from her. The other three men blocked the path back to her room. All six trained their weapons on her. She turned her focus to the lone man in the shadows.

He stepped into the light.

She gasped.

"Now where were you planning on going, child?" Sinclair asked.

Clarissa buried her head in her hands and cried. The guards reached under her arms. She didn't struggle as they lifted her and drug her down toward the open door Sinclair had come from. She braced herself for what was to come.

They pushed her through the opening. The room was painted off-white. A table filled the middle of it. Two chairs sat at either end of the table.

"Sinclair will be in to see you soon," one of the men said as they left the room.

CHAPTER 3

Bear paced the full parking lot. Row after row, he walked looking for signs of Clarissa.

Mandy followed close behind.

"Bear," she said. "I'm tired of this."

Bear glanced down at her.

"What are we looking for?" she asked

"Not what," Bear said. "Who."

Mandy sighed. "OK, then. Who are we looking for?"

"Ms. Clarissa."

"Did she know she was s'posed to meet us here?"

"No."

Mandy stopped and put her hands on her hips. "Then what are we doing here?"

Bear laughed at the girl's sudden attitude. "We're here because I said so. End of story."

Mandy sat down in the middle of the road. "I'm not going anywhere."

"What do you think you're doing?"

Mandy didn't say anything. She crossed her arms and turned her head.

"Get up," Bear said.

Mandy didn't move. "Did someone say something?"

"Now," Bear said. "Mandy, don't try me."

She looked at him out of the corner of her eye and quickly turned away again.

Bear walked up to her, stood over her. "You can be a good girl and get up now or—"

"La, la, la," Mandy said in a sing-song tone.

"—or we can do this my way."

She stopped and looked up at him.

Bear reached down and scooped the girl off the ground, threw her over his shoulder.

"Bear," she screamed. "No."

A family stopped and stared at them.

Bear waved.

The man dropped his bag and walked up to Bear.

"Is this man bothering you?" he said to Mandy.

"Yes," she said.

Bear turned so he faced the man directly. "I suggest you leave."

"We—" he looked back to his wife and two sons. "I'll call the cops."

Bear took a step forward.

The man jumped back three steps.

"She's just tired of walking," Bear said with a nod to the man's family. "You got kids. I'm sure you know how it is."

The man gulped. His bottom lip quivered.

"Get outta here," Bear said.

The man backed up and turned. "It's nothing," he called out to his family. They turned and walked toward the pier.

Bear followed them, Mandy still slung over his shoulder. He spotted a cop and risked talking to him.

"Officer," Bear said.

The cop nodded in acknowledgment.

"I'm trying to find my friend," Bear said. "I was supposed to pick her up here. She didn't show up. Here's a picture."

The cop took the picture from Bear and smiled at Mandy. He stared at the photo for a moment. "Doesn't look familiar."

Bear fought the urge to roll his eyes. "Well, she was supposed to be here. She's not. What can I do?"

"How long she been missing?" the cop asked.

"A day."

"Can't do anything for forty-eight, y'know. And besides, maybe she just wanted to disappear. It happens, y'know."

"Yeah, I know." He grabbed the picture from the cop and turned. "Thanks for nothing." He set Mandy down and led her by the hand.

"Hey," the cop said. "Wait up."

Bear turned.

"Gimme the picture, I'll make a copy and pass it around. Maybe somebody saw something."

"Thanks," Bear said with a nod and a curt smile.

The cop slipped off with the picture and stepped inside a small yellow building at the edge of the parking lot.

Bear pulled out his phone and dialed Clarissa's number. No answer. What's that, thirty times now? And still no answer. That couldn't be good. He tried Jack's number again. And again, there was no answer.

The cop emerged from the small building and walked back to Bear at a quick pace. "Here's the picture. Gimme a number to reach you at."

Bear spit out a forwarding number. Hell if he was giving a cop his cell.

The cop nodded. "I'll call you tomorrow with an update. Good or bad, I'll call. We can file a missing person's report then."

Bear nodded and said nothing.

"You should get outta here though," the cop said. "Some guy and his family are inside filing a complaint about a large man with a beard and a blond girl harassing them."

Bear laughed. "Frigging wuss, letting a little blond haired girl harass him."

"Say again?" the cop said.

Mandy laughed.

"Nothing. We're outta here." Bear turned and led Mandy back to the car.

An hour later Bear pulled off of I-95 and pulled into the empty parking lot of some greasy diner that apparently didn't see much action despite the constant flow of traffic along the interstate. He turned the car off and sat back. Panic flooded his system. He took several deep breaths. Closed his eyes. He worked his large muscles, tightening and releasing them. The panic subsided, for now, at least. Bear learned to control his emotions, any emotion, at a young age. Countless times he'd pushed through and controlled the symptoms in order to complete a job or get out of a sticky situation. And every time he did so, it made him stronger.

Bear looked over at Mandy. "Stay put, OK?"

Mandy looked up from her book and nodded with a smile.

He stepped out of the car, closed the door and moved toward the back. He kicked at the loose gravel as he reached into a deep pocket for his cell phone. He tried both Jack and Clarissa again, but didn't get an answer. He cursed under his breath and searched for Brandon's number. The phone rang.

"What can I do for you, Bear?" Brandon said.

"You find anything out about my friends?"

"Not looking good, my man."

"What do you mean?" Bear asked.

"Everyone's a ghost, Bear." The sound of Brandon tapping on his keyboard filled the ear piece. "I can't find a trace on any of them."

"Dammit," Bear said.

Brandon said nothing.

"I'm gonna need some favors."

"Name it."

"Not now," Bear said. "Not on the phone. I'm coming to New York. I'll call you when I'm close."

"You got it, man."

Bear hung up and climbed up on the trunk, the rear end of the car sagged under his weight. He studied the traffic light. Watched as cars lined up, blindly obeying a single red light for no reason other than that's what they had been told to do. The light turned green. The cars took off. A car door opened. Mandy stood in front of him. Tears welled in her eyes. Bear leaned over and placed his hand on her head. Stroked her hair.

"I'm sorry," she said softly.

"For what?"

"You're mad at me, I know." She looked down at the cracked asphalt and gravel. "I acted like a brat and now you're mad at me." She sobbed and sighed loudly.

Bear slid off the trunk and picked her up. Hugged her tight to his chest. "Listen to me, I could never be mad at you. Got it?"

"I love you, Bear."

Bear squeezed her and ran his large hands through her hair. For the first time in a long time, a tear fell from his eye.

CHAPTER 4

Sergei Ivanov stood still in front of the full length mirror in the corner of his study. He admired himself. Most men his age didn't have his physique. Hell, some men half his age didn't. He liked the attention it brought him. The stares it elicited from women. Of course, those stares might be due to the fear and power he held over them. He knew this, and it didn't bother him. There was no greater weapon than fear. It kept the masses in check. It kept those under him in check. He'd learned long ago how to use fear to his advantage.

He smiled at his reflection, wiped down his hair and eyebrows. He slipped into his coat and saluted himself. A smile crept up.

"Today," he said, "is a good day for fear."

A knock on the door caught his attention. He spun on his heel and walked to the other side of the room. "Who is it?"

"Julij."

Ivanov opened the door and waved Julij into his study as he retreated toward his desk.

"Sir," Julij said. "The American and the Frenchman are being prepped for trial."

Ivanov stared out his window at the bleak courtyard. Brown grass littered the ground. Dead trees swayed in the cold breeze. "Do you know what makes these men different from others?"

Julij shrugged and said nothing.

"What makes them," Ivanov continued, "different from even us?"

"They are an abomination—"

"No," Ivanov said, his hand held out. "All men, in their own way, are abominations, Julij." He sat on the corner of his desk, one leg on the floor, the other dangling in the air. He pulled a pack of cigarettes from his inside coat pocket. He lit one and offered it to Julij, who shook his head. Ivanov continued, "Even the pope had to claw and hack his way to the top. He didn't kill men. No. He couldn't, right?" Ivanov paused and took another drag. "He killed souls, though, during his pursuit to the top. Made back-room deals with others, others who may be of dubious nature, to secure his position among the elite and be remembered forever. It's been that way for centuries, Julij."

Julij nodded.

Ivanov straightened up and laughed at the younger man's blank expression. "You don't understand, do you?"

Julij's pale cheeks flushed. "No, Sir."

Ivanov turned his back on his young ward and looked out the window again. A woman walked with her son toward the playground where a few other children played. A smile crept up on his face as he watched the children. He cracked the window and tipped his ash outside. "Take another guess. Why are these men different?"

"They kill without purpose?"

"Are you asking or telling, Julij?"

Julij rubbed his hands together and shook his head.

"No, they have a purpose, my friend. Just as you and I have a purpose for killing. Only, our purpose has the power of belief behind it. Understand?"

Julij said nothing.

"These men—"

A rap at the door interrupted Ivanov. He frowned at Julij. "Who is it?"

The door opened and a young man stepped in and saluted. "Sir, they are ready for you in court."

Ivanov nodded and waited for the door to shut. "These men will kill anyone for money. They won't stop until it's done. We promise our own men freedom, power, and the ability to be feared. Yet some leave us the first chance they get in order to return to mundane lives. It doesn't matter what amount of money or other perks we offer them." He stubbed his cigarette out in the ashtray on his desk. "If we offered these men enough money, they'd kill their own leaders for us. They wouldn't question it. And they wouldn't stop until the job was done. Pit bulls, Julij. These men are pit bulls."

"Makes sense," Julij said.

"Of course it does," Ivanov said. He stepped toward the door. "Let's go."

"Sir," Julij said. "One more thing to discuss."

Ivanov turned. "Yes?"

"The documents, sir. The ones that were lost in transit a few weeks back."

Ivanov nodded.

"Intelligence found a blip."

Ivanov scratched at the short grey stubble on his face. "A blip? Where?"

"France."

Ivanov studied the ceiling for a moment. "Coincidence?"

"We could try to find out."

"I hate asking questions that I'm not sure I have the answer to, Julij. That's the kind of thing that can cause a problem for us. Find out."

The younger man nodded. "I understand, sir. We can pursue this at a later time."

"Let's get ready for court."

CHAPTER 5

J ack laughed at Pierre. "You look like a douche bag in that jumpsuit."

Pierre looked down and shrugged. "So do you."

Jack smiled. The dull grey and pinstripe combination made them look like prisoners in some crappy B movie. "We look like schmucks."

"Schmucks?" Pierre said. "I am not familiar with this phrase."

Jack stopped laughing. "Douche bags," he said with a smile.

"As you so eloquently said already. Douche bags."

Hearing Pierre say douche bags in his heavy French accent was more than Jack could handle. He bent over laughing.

"How can you laugh at a time like this?" Pierre asked.

"Shut up in there," the stocky guard said.

"Screw you," Jack said.

The guard turned away.

Jack's smile faded and his eyes hardened as he stared at the guard. "If I could only have five minutes alone with these guys."

Pierre nodded. "You and me both."

"Both of us?" Jack said. "Wouldn't be fair to them."

Pierre laughed. "Listen, Jack. If one of us doesn't—"

"Don't say it," Jack said.

"Jack," Pierre said.

Jack shifted and squared himself to Pierre. "You are getting out of here. I'm not."

Pierre leaned forward. "Who do you want me to tell if that happens?"

"Bear," Jack said. "Start with Bear."

"Anyone else?"

Jack stood up and moved to the cell bars. He turned his head trying to see where the hall led. One of the guards slammed his nightstick against the bars, close to Jack's face. Jack didn't budge. Finally, he turned, walked to the back of the cell and took a sip of water from the sink faucet. Clarissa deserved to know. But it would be best for Bear to tell her. After that, Jack couldn't care less who knew.

"No one else," Jack said. "Bear knows who to tell."

"I've got no one," Pierre said without prompting.

Jack turned to face him and saw Pierre staring over his head, eyes unfocused, as if he were staring out over the sea, or over the city of Paris from atop the Eiffel Tower. Did he really have no one?

"Well, there is one person, Jack. A young lady named Kat. Would you tell her?"

Jack sighed. He opened his mouth to tell Pierre that wouldn't be necessary, but stopped himself. Instead he asked, "Where can I find her?"

Pierre described Kat and gave Jack the location of the cafe.

Jack sat on the bench and leaned back against the wall, crossed his arms.

"Five minutes," the guard said. "Smoke now."

Both Jack and Pierre lit up. They smoked in silence.

Minutes later the stocky guard appeared on the other side of the bars. He barked orders in Russian and another guard opened the cell door. The heavy iron grates slid sideways and the clanking reverberated through the cell as the door locked into place.

"Get out," the stocky guard said, his gun drawn and trained on Jack.

"You know," Jack said, "he's more dangerous than I am."

The guard smiled. "That's why there are four of us."

Jack looked past him. Saw another guard with his gun out, pointed at Pierre.

"I tried," Jack said.

Pierre laughed.

"Shut up, now," the stocky guard said. "One more outburst and you'll need to be dragged out of here by your feet."

Jack contemplated taking the man up on his offer. Pierre must have read Jack's mind because he shook his head. Jack decided against antagonizing the guards any further. He needed a clear head for what was to come, whatever it was.

The guards led them through a maze of halls, each one the same as the rest. Jack stopped keeping track after the eighth turn. It didn't matter. He wasn't getting out of here on his own accord with handcuffs and leg shackles weighing him down. The hall narrowed and the floor sloped upwards. Going aboveground, he figured. Jack winced at the sunlight pouring in through the tall uncovered windows. *Definitely above ground.* He turned his head. Saw Pierre wincing as well.

"Eyes forward," a guard said.

The hall widened again. They walked shoulder to shoulder, no furniture or decorations to block them. Dark wood double doors stood at the far end. Two men dressed in fatigues and armed with semi-automatic rifles guarded either side.

The stocky guard behind Jack yelled something in Russian.

The other set of guards yelled back and stepped to the side. Jack stared at the one closest as he passed, but the man stood still, head forward, eyes trained on some imaginary spot at the end of the hall.

Good boy. Here's your dog treat.

The guards repositioned. Two in front, Jack and Pierre side by side in the middle, and the stocky guard and one other behind. They stepped into the room as a group. The two front guards stepped to the side. Jack felt the gun in his back pushing him to the front of the room. Four rows of wooden pews lined either side of the walkway. A few people sat motionless, looking ahead.

"Courtroom?" he whispered to Pierre.

Pierre nodded.

"Sit," the stocky guard said, pointing at two wooden chairs behind a plain table.

Jack and Pierre sat down. The chair felt hard and cold. Jack placed his hands on the table and winced as splinters invaded his flesh. He looked around the room. An apparent jury box sat empty.

"No court reporter," Jack said to Pierre.

"Don't expect one," Pierre said. "There are no more records of you and me."

"Always liked the idea of being a ghost." Jack smiled.

Pierre didn't.

Didn't matter. The smile was forced. Jack's stomach knotted as he braced for what was about to happen.

No clocks on the wall. No watch on his wrist. No discernible way to tell time. If Jack or Pierre spoke, the guards threatened them. So they sat in complete silence, like everyone else in the courtroom.

Finally, a door near the judge's bench opened. Out stepped a tall man with short, thinning brown hair. He had a square jaw and a hardened face. He looked directly at Jack without changing expressions. Jack studied the man. He looked familiar, but Jack couldn't place him. Maybe he just matched the stereotypical view Jack held of a Russian military leader.

The man stepped up onto a platform before taking a seat behind the bench. He placed a nameplate in front of him, but the Cyrillic alphabet was not one Jack understood. He nudged Pierre.

"What's that say?" Jack asked.

"General Ivanov," Pierre whispered.

Jack pushed back from the table and smiled at Pierre, impressed at the Frenchman's command of the Russian language.

Ivanov stopped adjusting his seat, looked up and glared at the men. His gaze was hard. His lips drew tight and his nostrils flared wide. He spoke in Russian and then pointed at Jack and Pierre. "Do not speak," he said in English.

Jack stared back but he made no sign of acknowledgment to the General. The name ran through his mind repeatedly. He knew it, Ivanov, but couldn't figure out from where. Not a target and not an employer. Eventually it would come to him.

A tall man dressed in a dark suit and seated across the aisle from Jack and Pierre stood and approached the bench. He didn't salute, so Jack figured him to be a civilian. He ran his hands through his dark hair and straightened his jacket before reading in Russian from a typed document.

"What's he saying?" Jack asked Pierre.

Pierre shook his head.

Jack sighed. Would the entire trial—if you could even call this a trial—be like this? Would they have anyone to represent them?

The man finished speaking and lowered the paper. He looked over his shoulder at Jack. His lips curled up in a smile, but his eyes narrowed.

"Thank you *gospodin* Zykov," Ivanov said in English.

Zykov nodded and turned to face Jack and Pierre. He approached their table and stood before them. His gaze shifted from Jack to Pierre then back to Jack. He lifted his hand and pointed. His lips were parted, as if he was about to speak. Instead he smiled again before returning to his seat, never uttering a word.

Ivanov addressed the court in Russian.

Jack nudged Pierre. "What's he saying?"

The Frenchman wouldn't respond other than to shake his head.

Ivanov stopped mid-sentence. He looked at Jack. "Perhaps I didn't make myself clear," Ivanov said in English. He nodded toward the guards and said something in Russian.

Pierre grabbed Jack's elbow and stood.

Jack shrugged him off, refusing to stand.

Two guards approached. One took Pierre's chair. The other pulled at Jack's chair. Jack put his hands on the table and took his time standing.

Ivanov said, "Now you stand for the remainder of this trial."

Jack exhaled loudly.

Ivanov narrowed his eyes and pointed at Jack. "Do not try me, Mr. Noble. I can—"

"What?" Jack said. "What are you gonna do?"

Ivanov lifted a gavel and slammed it down several times. "Bring him to me." He stood and left through the door behind the bench. The door swung fast and hard, slammed against the frame and bounced back toward the hall.

Two guards grabbed Jack's arms, pulling him by his elbows. They led him to the doorway and pushed him through the opening. The shackles drew taut, and he collapsed to the floor. He lifted his head. The dark hallway was narrower than the one that led from the cells to the court-room. He found himself back on his feet and the guards pulled at his arms again. They continued down the passage, every so often passing a closed off room. They came to an open doorway. The guards shoved Jack inside.

"Leave us," Ivanov said with a wave of his hand.

The guards pushed Jack to the ground and left as ordered, closing the door behind them. It clicked shut. Jack guessed they stayed right outside the door, ready to step in and shoot him if he tried anything.

"Mr. Noble," Ivanov said. "Are you trying to get yourself killed?"

Jack said nothing.

"Noble, speak."

Jack smirked. He was getting under Ivanov's skin. He still didn't answer.

Ivanov stepped forward and placed a hand on Jack's shoulder. His face softened. He smiled.

Jack stood still. Stared over Ivanov's shoulder, out the window at the dull grey sky.

Ivanov leaned in closer to Jack, his breath heavy and hot against Jack's cheek. He drove his free hand into the middle of Jack's stomach.

Jack had tightened his abdominal muscles, expecting the attack. He thought the General would go for the groin, but hoped for the abs. Still, the blow was delivered with enough force to cause Jack to buckle slightly, although the after effects were minimal.

"Now," Ivanov said. "Answer me."

Jack sighed and turned his head away, his eyes loosely focusing on the wall. He took a deep breath.

Ivanov pressed his body against Jack's. "You are nothing but a stupid American," he whispered into Jack's ear.

Jack fought the urge to flinch at the man's breath in his ear. Fought the urge to reach up and wrap the chain between his wrists around the man's thick neck. He clenched his jaw, teeth pressed tight together.

Ivanov delivered the shot Jack had been waiting for. Directly to his groin.

Jack buckled and fell to his knees. He refused to go all the way to the floor, though, and kept his hands above his waist. He looked up at Ivanov, keeping his face tight and hard.

The Russian stared down at him with a smirk, then turned and walked toward his desk.

Jack placed his hands on the floor and rocked back then forward, building momentum.

"Don't think about it." Ivanov turned and sat on the corner of his desk. "Besides, if you were going to do something, you should have done it when I stood next to you." He pulled two cigarettes from his pocket and lit them, held one out for Jack.

Jack shook his head.

"Take it." Ivanov leaned over and held the cigarette in front of Jack, the filtered butt toward Jack's lips.

Jack reached up and grabbed it. "Well, a big friggin' thanks is in order. I was trying to quit. Thanks for nothing."

Ivanov inhaled deeply and motioned to an empty chair, ignoring Jack's commentary.

Jack fought back the pain in his midsection, rose to his feet and sat in the chair. He kept his eyes on Ivanov, who was acting quite casual considering he was in the presence of a man on trial for single handedly killing five Russians.

"Jack, look at me," Ivanov said.

Jack blew smoke in Ivanov's direction. Didn't say anything.

"This might not go the way you expect, Jack." Ivanov turned toward the windows lining the back wall of his office. He walked slowly, his back to Jack. "If I wanted you dead, you'd be dead. You know that, right?" He didn't wait for Jack to respond. "You see, Jack, I think you can be a valuable member of my team." He looked over his shoulder and made eye contact. "Understand?"

Jack shook his head.

Ivanov turned and placed his hand on his oversized leather chair. His fingers traced the golden rivets along the top. "You'll need to prove yourself first, of course."

"How's that?" Jack asked.

Ivanov smiled. "Your loyalty to me, Jack, must be proven."

Jack tapped his cigarette against the glass ashtray on the antique wooden desk. "And if I don't? You'll kill me?"

Ivanov pulled the leather chair out a few feet and sat down. He placed his arms on the desk and leaned over them, motioning for Jack to come closer. "It's not that easy, my friend."

Jack cringed at the words.

"You see," Ivanov continued, "I don't give up on my goals that easily. If you refuse my offer, this offer I am making only this one time in here, for you to come to work for me, to be part of this great team, then we will return to the courtroom. I am the judge. I am the jury. I am the executioner. If I recall correctly, there were two men in that courtroom. I could choose to execute one of you on the spot."

"Pierre had nothing to do with this," Jack said.

"I don't care, Jack." Ivanov sucked on his cigarette. The end lit up, bright red, before dulling to ash as he lowered it. Smoke trickled out the corner of his mouth and his nose.

Jack rose and leaned over the desk.

Ivanov sat back and motioned with his hands for Jack to sit down.

Jack ignored him. "Listen to me. If I wanted to kill you, you'd be dead right now. You are—"

"By all means, do it." Ivanov stood, placed his hands on the desk and leaned forward, now face to face with Jack. "Take your best shot."

Jack froze. If he took a shot at the General, the door would burst open and *he'd be* shot.

Ivanov laughed as he straightened himself. He waved Jack off. "Just as I suspected. Can't take a man down while facing him. Typical assassin. Pussy."

Jack bit down hard and clenched his jaw. Forced himself back into his seat.

"As I was saying," Ivanov continued, "you have a choice to make, Jack. You can make it now, or you can delay the decision. There may or may not be consequences to you delaying the decision, though."

Jack's eyes met Ivanov. He said nothing.

Ivanov lit another cigarette and handed it to Jack. "Take five minutes, Mr. Noble, to make up your mind."

Jack had already made his decision, but he chose to sit in silence for five minutes enjoying the stale cigarette.

Ivanov sat back in his chair and kicked his heavy, black boots on top of the desk. He stared up at the ceiling, humming a tune. Not a care in the world.

Jack imagined the various ways he could kill the General. Some amused him more than others.

"What are you smiling about?" Ivanov asked.

Jack shook his head. "Nothing."

Ivanov looked at his watch. "Have you made a decision?"

"Yeah," Jack said. "Go to hell."

Ivanov laughed as he rose. "Very well, Mr. Noble. Let us return to court." He started toward the door, stopped halfway and looked back at Jack. "Just remember this. When you are lying in bed wondering how the hell you got yourself into this mess, remember that you had a choice."

"I'll keep that in mind."

CHAPTER 6

C larissa lost track of time while sitting in the white windowless room. She felt disoriented. And bored. She ran out of ways to amuse herself about an hour ago. She turned to singing show tunes to pass the time, something she and her mother did when she was young.

A rap at the door jarred her back to reality. The door opened and Sinclair stepped in. He had a folder in his hand instead of his black bag. His thin lips turned upward in a smile. His silver and black mustache now wrapped all the way around his pointed chin.

Clarissa felt the rhythm of her heart quicken. The pace of her breath increased. She countered by breathing slow and deep.

Sinclair placed the folder on the table and held his hands in the air. "Relax, child. I am not here to hurt you."

Clarissa took a deep breath and clenched her fists. "Whatever it is, I'm not talking." She dipped her head slightly and followed him with her eyes.

He smiled and moved behind her, placed his hands on her shoulders, squeezing gently. She felt his breath on the back of her neck. "I'm not here to question you."

Clarissa cringed at his touch. Her eyes welled up and a tear streamed down her cheek. She bit her lip and took another deep breath.

Sinclair let go of her shoulders. Walked around the table toward the door. He opened it and leaned out. "It's OK gentlemen. You can leave." He stepped back in the room, the door slammed shut behind him. He leaned back against it, reached into his pocket and pulled out a cell phone. The phone lit up as Sinclair tapped on the screen. He looked up, smiled, and then pocketed it. "Now, where was I?" He pulled a chair out from under the table and sat down. "Again, I'm not here to question you, only to ask you a question."

Clarissa leaned back, lifted an eyebrow, said nothing.

"Are you not intrigued?"

"Intrigued?" Clarissa said. "Last time you asked me a question you held a scalding hot ice pick to my face."

Sinclair grimaced and looked down at the table. He held out his hands. "Please forgive me for my previous actions. I was only doing the job my employer asked of me that night."

Clarissa shook her head and laughed. "That makes it OK?"

"It was only a scare tactic. I never meant to harm you."

"Say it enough times and I might believe it," Clarissa said.

Sinclair licked his lips and opened his mouth to speak, but said nothing.

She raised her eyebrows and held out her hands. "What is the question?" She stared into his eyes, beckoning him to answer.

"Perhaps," he said, "I should explain some things."

"Oh, this should be good," Clarissa said. "Please, explain away."

"Child, I'm not who you think I am."

"Then why the hell did you knock me out to get me here?"

"I admit, I did sedate you, but for your own good and only to get you here." He paused, his eyes wide and focused on her. "Would you have come on your own accord?"

"No," she said without hesitation. "And if you want to ask me if I want to leave, the answer is yes."

"I'm not asking you that. Not yet, anyway." He stood up and paced the room along the far wall. "Clarissa, you left quite an impression on me. I've never seen anyone stand up to the abuse you did." He stopped and smiled at her.

She didn't smile back.

"Right," he said. "Well, I've not been able to forget that." He pulled the empty chair out of his way and placed his hands on the table. He leaned over, placing his face close to Clarissa's. "The work I did for the old man that night, that was simply contract work. I don't work for him. I work for..." he stood straight and walked to the door. Opened it and checked the hallway again.

"You work for?" Clarissa said.

He rounded the table and knelt next to her, placing his face next to hers, eye to eye. Brushed strands of her hair back behind her ears.

She fought back the urge to flinch.

He leaned in and whispered, "I work for the government, dear." He rose and leaned back against the wall behind Clarissa.

She didn't move. Didn't say anything.

"You see, I can't state exactly who for, but I lead a team," he paused a beat and then added, "a highly specialized team. And I find myself in need of another operator."

"You want me to give up Jack?" She said it too quickly. She knew he had nothing to do with this.

Sinclair laughed. "Jack, no. He'd never join us. And not for a lack of trying on my part. I recruited him heavily years ago when he was coming off his two years with, well, if you know, then you know. If not, I shouldn't say."

Clarissa nodded. She knew all about Jack's time with the government after he left the Marines.

"I need someone like you," he said. "No, I take that back. I need you."

"Me?" Clarissa turned halfway in her seat and looked up at him. She cocked her head to the side. "Why me?"

"You're tough, for one. Tougher than the men I have in this facility." He placed his hand on her shoulder again. "I don't think I've ever met someone as tough as you."

Clarissa smiled. One thing she prided herself on was her toughness.

"Sexy, too. And don't be modest and deny it. You are quite an attractive woman. You have the sultry look that all men desire."

Clarissa laughed. "Give me a break."

"Guess I should add humble too, shouldn't I?"

Clarissa rose. She braced herself, ready for him to force her back down or smack her, but he didn't. She sat on the table and faced him. "What would I do on this team?"

"Infiltrate," he said. "You'd be a spy, most of the time, at least."

"Infiltrate what?"

"I—you see, child, I can't say much more than that without giving away the nature of the team I lead." He touched his fingers to his mouth. "I just can't do that. You'd know too much and there are people in Washington who wouldn't be too happy with that."

"Washington?"

"See, just like that." He smiled. "I can't tell you any more without an answer."

"What's in this for me?"

"I'm sure you're tired of stripping."

"I'm an exotic dancer," Clarissa said without hesitation.

"Sure you are," he said. "Those men come to the club for your art."

She lowered her head, eyes focusing on the floor.

"I'm sorry," he said. "You've only done what you needed to do. I know this. Losing your father so young didn't help."

She shook her head.

"Again, I'm sorry."

"So, if I can't answer yet or just say no, are you going to hold me here?"

Sinclair shook his head and pointed over her shoulder. "There's the door. You are free to leave if you want to go."

She didn't move.

"I don't see why you would, though."

Clarissa crossed her legs and stared up at the stainless steel ceiling.

"What is the deal with the steel ceilings?" she asked.

"The man on the boat, you knew him as Mike," Sinclair said. "We put him there."

Clarissa's eyes snapped down and met Sinclair's. She focused on his good eye. "What?"

"A test."

"You put my life in danger."

"Had to. He was only to subdue you." Sinclair paced along the back wall. "We gave him orders that if you made him—submit—then he was to leave you alone. We lost our tracking in the open ocean."

"Did you tell him to try and rape me?"

"No," Sinclair said. "That wasn't part of his orders."

Clarissa smiled. "Well he didn't get to. And he's dead. Well, I assume he is. He was still alive when he fell into the ocean."

Sinclair shrugged. "No matter to me." He stopped in front of her. "It's what I expected. That's why you are here now."

Clarissa said nothing.

"Now, what do you say? Will you join us?"

She shook her head. "I don't know. I need to find out about Jack."

Sinclair nodded. "You are free to go."

"I want to think it over." She slid off the table and stood in front of him.

Sinclair reached into his pocket and pulled out his phone. He tapped on the screen, placed the phone back in his pocket and smiled at her. He stood against the wall, hands in his pockets, with his eyes, both good and bad, on her.

Clarissa didn't move. She felt calm and wary at the same time. Could this be a set up? She didn't have anything else to offer as far as information went, unless they wanted Jack. But even then, she had nothing to give. She had no idea where he was or if he would ever return.

The door opened and a blond haired man stepped in.

"Mr. Montgomery," Sinclair said. "Will you escort Ms. Abbot to the house and see that she is set up in a guest room?"

"Yes, sir," Montgomery said.

Sinclair motioned to the door. Clarissa left with Montgomery.

"I'll be up to see you tonight, child," Sinclair called from the room.

CHAPTER 7

Guards escorted Jack back to the courtroom. They stopped at the doorway. Jack walked through. The chairs had been returned to the table during his meeting with Ivanov. Pierre sat at the table, back straight and hands in his lap. Jack sat next to him. The men nodded at each other, but said nothing.

Ivanov entered the room and the door slammed behind him. Conversations quickly fell silent as the General took his seat at the bench. He leafed through folders and papers then looked up at the room. He spoke in Russian for a period and then looked back at the papers and went silent.

Jack looked to Pierre for interpretation. As expected, he got none.

"Mr. Noble," Ivanov said. "Rise."

Jack placed his hands on the table, took his time getting to his feet. He looked around the courtroom. All eyes were on him.

Ivanov dropped his head a few inches and glared. "Approach the bench."

Jack stepped to the side then walked forward, stopping three feet from the bench.

Ivanov leaned forward and motioned for Jack to step forward.

Jack did.

"Last chance, Jack," he whispered

He turned his head toward the empty jury box.

"You stand trial for the murders of Grigori Dorofeyev, Fyodr Olkhovsky, and Mikhail Korzhakov," Ivanov said loudly so the rest of the room could hear. "How do you plea?"

"You forgot about Aleksandr and Viktor," Jack said. "The bodyguards."

Ivanov said nothing. His upper lip twitched and his face turned red.

"Although technically," Jack continued, "Viktor jumped in the ocean with a line tied around his waist. Aleksandr fell in shortly after. I tried to help, but the current, you know how strong the current can be at times."

Ivanov rose and pointed at Jack. "You will not make a mockery out of the murder of my men."

Jack smiled. "Too late."

"Plead," Ivanov shouted. "Now."

"I take full responsibility for the deaths of those men. I acted on my own accord. There is no one else in this courtroom that is guilty other than me."

It was a risk, but Ivanov had already tipped his hand. If there was any way to get both Pierre and himself out of here alive, Jack figured this would do it.

"Are you saying that the man at the table is innocent?" Ivanov's finger lingered in the air, pointing over Jack's shoulder at Pierre.

"Yes," Jack replied. "Pierre is innocent. I take full responsibility."

Ivanov shook his head at Jack. He mouthed something, but Jack couldn't decipher what the General was trying to say.

"Sit, Mr. Noble."

Jack turned and Ivanov said something else in Russian.

The courtroom fell silent. Pierre looked at Jack out of the corner of his eye and nodded slightly.

The door behind them opened. Jack turned. Two guards entered the room. They pulled Oscar by his elbows, led him past the table and to a seat next to the General's bench. The large man had marks on his face. His right eyelid was swollen such that it covered his eye completely. A bandage covered half his forehead. The thick hair on the sides of his head stuck out in every direction.

Did Oscar try to protect them?

"State your name," Ivanov said.

"Oscar."

Ivanov sighed. "Your full name."

Oscar blindly stared toward the back wall and didn't respond.

"It doesn't matter. We've already established your credibility." Ivanov looked past Oscar at Jack and Pierre. "Which man reached out to you to arrange the murders?"

Oscar's eyes slowly changed focus from the back of the room toward Jack and Pierre. He stared at Jack for a beat, then at Pierre. He returned his gaze to Jack and lingered there a few more moments.

"Well?" Ivanov said.

"Don't see him."

Ivanov leaned to the side and motioned with his hand to Oscar. "What kind of game are you playing?"

"Game?" Oscar said. "Not sure I follow."

"You told us a name before. You came to us with that name. Tell the court that name."

"You didn't ask for a name. You asked me to point out the man who contacted me." Oscar looked back at the courtroom, a slight smile pushing his chubby cheeks upward. "The man contacted me on the phone. Now tell me how I'm supposed to point him out?" He laughed as he finished his sentence.

Ivanov left the bench and pulled Oscar from his seat, shook him. "Give me a name, dammit."

Oscar stopped laughing. He placed his meaty hands over Ivanov's. The guards charged, separated the heavy man and the General, and threw Oscar to the floor. One knelt on his back and held a gun to his head.

"Last chance," Ivanov said. "Name the murderer."

"Pierre," Oscar said. "The man named Pierre arranged the hit with me."

"That's not true." Jack jumped up. "It was all me. I—"

"You will have your turn again, Mr. Noble," Ivanov said. "Sit down."

Jack stood motionless for a moment before returning to his seat.

"Get him out of here," Ivanov said.

Voices murmured throughout the room. Ivanov slammed his gavel to silence the courtroom. He pointed at Pierre. "Come up here."

Pierre did as instructed and stood before Ivanov's bench.

"Are you behind this or not?"

Pierre looked back at Jack, who remained expressionless.

"Look at me, Pierre," Ivanov said. "Answer the question, and keep in mind that if there are two of you, the sentencing might be more lenient. But if only one man," he nodded toward Jack, "is found guilty, then the sentence will be death."

"I," Pierre's voice shook, "had nothing to do with this. That man impersonated me to arrange the killings to fulfill his own agenda." Pierre's closed his eyes, kept his head high.

Jack smiled.

Ivanov rubbed his forehead. "Sit."

Pierre returned to the table and sat down. His shaking hands tapped on top of the table. The sound of his fast, laborious breathing filled the air between him and Jack.

"Relax," Jack said. "It's OK. I know what I'm doing."

Pierre shook his head, avoiding eye contact with the friend he just sentenced to death.

"Jack Noble," Ivanov said. "Approach."

Jack rose and moved toward Ivanov.

"Is everything this man said true?"

"Yes," Jack said. "One hundred percent true. I arranged it. I carried it out. I enjoyed it."

Calls for his life erupted from behind him. Jack smiled at Ivanov, who shook his head in response.

"You fool." Ivanov pounded the gavel into the wooden bench. "Return to your seat." Ivanov stood. "Fifteen minute recess." He left through the door behind the bench.

"Thank you, Jack," Pierre said. He finally looked over at Jack. His eyes red, cheeks stained with the remains of his tears.

"No need to thank me."

"You just gave your life for mine," Pierre said. "Of course I thank you."

Jack shook his head. "I'm not going to die." He looked around to make sure nobody was too close. "In his office, he asked me to work for him."

Pierre leaned in and raised an eyebrow. "Did you agree?"

"No," Jack said. "I figured this was the best way to go about it, get you out of here. I'll take my sentence. Once I know everyone is in the clear, I'll accept his offer and book it back home."

Pierre nodded. Crossed his arms and leaned his head back. "What if it doesn't happen that way?"

Jack shrugged. He opened his mouth to speak, but the banging of the chamber door opening interrupted him.

Ivanov stepped through the door and took his place behind the bench. He never took his eyes off Jack. Occasionally he shook his head and muttered something under his breath. "Rise, both of you."

Jack and Pierre stood together.

Ivanov pointed to Pierre and waved him closer.

Pierre approached the bench, standing with his head tall.

"I find you not guilty," Ivanov said. "You are to be held in our custody until transport can be arranged back to—"

"Just take him to the airport," Jack said.

Ivanov pointed at Jack. "You'll get your turn."

Jack waved him off and sat down.

Ivanov returned his attention to Pierre, trying to appear calm. His red cheeks and shaky voice betrayed him. "As I was saying, as soon as we arrange transport, you will be returned to Paris. Now sit."

Pierre nodded and returned to his seat, his eyes avoiding Jack.

Jack sensed his guilt and squeezed the man's shoulder.

"Approach, Mr. Noble," Ivanov said.

Jack turned and looked at the faces in the courtroom. Half of them looked back. The other half looked away. Interesting how split they were at the prospects of looking into the eyes of a dead man. He took his time walking to the bench. When he finally stood before the Ivanov, he held his head high, cocked back. He looked above the General, not at him.

"Defiant till the end, eh?" Ivanov tapped his fingers on the bench. "Is that how you want to be remembered, Jack? Or is it better to say stupid until the end?"

Jack shrugged. "Sounds about right."

Ivanov looked past Jack and scanned the courtroom. "Jack Noble, I find you guilty for the murders of Dorofeyev, et al." He focused his gaze on Jack again. "You are sentenced to death. You will await your sentence at Penal Colony number 6 Federal Penitentiary." A murmur spread throughout the courtroom. Ivanov added, "Also known as Black Dolphin."

Jack stood tall and said nothing.

"Have you ever heard of Black Dolphin, Mr. Noble?"

Jack still said nothing.

Ivanov smiled. "They say there is only one way out of Black Dolphin, Mr. Noble. Death. And I can assure you, death will be far more inviting than life in Black Dolphin."

Jack felt his face burn. Was this a power play? The only chance Ivanov was going to give him?

Ivanov raised an eyebrow, as if inviting Jack to say something.

Jack stared at the space above Ivanov's head and didn't say a word.

"Any last words before I make this official, Jack?" Ivanov asked.

Jack cursed at Ivanov and then spit on the floor.

"Take him away," Ivanov said. "Through there."

Two guards approached. One trained his gun on Jack while the other threaded a chain between the handcuffs on Jack's wrists. They forced him to the side of the room. Jack turned and nodded at Pierre. The Frenchman did nothing in return.

The guards led Jack through a door in the side of the courtroom and down a dimly lit hallway. They stopped beside an iron door and made Jack face the wall, legs spread. One guard unlocked the door, while the other leaned in next to Jack. "You'll be dreaming of this place once you are inside Black Dolphin."

Jack turned his head.

The guards pulled him back and threw him through the open doorway, into an empty room.

"We'll be back for you soon," one of them said.

The door closed. Jack scooted back to the wall, reached into his pocket for a cigarette, but found it empty. "Dammit," he muttered.

CHAPTER 8

"You ready?" Charles asked.

"As I'll ever be," Alonso replied.

Charles stepped through French doors onto the balcony overlooking Paris. He leaned against the railing. Watched the people pass below. Tourists, locals, whatever. Soon each would play their own part in the twisted web he was weaving.

"Who else should we bring?" Alonso asked.

Charles straightened up and turned, leaning back against the railing. A breeze blew across the balcony, carrying the scents of the city. He closed his eyes and inhaled deeply. It wasn't New York, but it'd do. It had its own flavor. "Just us."

"You sure about that?"

"Yeah," Charles said. "Anymore and I think it could cause problems. Problems we don't want."

Alonso nodded.

"We want to gain their trust," Charles continued. "If we show up with four or five guys that will put them on the defensive."

"Agreed," Alonso said.

A ringing phone interrupted. "Get that." He nodded toward the door and crossed his arms over his chest.

Alonso slipped inside and reappeared a moment later holding Charles's phone. "It's the old man."

Charles rolled his eyes. Grabbed the phone. "Yeah, what's going on?"

"Good morning, Mr. Charles."

Charles squinted up at the sun. "Guess it's pretty early there?"

"I have exciting news for you."

"The Jets are being disbanded?" He held up his hand and twirled his finger around in a circle.

Alonso shook his head and sat down in a wrought iron bistro chair. He held out a cigarette to Charles, who declined.

The old man laughed. "You know I could care less for your heathen sports."

Charles shrugged. "Yeah, chess is so much more exciting."

"Our friend," the old man said, his tone serious. "Mr. Jack."

"What about him?"

"Sentenced to death by the Russians."

Charles grabbed the railing and leaned forward, as if trying to get closer to the old man. "Say again?"

The old man laughed. "He's out of your way. Will never see the light of day again, as I hear it."

"This is," Charles rubbed his chin and upper lip with his hand, "good news."

Alonso shrugged and held up his hands. He mouthed, "What?" and propped his elbows on top of the bistro table.

Charles shook his head and held up a finger. "Boss, there's still the matter of his primary associate. And the woman."

"Why can't you forget the past?" the old man said with a sigh. "Leave them be, at least for now. You've got more important matters to attend to. Get Paris straight and then we can talk about cleaning up the rest of the mess."

"You're right," Charles said.

"He was with a French spy. Jack I mean. The Frenchman was or will be released soon. I want you to reach out to the spy."

"Who is he?"

"I'll send you details securely." The old man paused. "That is all, Mr. Charles. Good luck with your meetings."

The line went dead. "Yeah, meetings." He turned to Alonso and smiled.

"Well?"

"Jack's dead."

"Dead?" Alonso leaned against the wall next to the French doors.

"Gonna be. Sentenced to death by the Russians." Charles turned and wrapped his large hands around the railing.

Alonso stood next to him. "Excellent."

"Let's go."

Charles kept pace with Alonso through the maze of streets and alleys that make up the heart of the city. He hadn't had much opportunity to venture out since arriving. Too busy setting things up, selecting men for Western European operations and making—or bribing—a few local contacts. That's why he tasked Alonso with learning the city, even bought him a car to do so.

"Why aren't we using the car?" Charles asked.

"Too much of a pain. We don't have to go far. Why deal with this mess,"—he held his arms up and motioned toward the throng of people on the sidewalks and streets—"when we can walk for thirty minutes?" He looked back at Charles.

Charles shrugged. "Whatever."

"It's good for you," Alonso said. "The exercise."

"I look like I need more exercise?"

Alonso shrugged.

"You saying I'm fat?"

"Does it really need to be said?" Alonso pointed at Charles's gut.

True enough, he'd put on a few pounds over the last few years since settling into the sedentary life as the old man's right hand man, but he wasn't fat. He considered himself in decent shape. Better shape than those pencil pushing geeks who spent their lives with their butts in a chair pounding away at some stupid keyboard.

"Screw you," Charles said.

Alonso laughed. "Almost there."

Today's meeting was with two of Foster's top guys. His men were fighting over the leftover scraps of Foster's business that other crime bosses hadn't already swooped in and taken. Charles had every intention of relieving them of their duties while offering them the opportunity to work for him.

He followed Alonso without thinking twice. Sure, it could be a set up. Though if that were the case, best to just let it happen. If the old man wanted Charles dead, he wouldn't stop until the job was done. Besides, Charles thought he had a pretty good read on Alonso, and nothing in the man's body language indicated he was doing anything out of the ordinary.

"There." Alonso pointed at a building that Charles assumed was at least three hundred years old. Chunks of plaster were missing from the facade and the windows had the distinct look of hundred year old glass. They stopped in front of an old door, painted red. Chips of paint hung from the door and were scattered along the small porch. Tiny specks of red littered the concrete stoop, ingrained in the dimples.

Alonso knocked on the door.

A few moments later the door cracked open. A man stuck his head through the opening revealing spiky brown hair. His face was unshaven and his eyes darted around wildly.

Charles shot a look at Alonso. Alonso nodded.

"Who are you guys?" the man asked.

"Alonso," Alonso pointed at his own chest, "and Charles. May we?" He gestured toward the door.

The man opened the door and stepped back. "I'm Adrien."

Charles stepped through the door and waited for Adrien to guide them down the hall. The man walked by and looked at Charles a half dozen times for no more than a second per glance.

Nasty tweaker.

"Nice place you have here," Charles said.

"Yeah," Adrien said. "It's all right."

Charles heard chatter above them, light and soft, female voices. He reached out and tapped Alonso's shoulder, pointed at the ceiling.

Alonso shrugged and shook his head. He held a finger to his mouth.

Charles nodded.

Adrien opened a door and ushered the men into the kitchen. Another man sat at the table.

He stood and extended an arm. "Casper." His accent thick and French.

"Like the friendly freaking ghost?" Charles asked.

Casper blinked and said nothing.

"Tough room," Charles said.

"Please," Adrien said while pulling out two chairs. "Sit."

"You first," Alonso said.

Adrien shot him a look, eyes narrow, mouth open.

"Sorry," Alonso said. "You first, please."

Casper nodded toward Adrien, who took a seat opposite his partner.

Alonso took the seat against the wall and Charles sat down with his back to the open kitchen. The big man moved around in his seat and fiddled with his hands.

"Uncomfortable?" Casper asked.

"Don't like my back to the room. Know what I mean?" Thumps above caught his attention. He looked up.

Casper nodded. "Don't worry, we are the only ones here."

Charles glanced at Alonso, who remained expressionless.

Casper spoke. "Can we get you anything to—"

"Let's get right to it," Charles said. "I'm taking over these operations. From now on you report—"

"Like hell you are." Casper stood and kicked his chair backwards to the floor.

Charles responded in kind. The two men squared off.

"What my friend here is saying," Alonso said, "is that we would like to make an arrangement with you."

Tense silence filled the room. Charles and Casper stood inches apart, each ready to attack.

Casper took a deep breath, stepped back and picked up his chair, sat down, further from the table than before. "What kind of arrangement?"

"You need protection, correct?" said Alonso. "We can provide it."

Charles studied the faces of the men.

Casper held his elbow and tapped his right index finger against his chin. His lips puckered. His eyes looked at an imaginary spot on the ceiling. "You don't know this city, the way things work," Casper said. "How can you offer protection?"

"Through brute friggin' force," Charles said.

"That doesn't work," Casper said. "Not here."

"Yeah, man," Adrien said. "You won't get anywhere with that."

"Oh?" Charles slammed his fist into the side of Adrien's face. The impact of the blow spun the man around. He fell from his chair and collapsed on the floor.

"The hell?" Casper stood again and reached for his waistband. His hand tightened around the handle of a pistol that had been hidden under his shirt.

"Everyone just calm the hell down," Alonso said.

Charles stood and walked to the other end of the kitchen. He leaned back against the stove.

Adrien scraped himself up off the floor and pulled himself into his chair. His head wobbled.

"Listen," Alonso said. "We know what's going on. You guys are being pulled at on both ends by some pretty powerful people. We can help you with that. We have some pretty big backers ourselves."

"And if we say no?" Casper said.

"For Christ's sake," Charles said. He pulled a gun from under his shirt and shot Adrien in the chest.

Casper started to pull his pistol from his waistband. Alonso tackled him from behind and pinned him to the ground, knee in the man's back, elbow against his head.

Charles heard screams from upstairs.

"Ok," he said. "What the hell is that?"

"Thought you knew about our business," Casper said through labored breaths. "Those are the girls we sell."

"Sick bastard." Charles kicked the man across his face and Casper's body went limp.

Alonso stood up. "That went well."

"Screw 'em," Charles said. "Tie him up. He might be useful to us later."

Alonso dug through kitchen drawers and found some cord. He sat Casper up in a chair, secured the man's legs and torso.

Screams continued to penetrate through the ceiling.

Charles stepped over Adrien's lifeless body, being careful to avoid the pool of blood surrounding his torso. "Let's check that out." He walked back through the hallway to the narrow stairs near the door. He motioned Alonso ahead of him, and followed the man to the second floor.

"Hello?" Alonso called out.

Silence. Charles stopped at the landing and rested against the wall. Closed his eyes.

"In here," a voice called back, a mixture of hope and desperation.

A padlocked door prohibited their entry.

Alonso shrugged.

Charles rolled his eyes. "Step back from the door." He waited a beat, then kicked the middle of the door. It cracked and buckled upon the impact of his size 14 shoe.

Alonso stepped forward, pushed the door out of the way.

The men froze at the sight before them.

The room had to be no more than twenty by twenty feet. Fifteen young women, possibly teenagers, huddled in the back of the room.

"Jesus Christ," Charles said. "What the hell is this place? Who are you?"

None of the women said anything. They looked at each other, their faces twisted, eyes pleading.

Alonso stared wide eyed and slack jawed at the throng of girls.

The room had a rotten stench. The women wore tattered, dirty clothes.

Their hair tangled and unkempt. Some wept, others slumped to the floor. It appeared as though they didn't know whether to be happy or afraid.

Charles pulled out his phone and dialed the old man.

"Everything OK, Mr. Charles?"

"Feng, you gotta level with me. What's going on over here?"

"I'm sorry?"

"We're having a meeting with Foster's guys. This place," Charles paused a beat as he scanned the room. "It's like something out of a horror flick."

The old man said nothing.

"I mean, there are women, hell, girls here, being held in a room. A single tiny friggin' room."

"I heard something about Mr. Foster before," the old man said. "Into some bad stuff."

"I can confirm it," Charles said.

"Here is what I want you to do. Help the girls out for now. Don't do anything else until you hear from me."

"OK."

"I want you to reach out to the Frenchman. I'll have his contact information to you tomorrow. I'll send a man."

"OK."

"He'll be able to help and get those girls home."

"OK." Charles hung up. Grabbed Alonso's shoulder. "Go get Casper. Bring him up here."

Alonso slipped out of the room.

Charles turned his attention to the girls at the other end of the room. His heart cried out for them, their families who had no idea what had happened to their little girls.

"Ladies," Charles said. "I'm not gonna hurt you. We're gonna get you home."

None of them said a word. A few cried. A few hugged. A few stared blankly at him.

Finally, one stepped forward, slipping through from the back of the huddle. She tucked her dark, curly hair behind her ears. Her brown eyes burned. "Why should we trust you?"

Why should they? Charles couldn't think of a good answer. He opened his mouth, paused a moment, and then said, "I'm not a good man. I admit that. But, if I didn't want to help you, you'd be dead already."

A few of the girls gasped. The dark haired girl nodded. "It'll be OK, girls.

I trust him. Let's trust him." She turned to them, arms out, slightly bent over at the waist. "We've got to trust him."

Alonso's voice echoed through the hall as he and Casper approached the room.

Charles waited for them to reach the doorway. He reached out, grabbed Casper by the back of the head and threw him across the room.

Casper slammed into the wall and fell to his knees. He spun around and leaned back against the wall. Blood covered his chin, neck and shirt.

Charles lifted an eyebrow and glanced at Alonso.

Alonso shrugged.

"This man ever hurt any of you?"

The teenage women said nothing.

"There'll be no retribution," he said. "Did he?"

The dark haired girl spoke first. "He raped me my first night here."

Charles moved toward Casper, picked him up by his throat and slammed him against the wall. He reached down and undid Casper's thick black leather belt then shoved him into the corner of the room. He aimed his gun at Casper's head. The leather belt dangled from his outstretched arm, toward the group of women.

"Want to hit him?" Charles asked.

The dark haired girl paused. "Yes," she said. She stepped forward and took the belt from Charles.

He looked at her face. Her nostrils flared, mouth drawn wide, brows furrowed and her eyes narrowed. She lifted her arm high, letting the belt dangle behind her back. It twisted and turned like a snake. She whipped her arm over her head, brought the belt down across Casper's face. The heavy leather hit with a loud smack. It left a dark red mark and a cut across his cheek. Blood trickled from the wound.

"He raped me too," another girl said from the huddle which now spread out.

Charles didn't look back. He kept his gun and his eyes on Casper and smiled when the condemned man's eyes met his.

One by one, the girls took turns whipping Casper with the belt. Midway through Charles stripped him of his clothes. When the women were done, Casper's body looked as though he had been hit by a truck. Battered and bruised. His body convulsed. He wept on the floor.

Charles looked back at Alonso, who stood in the doorway, his face tight and drawn. Did he agree? Was he upset? It didn't matter.

Charles raised his gun in the air. "Should I?"

The dark haired girl stepped forward. "Let me."

"What's your name?" Charles asked.

"Missy."

"Ever killed a man?"

"No."

"How old are you?"

"Eighteen."

Charles studied her. Her eyes were focused, her breathing normal. She held her head high and her shoulders back. Defiant. Unafraid. He clicked the safety off, chambered a bullet and handed the gun to Missy.

She smiled as she looked at the heavy weapon in her hand. She admired the weight of it while balancing the pistol in her hand. Traced the barrel with her fingers. She seemed to enjoy the power. She looked powerful holding it. Like a natural fit.

"Any last words, Casper?" he asked.

"Screw you," Casper said, his voice broken and choked from the blood in his mouth.

"Never again," Missy said.

She knelt beside him, whispered in his ear.

Casper dropped his head to the floor.

Missy placed the gun to the side of his head. Pulled the trigger. The sound of the gunshot ripped through the air and echoed through the room.

Some of the girls screamed. Others sobbed. A few smiled.

Charles looked out the window. The street was empty, for the most part. He looked over his shoulder at fourteen relieved faces, looked at Missy on her knees, resting on her heels. She looked up. Their eyes locked. She smiled. Charles offered her his hand and she took it. He pulled her to her feet, leaned in and whispered in her ear. "I'm gonna take good care of you, if you want to stay."

"Yes," she said. "I've got nowhere else to go."

"How many showers does this place have?" Alonso asked.

"Three," one of the girls said.

"Wash up," Alonso said. "Quickly."

"Call for some cars," Charles said.

Alonso nodded and retrieved his cell phone from his pocket. He disappeared through the doorway, down the hall.

"We're getting you ladies out of here," Charles said. "And then getting you home."

CHAPTER 9

The hours melted into one another. Bear had been driving non-stop since leaving Florida. The New York state line approached. They wouldn't be going into the city. Not yet, at least. First stop would be an hour north. A small place he and Jack kept. A vacation home when one of them wanted to get away and do some fishing. Or just disappear. He looked over at Mandy. The little girl stretched her arms, yawned and opened her eyes.

"Where are we?" she asked.

"Almost to New York," he said.

She clutched at her seat belt. Her breathing quickened. "I don't want to go back to New York."

Bear reached over and placed his hand on her head. "It's OK, sweetie. We'll be out of the city." *For now.*

She took a deep breath, like he'd taught her, and seemed to control her emotions. "OK, Bear. I trust you."

He laughed. "I hope so." He waited, but she said nothing. "How about a movie tonight?"

She shrugged. "Guess so."

He didn't know what to expect from the girl. She'd been through so much the last few weeks. It'd be a good idea to contact his sister, a licensed therapist, for some advice. Of course, that would mean *contacting* his sister. They hadn't talked in four years, and he wasn't sure how receptive she'd be to the situation. Katie wasn't the biggest fan of his work. He brushed the idea aside, and focused on the highway and the traffic up ahead.

On cue, his phone rang. He looked at the caller ID. Brandon.

"What you got for me?" Bear asked.

"Some good news," Brandon paused a beat. "And some bad news, Bear."

"Give me the good news."

"I've got confirmation on your guys, Russ's team."

"OK, good. Hold the details. I can't take them right now."

"OK."

"What else?" Bear asked.

"I don't have double confirmation, but I think I've got enough to tell you that Clarissa's safe."

"Why can't I reach her?"

"I feel confident in saying you'll be able to soon."

"Where is she?"

"Really can't say anything else. It'll be up to her what to reveal."

"A mystery. Great."

Mandy slapped his leg and gave him a stern look.

Bear laughed.

"What?" Brandon asked.

"Nothing," Bear said. Reluctantly, he added, "What's the bad news?" He squeezed the steering wheel with his left hand, waiting for the answer he already knew.

"It's Jack," Brandon said.

Bear lowered his voice. "Dead?" Out of the corner of his eye he saw Mandy jerk her heard sideways.

"No, not yet anyway."

Bear waited, but Brandon went silent. "What is it then?"

Brandon sighed. "The Russians found him guilty of murdering those politicians—"

"Two politicians and a General," Bear said.

"And two bodyguards and a deckhand. That's beside the point, Bear. They found him guilty. He took the rap for the Frenchman, too."

"What's the sentence?" Bear asked. He already knew, though.

"Death."

Bear said nothing.

"Serving his sentence in a place called Black Dolphin," Brandon said. "Ever heard of it?"

"Yeah, bad place." Bear rolled down his window and spit, trying to get rid of the bad taste in his mouth. "We got anyone that can help?"

"I'm trying, my man, trying."

"I'll reach out to Pierre," Bear said. "Anything changes on Clarissa, you let me know. Send me the information on that other guy, too."

"Will do on both counts, man."

Bear hung up.

"Are we going to see Ms. Clarissa soon?" Mandy asked.

"Yeah," Bear said. He didn't know for sure, but why tell her that?

Bear spent the next two hours deep in thought, too many thoughts to make sense of. He struggled to find a way to help Jack, but came up with no solution. He only knew he had to do something. He pulled off of I-287 and took Skyline Drive north, toward Ringwood, where they owned a house near the Wanaque Reservoir.

Mandy awoke as the car slowed down. "Where are we?"

"Almost there," Bear said.

He guided the car along the winding road and pulled into a residential neighborhood. Two minutes later he parked the car on a paved driveway, behind the house.

"Stay here," he said.

Mandy pushed back in the seat and stared out the window.

Bear got out and walked through the light rain along the side of the house, across to the front, and to the other side. He went to the door and peeked in through the windows. Finally, he pulled out a key and opened the door. He stepped inside and his phone rang. He answered without checking the caller ID.

"Hi Bear," Clarissa said.

"Jesus, girl," Bear said. "Scared the crap out of me."

"I'm sorry."

"What happened?"

"Um, I can't really say," she said.

"What the hell do you mean? After what you put me through?"

"I said sorry, my God."

"Where are you?"

"I'll be back in New York soon," she said.

"You know the house on the reservoir?"

"Yeah, I've been there."

"I need you to come here, watch the girl. I got business in the city. Can you do that?"

"Sure," she said. "Don't want to go back to my apartment just yet, anyway."

Bear sighed. *Plan's coming together.*

"Crap, I gotta go, Bear."

"Wait, before you go I need to tell you something—," the line went dead. "About Jack."

Bear tossed the phone on the couch. He stepped through the door and waved Mandy out of the car.

The little girl slipped through the open door, ran through the rain, up the stairs and across the porch. She found the couch and TV remote, smiled as she flipped through the stations and found her favorite program, *Phineas and Ferb.*

So simple, so easy. All cares erased by the comfort of familiar faces and voices.

"Ms. Clarissa is gonna be here tomorrow, sweetie."

"Cool," the little girl said, barely turning her head to respond.

"Cool," Bear repeated. Very cool, indeed.

J ack sat alone on the bench seat positioned at the rear of the old bus. Diesel fumes filled the air. Nausea kicked in occasionally. That or his nerves got the better of him. He looked around the mostly empty bus. Just him, five other prisoners, four guards, and the driver. The driver looked back in the wide rear view mirror every few minutes. He had a broad face with red puffy cheeks that pushed his lower eyelids higher than they would naturally sit. Russian Santa Claus bringing a gift of fresh bait to the Black Dolphin. The guards didn't move unless someone said something. Only one person said something, though, and that beating he took was enough to keep the rest of the prisoners quiet.

The man had sat across from Jack, said something in Russian, then laughed. Two guards wasted no time, rushed him from the aisle. When they finished, blood poured from the man's mouth. Now he sat sideways in his seat, head back, with a trickle of blood streaming down his chin.

Jack turned in his seat and stared out the window at the bleak brown landscape that gave way to gray skies at the horizon. His mind wandered and started to recall everything that happened to land him in this situation. He quickly brushed the thoughts away. No point in going down that road. He figured he'd have plenty of time for that inside a prison cell.

Prison.

The thought made him nauseous.

He had no idea what to expect when the bus stopped. Pierre had tried to tell him about the place nicknamed Black Dolphin, supposedly one of Russia's oldest and most hardcore prisons.

Only one way out of Black Dolphin.

One of the guards stood and started walking toward the back of the bus. Jack sat up straight, eyes forward.

The guard stopped and looked down at Jack. The man had brown hair and light brown eyes. His face wasn't hardened like the other three. No, this man still had youth on his side. "May I sit?" he asked in English.

Jack nodded and slid toward the window.

"You are the man, Noble, yeah?"

Jack nodded and said nothing, eyes still forward.

The guard checked over his shoulder and lowered his voice. "I'm glad you did what you did."

Jack didn't move.

"Those men were bad news."

Jack looked at the guard. "You shouldn't be saying these things."

The guard shrugged. "No one here speaks English. I think."

Jack smiled. The guard had balls. Jack could respect him for that.

"If you had gone to a real court, you would have won."

A real court. Like he had a chance. Jack shrugged.

"You can appeal," the guard said. He looked up. "We're almost there. My name is Alik. I'll be inside and will do what I can to see that you are treated fairly, Mr. Noble."

Jack nodded at Alik. "Good, I won't have to kill you then."

"I like your confidence," Alik said as he stood. "Don't lose it. You're going to need it in there." He pointed toward the front of the bus.

Jack craned his neck and saw a circling double layer of barbed wire fences. Beyond the fence stood the prison, long and gray and two stories high. An arch roofed adorned the center of the building and was flanked by dormers. The bus stopped at the gate. The gate opened and eight guards stepped through. They walked along the side of the bus, shouting across at each in Russian, a cadence to their calls. The men circled and crossed paths in the back. Two entered the bus, walked to the back. Two more stepped on and stood at the front, aiming rifles at the prisoners.

The guards behind Jack whispered to one another in Russian and then laughed. One put his hand on Jack's shoulder.

Jack fought the urge to flinch. He wished he had a free hand. Jack watched as the other prisoners were escorted off the bus, one at a time by a single guard. The bus was empty except for him and the two guards behind him. He turned his head.

"Shall we leave, gentlemen?" he asked.

The guard closest brought his fist down across Jack's nose.

Jack's head snapped to the side and his eyes watered. He shrugged his nose up and down. It wasn't broken. He touched his upper lip with his tongue. No blood. He smiled.

Four more guards entered the bus. One stepped forward, pointed an assault rifle in Jack's direction and barked orders in Russian.

The guards behind Jack jerked him from his seat. Each grabbed inside his arms and pushed him forward.

Jack heard the deep, loud barks of what he assumed were very large dogs outside the bus.

The guard with the assault rifle backed up to the driver's seat. The other three guards slipped in between bench seats and trained their pistols on Jack's head.

He looked at his reflection in the wide rear view mirror and smiled at the sight of red laser beams dancing on his forehead. He nodded at each guard as he passed. None returned the greeting. When he reached the front, the guard at the head of the bus stuck the barrel of his assault rifle in the side of Jack's neck.

"Down the stairs," he said in English. "Nice and easy."

Jack looked down, through the open door. Two guards stood six feet from the doorway, both equipped with the assault rifles. Behind them, six additional guards waited, each holding a chain that connected to extremely large German Shepherds that had to weigh 150 pounds, if not more.

"They'll kill you on command," the guard said from behind him.

Jack took the stairs one at a time. Slow and steady. He kept his chained hands in front of him, held out as far as he could. He stepped off the bus. The two guards stepped back and waved him forward. He took three steps. They motioned for him to stop.

The remaining guards exited the bus and surrounded him. The guards with the dogs stepped to the side.

Jack felt two barrels in his back, pushing him forward.

"Move," a heavily accented voice said from behind him.

The convoy of guards shrunk to four after they entered the prison. Two in front, two in back. Faces pressed against thick glass as Jack walked through the open area of the prison. Most jeered at him. Some stared blankly at him. He stopped looking around and kept his focus forward.

"Stop."

Jack stopped.

The guard to his front right stepped forward, turned right and opened a door. Two guards hooked their arms around Jack's elbows and led him into a small bare room with a single locker in the far corner. The four guards piled in, positioning themselves in each corner.

One held out a key. "Come here."

Jack stepped forward.

"Your arms."

Jack failed to comply.

The guard punched Jack in the stomach.

Jack stepped back but didn't buckle over, which seemed to anger the guard even more.

The guard reached down and yanked Jack's wrists up. He unlocked the cuffs. "Strip."

Jack failed to comply.

The guard nodded at the man in the back of the room and Jack felt his hands on him.

One move, that would be all it would take, and Jack could end the man's life. That would probably mean the end of his life, too, so he shelved the idea for later.

The guard stripped Jack of his clothes. They poked and prodded him. He stood still. Stayed silent.

The guard in the far corner opened a locker and pulled out a black jump-suit and a black and white striped hat. He threw the clothes at Jack.

Jack caught the bundle. He held up the cap. "Seriously? What is this, a friggin' cartoon?"

"Humiliation is what it is," a guard said. "Put them on."

Jack dressed.

They moved him back to the hall. "From now on," the guard said, "this is how you will be transported." He nodded.

Two guards grabbed Jack's arms and pulled them to the side and up behind his back. The third grabbed the back of Jack's head and tried to push him forward, nose to the floor.

Jack resisted, pushed back despite the burning in his arms as the other guards twisted his wrists. Pain burned through his shoulders.

"Bend over and look at the floor," a guard shouted.

"Screw you," Jack said through gritted teeth.

A guard came around to the front and pushed his partner out of the way.

Jack rolled his neck.

"Here you walk like we tell you to walk," the guard said. "Arms back, head down, looking at the floor."

Jack said nothing.

"Now bend over."

Jack still said nothing.

The man smiled and slammed the butt of his assault rifle into Jack's midsection, causing him to double over. He felt a hand on his head. The guards pushed and pulled him through the white halls of the prison, shouting at him in Russian along the way. In between their shouts, the halls were dead silent. Not the way he imagined it. In his visions, this place looked like something out of an old movie, with men leaning against rusted bars banging cups and screaming obscenities.

They stopped. One guard opened a solid metal door. Behind the door stood another door, this one lined with bars. A cell within a cell.

"Your new residence, Mr. Noble," the guard said.

The pressure in his arms slackened. An arm wrapped around his neck and pulled him up straight. He stared into the room. It appeared to be solid concrete with bars lining the front and back walls.

"Looks homey," Jack said.

"Hope you enjoyed your time outside, Mr. Noble," the guard said. "You'll never see it again."

They pushed Jack inside the room and closed the doors behind him.

He stumbled to the floor. Pushed himself up and hopped to his feet. Turned to face the bunk bed and saw his new roommate.

The man sat up and Jack took notice of his dark, sullen eyes which were set deep in his bald, misshapen head. He put his feet on the floor and reached his thick arms out and up, using them to grab the bunk above him and pull himself from his mattress. He stood tall and looked down at Jack.

Jack looked up and estimated the man at close to seven feet tall.

The man rolled his broad shoulders and smiled, revealing a mouth half full of rotten teeth, half full of emptiness.

"I'm Jack."

"I'll kill you," the man said in English, his accent thicker than the guards.

"Nice place you have here."

"It's my place."

"What happened to your last roommate?"

"He asked too many questions."

CHAPTER 11

"We're almost there," Sinclair said.

Clarissa nodded. She stared out the tinted window at the Chesapeake Bay. The rhythmic sound of the car passing over the bridge's joints lulled her into a state of suspended reality. The car descended into a tunnel and dull yellow lighting filled the back of the stretch limo.

"Hate tunnels," Sinclair said.

"Really?" Clarissa said. "Didn't think you feared anything."

Sinclair laughed. "I fear lots, child. It's pushing through those fears that makes me who I am."

She nodded again. He'd been cordial the past couple of days, but she was ready to get home. That's why she agreed to the meeting.

"He's very excited to meet you," Sinclair said.

"What's he like?"

"Older. Smart as a whip and in excellent shape. Strong leader. Stern but fair."

The limo emerged from the tunnel and filtered sunlight penetrated the car. She rubbed her eyes and pulled her sunglasses over her face. "Langley Air Force Base?"

"Correct," he replied flatly.

"Did your homework on me?"

"Yes, but that's not why we chose Langley."

Clarissa shrugged.

"Besides, you've likely never been where we're going." He reached into his bag.

"Don't sedate me again."

Sinclair looked up and smiled. "Don't worry." He pulled something out of the bag and held it up. "Just a blindfold."

"Why?"

"You know the base like the back of your hand. Correct?"

She said nothing.

"Until you agree to join us, I can't show you the way. Understand?"

She sighed. "Just give me the blindfold."

Sinclair tossed the blindfold across the space between them. "You don't have to wear it yet."

Clarissa didn't respond. She turned her head and watched the trees, houses and buildings pass by in a blur alongside I-64.

Ten minutes later they pulled up to a security gate outside Langley Air Force Base. Sinclair cleared his throat and gestured with his hand.

Clarissa sighed, pulled the blindfold over her head and stuck her middle finger in the air. What a pain in the ass. But, he had a point. Clarissa had spent enough time on this base as a kid that she did know the layout fairly well. Perhaps something was not what it appeared to be. She heard the sound of knuckles tapping on glass. She held her breath. The sound of the window between the front seat and the rear of the limo lowering played a few feet in front of her. Sinclair said something to the driver, but his voice was too low for her to make out the words. Five minutes passed, then another five. Her patience wore thin.

"Quit driving in circles," she said. "I don't remember this place that well."

He laughed. "You are something else. How did you know?"

She shook her head and said nothing.

"Just take us there," Sinclair said to the driver.

A few minutes later the car stopped. She heard the driver's door open, then shut, followed by the sound of metal grating on metal.

"Can I take this off yet?" she asked, tugging at the corner of the blindfold.

"Not yet," Sinclair replied.

The driver's door opened and closed. The car dipped and bounced as the driver sat down. The engine started and the car pulled forward, stopped again. She heard voices in the background, indistinguishable. Chains clattered as what sounded like a metal roller door was being lifted. More voices from outside the car.

"Pull through," a man's voice said.

The limo started moving. She felt herself lifted out of her seat and forward. They were descending.

"Now?" she asked.

"Yes," Sinclair said. "Keep your head forward."

She took off the blindfold and tossed it at Sinclair. She looked out the windows and saw they were in a cramped tunnel. The car rolled inches from the wall on either side.

"I said forward."

"What's your problem? There's nothing to see here."

Sinclair sighed. "Are you always this difficult?"

"You haven't figured that out yet?"

"No wonder Noble's so drawn to you."

"What's that supposed to mean?" She narrowed her eyes and drowned a smile.

"A challenge," he replied. "You are a challenge."

She smiled.

Sinclair appeared to smile back, although he quickly covered it up with a fake yawn. He folded his arms across his chest, then placed them back at his side. His legs crossed and uncrossed.

"What?" she asked.

He frowned. "Nothing."

"Doesn't look like nothing," she said.

"We're almost there." He leaned forward and pointed at her. "Only address him as sir. Don't contradict him. And for God's sake, don't tell him no."

Before she could form a response, the limo stopped and Sinclair stepped out.

"Clarissa," he said.

She opened her door and stepped out of the car. They were in a bunker at least a couple hundred feet under the surface, judging by the angle of the road behind her and the time it took to get down here. The walls were high and painted grey.

Sinclair started forward and opened a door in the middle of the wall. Clarissa followed him, staying close as he led her through a maze of dimly lit corridors. A hundred questions raced through her mind, but she didn't ask a single one. They approached doors at regular intervals and her heart beat faster in anticipation.

"Up ahead." Sinclair pointed a narrow finger toward the end of the hall-way. The area widened and revealed a steel door with no windows. To the side was some kind of machine. Sinclair stopped at the door, slid over to the machine. He placed his hand on it and leaned forward. "Red tidal fox jump."

A series of beeps and clicks followed. He reached out and opened the door. "Follow." He led her down another long hallway and stopped in front of yet another solid door. "Wait here." He slipped out of sight.

Clarissa leaned back against the wall. The place looked solid. Carved from the earth and dressed in concrete. She'd heard her dad talk about places like this. Never imagined she'd be inside one, though.

Sinclair opened the door. "He's ready to see you."

"The leader of the alien revolution?"

Sinclair rolled his eyes.

Clarissa shrugged. "You know that was funny, Sinclair. Don't be such a fuddy-duddy."

"Don't say it again. And don't ever use the word *fuddy-duddy* in my presence."

"Fine." She followed Sinclair through another hallway. She felt more comfortable with him now, and his concern for her safety seemed genuine.

Finally, they entered a small room. She stepped through the doorway and smiled at the older man already seated at the table.

He nodded at her. He had a full head of grey hair, cropped close to his head, and deep blue eyes. His chin was square and gave way to a hardened jaw line. The man looked like he was cut from steel.

"Clarissa," Sinclair said. "This is—"

"Sir will do for now," he said. "Given her history, it's best that she doesn't know my name."

"My history?" she said.

The man cleared his throat. "I was getting to that, Clarissa."

She looked down at the floor.

"Your background, Ms. Abbot," he continued. "You may have heard of me before, and if so, it's best that you don't know who I am."

She nodded.

"And I'd appreciate it if you call me Sir," he added.

"Yes, Sir."

"Mr. Sinclair has filled you in on the details?"

"No," Clarissa said. "I have no idea what I'm doing here."

"I want you to be part of my team," he said. "You'll work under Sinclair. We think you have amazing potential and can work as our set up agent."

"Set up agent?" she asked.

"You'll work undercover, for the most part. You'll infiltrate groups we want to take down by getting close to their leaders."

"How will I accomplish that?"

"You'll have to be creative," Sinclair said.

"Yes," the older man said. "But that's not all you'll be doing. We'll train you in different areas and you'll do a great bit of intelligence work."

"Who will I work for?" she asked.

The men looked at each other, nodded and turned back to her. They said nothing.

"You can't tell me? Or you won't tell me?"

"At this time," the older man said. "We can't tell you."

"It's for your protection," Sinclair said.

"I can figure it out," she said. "There aren't that many options to choose from."

"More than you realize," the man said.

Clarissa sat back and studied him. His hardened face made it near impossible to get a read on him. She trusted Sinclair and he trusted this man. Plus, the job intrigued her.

"What about my regular life?" she asked.

"You can go on living it," the man said. "Only you won't have to worry about dancing anymore. You'll make more than enough money doing this."

"And my friends, family," she said. "Will I be able to tell them what I'm doing?"

The man placed his forearm on the table and leaned over. "You know the answer to that. But I'll reiterate it here." He paused making sure he had her attention. "No."

"They'll never know where I am when I'm away?" she asked.

"Correct," Sinclair said.

"What do you say?" the older man asked. "Will you join us?"

Clarissa clasped her hands together behind her head, looked up at the concrete ceiling. *Don't say no.* "I'll need to think about it."

The man sighed, nodded. "I understand. It's a lot to think about." He looked over at Sinclair.

"We've deposited a—" Sinclair rubbed at his jaw while he searched for the right words, "signing bonus of sorts into an account for you." He placed a folded piece of paper in her hand. "You can check the account balance out when you get home. You can let me know you accept or simply spend money from the account."

Clarissa tucked the paper inside her bra.

Sinclair stepped out of the room leaving her and the older man alone. She studied him but still couldn't get a read on him.

He broke the silence. "I knew your dad. Knew him well."

Clarissa smiled.

"Served together many years ago," he said. "After I left the Marines, came here, he continued to help me out."

"Is that why—"

"You're here?" he said. "No. This is all Sinclair. He's vouching for you."

Clarissa said nothing.

"Well, I hope you'll consider joining us. We need you." He stood up and walked past her, stopping to squeeze her shoulder before leaving the room.

Sinclair stepped back in. "Let's go. I have a flight to New York for you. It leaves in forty-five minutes."

CHAPTER 12

"What do you mean you can't help me, Michel?"

"Sorry, Pierre, there's nothing we can do."

Pierre clenched his jaw and took a deep breath. "This man put his life on the line for us. He lied during a tribunal to save my ass. Now you're telling me we can't do anything for him?"

"What do you want us to do?" Michel said. "Get a team and infiltrate Russia's most secure prison? That will go over real well."

"Screw you, Michel," Pierre said. "Keep working on this."

He slammed his phone against the porcelain sink. Stared at himself in the mirror.

"You coward," he yelled at his reflection.

He brought his arms up and punched the mirror with both fists. It shattered. His fingers bled. He ran them under cold water and bandaged them. Shards of glass covered the floor. He stepped over them and made his way through his apartment to the kitchen. He opened a cabinet and grabbed the first bottle of alcohol he could find without checking the label. He'd only been home a few hours, but guilt ate at him. It continued to grow with every passing moment. Perhaps alcohol would help to slow it down.

He stepped onto his balcony, leaned over the railing and lit a cigarette. Kids played in the courtyard below. Sunlight faded. So did his guilt as the alcohol worked its way through his body. It dulled his senses. Dulled his pain.

I'll get you out of there, Jack. Somehow.

He chain smoked three cigarettes and polished off half the bottle in the same time span. The sun set and the courtyard emptied, save for a couple making out in the corner. Pierre stepped back into his apartment, looked around. He had to get out. He changed clothes and hit the street.

The cool air felt refreshing on his flush face. He breathed in the smells of the city. *Home.* He'd been around the world, but no place felt like Paris. He wandered aimlessly for half an hour. Rounded a corner and saw *Le Cafe* across the street. He smiled. Perhaps he hadn't been wandering as aimlessly as he thought.

The patio was packed, every table full. He watched the patrons as they ate and carried on in lively conversation. He looked for Kat, but none of the wait staff were visible on the patio. He leaned back against a building and smoked.

Kat stepped through the door onto the patio carrying a tray of food. Her hair was pulled back tonight. Stunning was the only word that came to mind as Pierre watched her slip between the tables.

He crushed his cigarette and turned away and located the closest bar.
Time to refuel.

Forty-five minutes later he stumbled out of the bar and crossed the street. The patio of *Le Cafe* was nearly empty now. He fumbled with the gate latch. Gave up and hopped the fence and took a seat in the corner, his back to the road.

Kat stepped through the door.

Pierre straightened up and waited for her to spot him. He smiled.

She backed up against the door.

"Please," he said. "At least allow me to explain."

She shook her head.

Pierre stood, walked to her and took her hands in his. "Kat, I'm sorry. If I'd have known those men were following me—"

"Who are you?" she asked.

Pierre dropped his head. "I can't tell you."

"What can you tell me?"

"I can tell you that for two years I've watched you. Wanted you. Always convinced myself otherwise because of what I do. But now..."

"Now what?"

He sighed. "I'm tired of that life, Kat. I want to start anew."

"With me?"

"Maybe?"

"You don't even know me."

"I don't even know myself anymore."

"What?"

Pierre turned and looked up at the sky.

She placed her hand on his shoulder. "I'm off in twenty minutes. Let's go have that drink, Pierre."

"I could use a drink."

Pierre and Kat stood in the courtyard of her apartment building. Alcohol coursed through him and he could see the same in her. Kat's eyes were wide and glazed over. Her cheeks flush. She stood in front of him, arms at her side, mouth partly open. She blinked slowly. He reached out and took her hands. She stepped forward. He leaned in. They kissed.

"Come up," she said.

Pierre pulled her close. Her hair fell across his face. He inhaled her scent.

She stepped back and tugged at him. "Please?"

Pierre pulled back. "I want to. You've no idea how much I want to."

"But?"

"Kat, tonight isn't a good night. It's just not right."

She stepped forward. Wrapped her arms around his neck. "I can make it a good night." Her fingers ran through his hair, nails lightly scraping against his scalp.

"I don't doubt that," he said. "But there is something I need to take care of before I can do this."

She stepped back and smiled. "I can take care of anything you want."

"Go upstairs, Kat." Pierre turned around. "I'll call you tomorrow."

"Promise?"

"Yes."

Pierre started walking toward the archway that ran under the front of the complex. He didn't look back. He hadn't heard Kat go inside and knew if he looked back he'd never leave. That just wasn't acceptable tonight. He pushed through the heavy iron gate that stretched floor to ceiling. It slammed shut behind him. The sound echoed through the quiet neighborhood. He turned and saw Kat still standing in front of her building. He reached for the gate and pulled the handle. Locked. It was for the better.

She blew him a kiss.

He waved.

She turned and disappeared into the darkness.

Pierre took a deep breath and started toward home. Footsteps fell behind him, matching stride for stride with his. He looked over his shoulder and

420 / L.T. RYAN

saw two men, both dressed in dark suits. He turned at the next intersection, looked over his shoulder again. They turned, too.

They were following him.

He heard a car approach from behind. He looked back once again and saw the car driving slowly, next to the men. He reached inside his coat, only his holster wasn't there.

Dammit! You drunk fool.

In his haste and drunkenness he'd forgotten his weapon.

The steps behind him quickened. He increased his pace and turned on the next street. His mind raced, mapping out the streets ahead of him. Suddenly the car pulled up next to him and slammed on its brakes. Pierre stopped, turned, faced the car.

The door opened and a large man stepped out. He said nothing. The two men in dark suits caught up and stood on either side of Pierre. Finally, the big man spoke.

"Pierre, right?" He didn't wait for a response. "My name's Charles. You and I have a friend in common."

"Who would that be?" Pierre asked.

"Jack Noble."

Pierre felt his stomach knot. He glanced at the car and saw two more men inside.

"Yeah, no point in trying to run or fight," Charles said. "Get in the back seat."

Pierre pressed his lips tightly, stepped forward and slid into the back of the car.

Charles squeezed in next to him, pulled a flask from his coat, offered it to Pierre.

"No thanks," Pierre said.

"Suit yourself." Charles opened the flask and took a long pull.

"What do you want from me?"

"I'm new in town," Charles said. "I need all the friends I can get."

"I don't have friends," Pierre said.

"That's unfortunate."

"Isn't it?"

"Tell me everything you know about Mitchell Foster," Charles said.

"I'm afraid I can't speak on that," Pierre said.

Charles eyed him. "Why's that?"

Pierre shrugged.

"You have something to do with his—demise?"

Pierre shrugged again, looked straight ahead through the front windshield.

"I'm taking over Foster's operations," Charles said. "We met with two of his guys, but they weren't much use to us. Along the way we found out some pretty interesting stuff about Foster. You know anything about that?"

"Yeah," Pierre said. "We'd gotten wind of it before, but never could get the evidence."

"I've got the evidence now," Charles said.

"Are you telling me you plan to keep that part of his business running?"

"No," Charles said. "I'm trying to make an offer to you."

"I'm not a cop," Pierre said. "I can't make any deals with you."

Charles nodded. "You're like Jack then?"

Pierre held out his hands. "I'm classified." He pulled out a cigarette. "How do you know Jack?"

"He's done some work for us."

"Me too," Pierre said.

The car stopped. Pierre looked past Charles and saw his apartment building. These guys were good.

Charles opened the door and stepped out. He handed Pierre a card with his information on it. "You ever need a job, or even if you just want to freelance a bit, I can use a guy like you. Got it?"

"OK," Pierre said. He looked at the card. "I'll be in touch."

CHAPTER 13

Bear and Mandy sat at the table eating dinner. A rap at the door interrupted their conversation about *Captain America,* the movie they just watched.

"Stay here," he said.

He stepped through living room, grabbed his gun and opened the door.

"Hi," Clarissa said.

He tucked the gun behind him and pulled Clarissa through the door and hugged her.

She hugged him back. "It's so good to see you."

"You got no idea," he said. "Come in."

"Where's Mandy?" she asked.

Bear nodded toward the back of the house. Clarissa pushed past him and he followed her to the kitchen.

"Hey, squirt," Clarissa said.

Mandy dropped her fork, jumped up from the table, ran to Clarissa and wrapped her arms around her.

Clarissa scooped the girl up and held her close to her chest. "Oh, I've missed you." She tucked strands of hair behind Mandy's ears and kissed her cheeks.

"Me too," Mandy said as she buried her face against Clarissa's chest and wrapped her arms tight around her back.

Clarissa took a seat at the table and sat Mandy on her lap.

Bear watched from across the room, smiled. How many homes had a scene like this played out tonight? Hundreds? Thousands? Surely none under these circumstances.

"Hungry?" Bear asked.

"Yeah," Clarissa said.

Bear fixed her a plate of steak and broccoli and placed it in front of her. He walked back to the fridge, leaned against it. He scratched at the growth on his face for a moment. "There's something I need to tell you."

She looked up from her plate with a mouth full of food. "What?"

Bear opened his mouth to speak when his phone rang. He glanced at the caller ID. "I gotta take this." He stepped through the back door and waited for it to close behind him. "Brandon?"

"Bear," Brandon said. "I got them."

"Who?" Bear's mind raced with possibilities. Jack? The Russians? What if Brandon was playing Bear and said Clarissa?

"Russ and his crew."

"Where at?"

"Back of some Chinese joint. Tonight. Poker game."

"Security there?"

"Yeah," Brandon said. "But I can send my guys. You slip in, boom-bam-boom, slip back out. Simple."

"Yeah, simple." Bear stared up at the sky. "Where's this place?"

Brandon read off the name and address of the restaurant.

Bear knew the place. Even ate there on occasion until he read the health department's report. It was less than a block from the interrogation apartment. "Excellent. What time?"

"Nine tonight."

Bear hung up. Looked at his watch. Six-thirty. He walked back inside and stood in front of the table, fumbling over the words he needed to get out.

Jack's in a maximum security Russian jail with no hope of getting out. Just say it.

"Well?" Clarissa said, her arms out to the side.

"It's gotta wait."

Clarissa rolled her eyes. "Is it about Jack?"

Bear shot a glance at Mandy, who now sat at attention, listening intently to the conversation. Saying anything else would only stress the girl out even more, not to mention Clarissa. He couldn't do what he needed to do with that kind of pressure weighing on him.

"Wait till I get back, OK?" he said.

"OK," Clarissa said. "Where're you going?"

"Into the city. Don't worry about it." He grabbed his keys off the top of the refrigerator and opened the back door again. "Don't wait up."

"I will," she said.

Bear pulled into the lot behind the apartment building and parked his car next to the dumpster. A great place to park, he figured, in case you ever had someone shooting at you. The dumpster could take the hit and protect you. Plus, they made great places to stash a dead body.

He unlocked the door, stepped into the dark apartment, walked to the back room. Punched in a code and opened a locker and armed himself with two Smith and Wesson 9 mm pistols. He grabbed three stun grenades, one to get in, one to get out, and one for an *oh-shit* moment, which occurred far too often these days. And with that thought, he took off his shirt and put on a flak jacket. He had no misgivings that he'd be walking into a room full of unarmed men.

He exited the apartment through the front door, turned right, rounded a corner and stopped in front of *Ling's*, the local dine-in/take out Chinese joint with bad food and a fully stocked bar. Great combination. A tall man in a black leather jacket stood in front of the door. He watched Bear approach.

Bear nodded and waited for the man's response.

The man nodded back and stepped to the side, giving Bear a wide berth for entrance.

Brandon comes through again.

Bear entered the restaurant, which was completely empty aside from a few of the wait staff sitting at a round table playing cards and taking shots. The bartender was busy making drinks. At the back of the restaurant another man stood in front of a closed door. He was practically a clone of the first guard, only this guy was armed with an assault rifle.

Bear nodded again.

The man nodded back, stepped aside.

"You might want to go out front." Bear pulled out a stun grenade and held it up for the man to inspect.

The guard walked to the front of the restaurant without saying a word.

Bear waited for him to exit to the street. He took a deep breath. Pushed through the door and threw the grenade into the middle of the room. He closed the door before the explosion, counted to five and reentered the room. The flashes of light had stopped. Smoke enveloped the room. Four men littered the floor, dazed and confused.

Bear scanned their faces. He quickly shot the two he didn't recognize.

Direct hit, between the eyes, both men. He followed it up with a shot to the back of their heads while standing over them.

Russ staggered to his feet and Bear drove the gun across the back of his head and the man collapsed.

Bear pulled James Reston off the ground, held him up to the wall. "Like shooting at little girls and boys and killing their parents?"

James stuttered, but managed to speak. "What?"

Bear brought a large fist across the man's face.

James went limp.

"Wake up," Bear said as he put the barrel of his gun to James's head. He pulled him up off the floor and pinned him to the wall.

Russ groaned from the other side of the room.

Bear looked over his shoulder and saw the man getting to his feet again.

Bear fired two bullets into James, watched him fall to the ground. He turned his attention to Russ. "Where the hell do you think you're going?"

Russ cursed at him as he crawled toward the door.

"Who sent you?" Bear said.

"Wh-What?"

"Montana," Bear said. "Who sent you to Montana to kill the girl?"

Russ laughed. "Eat me, man." He had his hand on the doorknob.

Bear moved behind Russ and wrapped his arm around his throat. "You're coming with me."

He dragged Russ through the restaurant.

The bartender and wait staff huddled together by the front door. None of them made eye contact with Bear.

"I was never here," Bear said. "I seen all your faces. You got that?"

None of them said anything, they turned away in unison. Of course they got it. They knew how to be quiet. Criminals practically lived in the place.

Bear opened the door a crack.

"All done?" one of the guards asked.

"Yup," Bear said.

"We'll clean up."

Bear walked past the men. He held Russ up straight and pressed a gun into his side. The block was deserted. Not a single car passed during the short walk from the restaurant to the apartment. He led Russ up the stairs and stopped in front of the door.

"Where are you taking me?" Russ asked.

"Shut up," Bear said.

Bear opened the door to the apartment and pushed Russ through the hall, down the stairs and shoved him into the wall. "Don't move." Bear unlocked the reinforced steel door and pulled it open. Grabbed Russ by the back of his head and threw him into the room.

"Let's play a game," Bear said.

Russ got to his his knees, crawled to the concrete wall and pulled himself to his feet. He took a deep breath, said nothing.

"C'mon," Bear said. "Get through me and you can leave."

Russ didn't move. His eyes darted around, stopped and focused on Bear.

Bear stepped closer. "What d'you say?"

Russ swung his fist fast and hard. It caught Bear on the jaw. Caught the big man by surprise.

Bear stepped back, regained his balance and laughed. "That all you got?"

Russ stepped forward and took another swing.

Bear dodged, lunged forward and tackled Russ, landing on top of the smaller man, then he threw two quick punches into the back of Russ's head. Bear got to his feet, pulled Russ up and pushed him against the wall.

The man looked dazed as he swayed back and forth.

Bear delivered an uppercut that knocked Russ unconscious. He dragged him across the cell and chained his arms and legs to the wall.

Russ shook and came to. "Who are you?"

Bear ignored him, walked to the door. "Goodnight," he said as he closed the steel door. "If I don't see you alive again, it was nice playing."

The door clicked shut and Russ's screams faded, drowned out by the soundproof concrete room.

CHAPTER 14

Jack lay on the top bunk in the nine by ten foot cell. How the Russians expected two grown men to share such a space baffled him. It'd only been a couple days, but the routine was starting to settle in. The language barrier posed some problems with the guards. They beat him when he didn't react fast enough to their foreign orders. His tall roommate offered no help, only stared at him with dark burning eyes. Jack still didn't know his name, didn't care either.

The man paced the cell, never taking his eyes off of Jack. He'd stop occasionally and bare his few remaining gnarled teeth.

The first couple dozen times Jack offered no reaction, but this time he'd had enough.

"Make your move," Jack said.

The big man stopped pacing. He lifted his arms and pressed them against the ceiling. "When I make my move, it will be when you sleep. You'll wake to find me eating your flesh."

"Hope you like the—"

The guards started banging on the outer wall of the cell. Yells in Russian filled the air. The tall man bent over and backed up to the wall and placed his hands in the slot where the guards delivered their meals.

Jack didn't move.

"Enjoy your beating," the Russian said while the guards placed handcuffs around his wrists. He stepped forward a few feet and straightened.

The guards yelled louder.

Jack didn't move.

The solid door opened. A guard stepped forward and unlocked the door made from iron bars, the gate to the cell within the cell. He shouted and pointed at Jack, then at the floor. Three more guards entered the room. Two removed Jack's cellmate.

Jack flung his feet over the side of the bed and held his hands up.

The guards didn't wait. They pulled Jack off the bed by his feet. The bottom bunk prevented the back of his head from taking a six foot dive into the concrete floor. They twisted his legs and forced him onto his stomach, all while shouting in Russian. They cuffed his hands and pulled him to his feet. One stood behind, one in front.

"Assume the position," the guard in front said in English. A thick hard plastic club dangled from his hand.

Jack sighed, looked up and closed his eyes. No friggin' way these guys were going to break him. He knew what was coming, braced for it.

It didn't matter.

The club slammed into his midsection with the force of a small car. Jack doubled over. The guard behind him held Jack's arms high behind his back, preventing him from hitting the floor. It took a good thirty seconds before he managed to refill his lungs with air and rid himself of the painful burn in his oxygen-deprived lungs.

They dragged him from his cell into the hall. Guards positioned themselves on either side of him. He felt their hands around his elbows. One placed a hand on the back of his head, keeping him bent over and looking down. They forced him to walk in this position, a stress position. They came to a door where bright sunlight filtered in and reflected off the white tile floor. Jack felt another hand on the back of his head and his vision went dark as a blindfold slipped across his face. Same as yesterday. They kept the prisoners blindfolded so they couldn't react if something happened while they were being transported. They'd have no idea where they were in the facility. Brilliant.

The guards led him along a solid path. They continued shouting in Russian and he still didn't understand a single word. Dogs barked and growled in the distance. The guards stopped him. He heard the noise of metal scraping against rusted hinges. They pushed him forward, removed his blindfold and straightened him up. Jack rolled his head and saw his cellmate standing next to him, eyes forward. The guards unlocked another door and pushed the two men inside a large cage. The exercise room.

There was no prison yard where prisoners could gather at Black Dolphin.

This was it. Ninety minutes a day in yet another cage with the man you spent the other twenty-two and a half hours with.

Jack paced the length of the room. Above him guards patrolled on a catwalk overlooking the exercise rooms. Chain link fencing hovered fifteen feet above, parallel to the floor, keeping the prisoners away from the guards, and giving the guards easy access to shoot if necessary.

Would they shoot?

Jack stared at his cellmate. The tall man leaned back against the wall. A lit cigarette dangled from his mouth. The smoke streamed toward the open ceiling, wrapping around the man's large deformed head.

"Got another one of those?" Jack asked.

The Russian took a drag, exhaled and spit on the floor.

"Just one, man," Jack said.

The Russian pulled out a cigarette, snapped it in half and flicked it toward Jack.

Jack stopped mid-step and started toward him. A guard yelled from above. Jack stopped. Language didn't matter. He understood the tone.

The tall man smiled. He pulled another cigarette out, lit it and held it out for Jack. "Don't ever ask again."

Jack passed the next hour or so with a mixture of walking, sprinting across the room, and doing push-ups.

Finally, the guards started yelling from outside the room. Jack's cellmate backed up to the door first. Jack stood still. Made them come to him. Three guards surrounded him and he braced for the worst. They didn't beat him, though. This time they cuffed him and bent him over. He let them, too.

The blindfold went on and the guards led him back to his room. Ten minutes later they delivered lunch. Soup and bread. Again.

Jack let his food sit on the little table the men had to share.

His cellmate took that as an open invitation to help himself to Jack's lunch. He stuffed the bread into his mouth in one go and dumped the soup into his empty bowl.

"What the hell do you think you're doing?" Jack said.

The man turned his head to look at Jack. He laughed and small chunks of bread sprayed out, glistening in the air before falling onto the floor.

Jack walked over to the small table where they ate. The Russian pushed himself back, turned slightly to face Jack. Jack reached down, grabbed the bowl and dumped soup on the Russian's chest and lap.

The big man looked down, brushed chunks of meat and vegetables off his chest. "I hope you enjoyed your last cigarette," he said.

Jack smiled. One way or another he was getting out of that cage. He glanced around the cell for anything he could use as a weapon. Not much there that would be effective against a seven foot tall man. The size of the cell could work to Jack's advantage, though. It could also work against him if the Russian pinned him in a corner.

The Russian stood, stretched.

Jack didn't wait for him to finish. He threw his arms back and onto the top bunk, pushed off and delivered a kick to the man's midsection with both legs.

The Russian doubled over.

Jack dropped to the floor and drove an elbow into the middle of the Russian's back.

The Russian let out a groan, threw himself forward and pulled up on the cage enclosing the front of the room. He quickly turned around, arms in a defensive position.

Jack knew he couldn't wait too long. Guards would be there any minute. He lunged at the Russian, who reacted by throwing a right hook. Jack ducked and exploded upwards, slamming his fist into the Russian's chin.

The big man fell backwards, his body colliding with the bars in a thud.

Jack grabbed him by his shirt and started to swing him forward. The Russian managed to get an arm wrapped around Jack's torso, then his other arm wrapped around Jack's neck.

Jack felt his body lift and his feet were no longer touching the ground. He pried at the man's arm, but couldn't get the Russian's grip around his neck to loosen. Jack twisted his body and elbowed at the man's side, but he couldn't manage enough torque to do any damage. Finally, he reached up and behind and found the big man's eye sockets. He dug his thumbs into the man's eyes.

The Russian let go of Jack and fell to the floor. Jack twisted fast and drove his elbow into the Russian's stomach. The big man collapsed on Jack's back.

Jack reached back around the man's neck and flipped him over his shoulder. Moving quickly, Jack lifted the dazed man and pushed him forward into the opposite end of the cell. He grabbed sheets off the bottom bunk and wrapped them around the Russian's neck, and then threaded the ends through the cell bars.

Jack turned and started pulling toward the front of the cell, holding the ends of the sheet over his shoulders. He looked back, saw the Russian being lifted to his feet.

The big man clawed at the sheet wrapped tight around his neck, but could not get his fingers between the fabric and his neck. His feet slid along the floor as he searched for traction as his face turned dark and his eyes bulged.

Jack lunged forward a few more feet, looked back, saw the Russian suspended in the air, feet off the ground. Jack kept going until the man's head nearly touched the ceiling. He jerked forward several times causing, the Russian's body to bounce and finally his neck to snap.

The Russian went limp. Jack gave one more violent tug and then let go. The big man's body fell to the floor.

Jack checked for a pulse, found none.

Then, he waited.

The guards showed up moments later. They rushed in the cell, no words this time, just the guards and their clubs.

Jack managed to avoid the first two clubs swinging toward his head. He landed a punch on the third guard. Nearly made it to the door before the fourth guard's club came down heavy and hard against the back of Jack's head. He hit the floor with a thud. Black combat boots surrounded his head. He passed out.

CHAPTER 15

"Ms. Clarissa? Are you awake?"

Clarissa opened her eyes. Rings of blond hair dangled across her face, tickling her nose. She felt Mandy's hot breath as the girl whispered in her ear.

"Wake up."

"I'm up, sweetie."

The little girl stepped back and smiled.

Clarissa sat up, stretched her arms above her head and smiled back. She felt rested, but her back was tight.

"What time is it? Do you know?" Clarissa asked.

"Seven o'clock."

Clarissa looked around the room in an attempt to get her bearings straight. She stood, walked toward the kitchen, found the coffee maker and put on a pot.

"Have you eaten?" she asked.

Mandy sat at the table and shook her head.

Clarissa fixed her a bowl of cereal and filled a mug full of coffee for herself then she joined Mandy at the table.

"Aren't you going to eat?" Mandy said through a mouthful of cereal.

"Too early," Clarissa replied while rubbing her eyes. "Is Bear here?"

Mandy shrugged. "His room's empty."

Clarissa got up. "Stay here." She walked through the living room, didn't see him. She started upstairs and called his name from the top step.

No answer.

She checked his room.

Empty.

She made her way back to the kitchen and found her phone, dialed Bear's number and waited.

No answer.

She checked outside for his car, it wasn't there.

"What's wrong?"

Clarissa looked over her shoulder. Mandy stood on the porch, squinting against the sun.

"Nothing," Clarissa said. "He probably stayed in the city last night, that's all." She led the little girl back inside. "I think I will have some breakfast. What's good here?"

Mandy smiled and tilted her bowl of cereal. "This is."

"Hmm, good choice. I think that's what I'll have." She hadn't finished filling her bowl when the sound of a car pulling up caught her attention. She dropped the box of cereal and stepped outside. She stood in the doorway, half inside, half out, and waited. The car stopped, out of sight.

Bear appeared around the corner. "Sorry for not calling, dear."

Clarissa sighed. "Yeah, thanks for that."

Bear shrugged.

"Hungry?"

"Yeah," Bear said. "But wait a sec."

Mandy stepped out on the porch. "Hi, Bear," she said.

"Go inside, sweetie," Bear said. He waited for her to disappear. "Close the door."

Clarissa did. She walked down the stairs, biting her bottom lip. "What's going on?"

"I don't know how to tell you this," Bear said.

"Just tell me. What's happened to Jack?"

Bear looked down at the ground. He kicked at the grass with one foot. "He's in a Russian jail called Black Dolphin."

Clarissa wrapped her hand around the wooden handrail, her nails digging into the wood.

"It's not—not a good place, Clarissa," Bear said. He breathed heavily through his nose. "He's been sentenced to death."

Clarissa felt her lips tremble, her eyes welled with tears. She looked up, then to the side to avoid the fractured sunlight.

Bear placed his large hands on her shoulders and pulled her close.

Clarissa allowed herself to be swallowed up by his massive arms. She buried her face in his chest and cried, screamed, beat at his back with her hands. She felt her energy drain and her legs went weak. She collapsed, held upright only by Bear's embrace.

"What's wrong?" Mandy asked.

"It's OK," Bear said. "Ms. Clarissa is sad."

The sound of Mandy's voice brought Clarissa back. She pushed away from Bear.

He caught her eye. "We're doing what we can."

She looked up into his eyes. Reached up and placed her hand on the side of his face. "I know. And I know this hurts you as much as it does me."

Bear looked away.

"I've got a decision to make." She paused for a moment. "I have to make it soon."

He didn't say anything.

She turned, walked up the stairs and picked up Mandy. Carried the little girl inside and sat her down at the table.

"What's wrong?" she asked again.

"Just got bad news about a friend."

Mandy got up and hugged her. "I'm sorry."

Clarissa pulled out her phone and left the kitchen.

"Sinclair," she said.

"Hello, child."

"I need a few more days."

"Not a problem," he said.

She looked out the front window at the empty street. "Can you do me a favor?"

"If it's about Jack Noble, I'm afraid there isn't much I can do."

"Just make some noise."

"I'll try."

She stuffed the phone in her pocket and turned around.

Bear stood in the doorway to the kitchen, his large body making the entrance look small. "Who was that?"

"Nobody."

CHAPTER 16

J ack lay in bed, his head throbbing. The pain was worth it. He now had the cell to himself. Someone told him he'd have to go to court again, this time for the murder of Isai Goraya, his former cellmate. Jack just smiled. He was already a walking dead man, what difference would one more count of murder make? He'd told them that he'd kill any other men they stuck in his cell, and judging by the looks on their faces when he said it, they believed him.

He looked backward, through the opaque window that allowed sunlight in, but offered no view of the outside world. The thought of never seeing the sky or green grass depressed him. Would he be in the prison until he died? What kind of life would that be? He brushed the thoughts aside. He knew that something like this had always been a possibility. It came with the life he chose, the job he performed. A life had to be given for all the lives taken. It had to be that way.

And it was his life that had to be sacrificed.

He'd heard that only one person ever won an appeal and been released from Black Dolphin. Appeals didn't exist for Jack Noble, though, not the way he was convicted. He assumed that his sentence would be carried out soon enough. The sooner the better, because the ninety square foot room drove him crazy.

The sound of keys against the outside door of his cell disrupted the tranquil silence. He propped himself up on his elbows, prepared himself for what might happen.

Alik stepped through the opening and unlocked and opened the inner door. "Leave us," he said to the guards behind him.

Jack sat up.

Alik turned and nodded at him. "Mr. Noble, how are you?"

Jack shrugged, rubbed the back of his head. Said, "Better than Isai."

"I'm sure." Alik tossed a bag on the table. "Come on down here. I want to talk with you."

Jack rolled over the side of the bed and dropped his feet to the floor. His back was turned to Alik, and Jack paused for a moment, wondering if the guard would take a shot at him.

He didn't.

"Sit," Alik said.

Jack turned and took a seat at the small table.

Alik pulled a pack of cigarettes from his pocket and placed them on the table along with a box of matches. "I trust you won't try to burn the place down."

Jack lifted an eyebrow and shrugged. "Can't promise." He lit a cigarette and inhaled deeply. "You know what? I was going to quit."

"No point now," Alik said.

Jack nodded and smiled and said nothing. He studied the guard, noticed that the man came into his cell unarmed. Where did this trust come from? Maybe telling the other guards to leave was a show and they sat just outside the cell waiting for a signal.

Why else would Alik come in unarmed and leave the doors to the cell unlocked?

"Jack," Alik said. "I want to help you. You don't belong here."

"I don't belong most places."

"That's beside the point. Allow me to help you file an appeal."

"Why would you? Why risk your own neck?"

"I don't have to do anything if you prefer." He turned and added in a whisper, "If I could sneak you out of here, I would, Jack."

Jack stubbed his cigarette out. Sat back in his chair and placed his hands behind his head. He studied Alik. He saw trust behind the man's eyes. In that moment, Jack decided he could trust the guard.

Alik pointed to the bag. "Real food. Eat."

The brown bag sat on the table, the top folded down. Jack had been curious what was inside. He picked it up and dumped the contents on the table. "Where'd you get this?"

"I have my ways," Alik said.

Jack unfolded a paper wrapper and took a large bite of a thick hamburger. He savored the taste as grease and fat juices trickled down his chin.

"Good?"

Jack picked up the bag and looked inside. "No fries?"

Alik said nothing. He leaned back against the bars that made up the inner cell wall. He smiled. His eyes never left Jack.

Jack put down the burger halfway through, lit another cigarette. Said, "So, this appeal process, how would it work?"

Alik shook his head. "It doesn't really matter, Jack."

"What?"

"I've discussed this at length with Ivanov. He won't reverse the ruling."

Jack felt his heart race and his breath became shallow and rapid. Beads of sweat formed on his forehead, trickled down his chest and back.

What the hell is going on?

His stomach knotted, he clawed at his abdomen.

"First," Alik said. "The poison eats at the stomach lining in order to get into the bloodstream."

Jack got to his feet. His chest started burning. Was it the panic, or something else?

"Then it enters the heart, Jack."

Jack's heart cried out in pain. He clutched his chest. The man before him turned into a blurred mass. The world started closing in on him.

"The result is a massive heart attack. The kind no man can survive."

Jack felt his heart exploding in his chest. His oxygen starved brain ached, his vision started to fade black. He fell to his knees and reached out with his hand, searching for Alik. "Please," he tried to say, but what little breath remained in his body was all that escaped from his lips.

"Finally, Mr. Noble," Alik said, "you slip into that dark, deep sleep. The one you sent countless men to. May they never find your soul, you heartless bastard."

But, I have a heart.

"I'm finished in here, guards," Alik said.

Jack fell forward. He barely noticed the impact as his head hit the floor with a sickening thud. The cramping in his chest ceased. His dying heart thumped sporadically, the sound of it whooshing in his ears.

Thump-thump...thump...seconds passed...thump...

Then, nothing.

CHAPTER 17

Boris stuck the blade of the shovel into the ground, stepped on it and scooped it up. He tossed the chunk of dirt and grass to the side. He repeated the process another dozen times before stopping to light a cigarette. He propped himself up on the end of his shovel.

"You know what, Pasha?" he said.

Pasha lifted his chubby face up from his bent over position. His red cheeks glistened with sweat. He let go of his shovel and stood up, arching his back and groaning as he twisted side to side. "What, Boris?"

"They are wasting our time digging this grave." He inhaled deeply, waiting for his partner to reply with the obligatory why.

"Why's that?" Pasha said with a sigh.

"This man, this Jack Noble, nothing but American rubbish." He spit into the shallow grave.

Pasha shrugged and held out his hand. "Give me a smoke."

Boris reached into his pocket and tossed the pack of cigarettes across the hole.

"Rubbish or not," Pasha paused to light his cigarette, "he deserves a proper burial."

"Maybe so, but why not burn his body first? Wouldn't you rather dig a two foot hole instead of an eight foot one?"

"I get paid no matter what I do," Pasha said. "So a two foot hole would have suited me fine."

"You, sir," Boris said, "are a lazy bastard."

Pasha laughed as he tossed the pack back to Boris. "You and me both, my friend."

Boris looked around at the bleak landscape, up at the gray sky. "Rain'll be coming soon. We best hurry."

"A drink first," Pasha said. "In honor of our new friend, Jack Noble." He nodded to the pine box set fifteen feet away.

The men walked over to the box and took a seat on top. Boris kicked his legs out and let them slam against the side, one at a time, over and over, like a little kid sitting on a seat too big for him. He took the flask from Pasha and took a long pull.

"Good stuff," he said. "How about a drink, Mr. Noble?"

Pasha took the flask from Boris and tipped it over so that it poured through one of the seams at the end of the wooden coffin.

Both men laughed. They finished the flask then returned to their shovels.

Boris unzipped his pants and urinated in the hole.

"Wait until we are finished digging, you idiot," Pasha said.

Boris laughed. "Sorry." He stuffed himself back in his pants and returned to the job.

Half an hour passed as the men took turns burying their shovels into the soft earth to create Jack's final resting place.

"That's good enough," Pasha said. "You can take care of your business now."

Boris shrugged. "I just want to get inside. It's cold out here." He started toward the coffin, looked back, saw Pasha following close behind. "You don't have another flask do you?"

"No," Pasha replied. "Have another cigarette?"

Boris lit two, handed one to Pasha. They stood in front of the coffin.

"Poor bastard," Pasha said. "Can you imagine going like this. No one to see you off as you return to the Earth? Not a soul around that gives a care about you?"

Boris looked at his partner, placed a hand on his shoulder. "You don't shut up with that deep crap, it'll be you going in the grave. Not him."

Pasha laughed. Flicked his cigarette over the coffin. "Let's put this bastard in the ground."

Boris stood at one end, Pasha at the other. They grunted as they lifted the box, which must have weighed close to three hundred pounds.

"Better than the last one we buried," Pasha said as he struggled to keep the coffin off the ground.

"This guy is the reason for the last one," Boris said.

They reached the side of the grave and dropped the coffin on the ground. Both men caught their breath and squatted down, preparing for the final push.

"What the hell is that?" Boris said.

Both men looked toward the prison and saw a box truck driving toward them, flashing its lights, the horn blaring. They rose together and walked to the side of the road.

The truck stopped and Alik stepped out. "I've got orders to transport the body to—"

"Like hell you are," Boris said. "We just spent two hours digging a hole. We are putting a body in the ground."

"Then it'll have to be one of you two that goes in it," Alik said. "These orders come from Ivanov. They've negotiated with the Americans. Noble's body for some of ours."

Boris stepped forward, bumped Alik's chest with his own. "Show me."

"Screw you," Alik said.

"Then you aren't getting the body."

"Let him," Pasha said.

"What?" Boris said.

"Just let him. Maybe they'll send Mikhail's body back."

"Listen to the man," Alik said as he moved toward the back of the truck. He unlocked and lifted the door. "Bring him here."

Boris sighed and followed Pasha to the grave. "Let's just dump him in."

Pasha shook his head, bent over and lifted his end of the casket waist high. Boris did the same. They loaded the body in the back of the truck.

Alik closed the door and locked it again. "You two want to ride along?"

"I don't think so," Boris said.

"Come on," Alik said. "What are you going to do? Go back inside and chase turds?"

The gravediggers looked at each other and shrugged, walked to the front of the truck and climbed into the cab.

CHAPTER 18

Pierre walked alongside Charles. They stopped halfway across the Pont des Arts, a footbridge that crosses the Seine. Pierre stared out over the river, watching the boats float by. People passed behind them in a hurry, scurrying across the bridge. Normally, he'd judge each one as they approached. Today he didn't.

"So what's your answer?" Charles asked.

"I'm willing," Pierre said. "Side jobs, though. I still have my commitments to the agency."

Charles nodded. He tapped on the railing with his fist. "Can I count on you?"

"For?"

Charles spun and leaned back against the railing. "Missy, come here."

Pierre glanced over his shoulder at the young, attractive, dark haired woman as she crossed the bridge. She slipped her arm around Charles's neck and kissed him. Pierre felt repulsed.

"Missy," Charles said. "This is my new friend Pierre. He's going to be working for us from time to time."

"Charmed," she said.

Pierre nodded at her then returned his gaze to Charles. "What's she got to do with anything?"

"She was taken from her home in North Dakota. Sold into slavery." Charles paused. "Sexual slavery," he said slowly, drawing out every syllable. "First thing I want you to do is bring that ring down."

"Give me names and I'll take—"

448 / L.T. RYAN

"No names," Charles said. "Use your intel to make it happen."

"I can't use my resources in that manner."

Charles frowned. "Are you telling me no, Pierre? 'Cause I don't like to be told no."

"He doesn't," Missy said.

Pierre sighed loudly. "Do you know who I am?"

"Do you know who I am?" Charles said. "Who I represent?"

Pierre turned his head and looked over the river and said nothing.

"Can I count on you?"

"Yes," Pierre said.

"That's great friggin' news. I'm glad you—" His cell phone interrupted. "Excuse me a moment."

Pierre watched Charles walk away. Smiled at Missy, but kept his focus on Charles.

"Yeah, Boss," Charles said. He paused, nodded, turned to face Pierre and smiled. "That is excellent news, Feng."

"What's excellent?" Pierre asked.

Charles ignored him. He seemed to stare out at nothing. A big smile stretched across his face. He looked like a kid on Christmas staring at the toy he longed for all year long.

Missy walked up to him and draped herself to his side. "What is it, baby?"

"It's good," Charles said. "Oh, it's good."

Pierre leaned against the concrete wall, figuring Charles would tell him when he was ready. If he told him at all, that is.

"Go across the bridge, Missy." Charles walked over to Pierre, leaned against the bridge mirroring Pierre's stance. "You and Mr. Noble, you're friends right?"

"Yeah," Pierre said, trying his best to keep the worry off his face.

"I guess I should say *were* friends."

"What do you mean?"

"He died in prison yesterday."

Pierre dropped his head, closed his eyes. He fought back the tears that welled up behind his shut eyelids. He felt Charles's large hand wrap around his shoulder.

"While I might be happy, I do know how you feel. My condolences."

Pierre looked up through watery eyes. "I'll do whatever you need."

"I'll be in touch," Charles said.

C larissa sat in the swinging chair that hung from the porch ceiling. She watched Mandy as the little girl played in the front yard with a couple kids that lived across the street. Bear sat back in a wicker rocking chair, reading a book.

What an odd little family.

She cherished these moments, nothing happening, completely bored. And she didn't mind one bit. Not after the month she'd had.

"Whew," Bear said. "That was a good friggin' book."

She looked at him and smiled, turned her attention back to Mandy. A cool breeze passed through every few minutes, chilling her face. The setting sun warmed her cheeks when the wind died down. The sensation swept through her, leaving her calm and tranquil.

Bear's obnoxious ringtone went off, interrupting the moment.

"Yeah," he said into the phone.

Clarissa studied him as he stood up and turned to her. His face drew tight and he disappeared into the house. She got up and walked to the door, trying to listen in, but he must have gone out through the back door.

"Mandy," Clarissa said. "It's time to come in."

"But I don't wanna," Mandy said.

Clarissa looked back inside. *Still not there.* She fought back the pangs of panic.

Mandy continued to play in the yard.

Clarissa scanned the street looking for anything or anyone out of the ordinary.

"Mandy," she said again. "Come on. I need you to—"

"Clarissa," Bear said from behind her. The screen door slammed shut.

She straightened up and turned around, expecting to see fear or concern spread across Bear's face. Instead he looked at her with tears in his eyes and streaking down his cheek, settling into his beard.

"What? What is it?"

"Jack." Bear paused to wipe his face with his sleeve. "He's gone."

"What do you mean gone?" Clarissa stepped back, reaching behind her for something to steady herself on. Her knees felt weak, her head light.

"He's gone, Clarissa."

She dropped to her knees. "No, no, no..."

Bear dropped to his knees and pulled her close, wrapping her up in his arms. They cried together.

"What's the matter?" Mandy said from behind.

"Oh, baby," Clarissa said. "Come here."

Mandy wrapped her arms around Clarissa's neck, placed her chin on top of her head.

"Mr. Jack," Clarissa paused, looked to Bear for help.

Bear shook his head and looked away. His big body heaving as he fought through the pain.

"He's passed away, sweetie."

Mandy stroked Clarissa's head. "I'm sorry, Clarissa."

They barely spoke the rest of the night. Bear had left for a while, leaving Mandy and Clarissa alone. She held the girl close to her as they watched TV. She checked her phone every few minutes, hoping for a call or a text from Jack saying it was all a big mistake and he's OK. Alive. On his way to get her and take her away.

It never happened, though.

Finally, Mandy fell asleep.

Clarissa slipped outside and pulled out her phone. This time she placed a call.

"Hello, Clarissa," Sinclair said.

Clarissa stood, silent, the phone to her head.

"Are you there?" he said.

"Jack's dead," Clarissa said.

Sinclair cleared his throat. "Sorry to hear that. He was a good man."

"He was."

Sinclair said nothing.

"Are you going to do anything?" she asked.

"What can I do? Start a war with Russia over the death of a hitman?"

Clarissa said nothing.

"Join us and maybe you'll have a chance to avenge his death."

Clarissa paced the porch, stopped, looked up at the full moon. "I'm in."

"Excellent. We'll be up to collect you in the morning."

"I'm not at my apartment."

"I know."

The phone went silent.

Bear's car pulled into the driveway. He stepped out and lumbered up the stairs, joined her at the edge of the porch.

She leaned into him, noticing that he reeked of alcohol.

"Leaving?" he asked.

"Yeah," she said.

"Want to tell me where to?"

"No," she said.

CHAPTER 20

A gasp forced shriveled lungs to overfill with air, stretching them to maximum capacity. A struggle to exhale ensued. He gasped to fill his lungs a second time. A burning sensation tore through his chest as his heart erupted to life and began pumping blood through his veins at over 120 beats per minute, sending much needed oxygen to his brain and other vital organs.

His cold body tingled with sensation as his blood vessels and capillaries filled. Deadened nerves returned to life, screaming out in pain and pleasure at the same time.

He tried to sit up, but found himself confined, unable to move more than a few inches up, down, left or right.

He took a second, allowed his body to return to normal and let his senses take over. His eyes struggled against the dark.

Jack Noble steadied himself.

Controlled his breathing.

Took possession of his mind from the doubts and fears that ruin most men.

His sense of touch restored, he felt a cold, metal object in his hand. He played with the object, sliding it up and down. A rubber tab stuck out near one end. He pushed down and the space filled with light, a light so bright that he initially had to blink away the pain in his eyes while they adjusted to it.

He looked left, right, up and back at the panels of wood surrounding him.

Where the hell am I?

He made a fist with his other hand, felt and heard the paper crinkling.

He drew his hand up to his chest, pulled the flashlight over his head, focusing the beam on the paper. It was a letter from Frank.

Nice of him, Jack thought, *considering he's the one that gave me the job in Paris to kill Foster.*

Jack,

Sorry about killing you. It's the only way we could get you out of that hell hole. As you've guessed by now, you didn't really die. In the event that you haven't guessed, no, this isn't Heaven. You are alive. I'll give you the details later, if you want them. In the meantime, try to relax. You are in a pine coffin in the back of a box truck heading south through Russia. You may or may not hear gunfire along the way. Chances are it's the good guys firing the guns. If it's the bad guys, well, at least you already know what death feels like.

See you soon,

Frank

Jack closed his eyes, feeling the slight vibrations as the truck rolled along. He smiled. Someone did like him after all.

The truck stopped. Russian voices, one familiar sounding, echoed through the back of the truck and into the pine box. An argument ensued. Two shots ripped through the air. A door opened then closed. Another door opened, followed by two thuds, like the sound of bodies hitting the ground. A rap against the side of the truck filled the silent void.

Clicks and clanks filled Jack's ears. He pictured the man outside the truck, unlocking the door, heaving it up. He saw the door rolling up in his mind as the sounds of metal squealing against metal reverberated through the coffin.

Was he friend or foe?

"Wake up, Jack," the man said.

He knew the voice. It wasn't Frank, though. This was a Russian voice.

Alik.

Something smashed against the other end of the coffin. A crack formed in the wood, just a sliver. Sunlight spread through the coffin and filled Jack's eyes.

"You're a ghost now," Alik said. "And you're free."

I am free. A living ghost.

A smile swept over Jack's face as he waited patiently for the lid to be pried open.

Jack is back in *When Dead in Greece*. Read on for a sneak peek, or purchase your copy today!

Join the LT Ryan reader family & receive a free copy of the Jack Noble story, *The Recruit*. Scan the QR code below to get started!

WHEN DEAD IN GREECE: CHAPTER 1

Palaiochora, Greece.

Old men crowded the white-tiled terrace. They gathered at the cafe once a week for their backgammon tournament. They made bets. Talked trash. Winked at the waitress. Conned free coffee out of the establishment's owner. A few minutes after their arrival the aroma of dark roast overtook the adjoining Libyan Sea.

This was the first time I'd managed to stand long enough to watch the initial round of matches. I'd spent my first two weeks in Palaiochora on my back, recovering from my injuries. A collapsed lung. Bruised spleen. Hairline fractures to my jaw, right ulna, both tibias. Several broken ribs to go along with broken bones in my left hand.

The majority of the injuries had been sustained during a nasty fight with my seven-foot-tall Russian cellmate in the hellhole named Black Dolphin. The guards of that fine place were kind enough to do the rest of the damage.

Then there was the manner of how I escaped. Wasn't my own doing. But, damn, did the effects linger on.

Over the past month the physical pain had subsided. I still wasn't myself though. Fatigue set in fast. My strength was sapped. Mental acuity was nowhere near what I was used to. I presumed these were the side effects of whatever the Russian, Alik, had slipped me to send me into that deep slumber. It was hard to be angry with the guy. He'd only done what Frank Skinner had instructed him to do. And he'd managed to get me out of that shithole prison.

Life, and death, sentence served.

Half the old guys cheered as the final match of the first round wrapped up. They stood feet wide, hands up, palms slapped, as the losers pulled bills from their wallets and handed them over to the victors. The next stop for the old men was inside to replenish their food stores and refill with caffeine before the next round began.

So I stepped into the cafe first to beat them to the counter.

Isadora Georgiou stood behind the glass display case that housed a selection of breakfast pastries this time of day. Her fingers danced playfully along the stainless top. She tucked a strand of dark curly hair behind her ear. Her full lips spread into a smile when she saw me approaching. A spotless apron covered her jeans and faded red t-shirt, cinched tight at the waist and loose around her breasts and hanging off her hips. She was the kind of woman who was beautiful without a trace of makeup. There wasn't so much as the thread of a wrinkle on her face.

"Looking good today, Jack." If velvet had a tone, it was her voice.

The old men settled in line behind me. Their chatter quieted to a hum.

"Not as handsome as these gentlemen, though," I said to her.

She exaggerated a shrug with upturned hands and pouty lips. "True. You are not to blame, though. Not your fault you weren't born Greek."

A couple of the old guys got a chuckle out of her comments. One said something I couldn't understand. Presumably, the comment had been inappropriate, because Isadora chided him and sent him away with a discarding wave of her hand.

"Aye, these men." She tossed her hands into the air in mock exasperation. Smiling, she turned to me. "I know what you want, Jack. I'll bring it to you after I take care of them."

I retreated to a table and watched as Isadora and her uncle, Esau Rokos, handled the rush. Esau owned the place. For a while in the 80s, he split time between the States and Greece, running a chain of Greek diners in Virginia, near D.C. This cafe, as he explained it, was his retirement. Together, Esau and Isadora slung coffee, pastries, a few orders of eggs and lamb. One at a time, the old men hustled back to the terrace to eat and resume their game.

Ten minutes later, Isadora carried a steaming plate and a fresh mug of java to me. It smelled so good I could taste it before she set it down. She asked me if I needed anything else, then took a hiatus in the back office. I watched as she crossed the room, walking away from me, her hips swaying slightly. As her ass entranced me, I realized how thankful I was that the events at Black Dolphin hadn't robbed me of my appreciation of the female form.

The door shut behind her, and I turned my attention to the food on the table. The smell of eggs fried in butter and sautéed lamb enveloped me. I dug in.

The little town had grown on me. Relaxed me. A bit quiet for my tastes. But the folks were friendly. Everyone seemed to know each other. The smells and sounds of the sea were ever-present. Reminded me a bit of where I grew up.

Alik and I weren't sure how long we would have to stay in Greece. Only thing Frank had said was to stay put. He would send for me when he needed me. There would be no advanced notice. Until then, Alik watched over me, and I watched Isadora and the old men and the others who frequented the cafe.

Take your time, Frank, I thought. *No rush.*

"You really do look better." Isadora walked past me and stopped on the other side of the table. I hadn't noticed her approaching. Was I losing my edge, or was the food that good? Her perfume trailed after her. Smelled like lavender. My mother grew the herb by the dozens, and in several varieties. Couldn't walk in the house without smelling it. Isadora folded her arms over the back of the chair and leaned toward me. The legs of the chair scraped against the tile. "Almost look like you could throw a ball around. That's what you Americans like to do, yeah? Football and baseball and stuff."

"Something like that." I drained the remaining coffee from my mug and started to stand. "Anyway, coming back to life is harder than they make it look in the movies."

She gave me an odd look, then reached out and wrapped her slender hand around my arm. Her touch felt cool.

"I can take that for you," she said

"I need the exercise," I said.

"Stubborn man," she said.

"As opposed to what?" I said.

She winked and smiled and turned toward the counter. I waited a couple beats, then followed in her scented wash. She must've reapplied the perfume while in the office because I hadn't noticed earlier. Or perhaps I'd been too hungry so only the smell of food filtered in. Either way, I couldn't blame the lady for wanting to smell as nice as she looked.

Watching her round the counter, I paid little attention to the jingling as the front door opened, and hard soles slapping the tile behind me. But the person stopped too close. I glanced over and saw a guy about my age, a wide nose in the middle of a face covered with stubble. He was dressed in black trousers, a white button up, and wore dark sunglasses.

His shoulder hit the center of my back. His elbow and forearm found the tender spot on my ribs. I don't know if he got his leg in front of mine, or if I stumbled over myself. But I went down.

Hard.

First into the display case, then the floor.

The mug crashed on the tile and splintered into a hundred pieces. Ceramic shards flew in all directions. Several hit me in the face. One felt like it did a little damage.

"Get out of my damn way," the guy said, his accent deep and thick.

Isadora spun, her arms wide. She leaned over the counter and looked down at me. "Are you OK?"

I nodded as I planted my hands on the floor and pushed my torso up. The guy had continued walking past me. He entered the office. A minute later he returned, walked past me again on his way to the front door.

Isadora vaulted over the counter and headed toward the front door, firing off a torrent of words I didn't understand.

The man kicked the door open. The bells jingled all at once. He kept the door propped open with his right arm, glanced over his left shoulder.

He said, "Psolapothiki."

I wasn't sure of the literal translation, but knew he called her the equivalent of a *whore*. The insult stopped her. She looked back at me. Her face darkened and she turned to the front of the cafe again. She aimed an outstretched finger at the guy, then stormed toward him.

"Isa!" Esau's voice filled the cafe. His thinning white hair was disheveled. One cheek was redder than the other. Blood spotted the corner of his mouth. "Stop."

The guy at the door chuckled, said something I didn't catch, then left.

WHEN DEAD IN GREECE: CHAPTER 2

Random people attempting to get the best of me was nothing new. Seemed to happen wherever I went. Maybe it was the way I looked. The confidence I exuded. Someone always wants to take down the alpha dog. But most of the time I went somewhere for a reason. A mission. A job. Whatever.

That wasn't the case in Greece. Aside from Frank and Alik, no one knew I was here. Hell, no one else knew I was alive. Frank had even withheld the information from his superiors in Washington, D.C.

So why had this guy targeted me? Judging by the look of Esau, who now slumped over the counter, I figured I'd been in the way. He was the target. Not me.

I winced at the pain as I rose to my feet. Felt as though the guy had nailed me with a sap instead of his elbow. Might have. Damn ribs had almost healed, too.

Isadora stared at the front door like she expected it to burst open any second now. Her anger hadn't faded. She looked more pissed now than she had before her uncle yelled out to her. After a few seconds she turned and walked toward me. The anger on her face dissipated. Her eyes and lips softened. She reached and placed her hand on my elbow. Her touch wasn't as cool as it had been earlier.

"You OK?" I asked her.

"Me?" She stopped and looked me up and down. Reached out and touched my cheek. Her finger came away crimson. "You're the one that took a beating."

I shrugged, jutted my chin toward her uncle. "Don't think I got the worst of it."

"Uncle," she said, brushing against me chest-to-chest as she sidestepped past. Strands of her hair caught and lingered for a second before being tugged away. "What's going on? What did he do to you?"

Esau fought off her attempts at assisting.

"Quit being so stubborn, you old fool." She threaded her arm around his back and eased him into a chair.

Esau grimaced as he leaned back into his seat. A tiny stream of blood trickled from his lip and down his chin. He dabbed it with a napkin, then looked at the red patch as though it were an old friend he'd nearly forgotten existed.

Isadora had retreated behind the counter. She filled a bag with ice and wrapped a towel around it. I took it over to Esau. He held it to his cheek and closed his eyes and leaned his head back.

"What happened?" I asked.

He lifted his right eyelid and watched me for a moment. "Don't know what you mean."

"You gonna tell me that you walked into a door next?"

Esau closed his eye and said nothing. A ragged exhale slipped from his mouth. Stagnant hot breath reached me.

"Who was that guy?" I said. "Don't recall seeing him in here before. Thought I'd seen most of the town at one point or another."

"He was nobody," Esau said.

"You're a horrible liar, old man."

He muttered something in Greek, leaned forward, placed the blood-soiled napkin on the table. "I let you and your Russian friend stay here. I don't ask no questions, even though it's obvious something happened to you. Why can't you give me that same respect?"

I raised my hands in surrender. "Just seeing if I can be of help, Esau. That's all."

"Well I don't need your help." He stood and stumbled toward the office.

I glanced toward Isadora. She watched her uncle retreat. I waited a moment for the office door to shut, then approached her.

"What's going on here?" I said.

She sighed. "My uncle, he's...I'm not sure how to put it."

"In trouble?"

She studied me for a moment, perhaps deciding how far to let me in. She inhaled sharply. "I think you should honor his request and stop asking questions."

"Look, I'm just saying if you need help..."

She turned away from me and feigned busy work.

I took the hint and stepped out onto the terrace where the old men still gathered. If not for a couple curious glances, I would've thought they'd played through the entire incident. Were they concerned for Esau? Shamed at seeing me knocked over? Embarrassed because they didn't do anything to help? I nodded at those who glanced in my direction, then walked past and leaned against the railing. The waves were about waist-high and hammered the shoreline. Salt spray coated the wall below me in a fine mist. The steady breeze dried the sweat that coated my face and arms.

After a few minutes of staring out over the sea, I reentered the cafe and took a seat against the far wall. Isadora ignored me. Just as well. My heart rate had barely come down since being knocked to the floor. A sure sign I'd had enough coffee.

Most of the old guys came in, too. They'd made it through another round of matches. While some were winners, others were out of their weekly gambling stipend. They grabbed a snack or a drink or a mug and seated themselves at various tables. Chatter rose and filled the cafe. Took the chill out of the place. Felt like normal again. Sort of.

The front door opened, creating a wind tunnel for the salty breeze. Napkins lifted off tables and spiraled toward the door.

Alik stepped in. He nodded at Isadora, then walked up to me. If Esau was a bad liar, then I was even worse at hiding the fact something had happened.

"What's going on?" Alik said.

"Nothing much," I said.

"You've got a cut on your face."

I'd forgotten about the shattered mug. Perhaps that was what the guys on the patio were looking at. Maybe they had remained unaware that anything happened.

Not likely.

"I tripped," I said.

"You tripped, huh?" Alik drummed his fingertips on the table. "Do you think this is a game?"

"A game? What?"

"You have to remain invisible, Jack. You may not understand the power that Ivanov wields, but I do. He has puppets everywhere in Moscow. If he finds out you are here, this place will be crawling with his men. We'll both hang. So until Frank can get us out of here, you need to stay out of trouble."

"Jesus Christ," I said. "I got knocked over by someone hurrying out of here. That's all. I didn't start anything. Didn't say anything. Got an elbow to my side and my face planted into the floor. My mug shattered. That's why I'm bleeding."

He slid a napkin across the table. "OK, well, just consider that other stuff a reminder."

"Trust me, man. I just want to go home. The sooner that happens, the better. As nice as this place is, my heart skips a beat every time that door opens."

Alik nodded as though he felt the same.

Then we both turned as the door whipped open again.

Enjoying *When Dead in Greece*? Purchase your copy today!

ALSO BY L.T. RYAN

Find All of L.T. Ryan's Books Today!

The Jack Noble Series

The Recruit (free)

The First Deception (Prequel 1)

Noble Beginnings

A Deadly Distance

Ripple Effect (Bear Logan)

Thin Line

Noble Intentions

When Dead in Greece

Noble Retribution

Noble Betrayal

Never Go Home

Beyond Betrayal (Clarissa Abbot)

Noble Judgment

Never Cry Mercy

Deadline

End Game

Noble Ultimatum

Noble Legend (2022)

Bear Logan Series

Ripple Effect

Blowback

Take Down

Deep State

Bear & Mandy Logan Series

Close to Home

Under the Surface

The Last Stop

Over the Edge (Coming Soon)

Rachel Hatch Series

Drift

Downburst

Fever Burn

Smoke Signal

Firewalk

Whitewater

Aftershock

Whirlwind

Tsunami (2022)

Mitch Tanner Series

The Depth of Darkness

Into The Darkness

Deliver Us From Darkness

Cassie Quinn Series

Path of Bones

Whisper of Bones

Symphony of Bones

Etched in Shadow

Concealed in Shadow (2022)

Blake Brier Series

Unmasked

Unleashed

Uncharted

Drawpoint

Contrail

Detachment

Clear (Coming Soon)

Dalton Savage Series

Savage Grounds

Scorched Earth

Cold Sky (Coming Soon)

Maddie Castle Series

The Handler

Tracking Justice (Coming Soon)

Affliction Z Series

Affliction Z: Patient Zero

Affliction Z: Abandoned Hope

Affliction Z: Descended in Blood

Affliction Z : Fractured Part 1

Affliction Z: Fractured Part 2 (Fall 2021)

ABOUT THE AUTHOR

L.T. Ryan is a *USA Today* and international bestselling author. The new age of publishing offered L.T. the opportunity to blend his passions for creating, marketing, and technology to reach audiences with his popular Jack Noble series.

Living in central Virginia with his wife, the youngest of his three daughters, and their three dogs, L.T. enjoys staring out his window at the trees and mountains while he should be writing, as well as reading, hiking, running, and playing with gadgets. See what he's up to at http://ltryan.com.

Social Medial Links:

- Facebook (L.T. Ryan): https://www.facebook.com/LTRyanAuthor

- Facebook (Jack Noble Page): https://www.facebook.com/JackNobleBooks/

- Twitter: https://twitter.com/LTRyanWrites

- Goodreads: http://www.goodreads.com/author/show/6151659.L_T_Ryan

rmation can be obtained
Gtesting.com
ne USA
738290323
V00009B/424

CPSIA inf
· at www.IC
Printed in
LVHW021
742916L